Les is More

Jess Carpenter

ISBN-13: 978-1-7347798-0-6

Cover design by: Sarah Kil Creative Studio / www.sarahkilcreativestudio.com

Spanish translations: Lisa Torres
B.A. Spanish Studies, Texas Lutheran University / www.twitter.com/lisalovesrandom

Printed in the United States of America

To my mom, Colleen, for always being my #1 fan.

Contents

Chapter One

I t's what every girl like me dreams of. The warm summer air, students passing by with smiles on their faces as I twirl around in the grass, taking in my first day at West University.

Scratch—

Alright, you caught me. I'm not twirling around. Students aren't smiling at me. In reality, I'm sitting on a bench, people-watching, as 99% of the student population is texting and walking. Shouldn't there be some school-wide ban on that? I've witnessed five head-on crashes.

Get it? 'Cause their heads crash. I know, I know, it's never as funny when you have to explain the punch line.

Anyway, today has been pretty uneventful. Unless you think the old man sitting next to me, throwing back a stinky egg salad sandwich, is eventful.

I check my watch. Almost time for that last class. Of course, it's Business 101. My mom forced me into taking this course. Said it would make me more marketable for med school.

Who doesn't love thinking about their post-grad education three months before their freshman year?

"You a freshie?" Old Man asks, some egg crumbs sticking to his chin.

I give him a polite smile. "Sure am." Grabbing my book, I stuff it into my backpack and ready myself to leave.

He takes another bite and smacks his lips. "This year will be life-changing for you. I just know it."

"Thanks. I guess we'll see, huh?" I sling my backpack onto

my shoulder and walk away with a beaming show of teeth. If anything, I'm always nice. Probably a little *too* nice. At least, that's how I see things.

Like when I caught my best friend in middle school stealing my purse, I smiled and told her, "This won't define your life. You're bound for greatness."

Sure, a few hours later I thought of about a thousand different comebacks that didn't brand me as a grade-A doormat, but alas, I never did figure out how to build a time machine. As far as I know, she's not in prison for grand larceny, so maybe my pep talk worked.

Gah, West's campus is way too big.

I stare at my phone, trying to decipher this ancient photo of the university map. I enter what I'm pretty sure is the business building. Zooming in to get a closer look, I open the glass door and squint at the pink-colored illustration on my screen. I glance up and...

Smack!

Make that *six* head-on crashes. My phone slides a few feet away and some pencils roll out of the unzipped front pocket of my backpack.

The offender, a large, hot, muscly guy, is in front of me.

"I'm so sorry. Are you okay?" he asks.

My gaze meets some sexy blue eyes. Little speckles of green sparkle in the irises, and he hands me my phone and discarded pencils.

He's *gorgeous.*

Shut *up.* Egg Salad Guy was right. This is so cliché. It'll be the cutest meet-cute you ever did see. I can picture it now: Me and him dating through all four years of school, engaged at graduation, marriage, babies, the whole perfect portrait.

I brush a chunk of hair behind my ear and quirk my lips. "Yes. I'm so sorry. I wasn't watching where I was going."

He grasps my hand, and electricity shoots up my arm. He helps me up, and I stand in front of him, too far away. A gentle pull begs me to close the gap. His gaze travels up and down my body, and I'm stuck in place. My mind scatters, and I don't know what to say.

"Hey, babe," another man says. "You ready?" He leans in and kisses my rescuer on the cheek.

Everything in me deflates like a balloon. Of course he's gay.

Rescuer looks at me again, and what I thought was a smolder is actually just an embarrassed grin. "You sure you're okay?"

"Yes," I mumble. Only my ego and pride are hurt, thank you very much. Egg Salad Sandwich dude was wrong. If anything, this year is going to be exactly like every past year of my life—boring.

My feet drag on the way toward my next class. I'd question which room is mine, but I'm able to recognize it as soon as I see the *Peanut Free Zone* sign that's posted on the door.

Now let's just hope people actually follow it so I don't have to make a grand performance with my EpiPen.

I trudge down the stairs and find a seat right in the middle. Not too close, not too far. Like Goldilocks, it's just right. *Ugh*, I'd rather do anything than sit through a business class that's going to drone on and on about nonsense. Like I'll need that in the real world.

Fine, I know I'll need it in the real world. I'm not an idiot. It's just not what I'm interested in.

Maybe I can close my eyes for a minute. Catch a few Zs. I stayed up way too late watching Netflix's new murder documentary.

A loud bubble pops near my ear. A woman sits next to me, smacking gum that's literally the same color as her hair—bright freaking pink.

She holds out a hand. "*Hola. ¿Cómo estás? ¿Hablas español?*"

I point at myself. "Oh, um, I don't really speak Spanish." I clear my throat and run through my four years of high school Spanish. "Good, I'm good. You?"

"*Sólo estoy bromeando contigo.*"

I shake my head 'cause I got no clue what she just said.

She winks, and her eyeshadow looks like it came from an Instagram video. "What's your name?"

Isn't the other person supposed to introduce themselves first? I grin. "So, you do speak English. I'm Les."

Her hand is thrust out, so I shake it.

"Mhmm. Cool name, is that short for something?" She sticks her tongue through the gum and blows another bubble.

And this is what always happens. Which is why I hate telling anyone my name. Yes, Les is my name. Nothing more, nothing *less*. And yes, I've heard that joke way too many times to count. My dad's favorite thing to say was, "Just because you have half a name doesn't mean you should think any Les of yourself."

Hardy har har. So funny, Dad. That joke got old sixty seconds after I exited the womb. Although now, I guess it'd be nice to hear that joke again. I shake my head. "Nope, it's just Les. And yourself?"

She blows another bubble and pops it with a loud boom that I swear echoes across the lecture hall. "I'm Candy."

I giggle like a schoolgirl (no pun intended). "For real?"

Her face grows serious, and she pinches her brows together. "Something wrong with that?"

My face goes long. "Me? What? Pftt. No. Just the name... and...the gum." I clear my throat. "Beautiful. Beautiful name." Is it hot in here?

She gazes at me with a cocked brow before cackling. "Totally kidding! I got where you were coming from." She nods and it bounces her hair.

I get mesmerized by the perfectly curled, pink strands and drop my pen. The lecture hall angles down like a stadium, and the pen rolls and clunks down the steps.

Roll.

Clunk.

Roll.

Clunk.

Roll-*clunk.* Until a brown-haired dude reaches down and picks it up. He holds it in the air without looking back, and

I groan the second I see his hand. I'd recognize that heart-shaped birthmark in between his thumb and pointer finger anywhere.

Meet Ben. Future star of the West baseball team. A doctor in the making. Rich boy who everyone loves. And my ex-boyfriend who dumped me six months ago on senior prom night. He told me that he thought we should take a break to "explore other options." I told him that if he thought I'd wait around for him, then he could stick his pompous head right up his—

As fate (or karma) would have it, he's turning around.

"Les? Wow. Hey. It's so good to see you. I'll come up there." He gathers his things and steps up the stairs.

"Oh, uh, it's okay. You don't have to..." I stutter because seeing him after all this time has me flustered. Too many emotions are involved.

Candy mumbles, "This should be good."

Please don't sit next to me. Please, please, please.

His butt hits the seat beside me, and I bite my knuckle. A scream is building up, but I cough instead.

"Ben. What a surprise seeing you here." My cheeks burn as I strain to give him a smile. It's probably more like a Joker grimace, but can he expect anything else? We had two years of high school bliss and planned every aspect of our life together. And then, *bam*! It was all over. I hate that my stomach is getting all flippy-floppy looking at him.

He hands me my pen, and our fingers brush. "Really? I mean, we both planned to take this class. Since there's only three different ones offered, we had a pretty good chance of both being here."

My butterflies that were making their way out of their stomach chrysalises slowly board themselves back up. Ben's mansplaining has a way of doing that to them.

Candy snorts. I give her a frantic, little shake of my head, and she huffs out a laugh before staring at the blank whiteboard as if it's the most fascinating thing in the world.

"Thank you so much for explaining that for me." I brush

through my hair. "Can't believe I didn't think of that."

He pats my shoulder, so I angle away from him. And because he's as predictable as they come, he leans in closer. "You're welcome. So," his voice lowers to a whisper, and he looks around the room as if he's going to tell me the secret recipe for Oreos, "I've been thinking about you a lot lately, and—"

"And I'm going to stop you right there." I nudge his hand off of the little desk that's attached to my seat.

He throws his head back and then exhales with too much force. "I'm serious, Les. I just want to get some froyo or something. Catch up. I promise, nothing more. You're free after class, right?"

Ah, so he's going for the soft close of a salesman. I cringe like I just ate trash. "Oh, I can't. Sorry!" I smile and look toward the whiteboard. Where is everyone else? Class is starting any second now.

He groans. "Stop being difficult. I'm sorry, okay? I know I screwed up. I just want to talk to you."

Talk to me? Yeah, right. We both know how that will end. Spoiler alert: my bed won't comfortably fit both of us *and* his ego.

I sigh. Five minutes and he's already exhausting me. "Listen, I really am busy after class. Otherwise, I'd have no problem getting froyo. You know I'm the froyo queen."

Ben crosses his arms like the petulant child he is. "Oh, really? Then what're you doing?"

A sound like a snort mixed with a scoff comes out. Without a second thought, I place a hand awkwardly on Candy's arm. "I'm hanging out with Candy. Yeah, we've got big plans. *Huge* plans."

"You're overselling it, *chica*," Candy whisper-sings. I kick her shin, and she claps her hands, laughing like a high-pitched hyena.

"You're friends with her?"

The cackle cuts off. Candy moves her head to the side of mine. "*¡Un momento!* You have a problem with that, Bruce?"

"It's Ben." His brows furrow.

She shrugs. "Either way, it's a dumb name."

He looks at me, and the flirty smirk is gone from his face. "Great friends you've got."

I wink and give him a kissy pout. "Tell me about it, Stud."

He grips his pencil tighter, and I can see him clenching his teeth. "You're doing that thing again."

I draw circles with my finger on the desk. "What thing?"

"You know, your 'studio audience' thing. Where you react completely inappropriately to the situation at hand."

He wants to accuse me of that? Fine. Here's where the crowd would gasp. You know, *if* my life were a reality TV show. Oh, Ben. The problem with being with someone for two years? They know a thing or two about you. He always accused me of "talking" to myself. Which is ridiculous. Because who *doesn't* talk to themselves? He's the weird one. You guys agree with me, right?

I cluck my tongue. "Thanks for pointing that out. You're right, I totally was. I need to work on that, so I really appreciate you bringing it up." I don't have to mumble the name I'm thinking of calling him because my glare gets it across.

"I'm sure you do," he mutters.

The professor walks in, and Ben doesn't say anything else. He succumbs to looking at his shoes, a dejected frown gracing those full lips.

When the syllabi get passed out, he scribbles little dots and lines on the paper. I can't stop looking at him out of my peripherals.

Ugh, he's so tan. And he looks like he put on a few pounds of muscle. Gone is the roundness of the boy I knew. I don't even catch myself drawing the same shape of his birthmark on my paper over and over again. A little heart that's just bigger on the right than the left. But when Candy raps her pen against the paper and then motions towards Ben's hand, I crumple it up faster than I should.

The commotion causes Ben to barely glance my way. Maybe

his pout and silence is all a play. He's trying the opposite approach to what he would normally do, which is be as annoying as possible until I give into him.

Fine, I'll admit it. Whatever he's doing, it's working. By the time class ends, I feel a little bad I was so mean to him. As I gather my things, I put my hand on his knee. His gaze meets mine, warm brown eyes full of sadness.

"If you seriously want to get together, text me. We can set up a time."

He nods and bites his lip. "Yeah, okay. I've got a team thing I'm supposed to be going to anyway. Have fun with Candy, Les."

I give him a wonky thumbs up and follow Candy and her pink hair up the steps, knowing I just made a massive mistake.

As soon as we step outside and the fresh air forces its way down my lungs, obliterating the spicy scent of Ben, I double over panting.

Candy leans down with me. "The only thing you've been running is your mouth, so why are you panting like a dog?"

I glare at her, but the nonchalant face she wears makes one laugh come out. Then it's followed by another, and another. "I'm just—forget it." I wave her off. "Thanks for having my back in there. We're the best."

She takes a step back and pops another bubble, the gum sticking behind to her lips. "Who, me and you?"

"Well, I meant more like women in general, but yes. The way you supported me in there deserves some kind of reward. Preferably a chocolate one." I unzip my backpack and see the contents of lined notebook paper, a few pencils, and an apple that's probably as bruised as a UFC fighter since it's smushed behind a textbook. Yeah, that reward's gonna have to wait.

Candy glances at her phone and bites her bottom lip as she taps on the screen like she's sending the world's greatest text. "Alright, let's go." She walks away from the business building, almost like she expects me to follow. "You coming or what?"

I look up at the sky then down at the ground. Well, what do

I really have to lose? "You know I didn't really mean we had to hang out," I say, catching up to her tiny, but fierce, strides.

Candy mocks being hurt, hand over her heart and pouty-puppy-eyes. "You don't want to hang out with me?"

Considering I don't know anyone here but my ex, I should be jumping at this opportunity. "I suppose we can. I did get you into this mess."

Putting her phone in her pocket, she grabs out her keys and walks toward the nearest parking lot. "Why are you avoiding *guapo* Mr. Soul Eyes anyway?"

Soul Eyes? I snort. Unless she means those eyes suck your soul right out of you and stomp it to the floor with no care at all, Ben has no soul. "It's a long story."

She walks to a rundown Kia and circles her finger to me and the passenger side. "Tell me everything."

Chapter Two

I look out the window of Candy's Kia and squint at the passing road signs. "So, we were dancing, typical high school moment, crowns on our head from being king and queen, and he says, 'Well, maybe we should see other people.' Where are we going anyway?"

"*Tonta*, don't you know you shouldn't get in cars with strange people?" Candy asks, flipping the switch for her blinker.

I roll my eyes.

She pops another bubble. Not gonna lie, I wish I could edit those out for my studio audience. Makes me flinch every time she does it.

Yes, I'm a little jumpy. Freaking Ben and his stupid freaking accusations. If I *did* have a studio audience, life would be a lot more fun.

"*Estoy bromeando*," she says.

"Obviously," I mumble.

"Awe, you do know *español*!"

I wave my hand. "Unfortunately, not enough."

"That is unfortunate. We could've had secret conversations together in front of Brandon. Anyway, we're headed to Candyland, AKA, my apartment. Speaking of Brad, that seems fishy, what he said. What were you talking about before that dance?" She speeds up as a car nearly T-bones us and calls out, "Your side!"

This woman is going to kill me.

"We weren't talking about anything noteworthy as far as I remember. We were literally dancing. *To our song.* Reminiscing about our past and looking forward to our future." I bang my head against the headrest but it's completely unsatisfying because it's cloth.

Candy taps her fingers on the steering wheel to a Marshmello song. "That could be a slogan." She clears her throat and starts talking in a deep, male sports announcer voice, "Reminiscing about our past and looking forward to our future: How men have successfully oppressed women over the generations. Ooh, I need to put that on my Twitter." She searches the cupholders blindly as she drives.

I snatch her phone. "Girl, you are not putting that on your Twitter right now. I'd like to live long enough to see Candyland."

"Fine, but I'm sort of a big deal on there. Your words could've been famous."

"You an influencer?" I laugh.

She flips her hair over her shoulder in a wave of cotton candy clouds. "Sure am."

Doesn't surprise me in the slightest. "Good for you. I'm fine not being famous though."

Looking in the rearview mirror, she says, "*Mira,* all I'm saying is that Bruce was hot. *Bien guapo.*"

"It's Ben, Candy. *B-E-N.* You have to at least know his name if you're going to be my friend." I shake my head. "And who cares if he's hot? He dumped me on prom night!"

"Dun-dun-dun-dun," she sings along to the beat. "Wait—did you say Ben?"

Is she for real? Does she not listen to anything at all? "Yes."

She's quiet for a moment. "Shut up. So your couple name was *Lesben*? It sounds like—"

"Lesbian. Yeah, yeah, I know." Ugh, I thought that name died in high school. "Adorable if it were me and you and your name was Ben. But unfortunately, Ben's a man."

She laughs so carelessly that it makes me a little jealous.

"So, as you can imagine, it wasn't the best name for a hetero couple. Anyway, we'd have to be a couple for that to be legit. And we *aren't*."

Tears stream down her face and her giggles filter down to a soft ha and ho. "Oh man, that's good. Lesben. I love it."

A loud bang startles me, and my head hits my knees as I cry out, "Please! I don't want to die!" My heart beats at probably 5,000 times per minute, and my hair is in my mouth like bad spaghetti as I sputter to get it out.

Candy puts a hand on my forehead and shoves me back to sitting straight up. "*Para con eso.* It's just my car backfiring or something. Who knows, I need to take it into a mechanic."

I don't mention that Ben could easily fix her problem. Spoiled kid or not, he's always been obsessed with cars. It's why him and my dad got along so well. Seeing him in class is going to be awesome. You know, if sticking your face with porcupine needles is awesome. Plus, I can already feel how this is going to end, and it's not good.

We pull into a new apartment complex with stone lining the side of the building and ivy cascading down it, which had to be plastered on the wall like that, because ivy doesn't grow that quick. My heart rate is still through the roof, but I try to breathe through my nose to make it calm the freak down. "Nice place."

She waves me off. "On the outside. They built this complex so cheap I swear everything is breaking on the inside. We've had the repair man out like ten times already, and we've only lived here a month."

"Bummer. Who do you live with, anyway?"

She turns the key, the engine sputters out, and she takes it out of the ignition. The sun is beating down, and I doubt her AC had been working because it's hot as crap. "*Mi hermano* and a few of his friends."

Oh, great. She has a brother? And lives with *his* friends? I hope they're video game nerds or something. Candy is downright adorable, so her brother better be as tiny and cute and a so-not-my-type kind of man. Because it's been too long, and a girl needs company. Non-committal, don't-let-the-door-hit-you-on-the-way-out company.

She holds up some plastic key fob to the complex's side door, and it opens automatically. The hallways inside smell like a floral cleaning solution. It's not bad, but it's not really pleasant either.

Candy is a girl on a mission, and she trudges through the halls with her gaze fixated ahead. As we near a hallway to turn right, there's an unmistakable EDM song making the walls shake.

She growls, "I'm going to kill him. *¡Voy a matarlo!*"

So, you know, I'm thinking maybe it wasn't such a good idea to come here with her. In fact, as I walk to her side and see her narrowed eyes and curled lip, I'm wondering if I should run the other way. Dark hallway, a girl I barely know, loud music playing, and a den full of boys we're about to walk into. You think I'm an idiot, right? I don't even have to ask...I'm an idiot.

"Maybe I should go. I'll just catch an Uber or something," I whisper, half-hoping that she doesn't hear me and I can bolt before we go into whatever situation has her pulling out a can of hairspray...oh shoot, nope, that's definitely mace.

Candy grips my upper arm. "Um, no way. You're not going anywhere. I'm gonna need backup."

I try to pull away from her, but she packs a lot of strength in those hands. "What you're going to *need* is to let go of me so that I can *go*."

"*Cállate.* You ain't going anywhere, *chula.*"

You've got to be kidding me. I'm too young to die.

She doesn't let go of me and walks past three more doors. The music gets louder and louder the closer we get to the hallway's end. She stops at a door labeled 13666 and takes a deep breath. Now I'm really worried because seriously? You couldn't pay me to live at an apartment with both the numbers 13 and 666 in the address.

"*¡Abre la maldita puerta ahora mismo*, Carter!" Candy's

screams pierce my ear drums and make them explode.

Okay, fine, maybe not *actually* explode, but they might as well have. "Please tell me you're just pissed that the music is loud and that we're not going to be walking into some satanic ritual or something."

Candy taps on the door and furrows her brow. "Nah, we do satanic rituals on Tuesday. *Está bien.* I'm pissed because *mi hermano idiota,*" she yells and hits the door again, "is using my freaking speaker!"

Who is she? The door swings open, and a tall, scowling guy is standing in the way, glaring at the pink-haired girl next to me.

Alright...who is *he*?

Because I'm suddenly all choked up and can't form a proper sentence when he glances at me, looks me up and down with green eyes, then says, "Who the hell are you?"

"I-I could ask you the same question," I retort, but it lacks its usual punch, and he can tell because he quirks the corner of those delicious rosy lips.

He turns around and yells, "Shut off the music, idiots!"

He's like if Shawn Mendes and Diego Boneta had a baby that came straight from the fiery depths of Hell (isn't that where all hot guys come from?).

The bass fades out and the walls stop shaking. However, Candy, does not. She's like a bottled up piece of dry ice where all the steam rises, and it's going to *boom!* make some type of bomb. That's a thing, right?

Pretty sure that's a thing.

Her glower twists her glossy red lips up to her button nose, and Carter takes the opposite approach by beaming toward her. I swear, a sparkle just lit up on his teeth with his cutesy-boy grin. It's like a weird dream that I can't stop watching. They both make different facial expressions at each other, their eyes never straying from the other's face.

The longer my head moves back and forth, the more I feel like I'm watching the championship game at Wimbledon.

And then, more of their similarities and differences manifest. They've each got golden-brown skin and green eyes. Everything else, different.

Carter is easily 6'3". Candy is pushing, I don't know, maybe 5'2"? He's some sort of athlete, as is obvious from the way his muscles are straining his shirt sleeves. Candy is petite. And well, for one thing, as hot as Candy is, I'm not thinking about kissing her. But Carter, on the other hand, let's just say I wouldn't mind running my hands through his hair, down his neck, his chest, those abs—

"Do you forgive me now?" His husky voice shatters my little fantasy.

Candy sighs. "*No lo vuelvas a hacer, ¿de acuerdo?*"

"Did I miss something? You guys didn't speak one word." My neck is sore from moving between the two so much.

"*Probablemente,*" they both respond at the same time.

Candy shrugs. "You were too busy checking out *mi hermano.*"

My jaw drops. "I was not!"

Carter steps aside so we can walk in. "You were." He puts his hand on my back and ushers me through, closing the door behind us all. "*Está todo bien.* I returned the favor."

Aaaand, my cheeks are burning. Afraid saying anything else will lend me another chastising, I follow Candy into the apartment.

Inside, three other guys sit on a black leather couch. It's one of those modern-design, low to the floor ones, and it makes the couch look extremely small with how large each of these dudes are. "What're they putting into their Wheaties in the morning? They're all jacked." I say it under my breath to Candy so no one else can hear.

She laughs. "They look tough, but on the inside, they're a bunch of softies. You'll like them."

I'm not too sure about that, because the only one that's caught my eye is Carter. And I have a feeling he'll be off limits thanks to my new friendship with Candy.

"Want something to eat?" she asks, walking into the kitchen. "Welcome to the kitchen a la Candyland."

The guys grumble, and Carter rolls his eyes. "No way are we calling this place Candyland."

She places her hands on her hips, ready to square off with her brother once more. The least I can do is help. I mean, she had my back with Ben. "I think it's a cool name. Chicks will dig it."

To me, it comes out nonchalantly, but Carter's got that little smirk back on his face, so we can probably mark it up as a loss.

He plays with a rubber band on his wrist, eyes not leaving mine. His tongue darts out to moisten his lips, and I bite the inside of my cheek. The last guy I kissed was Ben, and that was six months ago.

"*Ay Dios mío*, just get a room already," Candy grumbles as she puts grapes into a bowl and washes them off in the stainless sink. "Les, meet my twin, Carter. Carter, Les. You didn't even ask for her name."

"Maybe *no lo necesito*." He walks toward Candy, steals a grape, and tosses it into his mouth.

"Whatever. She's unavailable, anyhow." She shoves him away from the bowl.

He quirks an eyebrow. "Is that so?"

"Um, no," I give Candy a disapproving glare, "it is definitely not so. But at the same time, slow down. Maybe I'm not interested."

Before I can say anything else, he walks over and slings a heavy arm over my shoulders. He smells like cinnamon, which is such a *strange* thing for him to smell like, but I want more of it. "Is that so?" he says again.

I nod and grab his hand, moving to take his arm off of my shoulders. Instead, he threads his fingers through mine, and I'm here for it. Settle down, stomach. With his perfect face and hair that's just slightly wavy, I could run my hands through it, pull him closer to me—gah! What am I doing? What I meant was with his perfect face, Carter is obviously a notorious hooker-upper. Wait, that's not a word. Although, it's not technically *wrong* if he hooks up with a bunch of people. Carter the hooker...upper?

Their apartment door swings open without a knock. "Sorry I'm late guys, I had class and—What the hell is going on here?"

"*Ben?*" My gut roils, and I scramble away from Carter's side. I shouldn't have anything to worry about, but the way Ben is standing in the doorway with his mouth agape makes me feel guilty.

Candy giggles, doubling over and slapping her hand on her thigh. "Bryce?! This day just got a thousand times better."

Ben pinches his nose. "It's *Ben.*"

Carter finally lets go of my hand, but not before using it to pull me into his side once more. "For the record, I *am* interested," he whispers in my ear and then saunters off to Ben, slapping him on the back with a devilish glare twinkling in his eye.

My fingers tingle where he held my hand. I must have carpal tunnel or something. Carter's going to be trouble, I can already tell. But it's the kind of trouble I'll gladly participate in.

"What're you doing here?" Ben asks.

Oh, right. *He's* here. "More like, what are you doing here?" I rake my hand through my hair.

He closes his eyes and shakes his head. When he opens them, he looks tired. "These are my teammates, Les."

Ooh, baseball players. Yikes, totally my type. Ben steps away from Carter, who checks his Apple Watch, then sighs.

My skin itches from Ben's stare. "Well, Candy is Carter's sister. It's not like I knew you'd be here."

Carter cocks his head. "You guys know each other?"

Ben looks at him and huffs. "She's my girlfriend."

I flinch. A weird, panicky feeling pangs in my chest. "Uh, no, I'm not. *Was.* I *was* your girlfriend. We broke up six months ago!"

I still haven't met the other three dudes on the couch, but

one of them sing-songs, "Awkward!" and it makes me want to tape their mouth shut. But, I don't condone violence, so maybe I can ask Candy to do it?

Carter chuckles. "Oh, *está bien*. I was going to say—"

"You were going to say what?" Ben takes a step toward him. They're about the same size, but Carter has an inch or so on him.

From behind the two, Candy grimaces at me as if she's saying, *uh-oh, abort! Abort!*

And if this *were* a show, I'd ask you to cut to commercial break. But, it's not, so I don't get any reprieve.

Carter shrugs, a simple up and down motion of his right shoulder as if he doesn't have a care in the world. "I was going to say that if she were your girlfriend, which she's *not*, that I wouldn't be able to shoot my shot."

Ben might as well have steam coming out of his ears. "You're not shooting any shot, Carter! She's taken."

What do they want with me anyhow? It's not like I'm even that great. Oh, wait. They probably don't want *me*. It's just the modern version of those old-timey gun fights. They've got to prove who's the macho-est man.

Carter takes a step back from him, and his body is relaxed, unlike the tautness of Ben's. "Nah, man. I don't 'got it.'" He air quotes. "She said you're not together. You need to calm down."

I should probably step in at this point, but honestly, both of them are starting to piss me off. I'm not some object to be fought over. Candy holds her phone upright against her chest, and she keeps peeking at it, so I can almost guarantee she's recording this. It'll probably show up on Twitter later for the world to see. She'll plaster crying-laughing smiley faces and a caption of, "Two idiot baseball players fighting over a semi-attractive girl. Who wins?"

Not a bet I'd make. I can guarantee neither of them are winning in my book. Ben groans then turns toward me, hands on his head like he was just put through the wringer. "Les, let's go.

I'll take you home."

I want to stomp my foot because that's what Ben does. He brings out an immature, petty side to me. But, I refrain. "I came here to hang out with Candy. If you don't want to be here because you can't handle seeing me here with *my friend,* then leave. No one's going to miss you."

The peanut gallery on the couch say, "Mhmm, girl's harsh."

But how am I harsh? He just demanded I go with him after staking some claim in the grass like this is the 1600s or something. He's a jerk, and even if I do miss him and wish we'd never broken up, he's pissing me off. You don't act that way to someone—especially not an ex.

He looks at me as if I've slapped him across the face. I spent the last six months wondering what I had done wrong, why he wasn't calling me, and pining over him while he probably slept his way through the baseball groupies.

I needed him this summer.

He had no right. *No right* to speak to me like that when he knows everything I've been through. The longer I stare at him, the more frustrated I grow. I bite my lip to keep from crying over something stupid like this. And it's probably not even him but rather that I'm hungry and today was freaking sucky. "You know what?" I ask. "I'll go. But not with you."

I push past him and leave the apartment, already pulling up the Uber app as I pass through the doorframe.

"Les, wait." Ben reaches for my arm.

"Not today, Ben." I shrug away, like Jennifer Aniston to Brad Pitt at the SAGA awards. As soon as I get outside and the sun hits my face, I feel better. It was too crowded in there, anyhow. Thanks to the guys on the couch and Candy's recording, I'll probably be known by everyone before I want to. They'll whisper about me at parties, and I'll have nothing to do but talk to myself and you all. *Great.*

The nearest Uber is fifteen minutes away, so I sit down on the curb and pick at a weed that's growing through the sidewalk. I could make up some cheesy quote about how the weed persevered even through concrete, but then I'd be comparing myself to a weed, and I'm better than that. Try to remember me as a beautiful flower or something, not a plant everyone wants out of their life.

"Hey, *estás bien*?" Carter's voice breaks my monologue, and he sits down on the curb next to me with his elbows on his thighs. He's so tall that he looks ridiculous sitting like that. His knees practically touch his forehead.

He's giving my stomach real butterflies and Ben just made a fool out of me. Could this day get any worse? And, that's rhetorical. Please, I don't need any more drama. "Yeah, I'm good."

He slings his arm around me and pulls me close to him, and I definitely feel some tingles in all the right places. "If it helps you feel any better," he drawls, "Candy wanted to come out and grab you, but I told her I got it. She's in there ripping Ben's *cojones* right off."

It's so unexpected that I bury my face in his side and break out into laughter. "I believe it."

His chuckle reverberates through me. "Seriously though, are you good? I told Candy I'd give you a ride home."

The Uber took a wrong turn and is now seventeen minutes away. Perfect. "I appreciate it, but I don't get in cars with strange men." I wink.

"Ah, *bien*. Then, it's a good thing you didn't get in a car with Ben." He shakes his keys in front of me. "*Vámonos*, I'll drive you." He smirks that panty-dropping smile, and I'll admit it, he seems like a much better ride home than Raquel, my Uber driver.

He pulls on my hand until I stand from the curb and follow him through the parking lot. I glance at the cars. "Let me guess, you drive some douchey car, like a Charger or...no! Wait! You drive a Mustang, huh?"

"*Chica*, where'd you get the impression I'm like that?"

Oh, I don't know, because you have the eyes to make every woman in a mile radius swoon? "Just admit it. It's probably a flashy red or blue color, too."

He shakes his head and presses a button on his keys. A white, Chevy truck beeps. It has a baseball window sticker with a #1 inside of it, and I'm not sure if that's his number or saying that West's team is supposed to be number one. We head around to the passenger side where he opens my door. I want to roll my eyes but then the smell of his car is like an assault of cinnamon gum, and I end up blinking back in surprise.

I hop in, and he closes the door, swinging in himself on the driver side. When he cranks the engine, it fires to life and doesn't backfire like Candy's car did.

"Where to?" He types something out on his phone and then puts it in the center console. More EDM, I think Kane Brown and Marshmello's "One Thing Right," comes through the speakers, but it's barely there unlike at the apartment. So far, that's his biggest flaw.

"I live off of Ben—Tenth. I live off of *Tenth* Street." I hope I caught myself early enough, but judging by his snort, I didn't.

Why is Carter being so nice anyway? Does he just want to get in my pants? If so, he'll be sorely disappointed. At this rate, there's probably enough cobwebs to serve as a chastity belt. "*Lo siento, señor*," I mumble, embarrassed that Ben is somehow overshadowing the whole ride.

He shrugs and laughs. "Nothin' to apologize for—except your accent." He chuckles again, and I roll my eyes. "So, you met Candy in class today, right?"

Cold air blows from the vents and makes me shiver, despite the heat outside. "Yeah, how'd you know?"

"She told me."

I scan through our encounter. "When did she tell you?"

He taps on his forehead. "Twin telepathy." His nose crinkles when he grins, and it makes me want to reach out and 'boop' it. It's so freaking cute.

"I think I'm in love with your sister, actually. She sorta saved me in class today. But then, she almost killed me right after."

He taps his hand to the beat on the steering wheel. "Everything she does is a thinly-veiled version of dangerous."

Maybe first impressions aren't always right. The way the music was blaring and their whole twin argument without speaking and the downright gorgeous smirks, I was sure he was just some womanizer. Maybe Candy is the womanizer. Or man-izer?

"What're you thinking about?" He reaches over and turns the A/C down, but his fingers brush mine.

I don't breathe. Because if I do, it's going to come out ragged, and come on. I can't let him know he affects me like that. "Nothing, why?"

He gives me a side-eyed glance as he stops at the red light. Not too far from my apartment now. The light turns green and the truck rumbles as he punches the gas. "You just had this glazed over look like it was something important."

Man, why's everyone all up in my business? Can't a girl talk to her studio audience without being questioned? "Nah, I was just thinking about Candy and how I didn't get her number."

"Oh." He pops open the center console and fishes around. Out comes his phone, and he hands it to me. "You can grab it from my contacts. While you're in there, put your own number in." Now it's his turn to wink.

And oh, do those winks get to me. Most guys are worried that they'll get a text or that chicks will go and snoop through their messages. The way he casually handed his phone over sort of makes my heart flutter. Ridiculous. I can hear everyone say, *Millennials, they're killing the romance industry.*

"Please, don't ever wink again."

He juts out his bottom lip. "How come you get to wink and I don't?"

He's being ridiculous, and I turn up my nose at him. "Because I don't make women abandon all their morals when I wink." I punch in my phone number.

A long sigh is his response. Then, "Well, your winks aren't half bad, either."

I sputter into laughter. "That's what I aspire to be. 'Not half bad.'"

He flicks my nose gently. "Relax, Les. I was just kidding." But then he winks *again*.

Is he flirting with me? I want to say yes, but maybe he just thinks I'm funny and is playing along. He pulls onto Tenth Street, and I point to a brick building with new, industrial-style condos. I know. So fancy, huh? Blame my mom for that. "Right here."

The truck shakes as it's put into park. I hand him back his phone, and he bites his lip at the screen with my name, number, and a quick selfie I just took as the contact picture (where I'm winking, of course). As I'm about to close the door, he leans over the center console and keeps it open. "Don't be a stranger, aight?"

I shrug and feign nonchalance. "No promises." I blow a kiss and wave, not daring to look back.

Chapter Three

I figured I'd live in the dorms, but my mom insisted on me having my own apartment. She didn't want any other "residents" distracting me from my studies. My parents always said everything is paid for—so long as I go to school. Once I get my degree, Mom sends me on my merry way into the real world.

But, even that can be argued considering the trust fund unlocks when I turn twenty-two, which is right after I should finish my degree. Of course, should I stop at just a bachelor's degree, my mom might disown me. She plans on me being her protégé. Unfortunately for her, I'm really not a fan of brains.

Unfortunately for *me*, she's not a zombie. Because that would be way cooler. She's a neurosurgeon, one of the toughest people I know, and her name is currently flashing across my phone screen. And I have no choice but to answer it because...well, 'cause she's all I have left. "Hey Mom, what's up?" I kick off my shoes and catapult onto my bed.

"What was that noise?"

Alright, cool, so obviously not that important of a call or she would've opened up with her news. Which means, what the hell is she calling about? Apparently, my silence is all she needs to continue. "I have ten minutes. Your first day? Good?"

She never speaks longer than she needs to. It's as if she thinks her words hold so much weight, everyone should already know what she's trying to say. "Yep, it was great."

"You saw Ben?"

What the... "How did you know I saw him?"

"Ben has a good head on his shoulders." Oh, *now* she'll talk. Ben's the favorite no matter what, and he's not even her kid. "He's going to make a great surgeon and he's on scholarship for the baseball team. It'll look great for his med school applications. You could apply to the same school. Think of your future, Les."

Something's pounding at my forehead. Okay, it's my fist hitting my brow over and over again because is she for real? I barely hold in an eye roll. "That's the thing, Mom. I shouldn't have to think of my future. I'm a freshman in college. Let me find myself before you make up my life for me."

A sputtered breath comes through the phone on the other end. "Finding yourself is just a millennial term for 'goofing off.' You never should've broken up with Ben."

"I didn't break up with him. He broke up with me."

"That's not what he said."

I want to tear out my hair. "Well, whose side are you on?"

"The side of rationality."

I can't do this. "I'm going to hang up before I say something I regret. Goodbye, Mom. Love you." I press end before she has a chance to say something else. And since rude thoughts about her could hang around my head for the next five hours, I pull out my syllabi and look them over. I'm taking fifteen credits, but that shouldn't be too hard. Regardless of what my mom likes to think, I'm smart.

So, why do I feel like Phoebe on *Friends* right now? Which, by the way, is a great show. Ben would always groan about how old it is whenever I wanted to watch it. Stupid. Ugh, I don't even want to think about him. His annoying little grin and warm brown eyes, and...GET OUT OF MY HEAD!

If you think I've read the first paragraph of my Criminal Psych syllabus five times, you're right. And the only thing I've retained is that the professor's last name is Douché. I'm not even joking. Poor guy. From one weird name to another...I feel ya.

Maybe I should just give up on today and take a nap. But

then my mom will get mad and go on and on about how "naps mess up your circadian clock, Les." Heaven forbid.

Wait. She's not here. I can totally take a nap without judgement. Ha!

I hop off my bed with renewed energy and shut off the light. With an overdramatic swipe, all my books and syllabi scatter on the floor. I cozy under the covers and smell the fresh scent of my fave laundry detergent. And I close my eyes with a smile on my face. Screw you, circadian clock.

My phone buzzes. I groggily reach for it because I literally just closed my eyes. My fingertip touches it, but I forget the direction I'm in and push the phone to the floor. It clatters against the hardwood. But it keeps buzzing.

I open my eyes. And...it's dark. As in, like, no light coming in from my blackout shades whatsoever. So maybe I didn't *just* close my eyes because my Apple Watch is saying it's 8:05. Yep, three hours later. *Whoops*.

My cell stops buzzing for 0.3 seconds and then starts up *again*. I reach off the side of the bed and, thanks to my silk sheets, slide right off and land in an undignified pile on the floor. Maybe my mom wasn't so wrong about me living alone because at least that wasn't caught on camera by my roommate.

It's not a number I recognize, so I answer with, "Hi, this is Les."

In response? A laugh. A high-pitched, feminine laugh. One that belongs to a woman with light pink hair. "I hate to inform you, but this isn't some employer calling. Just little ol' me."

I rub at my eyes and sigh, but my lips twitch in response. "What's up, Candy?"

"We're outside your building! Grab a swimsuit and come out here!"

There's probably drool all over my face. I can guarantee I'd make a great advertisement for the newest racoon-style makeup trend that will never be in. "Um, who's we?"

"Don't worry, we're Brody free."

I'm tempted to correct her, but I think she just refuses to say Ben. Which is fine, because that's an awesome friend to elevate my ex to the same level as Voldemort. "Who else is with you?"

She shushes whomever she's with and says, "*¿Por qué?* You looking for Carter?" She says this all with a valley girl accent, which sounds suspiciously like me.

"Um, *no.* Give me two minutes and I'll change."

"Thanks, *chica*," she says, and the line goes dead.

My swimsuits are still packed away, but thankfully, my mom was meticulous with labeling. In fact, I know exactly which box my bikinis are in because it's labeled "Les's Hooters' Uniforms." Obviously, the dignified neurosurgeon that she is has never been to a Hooters or she'd know they wear shorts and tanks. I grab the first bikini that matches and run out the door.

I see a Jeep parked below, and Candy sticks her upper body out of the window and waves. Is she drunk? She's gotta be drunk.

"What's up?" I open the rear door and hop inside, sliding in next to a tall, hot, dark wall of muscle. "Who are you?"

He flashes a bright grin with a large gap in his front teeth. "'Sup, girl? I'm Rykard." His pecs suspiciously flex, and he has a tattoo of some bird over the right one. "Must've not made a good impression earlier."

The guy driving turns around. "Yeah, that mess was golden. I'm Tom, by the way." He smiles, and his teeth are such a stark contrast against his black skin that they nearly glow. I must ask him his teeth whitening routine. He shifts the car into drive and pulls out of the parking lot, throwing his hand palm up behind him so I can high five it.

The last guy in the third row is cute and blonde. "You tore B apart! I'm Jared," he says, leaning over on my seat.

Don't you worry, I'm getting lost with all the names too. "Nice to meet you all," I mumble, wondering why I agreed to coming anyway. The attention is on me, and I feel awkward.

Candy turns around and claps her hands. "Thanks for coming, I didn't want to be stuck with all my roomies tonight."

"Then why'd you come?" Tom asks, turning the radio on.

She rolls her eyes. "Men." She sighs, then runs her hand through Tom's curly brown hair before lacing her fingers with his.

"So," I half-yell over the loud music, "where are we going?"

Rykard unbuckles his seatbelt and scoots into the middle seat next to me. "The hot springs, duh."

"Don't people mostly go there in the winter? You know, when it's cold out?" Who wants to hot tub in September?

Jared leans forward and puts his head between the two of us, wrapping his arms around Rykard's neck. "Nah, it's in the mountains, so it's a bit cooler once we hike up there. You'll like it."

Candy screams some words to whatever song is playing. It pretty much sounds like the devil's soundtrack. The guys begin talking (yelling) about training for the spring games and their grueling schedule. It makes me tired listening about it.

I scroll through Instagram as we drive, mindlessly getting lost in everyone's updates. I'm twenty minutes deep when Ben's username flashes at the top of the screen with the words, "Look, I'm sorry about tod..."

Ugh. I click on my inbox and find his dm.

B_maldon5: *Look, I'm sorry about today. I was wrong and acted like an ass. Will you please call me?*

Of course he wants *me* to call. I tap my fingers against the screen way harder than I need to.

Lesisbest: *Why don't you call me if you want to talk to me so bad?*

I go back to the picture feed and see that Sheila from high school is engaged. She also announced her pregnancy last week. Bet her parents threatened to cut her out of the trust fund if she didn't get married to the guy. #yayrichparents

B_maldon5: *You blocked my number.*

Drama king. I did not block his number. And just to prove so, I go to his contact in my phone, scroll down, and...

He's right. Well, too bad, so sad. I'm here with three hot guys, my new best friend, and we're going to get in some warm water. He can suck it.

"Just checking," I lock my phone and shove it in the seat-back in front of me, "Ben's not going to be here, right?"

Candy shuts off the music, and I swear I hear a cat yowl and a record scratch. "I said we were Brock-free. He's not coming."

She's kinda scary when she's pissed. I wave my white flag and put my hands up. "Okay, okay, I just wanted to make sure."

Tom pulls onto a dirt road and follows it for a few minutes before turning into a larger area where maybe twenty cars are parked. He turns off the ignition and opens his door. "Up and at 'em. We got a mile and a half hike."

"You call that a hike?" I laugh. "Please, that's a stroll."

"He conveniently forgot to mention that it's all uphill, doll," Rykard says, hopping out of the car. "And there's snakes, so be on your watch."

Jared rustles my hair. "Can you press the side latch once you get out? I don't want to be forgotten back here."

I ease out, swimsuit and phone in hand, and press down on the latch. The seat flings forward like it's on some sort of sling-shot and slams into my hand on the seat. "Don't worry, I'm good," I groan out. "But, Jared?"

"Huh?" His floppy blond hair swings with his head. "Oh, man, you good?"

Do men ever listen? "Could you maybe pull the seat back up? It's on my hand."

He grips it by the headrest and lifts it a few inches. I move my hand and shake it out as I walk toward where Candy grinds up on Tom. They already have their Bluetooth speaker hooked up blaring country music. And apparently, this group of people doesn't have one type of music genre they like because first it's EDM, then it's rap, then it's pop, and now country. You can't hike in the woods without listening to country music.

She unlatches her hips from his and puts an arm around me.

There's no alcohol smell, which means she's always like this. I love it.

"Let's go, party people! Everyone else is waiting on us!" she shouts.

We let the boys lead the way so they're the first ones bitten by rattlesnakes. On the way up, a few people pass by us, soaking and smelling like sulfur.

"Gosh, that stinks."

Candy pinches her nose. "I know, right? We'll get used to it the closer we get. I need to tie my hair up though. The last thing I need is that *agua* ruining my dye."

"Mhmm. So, you and Tom?"

She stumbles on a rock, but I catch her before she falls. Shooting me a full-lipped smile, she crinkles her nose and shakes her head. "*No es mi novio...*anymore. Actually, I'm saving him for later."

I full-on stop walking. Letting the guys get a little bit ahead so they can't hear us, I shoot her a look that hopefully says *WTF are you talking about?*

And then I actually say, "WTF are you talking about?"

"Like, not dating him now, but totally dating him later."

I snort. "Can you do that?"

She taps her cheek with her pointer finger. "I don't know. Let me check the book of life...*sí, está bien*. Who says I can't?"

"How does Tom feel about that?"

"He gets to sleep with whatever ball-girls—"

I rear my chin back to give me at least fifty double chins. "Huh?"

She waves me off and starts walking again. "The ball groupies. He gets to sleep with whatever ball-girls he wants. In the meantime, I date around, travel the world through men, so on and so forth."

"That is...definitely an interesting arrangement, I'll give you that." The dirt trail opens up a bit wider, and the smell of sulfur gets stronger with each step. "Hey, we almost there?" I yell to the guys ahead.

"If you slowpokes ever hurry up!" Rykard yells back.

Tom slaps Rykard's head, and the big guy pouts enough to see it from this far back.

The rest of the hike up, Candy tells me about her Twitter platform. She's got quite a following on Instagram too, but she's building both daily. She talks about how last year, there was a riot over the university reporting a student to ICE, which helped her decide she would start fighting for immigrant rights. It's intriguing, and the passion behind her words just tells me she's doing everything she always wanted to do. Clearly, she's living her dream.

I admire it.

She smiles. "Don't worry, we'll make a political girl out of you in no time, Les."

I laugh. "I'm sure you will."

A few minutes later, the bubbling of water sounds, and the pools come into view. It's dark, but enough of the people in the water have lanterns and their phone flashlights on to see. There's a smaller pool up at top with a trickling waterfall that leads into the larger three pools that cascade down toward us. People pack in, and everyone says their heys and hellos to the guys.

Candy fits right in, waving toward a few people tossing a ball back and forth. "Let's get in!"

"I'm not in my swimsuit yet."

She points off to the side. "Just change behind that tree."

"You said there were snakes. What if a snake bites me?" Call me a scaredy-cat, but there's no cell service up here and the chances of me getting to a reputable hospital in time for the antivenom for a snake bite is slim to none.

"*Bien*, I'll come with you."

"Thank you." I stomp ahead to the largest tree I can find. There's a lot of people, and I really don't want to flash my goods to anyone. "Can you cover me?"

"I'm like six inches shorter than you. How am I supposed to do that?"

"Just do it!"

"*Dios mío*. You don't have to be so bossy," she mumbles, standing in front of me, arms spread wide like a cross.

I quickly undress, bottoms first, then top. In record time I change into my *Hooter's uniform*, but then Candy says, "Your bottoms are on backwards."

Huffing a sigh, I switch them inside out and barely get them over my butt before Candy shouts, "Carter! You said you weren't coming!"

I blow out a forceful breath and turn around with a hopefully-composed smile. Then it melts on my face like ice on a hot summer day because Mr. Carter McHottie Pants has some *Sports Illustrated* model attached to his hip.

Which is fine. Like, *totally fine.* Because why wouldn't he have a girlfriend? Standing here in my bikini is kind of cold, so I should probably go into the hot springs. Where's Rykard, Jared, and Tom? They're easy friends.

Carter hugs Candy. "Yeah, I didn't think we were. Kinda last minute," he says, lifting his chin toward me. "Hey, Les. How are you?"

"Good. Good. Great. Candy, I'll be over with the guys, okay? Carter, nice seeing you again." I nod and ease my way away from the tree. Two steps later, I feel an unmistakable pull on my bikini top. I grab my boobs so that my top stays up and slowly back myself up toward the branch holding my string captive.

"Little hung up there, are we?" Carter bites his lip and chuckles.

I yank at the tie that got caught up on the branch until it pulls free. "Not. Another. Word," I hiss.

Thankfully, I spot Rykard's tall, dark, and handsome body up ahead. I tie my top, making sure to double knot it, as I make my way over to him, hearing Carter's lyrical laugh the whole way.

Rykard's brown eyes sparkle against the lantern light. "'Sup, Les. Wanna play some volleyball?"

"Why, yes I do." I step into the hot spring. The water isn't quite as hot as a jacuzzi, but definitely hotter than a pool.

Rykard introduces me to a few other people, and we pair off into teams. We play three games, and I rock (since I played in high school), so we win two out of the three. Candy joins in halfway through, drinking more than she spikes the ball.

We wind down and slide into the warm water. It hits right at my shoulders. I can't smell the sulfur anymore, so at least my nose has adjusted.

Candy sits beside me and leans her head against mine. "It's been a fun night, right?"

I pat her head. "The best, Can-Can."

"Good," she whispers.

"Hey," Tom walks up to us, holding a girl's hand, "are you guys cool with catching a ride with Carter? I'm taking Jiah home."

Candy's head pops up. She scans the other pools and yells out, "Carter! Can me and Les drive back with you?"

"Yeah!" he yells back.

She pulls my arm until I'm standing. "We're good. Thanks, Tom. See you back at home."

Weird dynamic, those two.

She stomps through the water, not letting go of my hand until we're in front of Carter. "I'm ready to go."

Carter is sans-Sports-Illustrated-model, and he waves to the group of guys he was talking to. "Your wish is my command, little sis."

"We're twins."

"I was born first."

Candy hands me the empty beer bottle she'd been holding and crosses her arms. "By like thirty seconds."

"Still counts."

"Hardly."

This is going to be a fun ride home.

Chapter Four

Halfway through the hike back to Carter's car, Candy proclaims that she's too tired and makes him give her a piggyback. Let's just say that Candy is a very high maintenance drunk.

"Is she asleep?" Carter nods his head toward his back.

I take a peek at her squished up face on his shoulder. "It would appear so."

He laughs. "She's the worst drunk. I don't even want to say she's my twin when she gets like this. She's snotty, lazy, and—"

"I heard that," she mumbles.

"I know." He winks. "That's why I said it."

"So," I kick at a rock as we hike downhill, "Candy said you weren't coming to the hot springs."

Candy's legs slip, so he readjusts her, and she mumbles something incoherent. "Keeping tabs on me, huh?"

"*No*," I protest.

He bumps me with his shoulder and quirks up the right side of his lips. "Nah, I hadn't planned to. It'd just been a while since we'd been here. I used to come here all the time as a kid."

"Oh, no way? That's cool. I didn't realize you two were from around here."

"Yeah," he hikes her legs up once more, "born and raised. What about you? You from around here?"

Thankfully, no, but I'm not going to insult the guy. "No, I'm from Glenbrook, Nevada. Little town on Lake Tahoe. About three hours northeast. My mom really wanted me to go here,

34

and since I got an internship with a really good doctor up at the hospital, it just made sense."

Crickets chirp, and the sound of frogs echo. My thighs burn from going downhill in flip flops and playing those three games of volleyball. I'm going to be sore tomorrow.

Carter nods. "Is it just you and your mom?"

I trip on the same rock I've been kicking. He reaches out his arm before I slam into the ground, holding Candy up with his other. "Ah, ha. Ah, yep. Yeah, just me and my mom."

"Cool. Are—"

"My dad actually passed away in March." I hate saying it. And I'm apparently a super awkward person because who just drops that into the convo?

Carter squeezes my arm before gripping Candy's legs again. "I'm sorry. That sucks. Were you guys pretty close?"

My smile wobbles, and it feels like I get an uppercut to the chest. "Yeah, we were." I don't tell him of the irony that a neurosurgeon's husband got inoperable brain cancer. I don't tell him that most days, I sit at home staring at the wall nervous that I'm going to make a wrong decision without his advice. I don't tell him about the last six months of therapy and how I thought I was fine, but now, I'm not so sure.

Thankfully, I'm spared from the rest of the pity-filled conversation because we step up into the parking lot, and he points out his truck with his chin. "I can't wait to put her down. My back is burning something fierce."

"Oh, is it, Mr. Baseball?"

He presses the unlock button, and his headlights flash, making it easy to see his smile. "That's Mr. Baseball Captain to you, Les."

I laugh sarcastically. "Wait, are you really team captain?"

As he puts Candy in the backseat and buckles her seatbelt, I go to the passenger side and hop in. Again, his car has the same strong cinnamon smell.

"Yeah, but don't get your panties in a bunch. It doesn't mean the same thing in baseball as it does in other sports. It's really not a big deal. Pretty sure they gave it to me out of pity." He pushes the ignition, and the engine fires up with a loud purr.

"Pity, huh?" I pull on the glovebox handle 'cause I'm nosy. It clatters open. The little light inside illuminates a few juice boxes, fruit snacks, honey sticks, and applesauce packets. "Geez, are you an Uber driver on the side? Talk about hooking up your ride."

He looks in the rearview mirror as he pulls out and starts on the gravel road. "Ha, yeah. No, I'm not an Uber driver."

"Ah, I see. Breakfast for your hookups, right? Well, at least you're a gentleman." I hold up the applesauce. "I'm stealing this, by the way."

"Help yourself."

I didn't realize how hungry I was. Correction: Am. I *am* hungry. This applesauce isn't going to do anything for me. Nor did I realize how late it is. It's a quarter past midnight, so not much is going to be open.

"You hungry?" he asks the same time I say, "We should get food."

We look at each other with mock-horror expressions. I gasp. "Oh gosh, I'm taking on the twin telepathy since Candy is asleep."

He reaches over and taps my nose. "I dig it."

"You dig that I'm like your sister?"

His lips scrunch up. "Well, when you say it like that, it sounds weird."

Because it is weird, weirdo. "Alright, we got like, what? Forty minutes till the first In-n-Out pops up? Give me that phone. Let's get some tunes going."

"Tunes?" He cackles. "You sound like an old mom trying to be hip."

I can't help the big grin that comes on my face. "Phone. Now, *por favor.*"

He hands me his phone. His lock screen is a photo of him with two young boys. They've got curly mops of light brown hair and green eyes. One boy is missing a front tooth, and the other boy still has all his baby teeth. All three of them wear backward baseball caps. "Those are my nephews. Mateo and Adrian."

I can't help but stare. Carter looks so happy next to them, like they're his entire world. What would it be like to have family like that? I can't imagine because I don't. I meant what I had said. It's just me and my mom. "They're adorable. Twins?"

"Oh, yeah." He glances at me sideways from the road. "My sister, Carlotta, was pissed. You should've seen her."

I look at the picture for a second more and then swipe up to get to his music. "Alright, what app do you use? Pandora? Spotify? Apple Music? Come on, where's the playlist full of old K-pop songs that I know you have?"

He pretends to flick his hair off his shoulder. In a mock valley girl accent (which, again, sounds *suspiciously* like me) he says, "The Bangtan Boys could do me in the middle of a forest, and it'd still be the best thing that ever happened to me."

"Okay, ew!" I can't stop laughing. "You're so weird!"

"Psh," he sputters, "you're judging me? Don't ever let me show you my room then. I have shirtless pics of Jimin all over my ceiling so I can fall asleep looking at his abs."

I playfully push his arm that's way too muscly for its own good. "Oh, stop. For real, favorite artist. Go!"

He taps on the steering wheel and readjusts in his seat. "That's too hard. Plus, my music is kinda weird. I bounce between genres a lot."

"Eh, Ben used to say the same about mine." It pops out so easily, and my cheeks heat. "So give me your top three or something."

He's silent for a minute as he brushes the palm of his hand against his jaw. "Alright. Top three I'd have to say Marshmello, Lord Huron, *and,*" he sighs, "I feel like I'm betraying other bands. Okay, final answer: Marshmello, Lord Huron, and Amber Run and NF."

My jaw drops, and then I raise my eyebrows to the roof of the car. "Shut up."

"What?"

"Well, first of all, that was four. But, I'll forgive you. I *love* Amber Run."

"No way? We're musically-compatible. That's like an automatic best friend, right?"

"Duh!" Which I guess means I'm friend-zoned, but I'm too excited someone else likes the same sort of music as me that I don't even care. This moment should be captured for my studio audience for sure. "Favorite all-time song by Amber Run?"

"Is that even a question? Obviously it's 'Neon Circus.'"

I hiss. "Oh, yeah, you didn't pass that test. It's clearly '5AM.'"

He rolls his eyes. "Are you going to play a song or what?"

"Someone's cranky. Do you need one of your five thousand packs of fruit snacks to cheer you up?" I pause for effect and also to see him flip me off with his ring finger, not his middle one, which just makes me laugh harder. "And yes, I'm playing a song. But I'm going to let Pandora decide what song needs to play so I don't have to decide."

I type in a new station and set it as Amber Run Radio, which begins playing "Waves" by Dean Lewis.

Carter yawns and grips the steering wheel, leaning forward to stretch his back. "Favorite color?"

"Pink. You?"

"Blue. Favorite flower?"

Hmmm. "Lilies. But only if they're planted. I hate receiving flowers. Don't give me something that's going to die, you know? Give me something I can digest, like chocolate or Sour Patch Kids."

"Oh, for sure. Never understood giving a girl flowers."

I scoff. "Well, yeah, you'd have to do more than hook up to get to that point in a relationship."

I lean my elbow on the center console and prop my cheek up. Even with that nap earlier, I'm freaking tired too. "Favorite animal."

He shifts in his seat and his shoulder brushes up against my hand and stays there. "That's so random. Who has a favorite animal that isn't a dog? A hundred percent dogs."

"True. Dogs are great." Music plays softly in the background and everything is so natural that I almost forget I nearly flashed him my boobs earlier.

We go back and forth, talking about everything random from pizza to his hopes of skydiving. He tells me more about his nephews, his family, and why he loves baseball so much. (Side note: Apparently, it's not for the hot baseball butts. He *actually* likes the game.)

I'm about to rest my eyes for a minute when he asks, "So, what was your dad like?"

I flinch. "Um, my dad was...great." Glancing out the window, I bite my bottom lip. "He was funny. Spontaneous. He had a way of making every person he met his friend." I chuckle thinking about all of our memories.

Carter places his hand, palm up, on the center console, and I lace my fingers with his. "There was this one Fourth of July when we went bike riding through our neighborhood. He pushed the wrong brake and flew over the front of the bike. Split his chin open and blood poured everywhere."

Carter grimaces. "Yikes. That's a good memory?"

I laugh. "Well, yeah, because he didn't even act like it was a big deal. The concrete had his blood stain for, like, a year after that. But that was just him. He was back from the hospital in an hour or two, and he still threw a huge party that night. I know everyone says it, but really, my dad was basically perfect."

Carter checks his rearview mirror before putting on his blinker and switching lanes. "He sounds pretty great."

"Yeah." I could tell another thousand stories about Dad, but it feels weird. Carter didn't know him. So... "I'm tired, but the thought of animal-style fries is keeping me awake."

"That's what I like about you, Les. You've got your priorities clearly figured out."

"Duh." A happy calm spreads across my chest. I rest my eyes for the next few minutes, listening to a nearly-perfect Pandora station and the hum of the road beneath us. When the car slows down and he makes a slow, left turn, I open my eyes to Heaven.

And no, we didn't get in a car crash. We've arrived at the In-n-Out drive through. "Candy," Carter reaches back and pushes on her arm, "do you want In-n-Out?"

"No," she mutters, and then her breaths steady before turning into an awful snore.

"What do you want?" he asks, rubbing at his eyes.

"Cheeseburger and animal-style fries." I settle back into my seat. "In-N-Out is the best. No worrying about what I can and can't order."

"What do you mean?"

Oh, right. "I, um, have a peanut allergy." I always dread this. People ask a million questions about why, how, when, what, and where, and I end up feeling like a weirdo. Not to mention, any guy interested in me automatically sees a blaring warning in their mind of *Don't do her! You'll never eat peanuts again!*

Carter beams. "For real? Huh. It's a good thing I hate peanuts then." He winks and rolls down his window.

I don't think he realizes how sexy that just was.

The drive through lady says, "Welcome to In-n-Out, will you be eating in your car today?"

"Yep. Can we get two cheeseburgers, two fries, one animal style, two waters, and…" He turns toward me. "Do you want to share a Neapolitan milkshake?"

Is he really asking me that? "Of course." I furrow my brow. "The answer is always yes."

The light from the menu illuminates his features from behind and he quirks his lips into a sideways smile. "And a Neapolitan milkshake."

She gives us our total, and we pull behind the few cars in front of us. Carter checks his watch, reaches into his pocket, and pulls out what looks like some sort of old Blackberry phone. While we idle, waiting for the other cars to pull ahead, he clicks a few buttons then puts the phone back into his pocket.

He's got two phones? Seems strange. Okay, yes I know, it seems more than just strange. It seems super fishy.

The brake lights ahead flash off, and we slowly creep up until we're at the window. Carter hands over his card to the woman, and she sends us on our way to the next window. A shrimpy dude hands us our order, and we're finally ready to eat.

The first bite of fries is euphoric. Holy crap, I'm hungry. And also, something is wrong with me because the thought of putting my lips on the straw that was just in Carter's mouth is turning me on. Shh, it's been a *very* long time, okay?

"I'm just going to say it."

His cheeks look like he has four marshmallows in his mouth. "What?"

"If I died right now, I'd die happy."

He puts his blinker on as the streetlight ahead turns from yellow to red. "Aw, Les, that's so sweet. I knew you liked me."

"From the In-n-Out."

"Nah, you can't take it back now." He does one of those horrible winks. Why is winking suddenly a thing?!

"Whatever." I playfully slap him. "You're so annoying."

He chuckles, and then we meld into comfortable conversation, music, and the occasional Candy-snore. By the time we pull up at my apartment around two in the morning, I'm a little bummed.

I grab my stuff and sigh. My apartment is so lonely. Just me, my anxiety, and I. Oh, and don't worry, I would never forget about my studio audience. But seriously, I don't think you can jump in and stop a murderer, so sleeping alone is kinda scary.

"We've got to stop meeting like this," he mumbles.

I turn toward him. His hair is in all directions, probably from the hot springs and him running his hand through it. "Meeting like what?"

He looks down at me with those swirling green eyes and slowly blinks. "At your apartment without you inviting me in."

Oh, he thinks he's smooth, huh? I draw my lips up and pout, lean into him, and put my arms around his neck. Two can play that game. "Who says I wasn't going to invite you in?"

He clucks his tongue and moves out of my embrace. "Thanks for the invite, *cariña*. I mean, I'd love to, but I can't do that to *mi hermana*."

"I didn't even invite you!" I roll my eyes.

"Close enough." He smiles victoriously as if he's just won the Flirting Olympics. "Want me to walk you up?"

"Actually, yeah. I know it's dumb but I'm kinda scared." I giggle like a schoolgirl and play it off. But legit, it's the middle of the night in a college town city. I'm not an idiot.

With the car in park, he gets out and walks with his hands in his swimsuit pockets. I lead the way up the stairs and to my front door. "This is me," I whisper. Don't need the annoying neighbors getting mad at me.

"I had fun tonight. I'll see you around." He kisses my cheek and walks backward with a grin that rivals insert-whatever-celebrity-you-think-is-hot-here.

Before I can ask him what the hell that peck was for, he spins around and disappears down the steps. Right as I turn the lock, my phone buzzes. Thinking I left something in Carter's car, I don't waste time answering.

But it's not Carter.

"You finally unblocked my number." It's Ben. And he's drunk.

"Is everything okay, B?"

"Les, I—" Katy Perry's *California Girl* plays through the speaker. Is it 2000s night at the club?

"What's wrong? It's 2AM. Are you okay?"

He groans, and from the sound alone, I can almost see him picking at his lip in frustration. "Les, I still love you."

Chapter Five

When your ex says he's still in love with you, what do you do?

A. Tell him you love him back.

B. Say you're sorry, but you don't love him back.

C. Tell him he's drunk, and that you'll talk a different day.

D. Drop your phone from shock, shatter the screen, and accidentally hang up while trying to pick it up without getting glass shards in your finger.

I'll give you a hint—I'm on my way to a phone repair shop right now. Thank whatever deity you believe in because it's located right on campus in the Union building with a bunch of other handy eateries and shops selling West University apparel.

But even a broken screen can't keep out my mom. She texts me three times then calls me. That's how I know whatever she's about to say is serious. "Hey, Mom!" I plaster on my good-girl voice and even smile. People can hear whether or not you're smiling.

"Les, the internship."

Again with her short words. "Yep, I'm about to head that way. She said to show up at one."

She sighs. "It's twelve-thirty."

Am I missing something? "So I have thirty minutes?"

"On-time is late. You need to be early."

Why does she even care? "I'm going to be there early. It's

literally a ten minute walk from where I'm at right now. I just have to drop off my phone."

"Don't snap at me."

"Mom, I'm not!" I probably sound like a whiny toddler to anyone walking by me. So far, my reputation is sweeeeet. "This internship is just as important to me as it is to you. I'd even argue that it's more important to me. It is *my* career and *my* life, you know."

"Yes. I checked beforehand with your schedule. The internship collides with your current calculus class. I've switched classes for you. It's before Business 101. Try not to miss it."

She thinks that just because I'm not with golden boy Ben that I've suddenly dropped all my life plans? This internship with the top research doctor at West's University Hospital is a big deal. I know that. It's why I applied for it and worked my butt off to get it.

Ever since they asked on my first day of kindergarten what I wanted to be, the answer was doctor. But, not like how every other kid said it. I've been studying for the MCAT since eighth grade, volunteering at local hospitals, and even shadowing my mom on occasion. I won't stop until I make my dream come true, but which type of doctor I want to be is still up in the air. Secretly, I think it kills my mom that I don't want to be a neurosurgeon like her.

"I promise I won't make you look bad."

"I'm not worried about that," she clips.

Lately, it seems as if I can't do anything right. Everything I do and everything I say is wrong. She's been so snappy, cold, and...neurosurgeon-like the past few months. It sucks. "Okay," is all I mumble.

The call ends before I can tell her that I love her, which hurts. But, she's right. I do need to hurry to my internship.

∞∞∞

I make it with five minutes to spare to Dr. Guilliod's office. Let's just hope she's liquid-blind and can't see all the sweat running down me. With a few calming breaths that do *not* calm me, I open the door and flash a giant smile that feels painted on.

A petite woman with shaved platinum hair smiles up at me. "Hi, can I help you?"

"I'm here for the first day of my internship."

"Oh!" She shuffles a few papers and points to the chair in front of her desk. "I'm so sorry. Dr. Guilliod's wife is in labor. But she told me to have you fill out the onboarding documents, and she'll be back on Monday next week for your first official day."

Psh, see? Mom was worried for nothing. I sit with the clipboard and fill out too many papers—with everything from my social security number to where I've lived the past five years. So, here's hoping they shred these afterward because I'm about to get a call from the credit bureau saying there's an unpaid $20,000 balance in my name down in the boonies of Florida or something.

Once they're all filled out, the secretary dismisses me. It took a grand total of forty-five minutes. The phone shop said my phone would be fixed in an hour, so I make my merry way down there in the lingering heat. Thankfully, this walk is downhill not uphill like it was to the hospital. The shop bell rings as I open the door, and the guy from earlier hands me my phone as I hand him my card.

I'm walking out, brand-new screen in hand, when Ben calls. Considering my avoidance last time ended with a $100.84 bill, I answer. "Hey, what's up?"

"Hey, Les." He clears his throat. "How're you?"

He's seriously going to act like last night didn't happen? Or maybe he doesn't remember it. Either way, "I'm good, you?"

"Yeah, same. So, uh...according to my roommate, I called

JESS CARPENTER

you last night. And I may have said something strange. Can you confirm whether that did or didn't happen?"

I bite my lip to keep from smiling. His embarrassment is actually sort of cute. His nose and cheeks tinge with pink whenever something bothers him, and I can picture it so clearly through the phone. "It happened."

He groans.

"Yep."

"I'm sorry."

I put my hand up even though he can't see me. "Whoa, did you seriously just *apologize*?"

He chuckles. "Oh, whatever. Don't pull that with me. I'm pretty sure I'm the only one who ever apologized in our relationship."

"Well, yeah, 'cause you were the only one that did things wrong." I pass through a million tables and signs with clubs and sororities trying to recruit members. It's a relief being on the phone.

"I'll be the villain if you need me to be. Can I see you?"

For whatever reason, my chest gets tight. But it's in an anticipation kind of way. "That depends. What're you wearing?"

He mock-gasps. "You're objectifying me already?"

"Duh. Come over in those shorty-shorts of yours and you've got yourself a deal." I laugh as a woman hands me a flyer about STIs. Typical.

"Chinese takeout?"

I hear a jingle of what I can only assume are keys, and I question why I'm letting this happen. But, I did promise him we could meet up, and after last night's little truth-bomb, it's only right to talk it out. "Order kung pao chicken, and you're dead to me."

"I wouldn't dare, babe. Moo goo gai pan?"

What is going on? Why is my lower half tingling? "Yeah. And Ben? Use *Spokin* to find a safe restaurant, okay?"

"Yeah, for sure. The only shortness of breath you're gonna have is from my shorty-shorts."

46

I laugh. "I'll text you my address. Let me know when you're on the way. Lo—"

I hang up before finishing because *gahhh* did I almost just say 'love you' to him? It's just habit.

We spent over two years together. A billion phone calls. So, obviously, the first time I'm on the phone with him again, I'd try to say it before hanging up. I say it to my mom too. It was habit. Get off my metaphorical balls.

Texting him the address, I speed walk to my car. Not promising anything, but I may have set a new record with how fast I walked. Anxiety will do that to ya.

The whole car ride home, I fidget and twist and also try to contain a bubbling squeal and scream. Does that make sense? Because I'm freaking out, yet a part of me is weirdly excited.

Rushing into my apartment, I make like the Flash and shove boxes around to make it look like I've unpacked way more than I really have. A mere thirty minutes later, I open the door to a mop of brown hair and a Chinese takeout bag in each hand.

"Hi." I side-step and let him in.

"Hey." He sets the bags on the counter and starts to unpack everything. His back is toward me and he's wearing tight jeans and ahh, his butt looks good.

"So…"

He grips the counter, and the muscles shift under his shirt. When he looks up at me with shining eyes, I relax.

I know him. He knows me. *Really* knows me. All the good. All the bad. And he still loves me. Did we make a mistake breaking up?

I take a step toward him.

He takes a step toward me, closes the gap, and kisses me.

Threading my arms around his neck, I jump. He grabs my thighs, hoisting me up around his waist and walks until my back is against the door. It feels so new, foreign, and yet, completely the same. Electricity laces up my spine and down every nerve as his tongue traces my lips. Sense is so far away, and I don't want to stop and look for it.

He pulls away and trails down my neck, kissing then biting right at the curve. I moan, and he presses harder against me. His hand moves up and around to my stomach, crawling up my side.

"Ben." I gasp, writhing against his hips.

His hand freezes. He untwists my legs and sets me down, stepping back and running a hand through his hair. "I'm sorry. That was not what I came here for."

I'm still sort of out of breath and grumpy that he stopped things. "Okay?"

"I just," he looks me in the eyes and then glances to the side, "don't think it's smart."

Again, all I can say is, "Okay?"

"It's not that I don't want to. I want to. But, I can't."

"*Okay?*"

He picks at his lips and then sighs. "This is coming out wrong. I, uh, I think I meant what I said on the phone last night, whatever it was."

Oh. *Oh.* Is he wanting me to say it back to him? Cue the gasps and utter shock.

Fidgeting with the hem of his shirt, he mumbles, "But I don't, like, need a response or anything." He glances up. "I just, I don't know. I wanted to be near you. And apologize. I'm so sorry for everything that happened between us because I don't know what went wrong, and you iced me out."

"Because you dumped me the day after my dad died, B. What was I supposed to do? I needed you, and you weren't there." He really wants to do this heavy crap? Fine, lay it on me.

"That's the thing, Les, I didn't dump you." He throws his hands up in the air like I'm the most frustrating person in the world.

"Then tell me what, 'maybe we should see other people' means." I sit down on the couch and bite my thumbnail. What was I thinking? That this could be some regular get together with an ex? This is why you don't have exes over. It's never a good time.

"I literally said that because you were all in your head and asking me questions like, 'What if you'd never have met me? Don't you think you want to see what else is out there?'" He air-quotes then rubs his palm into his eye. "The answer was always no, by the way. Because I'm so freaking in love with you that it hurts."

I scoff. "Oh, spare me. I don't remember it going down like that at all. If you were so in love with me, why were you posting pictures of girls on your Insta every single week?"

He sits down a few feet away from me on the other side of the couch and puts his elbows on his knees. "Because I'm an idiot."

"Well, at least we can agree on one thing."

The bags of Chinese food mock us. He must see where my gaze is because he blurts out, "Are we going to eat or not?"

I cock my head. "You think by feeding me I'm suddenly going to be nice?"

"Yes."

I mean, he's probably right, but I don't want to press pause on our conversation. It seems important. But then my stupid stomach betrays me by growling, and he puts on a smug smile with straight, white teeth and full lips and whew, those lips were just on me.

He bites his lip. "You're turned on."

"Me? Uh, no. By you? Puh-lease. Boy, bye." I take the scrunchie from my wrist and put my hair in a bun.

Somehow, his grin seems to grow even larger. He goes to the counter, grabs the different takeout containers, and hands me mine with some chopsticks. "Remember when we used to talk about moving into an apartment together and eating Chinese takeout naked?"

"I'm going to throw a water chestnut at you if you don't quit it."

He laughs. "Good times."

I grab the remote and flip through the channels on the

TV until I find some rerun of *Harry Potter*. It's about the only movie we can agree on, so it's a good thing Freeform pressed their we're-out-of-show-ideas-so-let's-run-a-Harry-Potter-marathon button.

I shovel chicken and veggies and rice into my mouth, not caring if I look like I'm trying to win a hot dog eating contest. If he's "so in love with me," then he'll deal. No way he actually meant that. I can't even count on two hands how many women he's posted photos with. Boating, literally doing a body shot off a redheaded woman in a bikini, and dozens more. He lived up the summer like some B-list celeb on Lake Tahoe, and I lived it up by studying for the MCAT and packing up all Dad's belongings. So, yeah, I'm a little annoyed. Had he told me he was in love with me the next day, week, or month, we'd probably be doing this every night and living together.

If I'm being honest, it makes me a little sad. My dad loved Ben. My mom loves Ben. So why couldn't he have told me he loved me back then?

I don't know how it happens, but Harry's about to play quidditch for the first time, and Ben's rubbing my feet. Again, how did this happen? No idea. With every minute that passes, Ben scoots an inch closer. By the time the movie ends and the next one begins, we're spooning on the couch like an old married couple. His arm is slung over my belly and he starts to trace circles right above the button on my pants. I'm squirming, and he knows it, but he doesn't make another move.

So, because I apparently like trouble, I turn toward him so we're chest-to-chest. Our noses and foreheads touch. But when he tries to close the gap between our lips, I pull back a fraction of an inch. He squeezes my side, and I laugh.

"You tease," he whispers. Then he kisses me, and I let him.

I straddle him and moan when he pulls up my shirt as he moves his hands on my back. But again, he stops and breaks our kiss with a, "I should probably get out of here. It's getting late."

It's like nine, but I do have an early class tomorrow. "You're right. I have Calc tomorrow."

He pushes himself up to sitting, slumping down with his legs spread out. "I still can't believe you tested higher than me in math."

Um, excuse me? "Why? Because you think you're smarter than me?"

Stretching his arms above his head, his shirt shows the littlest bit of skin right above his pant line. The same pant line I've looked at a thousand times, but my pulse thrums. "I don't think I'm smarter than you. But I did test higher on every single subject except math, so..."

Now he has my pulse thrumming for a whole different reason. "Yeah, well, I took that test a week before my dad died, so..." I flip him off.

"Come on, don't be like that."

"Be like *what?* Sane and rational because you're being an ass? Oh, excuse me, I'm so sorry for reacting completely normal to your idiocy."

He reaches out to grab my hand, but I yank it away. "Don't touch me."

"Seriously, Les? Stop being so sensitive!"

My jaw drops. "I will—when you stop being such a douche!"

Ben grabs his keys off the table and stomps toward the door where he slips on his shoes without untying them. The tongue of the sneaker gets bunched up to the front, but he either doesn't care or is too annoyed to notice. "I'm leaving. But you better not act like tonight never happened. When I call tomorrow, you better freaking pick up."

I scoff and roll my eyes. "Okay, Dad." And then I remember how bad those jokes hurt. Because he's not here anymore. "Get the hell out." I'm not going to cry in front of him.

He opens the door and stops because there's a five-pound bag of Sour Patch Kids blocking the mat. "Do I even want to ask why you have those?"

I don't remember placing a grocery delivery order, so I don't know. But I don't owe him any explanation. "Nope. Now, go!"

I grab the Sour Patch Kids and slam the door shut, locking the deadbolt and chain.

What am I doing with my life?

My phone buzzes on the kitchen counter, relieving me from the tension that just went down with Ben. Setting the candy down, I open up the unknown number's text message.

It's a picture of Carter with a Sour Patch Kid stuck up each nostril. He's smiling, his tongue out, eye shining, and his tongue licking the red piece of candy in his nose. A smile creeps up on my face, and then I read his words: *Are we candy compatible too?*

I'm in such a no-nonsense mood that I rip open the bag, grab a green and yellow kid and stick them up each nostril. Putting the camera forward-facing, I snap a picture of me, my lips in a kissy face.

Les: *I'm blaming you for the five-pound weight gain I'm about to experience.*

Les: *Also, ouch. The candy burns lol.*

Carter: *Yeah, should've warned you. I was hoping you wouldn't copy me.*

Les: *What can I say? I'm a follower.*

Carter: *Ha! For some reason, I highly doubt that.*

Les: *Seriously though, thanks for the candy.*

Carter: *That picture is your new contact pic. So, thank YOU. Seriously though, you're welcome. So, cute thang, if I haven't annoyed you yet...we're doing game night at my place tomorrow. Wanna come?*

I should say no, right? I just got it on with my ex. So, why am I considering saying yes? Three dots appear because he's typing and then disappear. I don't want him to rescind the invite.

Les: *Sure.* ☺

"Ah! What is life?" I grab a handful of candy and then run to my room where I cocoon myself in my sheets. My phone buzzes again. I should really just, like, not look at it. But my eyes betray me.

Carter: *It's a date.*

And the text doesn't make me smile, it's just my face's natural reaction to the sour candy.

Chapter Six

I wake up to my phone going off. Picking it up without looking at the caller ID, I groan, "What?"

"You're asleep." Utter distaste in my mother's voice. "Your new calculus class starts in thirty minutes."

The clock says 8:00. She's right. "I'm not asleep. I'm getting ready right now."

"I'm driving there."

What the...? No. Absolutely not. "I don't think that's a good idea, Mom. I've got classes all day today."

"We can go out for dinner. Bring Ben?"

"No!"

She clears her throat. "Excuse me?"

Ugh, why is she so scary? "I, just, um. Ben and I aren't speaking, remember? We broke up." Come on, I know she doesn't have memory issues.

"You have class together."

I hear the beep of her car unlocking, and I swear, it's a shot to my heart. "Mom, please. Not tonight."

"Tonight is the only night," she says. "I have a triplet separation surgery starting tomorrow afternoon. An over 24-hour surgery. I would like to see my daughter."

Putting the phone on mute, I cover my head with a pillow and scream. The pillow's a precaution—that woman can probably hear through mute. She lays the guilt trip on *so* thick. I take a deep breath and put a smile on that I know she'll be able to hear. "You're right. I'll make tonight work. Text me when you get in, and I'll give you the code to the apartment."

"No need. I already have it."

But I didn't give it to her. "Um, okay. Bye, love you." I hang up and want to throw the phone across the room, but I also don't want to pay another hundred bucks for a new screen.

What is she talking about that she already has the apartment code? And what gave her the idea that I should be inviting Ben to dinner? If everyone was so freaking gung-ho about me and Ben, why didn't they say something the entire summer?

Today is not the day to try and figure out the two most impossible people on Earth. I need to hurry up and get to class. I brush my teeth, nearly stab my cornea with the mascara wand, and grab an Enjoy Life granola bar for breakfast. As I rush down the outdoor steps, I side-swipe a tall woman with an, "Ah, I'm sorry! So late!" then sprint toward my car and blast the AC because my pits are sweating, and it's only 8:25.

My tires squeal as I pull out of my apartment's parking lot, and I am too stressed to turn on music as I navigate my way to the closest parking near the mathematics building. It's 8:29 and I'm right back to the first day, squinting at my phone to figure out where I'm supposed to go.

By the time I get to the door labeled 4600, I yank it open expecting a lecture hall. But, of course, it's not. It's a small room with maybe twenty students, and the professor, a small Black woman with curly pigtail buns and bright pink glasses, stops talking.

"And, who do we have here?" she asks.

"Sorry. I'm Les."

"Les?" She glances down at her iPad and scrolls a bit. "I don't have you on my class list. Is Les short for something?"

I should've seen that question coming. "No, I just transferred in yesterday."

She smiles and gestures to the shared tables. "Ah, okay. Well, find a seat. Anywhere you'd like. My TA will hand you the syllabus. I have a strict no make up policy, but because you've only missed one assignment, you can email it to me by tomorrow."

I nod. "Okay, thanks."

"Pssst."

I turn to the right.

Candy sticks out her tongue. "Sit down."

I sigh. Thank the holy math gods that I know someone. "Two out of five classes together? Meant to be."

"I know," she says under her breath. "We'd be a much better couple than *LesBen.*"

"Don't repeat that name!" I giggle, and Professor Butler glances my way, so I hush.

Candy slides me a note. In hot pink (of course) marker, it says: *Get home okay last night? I'm the worst. Sorry.*

Notes? Are we back in fifth grade? I steal her marker and write, *Yes,* before handing it back and pulling out my laptop.

She scribbles for a moment and slides the paper toward me again. *This class will be easy. P. Butler is a student-teacher, and Carter is the TA. Not positive, but I think they're hooking up. Lol*

Lmao, cool, I respond and hope she doesn't send me another note. I legit need to focus because now Ben has me all psyched out that I can't handle a class like this. But, I glance behind me and sure enough, there's Carter, biting at the end of a pen and wearing glasses. Glasses! Gosh, I hate that I have to cancel on tonight's game night 'cause of my mom. I was hoping I could wait until later to text him.

Professor Butler does an intro on limits and functions—everything we should remember from pre-calc. Key word: Should.

I don't remember anything. My hands cramp as I type line after line of notes. A brief thought passes through my mind saying, *you're going to fail.* And it's probably correct.

By the time the class ends, I'm so overwhelmed I could shed a river of crocodile tears to get some sympathy. I'd be a perfect contestant for *The Bachelor.* Tears are easy for me to whip up. Just stress me out enough, and I'll supply a wave pool.

"See," Candy bumps my shoulder, "told you this class will be easy."

But it wasn't easy for me. So, that's when I know that Ben isn't the only mistake I've made this semester. It sucks that I need this class for med school. Not only is it necessary, but without a good grade, I might as well pack my bags for the Caribbean because that'll be the only school to accept me.

"Mhmm, yep. Definitely," I mumble, following her toward the door.

Carter sits on the front of his desk, giving us a nod. "What's goin' on?"

He hands me the syllabus and bolded on the top is *No make ups for tests and/or assignments. I don't care what your excuse is. Absolutely no make ups!!!*

I stuff it in my backpack and glance back toward Carter. Might as well confess now. "So, I have some bad news." My puppy dog eyes are pretty good, so I'm using them right now. He *did* say he liked dogs.

He holds the door open for us. "Lay it on me."

"My mom's coming into town today, so I don't think I'll make the game night tonight."

Carter shakes his head and traces a finger horizontally across his neck at the same time Candy says, "Oh! Who's hosting?"

Whoops, my bad. His shoulders slump, but he winks at me. I'm about to be caught in sibling crossfire.

"*¡Dios mío!* You weren't going to tell me there was a game night?" She's crosses her arms.

I grab her elbow and drag her away from where we're blocking the door when a blonde chick says, "Um, can you move?" And from that exchange alone, I can tell she probably asks to speak to the manager 9/10 times she's at a store.

"Relax, I was going to tell you." Carter waves her off. "I was just waiting until tomorrow 'cause you have that thing tonight."

"Oh." She brushes away an errant pink curl. "Wait! The game

night is tonight, *tonto*."

I can't hold back my laughter any longer and pinch the bridge of my nose to try and calm down the giggles.

Carter chuckles too. "*Cálmate*. We're hosting tonight, okay? I didn't tell you because you already had plans, and I didn't want to mess things up. Just don't be pissed when Tom is with Jiah tonight."

Ooh, spill the tea. "Who's Jiah?"

Candy glares at me as if I shouldn't dare utter the name. "That girl from the hot springs the other night."

I point at Carter. "With you?"

"Nah, with Tom. Why'd you get her started?" Carter groans. "Can we at least go get brunch if you're going to torture me?"

"Class?" Candy asks me.

"Nope. Not until one. Let's brunch!" I hook my arms through both of theirs. "Just like Dorothy and her compadres. We're off to go eat brunch. Some wonderful, wonderful, brunch!"

Candy furrows her brow and looks toward Carter. "What the hell is she talking about?"

Has she really not seen the *Wizard of Oz*? There's no way. "Dorothy. Tin-man. Lion. Scarecrow. Wizard!"

Carter shrugs. "No clue."

Ugh. I glower and drag my feet because my mom is right: Millennials ruin everything.

But then Carter and Candy high five each other across me and start cackling.

"Freaking twins!" I let go of them to cross my arms. "You're the worst."

"Lmao," she drags out the last letter and pretends to shoot a basketball, "touchdown for the twins."

I throw my arm around her shoulders. "Settle down, Lebron Brady, you made one joke." But it feels like a permanent happiness is tattooed on my face.

Carter snorts. "Yeah, Candy. *Te amo*, but come on. You gotta get your sport references under control."

She tightens the strap of her bag and marches with her petite feet. "Whatever. Let's go to Anna's, that diner by the frat houses. Then we don't have to Uber. ¡Vámonos!"

Thankfully, Anna's is really good with allergies. I go back to the cook, and lucky for me, his daughter has a tree nut allergy, so he understands everything he needs to do.

I'm elbow deep in a waffle when I finally ask, "For real though, what's with you and Tom? You can't be mad that he's seeing someone else if you won't see him yourself."

Carter sips some water, and his bicep becomes that much more enticing as it ripples across his shirt when he sets his glass down. "Ah, she hasn't told you."

"What?" I set down the fork and syrup bottle that is now, surprisingly, empty. Stop judging, I like my sugar. "What haven't you told me?"

She rears her chin back and then points to her full mouth. "Sorry, too muff pancake. No talk."

A guy walks by, and Carter and him do that weird bro-shake-hug-fist-embrace thing. He sits back down and then pulls out his second old-fashioned-BlackBerry-looking phone. "Tom is a lotion conspiracy theorist."

I choke on too big of a waffle bite. The coughs overtake me, and I can see it on my gravestone now: *Died happy while stuffing her face.*

Okay, that wasn't a good joke.

Carter presses a few buttons and then glances up at me. "Geez, chew your food, dude."

By the time the waffle is down, I almost forget what made me choke in the first place. (I rescind my earlier too much waffle reasoning.) "What in the world is a lotion conspiracy theorist?"

Candy drops her fork onto her plate. It clatters, and a few people whip their heads around to our booth, but she doesn't seem to notice. She slaps Carter's arm. "Knock it off! That is not the reason."

"Reason or not, I gotta know." I'm already folding up tin foil into a hat so I can place it on my head.

She puts her head in her hands. "He thinks lotion is created by lotion companies."

"Um...it is?"

"No!" She throws her hands in the air. "He thinks that lotion actually dries your skin out over time, and then you need more lotion to make your skin soft again. So, the only reason we need lotion in the first place is because of lotion."

I pick up my fork. "That is...oddly specific."

Carter presses one more button and shoves the second phone into his pocket. He raises his hips up to do so, and I'm not leering, you are. "Yeah," he joins in. "He's weird, but we love him."

Candy shoves bacon into her mouth. "I told you, I'm saving him for later. We're exes. I can't get back together with him until it's almost marriage time. I want to have lots of experiences to share with my pink-haired kiddos."

They're *exes?* It's possible that she's either a genius or idiot. Maybe a little of both. "Huh, well, okay. I can respect that, I guess."

We spend the next little bit eating, joking, and people-watching. A couple in the next booth over is fighting, and let me just say, the dude, Gary, should probably sleep with one eye open tonight.

Carter's watch dings, and whatever he reads has him pulling out some cash and saying, "Gotta go, I've got an appointment with the team doc."

I shove his money back to him. "I've got it. You paid the other night." Plus, my trust fund may not be unlocked, but the so-called allowance that my mom gives me is ridiculous. Even I know that.

He shrugs. "If you insist. Are you for real out tonight? Game night doesn't start until ten."

The water I guzzle comes shooting out like my mouth is a firehose. "Ten? At night? Are you secretly all nocturnal trolls?"

Candy rolls her eyes. "Freshmen."

"Never cease to amaze me," Carter agrees. "See you tonight." And with a final wink, he's gone.

"Wait, you're not a freshman? But we're in two of the same classes."

"Nah, technically, I am. Second semester freshman here though." She levels her fork with my eyes. "Carter's a sophomore. I took a gap year and traveled."

People actually do that? "Huh, that's cool. So, I've been meaning to ask you something."

She chews her food and widens her eyes, which I'm guessing is a signal to go on.

I grin. "Do you watch *Bachelor in Paradise?*"

"Hell yes, I do." She makes her hand like a wave. "You better be inviting us over to watch. Rich girl like you probably got a whole wall-screen TV."

"Who's us? And what makes you think I'm rich?"

She scoffs and cocks a brow. "*Chica,* I know the cost of your shoes. And your basic shirt screams uppity. Now hurry up and let's go, we got Brock to torture."

Ben, Candy. It's always gonna be Ben.

Chapter Seven

I successfully ignore Ben the entire class. He tries passing me note after note, which I either tear up or shove into my bag.

After class, I drive home. Everything is peaceful. I'd even dare to say serene.

But I can feel the tension building like a wave. Everything before this was the calm before the tsunami. The pulling back of the water before a giant freaking wave comes and wipes away everything. So when I stand outside my apartment door and feel the pulsing energy coming from within, I know.

She's here.

I mean, I saw her Range Rover in the parking lot, so I already knew. But still, it's more dramatic like I said it. With a deep breath, I punch in my keycode and the smart lock unlocks. The door eases open with a gentle turn and push of my wrist. "Mom? Hi."

She comes barreling around the corner, heels clacking against the hardwood floors. Her hair is pulled back in an always-chic pony, and she reeks in the way that all rich people do—expensive manicures and face cream. "Les. I've finished your unpacking, besides those boxes in the corner."

For real? Why does she do this stuff? It's like she thinks that it's helpful, but it only makes her secretly resent me and me secretly resent her. "Wow, thanks, Mom. I know I should've cleaned up—"

"Mhmm."

"—but I'm so happy you're here." I embrace her, and she

leans her head down onto mine and pats my back.

When we break apart, her gaze travels from my toes to my hair. "You're not wearing that to the restaurant, are you? I secured a last-minute reservation at Fig."

I nod. "Sounds pretentious. Cool, just let me change."

"I laid out your lace Valentino dress."

My breathing stops.

As in the same black lace dress I wore to my father's funeral? Is she asking for a breakdown? Remember what my therapist, Judy, said: *Deep breaths. In. Out. In. Out.*

But it's not really helping. Mom's dressed in a gray pantsuit, so I'll be damned if I'm about to wear a morbid AF funeral dress to dinner. I bury the pain with an, "I want to match you! Wait here, I have the perfect strapless dress in that same gray. It'll be so cute."

I hightail it out of my own living room, close the bedroom door, and slide against it and onto the floor.

From the other room, she calls, "What was that noise?"

"Just my purse!"

"Your purse is out here."

I strangle the air. "My other purse!"

Why is she so hard to be around? Okay, the sooner I can get this dinner over with, the sooner I can send her on her merry way. Maybe I'm being rude, but I just *can't* with her lately.

Thankfully, I wasn't lying about the dress. I push the hangers to one side like I'm in some amazing rom-com picking out a dress for a date. Except, I'm not, 'cause it's a date with my mom. And the only romance in my life is an annoying ex.

I strip down (hey, don't look) and pull the dress up and over my hips. Zipping up the side and slipping into some classic, ankle-strap heels, I smile, eyes nearly closed from the intensity of it, and meet my mom in the living room. "See? Matching! Okay, let's go."

"Not going to grab your 'other purse?'"

"Psh." I wave her off. "No way. That one has all my illicit drugs. Hence why I took it into my room."

She rolls her eyes. "Hm. Classy. I'll drive."

Clack-clack-clack. Her heels make the obnoxious sound with every step. It sounds a little like a ticking bomb, and I'd be lying if I said I couldn't see a lecture coming from a mile away. She probably drank her morning cocktail of guilt trip and despair just for this dinner.

We get into the car, and even though the heat is blazing outside, somehow the interior manages to feel cold and sterile. As we drive through the winding hillside roads, there is no soft-playing music, no talking, and definitely no jokes. My dad and mom were opposites. You know what they say: Opposites attract. And for them, I guess they did.

My mom's phone lights up with a notification, and I glance at the family photo she has as the lock screen. She's smiling, but my dad is sticking his tongue out, and I'm putting bunny ears behind my mom's head. We got the silent treatment for a few days after that photo. So why she has it as her lock screen, who knows.

It's not fair that my dad was the one who died. And I know she's trying in her own way. But my dad was the one who always raised me. Sure, Mom's card was there to be continuously swiped should I ever need anything. But beyond that, every volleyball game and dance performance, it was my dad cheering from the sidelines.

It just hurts, I suppose. And seeing all these tall trees, the lush vegetation and smell of fresh air, it reinforces the fact that he would've loved to be here with me. But he's not, and that sucks.

I swipe at a very impolite tear that had the audacity to escape my eyes and disguise a sniffle as a deep breath. "So," I clear my throat, "work is going good?"

"Same as always, Les."

"Right," I whisper. The next twenty minutes, until we pull into the restaurant parking lot, I don't say a word.

We get out of the car, and I follow her to the cabin-style restaurant that is set up high upon large rocks. There's about fifty steps, which is just asking for a lawsuit, that lead up to the amber-lit door.

"Welcome to Fig," a man somewhere in his mid-thirties says.

"Reservation for Elizabeth Watkins."

"Of course." He bows his head. "Right this way."

The restaurant smells delicious, so that's a plus. Though it'd be nice to have a flashlight to actually see where I'm going in this dim lighting. It's clear this is some fancy-shmancy-only-made-for-millionaires type of place.

I hate it.

The waiter hands us a menu (with a built-in reading light) and leaves us to "discuss the options." But of course, we sit in silence instead.

"Do you know what you want?" she finally asks.

"Um, well, I didn't get an allergy menu or talk to the chef, so no." I always forget to ask until the waiter leaves.

"Everything's peanut-free tonight. Called ahead."

Did I say this place was pretentious? Well, call me Ms. Queen 'cause I'm about to blow this place up with my order. Does that say fresh baked brownie? Salted caramel crème brûlée? Fine, Mom won some brownie points in my book—pun intended. You know, as long as she isn't lying in some longterm scheme to murder me and collect a life insurance policy under my name or something.

I've gotta stop watching *Dateline.*

After placing my order with the waiter and handing back my menu, I'm just about to take the first sip of my sparkling water when she says, "Courtney called me yesterday. You remember her, right?"

Ben's mom. "Ben and I broke up, Mom." Slightly crazed smile here. "Didn't suddenly develop memory loss."

"Well, Courtney said that she was heartbroken to hear the two of you broke up."

How much longer am I going to endure this? Courtney *should* be heartbroken, but not for me. For herself because she raised Ben. "Is that so?" I fiddle with the napkin on my lap. "Maybe she should talk to her son about that."

It doesn't derail Mom's planned speech. "And how the Maldons will especially miss you when they travel to St. Maarten for Thanksgiving."

Where is she going with this?

Mom tucks a small section of hair behind her ear probably to show off delicate pearl earrings. "Your ticket was bought last December. Courtney said they'd still love to have you along."

And, there it is. I sip my drink. Keep sipping, more, more, more, *gurgle*—crap, it's gone. Mom blinks at me with expectant eyes. I choke out a hesitant, but polite, laugh. "That's nice of her, but I think it'd be a little awkward going to an island with the world's most perfect couple when me and her son are broken up."

Her brows raise, but no wrinkles appear on her forehead. "Think about it, Les. That's all I ask. They are a great family with many connections. Your father—"

"Can we not do this tonight?" I don't want to talk about Dad with her. Not now, not ever.

"Consider it."

I nod, but it's not happening. She can't ever find out about the kiss with Ben. It would only fuel her fire. Thankfully, our food comes out, and we focus on that. Roasted duck with an orange glaze, fingerling potatoes, and garlic butter spinach nestle in my stomach as if I'm some glorious new home for them. And you'd think my inn would be full, but when the dessert comes out, I'm all, "Come to, Mama."

Mom gives me a strange look over her phone, but who cares if I look like the wolf about to eat three little pigs? If I don't leave a restaurant looking at least five months pregnant, it's not worth it.

As the waiter passes by, Mom holds up her pointer finger and says, "Check please," because she can't *wait* for a waiter to hand over the check. She has to be the first one to request it.

She hands over her card, and I eat the rest of my brownie. When the waiter comes back, Mom quickly signs her name and puts her wallet away.

A busser, who is tall, fairly handsome, with curly brown hair that hits his shoulders, walks by with a too-full tray. My mom scoots out her chair, knocking into him, and a fork falls from his stack, clattering to the ground.

Mom gasps and quickly retracts her foot as if the fork is poison.

Setting the tray on an opposite table, he apologies as if his job depends on it, but it comes out broken and stuttered. With a tight-lipped frown, she nods and waves him off.

The man walks away, but I notice a hint of purple on his cheeks.

She sighs. "He needs to be written-up for that kind of behavior."

I'm not usually one to disagree with her (in public), but something about this is rubbing me the wrong way. She gets annoyed by these things, but once they're out of sight, that's usually the end of it. So, what about this busboy is different? "You mean for his mistake?"

"When you come into this country and work an honest job, you can't afford mistakes. Who knows if he was even legal by the looks of it."

My jaw drops, and I scoff. Was she seriously just blatantly racist? "Right, you don't know. Nor does it matter. Are you saying you've never made a mistake?"

"That's different. I'm a surgeon. There are plenty of opportunities for mistakes. But at least if I make a mistake, I know how to apologize in English." She taps at her phone then says, "Let's go," before I have a chance to respond.

As we get into the car and drive off, it's my own silence that's haunting, not hers. I should've said something. I should've *done* something. Which is weird because I haven't felt like this before. But at the same time, has she ever acted like that before? I would've noticed...right?

It takes a whole drive of silence for my anger to reach a crescendo. It's not okay. When we pull into my apartment's lot, I hurry to grab my purse. "You don't need to walk me in."

Her hand pauses on the ignition, but her face shows no remorse. "I'm staying in town tonight and will be heading back in the morning for tomorrow's surgery."

You've got to be kidding me. "Are you staying at my apartment?"

"No, I have someone to visit."

"Okay. Thanks for dinner." I yank on the handle and open the door.

"Happy early birthday, Les," she says. "I love you."

"Love you too," I mutter, closing the door with a gentle click. But if she loved me, she would've known that she's the last person I'd want to spend my birthday with.

I watch as her brake lights flash. She pulls out of the lot, turning left. Tomorrow's the first birthday my Dad isn't here for. The first birthday of many Dad-less birthdays.

I hurry into my apartment before the dam breaks. Grabbing a few tissues off the kitchen counter, I push them into my eyes as the tears flow so mascara doesn't run down my face. Is this how life is going to be? I'll go a few months thinking I'm fine and then everything will shatter again?

My body wracks with sobs, and I feel stupid for crying here. I need a cat or dog or something because crying by myself just makes me sob harder.

If my dad saw me right now, he'd probably throw a candy bar in my direction and slowly back away like I'm a rabid dog. The thought alone makes me cry harder because I'll never get consolation chocolate ever again, and how am I supposed to live without consolation chocolate?

The stupid rhinestone case I got for Christmas—from Ben—rattles against the hardwood over and over and over as someone calls me. I throw the tissues across the room and pick the phone up. Facetime call from Candy. "Hey."

"Hey, girl. What's—have you been crying?" Her eyes get

closer to the screen, and she squints one. Her eyelids are covered in gold sparkles and I see her contact lens through the camera.

"No," I sniffle, "I just have really bad allergies."

She grimaces. "Like...from your apartment?"

I wave my hand around. "This isn't my apartment. It's actually a really cool, posh restaurant."

"Uh, pretty sure that's your apartment." Someone tries to come into the picture, but Candy pushes them out. "What's wrong?" She draws out the last word for three whole seconds.

"Nothing is wrong!" I blow some loose strands of hair from my forehead.

Candy purses her lip and cocks a brow. "*Está bien*, hon. Come to our game night. It'll be fun."

"I don't really play games," I mumble because I'm pretty sure she won't take no for an answer.

"You'll be fine. Plus, we have jello shots here. It'll be *perfecto. Un segundo.*" She puts the phone further away from her face and cups one hand around her mouth. "Carter! I need you! We gotta go pick up Les!"

I groan. "Why does your brother have to pick me up? You just come yourself. Or I'll Uber." I really don't want him to see me crying.

She shakes her head. "Nah. I can't do *mi amiga* like that. Plus, the Ubers at this time of night are freaking creepers. You can't drive while crying, and Carter is coming with me to pick you up because, hello? Did you not hear me? We have jello shots. I've had like *cinco.* Carter! *Vámonos, por favor!*" She puts some gloss on her lips using the phone as a mirror. She pops them once, twice, three times, and smiles. "Hold tight, sad *señorita.* We are on our way!"

I hang up and sigh. My phone buzzes again with a text. When B's contact shows up, I don't read what he has to say. Instead, I turn my phone off. Tomorrow's my birthday, so I'm gonna choose myself for once. Forget him.

Clicking my toes together like a backwards Dorothy, I say,

"There's no place like Candyland." Maybe it's exactly what I need to take my mind off of everything.

Chapter Eight

W iping the mascara from underneath my eyes, I look out the window until I see Carter's car pull up, and then I head out the door.

"Look what I brought!" Candy dangles a loose piece of jello until it falls to the concrete in a splatter. "Aww, Carter. I broke it."

He puts his arm out the window and shoves her back into the car. "Yeah, you're going to be next if you don't sit down and buckle your freaking seat belt. Hey, Les. Glad you could make it after all." He juts his chin out, and his eyes graze over my outfit. "Nice, *mami*. I like the dress."

I adjust my hoop earring, pulling at it gently. "Ha, well, thanks. You don't look too bad yourself."

He opens his mouth to speak, but Candy hangs out the window again and yells, "*Vámonos, muchacha!*"

I jog as much as these heels will let me over to the passenger side. Carter leans over and opens the door for me, so I hop in and stick out my tongue with a wink like my fave emoji. "*A la fiesta, señor!*"

Carter throws his head back with laughter. "Aw, girl. We're really gonna have to work on that accent of yours."

Candy inserts herself between us and nods much slower than necessary. "Yeah, you sound really white."

I pull at one of Candy's pink curls. "Well, I am."

The car lurches forward, and my head slams against the back of the seat. "Geez, are you trying to kill me?"

Carter's fingers tap against the center console as he raises his eyebrows and smiles. "Definitely not."

"I have the perfect song." Candy squeals. "You're going to love it, Les." She scrolls on her phone and then seems to find whatever song she was hoping for because "DNA" by BTS starts blaring through the speakers.

I humor her and start singing Jungkook's parts at the top of my lungs. Carter rolls his eyes, but two songs in, he's singing along too. By the time we pull up to their apartment complex, I'm draped across Candy in the backseat, and our voices are nearly lost.

We get out and walk to the door arm-in-arm. Carter follows behind us, pulling out the key fob to let us into the building.

Candy pats my shoulder. "So, are you going to tell me why you were crying?"

And here I thought I was getting out of it. "Girl, I wasn't crying."

She untwists her arm and turns in a circle, swaying her hips to the music I hear blaring down the hallway. "*Mentirosa.* That's like me saying I'm not buzzed!"

"You're beyond buzzed!" The song is some sort of dub-step mix. Pretty sure my heart is now beating in sync with the bass, and I'm not even in their apartment yet.

We step up to their haunted 13666 apartment and the door flies open with some chick screaming, "Suck it, Ryker! I knew I'd beat you at Go Fish!"

Candy pulls me through the doorway where two dozen or so people are slapping cards on the kitchen table and shouting across a board game on the coffee table. And there's a random couple that makes out on the end table. *Sanitary.*

We stop at the kitchen counter that's lined with blue, orange, red, and green little cups of jiggling mixture. "These are the special jello shots."

A bad flutter flies from my stomach into my throat. I don't know what's in the jello shots. Or what if whoever prepared them had peanuts before? The risk of cross-contamination is too big. I pat my dress as if it might have an EpiPen hidden in the pockets. Crap. I didn't even bring it. Suddenly, nausea swirls in my gut. How could I be so stupid? If I have anything here that has been in contact with peanuts, I could die from an allergic reaction. Sure, the hospital's close by, but who knows if I'd make it.

Plus, I can literally hear my mom talking over my dead body saying, *well, she shouldn't have been involved with such lowlifes.* She'd probably even have a bedazzled sign on my grave saying *I told you so.*

"Which color do you want?" Candy's voice breaks my panic spiral.

"Uh, I can't. The risk of cross contamination is too much. If you or someone else had leftover peanuts on their hands, I could die. I didn't even bring my EpiPen."

She waves me off and her hands look like little cat paws. "*En serio?* Scary. I'll give you a free pass this time. Next time, you can make them with me. But for the record, I'm like 80% sure they're safe." She's so confident in her answer that I can't help but laugh.

"What?" She smiles with full lips.

"I appreciate your 20% margin of error with my life."

She scratches at her head and musses her hair. "That was being generous."

I fold my arms. "Take your shot."

"*Bien,*" she grumbles.

I rub my hands together. "Alrighty. Let's get to the games."

She dances with her empty shot cup, nodding to the others. "Drumroll, please."

Rolling my eyes, I mimic a drumroll.

"We have Go Fish, Cards Against Humanity, Candyland, which I'm obviously *la reina* of, and Carter's got some Xbox game set up. *¿Qué quieres?*"

"Cards Against Humanity first, for sure."

She nods as if I've just given her war orders and marches over to the kitchen table. After introductions, I sit down and share a seat with Candy, which makes it incredibly easy to look at her cards. She's basically fanning them to everyone at this point.

I play as best as I can, and after coming in second on round one, my mind wanders. I'd be lying if I said my attention wasn't just a little bit on Carter. Haven't seen him since we got here 'cause he's probably playing that Xbox game. But, surely I need to thank him for the ride here, right?

After three rounds of Cards Against Humanity, my heart definitely isn't in it. "Hey, you know where your brother went?"

Candy frowns. "Am I my brother's keeper? Nope." She pops her lips. "Go find him, if you want. I'm crushing this game."

She is one hundred percent not crushing the game. But, I'll let her believe it if that'll make her happy. I slide off the chair and go down the hallway. It's sort of hard to hear much over the loud music.

I peek in the first room on the left, then immediately peek *out.* That is definitely Tom, definitely kissing a girl who is not Candy. It's irrational, but my heart beats fast, and I feel like a little girl getting in trouble at school. Please say that they didn't see me. That would be so...awkward.

Onto the next door. The one on the right is Candy's, but there are still two more rooms. The next one is closed, so I knock gently, hoping whoever's in it can hear me.

"Come in!" Carter shouts.

I breathe a sigh of relief and open the door where he's chillin' on a beanbag, shooting zombies on Xbox. He glances up. "Hey, what's up?"

"Oh, nothing. Just seeing what else everyone else was up to."

"Are you even paying attention? I'm getting slaughtered, man!" he says into his headset. He throws one last grenade, rolls his eyes, and sets the controller and headset down, succumbing to the zombies that quickly attack.

Men and their video games.

Carter turns toward me and quirks his lips. "You were 'just

seeing what *everyone else* was up to,' huh?"

I can feel the heat crawling into my cheeks. "Yep."

"Hm. And what is everyone else up to?"

I shrug. "The usual. Games, Candy swearing at everyone in Spanish, random people making out with each other, you know. The usual." Crap, I already said that.

"Fun times." He winks.

There's a pause, and I awkwardly shuffle between my feet, glancing around.

The room is pretty bare. Just the two twin beds, night-stands, plus a big screen TV taking up most of the wall. Oh, and the inevitable mountain of clothes that every man seems to have stacked up in the corner of their room.

"You can sit, ya know." He points toward one of the twin beds.

I sit down on the bed, now somewhat unsure of myself. So, I say the first thing on my mind. "Well, it's game night. Wanna play a game?"

That was not a good question. Who am I? Jigsaw?

Carter stands from the beanbag, and somehow, he even manages to make *that* look sexy. When he sits down on the bed next to me, his thigh is touching mine. I'm just gonna ignore the tingles and heat I'm feeling there.

He nudges my knee with his. "Truth or dare?"

I laugh. "What is this? My seventh grade sleepover?"

"Hey," he chuckles, "you're the one who asked to play a game. Come on, girl, answer the question. Truth or dare?"

I stick my tongue out at him. "Truth."

"Did you or did you not come in here just to see me?"

Oh geez, don't look at my burning cheeks. "Fine. Yes, I did. Your turn. Truth or dare?"

"Truth," he says, leaning back on his hands.

"Bor-ring."

He mock-gasps, shifting on the bed until he's right next to me. Deep breaths. No, wait, his cologne smells too good. Shallow breaths. You know what? Imma just stop breathin' for a second.

His hand is barely an inch from mine, and I can feel a pulse in the gap. "You chose truth, too," he says.

"Yeah, but I had to go first. The first person always chooses truth."

With a smile, he shakes his head. "Just ask me my truth already."

"Okay, okay. Truth." Our gaze lingers, and I drop mine to his lips. There's a pause, and I can feel my heart in my chest. *Be bold, Les. Be bold.* (That's what you're saying, right?) So, I guess I'll listen to you. "Do you want to kiss me?"

He glances at my lips, then meets my gaze again. "Yes."

I feel the word all the way to my toes, and when he leans in, the loud music seems to get drowned out by my heartbeat. He cups my chin when his Apple Watch chimes.

Not a big deal. I'm used to it. Carter leans in, our lips almost brushing when his watch sounds again, louder and longer this time.

"Um, okay," I say, pulling back. "Maybe you should get that."

"*Chingao.* I'm so sick of this stupid thing." He takes it off, throws it on the bed, then stands up and leaves the room.

And then you have little ol' me. Just sittin' here, wondering what the hell is going on. 'Cause, like, huh? Is he sick of his Apple Watch? Just get rid of it, dude.

But also like...is he coming back? Should I just chill here? Seems pretty frickin' awkward to hang out on a bed that's not mine.

I barely have enough time to think before Carter rounds the corner with juice boxes, fruit snacks, and Sour Patch Kids piled high like snack Jenga. Candy's pushing him, and both of them are shouting at each other.

She groans. "*Lo vi.* You're welcome, by the way. You can't be so careless, Carter! What could've been so important that you ignored the first warnings? Your stupid zombies?" she yells, thrusting her hand out toward the TV, sounding way too sober for the amount of jello shots she's had. "You're lucky I was prepared."

He rolls his eyes so far back into his head that he can probably see his brain. "Thanks, sis. Heaven forbid I have to walk five more steps into the kitchen."

Candy lays on the other bed and flushes with a deep red. But, then the Spanish comes in. And they're shouting so quickly and furiously that I don't have any idea what they're saying.

It's not my battle, and it's awkward that I'm here, so I try to get up from the bed to leave. But the second my butt moves an inch, Candy says, "No, Les. I'm going to be the one to leave because I can't stand to be next to the world's biggest *idiota!*"

He jabs the straw into the apple juice box. "Wow, congratulations. You're the world's biggest drama queen. You are the last person who should be giving me a responsibility talk."

She crosses her arms, but it puts her off balance, and she catches herself with her hand on the mattress. "Because I had a few shots? Oh, wow. Except I couldn't *die* from my lack of responsibility!"

It seems like an inappropriate time to butt in and tell her that she actually *can* die from alcohol, but as long as you all know...

She doesn't stop there. "You can't ignore your warnings. You don't get to *accidentally* forget to eat. You can't make mistakes, Carter! Your mistakes could cost you your *maldito* life!"

"I'm so confused." I bounce back and forth between their faces. But it's also hard to take this seriously when Carter sips on a juice box straw until the last few drops noisily suck through. Candy sniffles, and wait, for real? She's crying?

I twist my ring around my thumb. "Um, Candy, are you okay?"

Carter crushes the juice box and sits on his beanbag. "She's fine. It's not a big deal. My blood sugar just got a little low."

Candy spits. "His blood sugar doesn't 'get a little low.' He has diabetes. He could literally die!"

He thrusts his hand in her direction. "*En serio,* Candy? Not cool."

Wait...The juice boxes, fruit snacks, and applesauce in his car. He's not an Uber driver. Nor does he have secret children. Nor does he give his hook ups snacks. And he didn't stop our kiss 'cause of my breath? I mean, that's nice to know. Really, this knowledge is a relief, if anything. "So, you're a diabetic?"

He sighs, pulls up his shirt, and points to the back of his hip where two devices, one circular and one cylindrical, attach to his skin a few inches apart. "*Sí*, type one. Meet my insulin pump and CGM."

"Are those always there?" I feel like I'm the weird elephant in the room, but I can't escape now. Plus, I'm intrigued. "Wait...so why didn't you say anything before?"

He drops the hem of his shirt and shrugs, grabbing his watch off the bed. "Hey, I'm Carter, I'm a type one diabetic. Sounds like a kinda weird way to introduce myself, right?"

I'm an idiot. "No, right. Of course, you're right. I just thought—" Well, I don't know. I guess I thought that maybe because I talked about my peanut allergy, he'd share his health problems? But that's not my place at all, so the words die in my throat.

If anything, I should completely understand.

Carter rolls out his wrist, and I notice his watch screen has his heartrate and a few other numbers on it. He sits down next to Candy and squeezes her shoulder. "*Lo siento*, okay?"

She pulls away. Though, I'm still not entirely sure why she's so freaked out. He said it wasn't a big deal.

He looks at me and then back to Candy. "Candy, can you give us a few minutes? I promise I'll retest again to make sure I'm good. You don't have to babysit me."

"That's the only reason I'm here." She scrambles off of the bed and storms out, slamming the door shut.

It makes me jump.

Carter scoots next to me so our shoulders touch. "I wasn't trying to hide it."

"No, honestly, it's fine. I get it. I always get kind of awkward when I tell people about my peanut allergy too. I'm just...confused. You said it wasn't a big deal, but Candy clearly thinks it is."

His elbows are on his knees, and he twists his foot on the floor. "I, uh, I was just diagnosed last year."

"Isn't that kind of late?"

He smirks and raises his brows. "Yeah, you could say that."

It seems like there's more to the story, but I bump his shoulder. "So, what happened tonight?"

Carter fiddles with the rubber band on his wrist. "My pancreas doesn't produce much insulin, so I have this pump to send me more." He points to one of the devices. "But, it sent me too much. So, my blood sugar got low." He puts his hand on my knee.

Now all I can do is stare at his fingers.

He keeps going. "Anyway, a low blood sugar number isn't usually bad. I just eat or drink something." Reaching into his pocket, he pulls out the clunky phone I've seen. "This little thing is my controller where I tell my insulin pump how much insulin to give me. Then I have a CGM that monitors my blood sugar. That's this other thing on me. They stay there. I mean, I change out the Dexcom, my CGM, every ten days and my pump, I change every three days. But, they're always attached somewhere on me. But it's no biggie. With my app, I have alerts set for when it hits eighty-five and is shown to be dropping. It'll keep sounding, which is why you heard it. Usually I catch low blood sugar fairly quick, but I was...distracted."

Okay, his fingers on my knee distract *me* for a moment. But, I'm good. I focus. And what I'm hearing is that it's a lot. Like, Candy has good reason to worry about him.

I've heard the horror stories of type one diabetes. And lately, there has been a ton of news about the rise of insulin prices. But I've never personally known a diabetic. "Can't you, like, die from type one?"

Eek, yeah, that's awkward. I shouldn't have said that. I vaguely remember watching the movie *Steel Magnolias* where —never mind, sorry, spoilers.

He sighs. "I'm fine. If I hit a low, I get some fast-acting carbs in my body, retest manually in 15 minutes if Dexcom doesn't show that my blood sugar is on its way up, and I'm good to go."

Why's he skirting around my question? "Okay, well, why is Candy so freaked out then?"

"I hate talking about this," he whispers.

"Oh. Well, you don't have to if you don't want to."

"Better now than later, I guess." He scratches his nose and adjusts the shorts he's wearing. "It's not a big deal, but because I didn't grow up with it, it's been sort of hard figuring it all out. And getting diagnosed was a problem too. I went into the ER three times feeling sick, and every time, they dismissed me. The only reason I was diagnosed was because at a game, I was pitching, and it got pretty bad."

I cock my head to the side. "What do you mean?"

Carter runs a hand through his hair. "I, uh, pretty much collapsed and started vomiting. Couldn't breathe. I went into something called diabetic ketoacidosis, which meant my blood sugar was too high. But I didn't know I had diabetes, so..."

Again, I'm on Team Candy here. I don't want to see Carter collapsing or dying either. "That's...intense."

"Yeah, sorta why Candy started her platform."

I draw my eyebrows together. "But I thought she was fighting for immigrants."

He smiles in a way that shows I don't understand. "She really fights for minorities as a whole, but immigration is always a hot topic, so yeah. But, she thinks I wasn't diagnosed early enough because I'm Mexican-American. Anyway, it's not really a big deal."

"Uh-huh." He keeps saying it's not a big deal. I glance at his shirt where the monitor and insulin pump hides. "So you think a white person would've been diagnosed earlier?"

Carter shrugs, his shoulders drawing up to his ears. "That's the million dollar question."

There's a moment of silence, and for the first time with

Carter, it feels awkward. I don't know what to do or say. He says it's nothing, but all of it sounds like a pretty big deal. And now I'm worried I handled it completely wrong. I just...*ugh*. It seems like he's possibly embarrassed, and now I want him to know that I see him, no matter what.

He's leaning back on his hands, and I put my hand on top of his. "You know I'm not gonna look at you differently because of your diabetes, right?"

His smile drops into an unreadable expression. "I think that's easier said than done, *chica*."

I trace his fingers with my nails. "Well, *I* think you're badass. I don't get it. Is it usually a problem for people?"

He shakes his head. "I don't know. I haven't really been with too many girls since I was diagnosed. It's not like I want to be with a chick and have to say, 'Shoot, hold on. Let me throw down some fruit snacks before we continue.'"

He mocks himself while staring up at the ceiling, and I snort.

"What?" he deadpans.

I'm in a fit of giggles, and his frown starts to ever-so-slightly change.

I crinkle my nose and smile. "What more could a girl ask for? Snacks and an intermission? Seems like a sweet deal."

He covers his face with his forearm, but I see his smile underneath. "*Ay Dios mío.* Who are you?"

I grab at his arm and take it away from his face. Then I hold out my hand. "Hey, I'm Les. Any guy I'm with pretty much has to swear off peanuts forever. I can't kiss random people or I could die because I don't know if they had a peanut butter sandwich for lunch. My biggest fear isn't sharks or alligators, it's walking into a Texas Roadhouse."

He chuckles.

I wink. "I have a gnarly scar on my hip from falling off my bike and onto a sheet of metal. Nice to meet you, dude. Also, full disclosure, I used to tell people that scar was from a shark attack, and they believed me."

He shakes his head and places a hand on my hip. "Hey, I'm Carter. I'm more of an almond butter guy, I've got type one diabetes, and I also have four screws in one leg because I tripped and fell off a stage when Candy forced me to be her ballet partner in middle school. Nice to meet you."

I lean my head closer to him and his full-lipped smile. "You poor kid, forced to be a ballerino."

"Mmm, I still got some sick moves I can show you if you'd like."

"Okay," I say as he closes the gap between us, and our lips touch.

It's soft and warm, and it races down my mouth and into every part of me. It's the something I didn't know I needed, the small piece of remembrance, the feeling of coming home. His kiss isn't fire and ice but a steady pulse sustaining me. All I know is I want to feel this feeling for a very long time.

He pulls back when the bedroom door opens.

Candy pokes her head through the door. "Did you retest?"

He holds up his phone. "No need. Dexcom is mapping it, and my blood sugar is on its way up. I'm fine. Now get out, Candy."

She flips him off and closes the door.

Overprotective sister. Wait a sec, it all makes sense. "Candy didn't really take a gap year to travel, did she?"

"Nah, she did." He taps on his phone and then slides it into his pocket. "It just wasn't supposed to be only a year. Sort of a permanent, *adios* mom and dad, I'm gonna find myself in the Himalayas type of thing."

"She came back for you?"

He looks proud, albeit a little sad. "We're twins. I was there for her. She's here for me."

"Wish I had a twin," I mumble.

Probably would've been a lot easier to get through my dad's death if I had someone to share it with. But no. Instead, I was holed up in my room with a broken heart, a broken spirit, and a broken mom. Which just reminds me that it's technically my birthday, and I should be having fun, not being sad. It's a shame

I can't cut to a commercial break and get a moment to myself.

Carter lifts my chin up until I'm staring into his green eyes. "Hey, what's wrong?"

I shrug. "It's stupid."

"Are you a sad drunk? Let me get Candy—"

"I'm not drunk! I definitely didn't trust those jello shots. But either way, no, I'm not a sad drunk. Wait, why aren't you drunk? Pretty sure Candy is." I ramble on because anxiety is cool like that.

He throws his hands up in false frustration. "Blood sugar. Gets weird with alcohol. It's already all over the place with sports, so it's not really worth it to me. I'd rather play baseball."

"Right, my bad. Sorry, I'm not that great with this stuff. Mom's a brain surgeon, not an endo."

"I'm surprised you even know what an endocrinologist is."

I give him a stare that rivals a spanking—and yes, my mind just went there too. Carter's got the perfect baseball butt.

He puts his arm around me and squeezes as I lean against him, nose to armpit.

Unfair. He even smells good in his armpits.

"We're getting off topic," he says. "What's wrong? You look all sad. You've got a mean set of puppy dog eyes."

I laugh. "Good. I'll use that to my advantage now that I know you're susceptible." I lean off of him, careful to put my hands on his thigh, not near his, ya know. (His insulin pump, *come on.* Get your mind out of the gutter.) "Tomorrow's my birthday. And, it's my first birthday since my dad died."

"Hold up. It's your birthday?" He grabs me by my hips and pulls me onto his lap.

Hey, I'm not complaining. "Yes. Happy birthday to me, right?"

He spreads my legs so I'm straddling him. "Yes, happy birthday to you. I can't believe you didn't tell us it's your birthday. I would've gotten you something."

I'm blushing. I can feel the heat rise in my cheeks. "What

would you have gotten me?"

He kisses the crook of my neck. "Something cool. What would you have liked?"

I can barely focus as goosebumps rise everywhere his lips touch. "Um, I don't know." My words come out between short breaths. "Uh, um, a bracelet?"

His hands tangle in my hair, and he kisses me, biting gently on my lower lip. So, now my head's spinning.

"Hold on." He gets up and walks toward his dresser. I take a moment to admire the way his shorts hug his butt. He rummages through his top drawer before pulling out a braided string friendship bracelet that's purple and pink.

"What is that?" I laugh.

He shoots me a goofy grin, tipped up on one side. "I got it at our baseball fundraiser last year. It was some carnival to raise money for kids' baseball camps. Honestly, I forgot I even had it. But then you said bracelet, and it sparked the memory."

I bury my face in my hands because why does a string bracelet make my heart feel like it's going to explode into glitter and happiness? When I look back at him, I shake my head and bite the side of my mouth to hold in the world's biggest smile. "And you want to give it to me?"

"Yeah, *cariña*. Unless it's stupid. This is stupid." He goes to put it back.

Pulling at his arm, I say, "Absolutely not! This is the best birthday present ever."

He rolls his eyes, but chuckles. I dangle my wrist in front of him like I'm in some Audrey Hepburn movie trying on a delicate diamond bracelet. He carefully ties it on, knotting it three times.

I run my finger over the braided pattern. "I love it."

"Ah, well, good. *Feliz cumpleaños*." He intertwines his fingers with mine, fiddling with the knot in my bracelet with his thumb. "What are we doing in here? Let's go demand you win every game. It's your birthday right."

He sits down and squeezes my side with his other hand. I

yelp. "Carter, you *loco hombre.*"

"*Chica,* your accent. No, no, no." He laughs, and our foreheads touch. "Plus, it'd be *hombre loco.* You know, if you want to call me that again."

I sit in his lap, trying to ignore the fact he's lighting my body up with a tingly feeling. "Whatever. My accent is da best. But okay *hombre loco*, let's crush those games." Yep, can't ignore the tingles. "But make out with me first."

He lays back on his bed, pulling me on top of him. "Don't have to ask me twice."

Chapter Nine

"What...is...that...noise?" she groans.

Why is there a woman talking in my ear, and why is she talking at all, and why does it feel so early? I open my eyes, and light spills through the blackout curtains that were not properly closed last night. Which is weird, because I *always* properly close my curtains.

What's in my mouth? I sputter and pull at a wad of pink hair. What is going on? Candy is to the right of me, forearm across her eyes, groaning. Then I look to my left, and Carter is there, breaths steady and hands clasped on his bare chest, sleeping.

And oh boy, is it a chest. But also...why is he in my bed half-naked?

I look to my left and right. Candy's in a tank and shorts. I'm in a long tee that barely covers my butt. "Oh, no. Please do not tell me some weird freaky threesome thing happened here."

Even whispering hurts my throat. Probably slept with my mouth open all night long. *Sexy.*

I tap on Carter's shoulder until he opens one eye and groans just like Candy did.

"What did you say?" he croaks and rubs at his eyes.

"Why are you guys here? In my bed? With me in the middle!" I'm not usually so confused in the mornings. But I'm also not usually roused from sleep mid-dream. *Think, Les.* Think!

Candy sits up and palms her brow. "Honestly, I have no idea. But what you said is disgusting. He's my *hermano.* And he's not even the good-looking twin."

"Am I the only sane one this morning?" Carter groans, his voice still thick with sleep. "I took you home last night, with Candy, so you two could have, and I quote, a 'slumber party.' Then you, and, once again I quote, said, 'Please, please, please stay the night with us, Carter. If you don't, I'll sue you and your family for everything they own.'"

And who says romance isn't dead? Threatening to sue? Adorable.

I hum. "That sounds like a lie."

He shakes his head. "It was maybe thirty minutes after you'd taken Benadryl. You said you didn't feel very well? I'm honestly not totally sure, I'm exhausted."

Well, Benadryl would definitely explain the lapse in judgment.

Oh, *wait.* No, no, no. I remember the real reason. Even hopped up on Benadryl, I'm smart. It was that chick Tom was with. Everyone else had left but her, so as the best friend, I made up a story to save Candy the heartache. Carter though? Yeah, that was probably the Benadryl talking.

I cough. "Oh, yes. Sorry. Benadryl. Super great drug. But I do tend to get a little needy on it." I grin so wide it hurts. It's possible I'm overselling it.

"Honestly, it was a little dramatic," Carter cuts in. "Worth it, though," he whispers, kissing my cheek.

Candy retches. "Gross."

But my attention isn't on them because I hear footsteps outside my bedroom door, and my feet go cold. I stutter, "Psh, what? No, no. I'm never dramatic. Candy, did you say there was a noise?"

Carter stretches his arms.

"Oh yeah! What was it? Like some beeping noise?"

Beeping? As in, my smart lock on the front door? Uh oh, the footsteps are getting closer. I pull at the covers. "There's someone—"

The bedroom door opens with a, "Happy birthday—ah!" My mom drops a box that looks like it could hold donuts and covers her eyes.

I scream. Mostly for the donuts, but also because she's *here.*

Mom huffs. "Really, Les? You couldn't make it past a few weeks in college before your first ménage à trois?" She opens her eyes and then scowls. "And with...I'm sorry, who are these people?"

The twins glance at each other, making us all a mortified sandwich. She's being rude. Why is she even here? "It's not what it looks like, I swear."

And, apparently, it's not what it looks like on her end either because Ben steps from behind my mother's shadow. "Uh, hey, Les." He clears his throat and rubs at his neck. "Carter. What's her face. Happy birthday."

I can feel Candy about to jump down Ben's throat, so I nudge her hard. "Mom, these are just my friends. Carter and Candy. They're, er, they're twins. So, no on the whole ménage-thingy. They stayed with me last night as my *friends.*"

Mom sighs. *"Oh-la, me llamo—"*

I try to scramble off my memory foam mattress, elbowing Carter somewhere soft. He groans, and my legs fly up in the air trying to pump some momentum into getting off the bed. "They speak English!"

"That's even worse." She waves at them sarcastically.

I'm not sure what she means, but I know she's being ridiculous. Nausea threatens to turn into throw up as I finally stand up from the bed much too quickly.

"Right," I say. "Um, Carter and Candy were *just leaving.*" I signal at them both behind my back, and they scurry out of my bed.

Candy grabs her jacket, and Carter pulls his shirt on over his head.

"That's for the best." Mom tucks an invisible flyaway behind her ear. "However, I'm leaving as well. I have surgery in a few hours but wanted to say happy birthday to my only daughter before I go. Goodbye, Les. I will call you when the surgery ends." But it pretty much sounds like she's sending herself off to war and isn't sure whether or not she will ever talk to me again.

I grit my teeth. "Bye, Mom."

"Uh, catch you later, Les?" Carter follows behind my mom, walking backward with his eyebrows raised as if he's asking whether or not he should save me from Ben.

Candy nods toward Ben. "You want me to stay 'cause of that fool? I can kick his *culo* out. Just grab him by the *cojones* and—"

"I'm good." I smile. "I appreciate the gesture, though."

Candy shrugs. "Your loss, *amor.*"

I wave to Carter, biting my cheek with uncertainty. He furrows his brow as Candy pulls him along and out the door, leaving Ben and me in my room alone. And I feel horrible for letting Carter leave without me telling him to stay. Because what am I doing? I just had a great night with him, but I let him leave me here with my ex, who I made out with the *other* night.

As soon as I hear the door close, I yell, "What the hell are you doing here?"

"Listen, I texted you last night. I knew you wouldn't like this surprise, so I wanted to give you a heads up."

"Well! I turned my phone off. Why did you even come?" I throw my hands up in the air. "Ben, why can't you get it through your brain that we are *done*?"

"Are we?" he shouts, his eyes wide. "Because it wasn't over when you were moaning my name on freaking Tuesday, was it?"

I scowl. "Oh, you're such a piece of work. And how dare you have *your* mom contact mine about some stupid Thanksgiving trip to St. Maarten. I don't want to freaking go to St. Maarten with you!"

Ben squats and picks up the box of donuts my mom dropped. For whatever reason, this just makes me madder. "Leave the donuts alone!"

"I'm trying to help you!" He picks the box up anyway. His golden brown hair is slicked to the side, not a single strand out of place. He's like a freaking Ken doll. "Why can't you let anyone help you?"

I take a deep breath. "I don't want to do this today."

"Yeah, me neither. I just wanted to tell you happy birthday. Your mom roped me into this, and you know her. I couldn't say no." He turns and leaves the bedroom, donuts in hand, joggers slung low on his hips and hugging his legs.

Because I'm starving (for food), I follow him into the kitchen where he puts the donut box on the counter and opens it. The donuts spell out, "HAdYB PRVOIDYL WE HATE YOU" with different pastel-colored icings and sprinkles covering them.

"Lemme guess, your idea?" I cock a brow.

"Definitely wasn't the Ice Queen's idea." He smiles and looks down at the donuts. "Oh, wait, no. That was not my idea. It was supposed to say 'Happy birthday, we love you.'"

I snort. How ironic. I guess I really do need a reality TV show because this stupid stuff is so dumb that thousands would probably watch it.

But, I guess it's the thought that counts because those donuts are looking way too good. "Thanks, B." I turn toward him and draw up my lips like I've tasted something sour. "It was...somewhat nice of you, I guess."

"Come here." He inches his finger, and I roll my eyes as I lean in closer. "Say it again without the constipated face."

"Oh my gosh." I push him away and laugh. "You're so annoying."

He sticks out his tongue and crosses his eyes. Then he checks his watch. "I've gotta go, but I was hoping we could meet up later? There's something I wanted to talk to you about."

And what else can I say? The man just brought me donuts. "Better be a freaking apology for what you said the other night. And we're still done"

"Uh, huh. Sure." He smiles that millionaire smile. "Happy Birthday. Enjoy the donuts."

I pick up the L and he reaches around me and grabs the B. With a quick kiss on my cheek that burns like a brand, he leaves the apartment. And once again, I'm left wondering why I agreed to see him later.

I'm frustrated, but these donuts are possibly the best thing I've ever eaten in my life. Unfortunately, they don't stop the sick feeling in my stomach, which exists for many reasons.

From the look my mom gave Carter and Candy, I probably just lost my only two friends here at West. I love my mom, I do. but lately, it's like she's become this horrible person. Or, maybe I've just started noticing it. I don't know.

I sigh. It's my birthday. Last year, my dad would've already had picked me up with activities planned. For the rest of my life, I'll have to plan birthday activities by myself. Probably just end up holed in my apartment with fifty cats.

Every year, my dad and I did something different. We'd go for a helicopter trip, zip lining, to an amusement park, anything and everything that would get our hearts racing. Even last year, when his memories started fading and he was more weak than strong, he had Ben take us to an arcade, one my mom would've hated, and we played until we had enough tickets to get me a pink crown that was meant for a two-year-old.

So many of my memories include my dad. And so many memories with my dad include Ben. I thought I was fine. I went to therapy for all of this. I had "accepted" my dad's death. And then I see Ben, and...it's bringing everything back.

I don't know how I feel about it. Maybe that's why I agreed to see him later. He's the only tether to my past. I can't talk about my dad with my mom. The only person I can talk to about it is the person I paid, my therapist. But Ben, he *remembers*.

I should go out and have some fun, get a manicure or something. But my manicure is fresh. So unless I want to go to a restaurant alone, there's not much to do.

My apartment's ceilings are two stories tall. Still, I can't help but feel claustrophobic. The walls are decorated with stupidly expensive art, splashes of monochromatic gray and white, and I feel hollow. The worst part of it is I don't even know why.

It has me longing for a reality TV show where I really am the star, where at least I could talk to my producer or something. Pathetic, right? But it feels like I have no one of substance. No one I could cry and talk to or explain what's going on in my life. All of high school was spent with Ben attached to my hip. Sure, we had other friends, but not real ones. Not ones that will last now that we're no longer sitting at the same cafeteria table.

I need to get out of here. Which means, it's time to get ready for the day.

The bathroom is clean, but there's a leather band by the sink that's never been there before. I pick it up and the universal medical sign is burnt into the center. On the inside, a piece of engraved metal says *T1 Diabetes*.

Carter.

Maybe I'll stop by and give it to him after showering. If he even wants to see me after the scene my mom just made.

He probably thinks I'm some elite, white supremacist. Heaven knows I feel like one after my mom was blatantly rude and racist. That's *two* times she's done it in front of me within 24 hours. I should've done something. I should've *said* something to try and make the situations better. Instead, I just sat there while my mom was racist and rude.

Carter's words from last night about not being diagnosed early enough because he's Latino impacted me. I don't *ever* want to be a medical professional like the ones he had. But now? Hardy-har-har, I just became the freaking poster child for entitled white girl.

Cranking the shower handle as far to the hot side as it will go, I slip out of my pajamas and hop in the shower. I give my marble tile shower the best ten-minute Adele serenade my scratchy voice can muster, then hop out into a deliciously fluffy towel.

I'm going to do the work I need to so that I can be an ally.

Yes, I made two mistakes earlier, but next time, I'll be prepared. Once I have some makeup on, I'll sit down and read.

Education—it changes people. So, I need to educate myself some more. I feel good about it.

It's time I get outside of my rich-Glenbrook-bubble and into the real world. And with the special election coming up for California's state senator position that just opened, it's like I have a trial run of voting in November. Like Candy said, she'd make me get into politics.

But she shouldn't have to make me, I should *want* to. And, I do. It's important to me. I don't have to be my mom. I don't know if it's this realization, my tea tree shampoo, the foam body wash, or my towel, but I feel renewed.

That is, until I go into my room.

I've been here, like, a month? How is my room already this messy? The clean clothes are piled up in the laundry basket, so I start folding them. Then, I put them away. And then, I see that there's some dust. Reading is not in the cards. So, I do a quick search for podcasts that talk about race, download an episode on my phone, hop into a silk robe, and clean.

Cleaning. On. My. Birthday.

Is this what adulthood is like? Take me back to when I was thirteen, please. But at least it goes by quickly, and one podcast episode becomes two, which becomes three.

When I finally make it back into the bathroom to clean the mirror and sink, I remember what I was going to do originally —my makeup.

But three strokes of mascara deep on my right eye, the doorbell rings. Glancing at my phone, four texts from Ben sit on the lock screen. I guess it *has* been two hours since he left. What is it he even wants to talk about?

Not too worried about being in my silk robe, I open the door and—

"Oh, shiz." All coherent thoughts bleed out of my brain.

Carter's hand flies up to cover his eyes. "I'm guessing you thought I was someone else."

And that makes it worse because he assumes I'm dressing in a silk robe for someone? After making out with him and copping a feel of his butt 5.8 times last night? Great. "You don't have to cover your face. It's not like I'm nude."

He lets his hand down and shrugs. "Honestly, I was peeking through my fingers anyway."

I laugh. "I wouldn't expect anything different." I step aside, and he walks past me dressed in khaki Under Armour shorts and a navy crewneck. He looks hot. And now I'm hot. Temperature wise, but also figuratively. But probably not right now because with my mascara wand in hand, I remember I only did one eye.

His smile falls into an unreadable expression.

"Look," I start, "about my mom..."

"Ah, no big."

But it feels like a 'big.' Like a really big *big* that I didn't say anything to her as she ridiculed them. "Um, okay. So, you probably came—"

"Do you want to do something today?" he cuts in, hands shoved in his pockets.

"You didn't come for your bracelet?"

"My bracelet?" He lifts up his wrist then nods. "Huh. Didn't realize I was missing it. But nah, I just figured since it's your birthday and all, maybe you'd let me take you out?"

I gasp and put my hand over my heart. "Carter DeLeón—"

"Shoot, you can't even say my last name right."

"—you want to take little ol' me on a date?"

He grimaces and looks toward the door as if he can escape. "Ah, I meant more like friends. I sort of felt bad for you, here, all alone on your birthday..."

I run and jump, throwing the mascara wand and bringing my arms around his neck. He grips my thighs and holds me at his waist.

"You're lying." I put my forehead to his.

"You're forward."

"Shh," I bring my finger to his lips, "stop changing the subject."

"I'm kidding. Of course I want to go on a date with you. But I actually have something better in mind." He squeezes my love handles, and I yelp and swat at his hand. "Did you know that we're only two hours from the beach?"

"Are we?" I squeeze my legs around his waist.

He groans. "Don't do that."

A smile creeps up my face. "No, I didn't. But, yes, take me. Let me grab my bikini." Unwinding my ankles, I drop to the ground and nearly skip to my room knowing the effect I have on him.

"You may wanna take the makeup off of that one eye too! Otherwise you're gonna look like a raccoon by the time we're done!" he shouts.

"Ay, ay, captain!" I change into some shorts and a tank, grab my itsy bitsy *pink* polka dot bikini and a makeup wipe, and head back into the kitchen where Carter rocks on his heels and shakes his head.

Looking me up and down, he bites his lower lip. "Okay, *mami*. Those shorts are doin' it for me."

I shake my hips and give him my best spirit fingers. "Thanks. Now let's go to the beach, Mr. DeLeón."

"*Ay*, come on, *chica*. You have to at least say my name right. It's DeLeón."

"That's what I said. Day-lee-own."

He brushes a hand down his face and crinkles his nose up. "Get yo' white ass out this door, and let's go."

I lift my chin, grab my purse, and walk out the door. "How do you know my butt is white? It could be tattooed with inspirational quotes like 'live, laugh, love.'" I grab a piece of gum from my purse's side pocket.

He waits against the iron railing outside my apartment while I press the lock symbol on the smart lock. When I turn around, he grins with perfect straight white teeth and fuller lips than should be allowed. "Because you threw your dress at me last night while getting into your pajamas. And your butt is definitely tattoo-free."

I inhale sharply, and my gum lodges in my throat. I cough, wide eyed, head shaking. He whacks me on the back, and I roll my eyes. Once I can breathe again, I say, "That did not happen. Who do you think I am? The strippers down at *XXX*?"

He puts his hand to my lower back as we walk toward his truck. "Hey, those women make an honest living down there. They work hard."

My shoulders shake from laughter. "Alright, fine. You caught me. My butt is white. But I did not throw my dress at you."

Fishing his keys from his pocket, he raises his brows and sucks in his lips. He hits unlock, and the car's lights turn on. Then with a quick step, he's in front of me opening my door. I step up into the passenger seat and reach for my seatbelt, but I'm distracted by the scent of cinnamon.

Leaning in, Carter whispers, "Whatever you have to tell yourself, *señorita*," with a kiss on my forehead. And *dayummm*, I'd be lying if I said I don't feel like freaking Camila Cabello in her music video with Shawn Mendes.

He closes the door, and I bite my tongue while simultaneously clenching my thighs, and, yeah, it's gonna be a long day.

He hops in and starts the car. The air blows with the force of a category IV hurricane, and he quickly turns it down. I scrub at my eye with the makeup wipe as he pulls out of the apartment complex and turns toward the freeway.

"So, what's with you and cinnamon? It smells like Christmas and Big Red had a baby in here."

"Eh, better not to talk about it."

Which is a suspicious enough response, but then music starts playing *suspiciously* loud and he shudders. So, yeah no. Now I need to know. I open up his glove box. All the sweets are there. I bring one of the hard candies up to my nose and give it a satisfying sniff. Not cinnamon.

I close the glovebox and open the center console. There's a wallet, a baseball, and no freaking cinnamon. "Where is the cinnamon?" I slap my thighs. "It's gotta be around here somewhere."

He pulls at the collar of his shirt, looks at me, looks back toward the road, then out his window. "If you must know, the cinnamon is in the floorboards."

Huh? "Why is there cinnamon in your floorboards?"

"Cinnamon essential oil."

I stare at him in dumbfounded silence as we pass large stone cliffs. He turns the music off, and there's only the sound of our breathing and road noise. "I...am so confused."

He sighs. "I used to hate cinnamon."

"Is this your way of trying to get over that?"

"No." He tucks some of my hair behind my ear and bites his lip. "Definitely not. I, uh—Well, my ex sort of, um, doused my car in cinnamon essential oil the night that we broke up. Ten car details later and it's still here."

I gasp. "What did you do to the girl?"

His hands fly up and his chin drops. Then he seems to realize that he's the one driving the car and quickly puts them back on the steering wheel. But not before the car ventures over to the edge of the freeway where the annoying humming noise to wake up drowsy drivers is. "I didn't do a thing to her! We broke up. We were going in different directions."

"'We were going in different directions,'" I mock in my finest surfer dude voice. "You probably even pulled the whole, 'we can still be *amigos*.'"

"*Sí*, how'd you know? Were you also in that coffee shop?" He sticks his tongue out and grins.

"You did it in a coffee shop?" I shout. "You deserve the cinnamon!" And I'm not sure how I feel about that because I guess I have his ex to thank for his delicious scent? Boring. She was probably some super-hot girl, and now here I am, awkward, anxious, and a barely there butt on a good day.

He reaches over and messes with my hair as if I'm his little sister. "Well, whatever. I'm glad she did it because you like it."

"I never said I liked it."

He smirks and looks back toward the road. "Oh, yes, you

did. Last night as you laid on top of me and fell asleep you murmured, 'Carter, you're so hot and sexy and smell like cinnamon. It's so *weird*. But I love it.'"

"Wow," I dip my chin toward my right shoulder so he can't see me, "do you get off on lying or something?"

He lets out a loud cackle, and then leans over and kisses me on my temple. I turn toward him with my nose crinkled up. And because I don't want us to get in a crash by starting a full make out session with that mouth of his, I interlace our fingers.

But it's almost just as good.

∞∞∞

I don't remember falling asleep, but Carter wakes me up by squeezing the life out of my hand.

"Les, we're here."

Yanking my hand from his, I stifle a yawn and rub at my eyes. We're pulled over on the side of the highway, and right outside his window is the beach. With caramel-colored sand, the smell of salt in the air, and a tall cliff with green brush growing on the top of it, I think I've found my one true love—I'm beach-sexual.

"Oh my gosh, it's so pretty," I squeal.

"You're so pretty," he says in his valley girl accent.

I roll my eyes. "Thanks."

"*Claro que sí.* I meant it though."

Covering my face with my bikini, I say, "Come on, let's change." Heaven forbid the boy sees me blush. "Close your eyes, and I'll just throw it on in here. But you better not peek."

"For real, this time I won't. I'll even put my shirt over my face."

I laugh. "Okay, whatever."

He pulls at the back of his collar and takes his shirt off

over his head in that sexy way only guys do because they are heathens and don't care about stretching out the neckline of clothes. But, that's not the point here. *Focus.* And when I say focus, I mean focus on that six pack of abs—scratch that— eight pack. "Do you freaking model for GQ on the side or something? Why are there so many rectangles on your stomach?"

His response is a muffled, "Oh-em-gee, you said you wouldn't peek!"

"No, you said that." I hurry and undo the button of my shorts, pulling them down and yanking my swimsuit bottoms up. Then I slip my bikini top under my shirt, tie it around my neck, and undo my bra while keeping my shirt on. "Alright, your turn."

He rips the shirt off of his head. "Nah, these are swimsuit bottoms and shorts. Under Armour for the win."

"Men's clothing is so not fair. You guys get the pockets, versatile styles, and cheap prices."

"Alright, drama queen. Let's go before your complaints stink up the car."

I slap his arm, and he cradles it while mock-crying. But the sound of crashing waves is coming in from the cracked window, and it's too hard to resist. I check for cars, then step out and circle around to the driver's side.

When he gets out, he holds my hand and actually locks his car for once. "I'm putting the keys inside the towel in case you need them."

Why would I need them? And I guess the confusion shows on my face because he turns to the side where his insulin pump is. *Oh.*

"Right-o. I gotchu boy. Snacks, snacks, snacks, snacks," I sing to the tune of 'Shots.'

There's a concrete barrier separating the road from the sand, so he hops over it and then grabs me by my hips, hoisting me over as I scream, "Put me down, you're going to drop me!"

In my defense, I swear I saw his arm wobble.

But then he cradles me, and I have my arms around his neck,

and he doesn't put me down, which quite honestly, I'm *very* happy about because I'm pushed up against his gloriously hot chest—figuratively and literally—and he's, "A golden sex-on-a-stick."

Crap, I just said that.

He whistles. "Well, alright then."

I furrow my brows. *Play it off, Les. Play it off.* "Alright, what?"

"You just called me sex-on-a-stick."

I bury my head in his chest and inhale like an addict snorts a drug. "Shh, no. You're hearing things."

The wind blows slightly, as it does wherever the ocean is, carrying salt along the breeze. Waves crash against the shore, and it's mostly bare except for an older couple a few yards down, walking away from us. When he sets me down, I slip off my shoes and wiggle my toes in the warm sand. There's not a cloud in the sky, and it's not too cold. Probably somewhere in the 80s, which is perfect in my opinion.

Carter lays out a towel that says *Playa del Carmen.*

"I love that place." We went there three years ago, just my mom, my dad, and me. It was before the cancer, before everything went wrong. I think it was actually our last vacation with just us. Every other vacation included Ben or my dad's home nurse. Once the cancer metastasized, flying internationally was no longer an option.

"No way? Me too. I have some family down there. They own a few vacation homes and run a tourist boat ride over to Cozumel. It's a really pretty area." He smiles, and the sun shines in his eyes, so he squints one, and his green irises seem to light up even more.

It's crazy how different his life is compared to mine. Or, maybe that isn't the right word. I just know my mom wouldn't be caught dead with *family* who ran a *tourist boat.* Guess you'd have to have family for that, which my mom does not.

I shake the thoughts from my mind. "So, is it your dad who's from there then?"

He nods and puts his hands on his hips as he gazes out to

the water. "Yeah, he's from *Puerto Morelos*. My mom went for spring break right after grad school, and one *salsa* dance led to the next. They were married a few months later. Moved here about two years after my sister Carlotta was born. We go back there every January to see family and vacation."

"That's awesome." I take a step toward the water and then turn to face him. "First one to the ocean wins?"

He reaches down into the sand and gets into a runner's position. "Go!"

I squeal and run off, not daring to look back, and pump my legs as fast as my haven't-worked-out-in-three-months body will let me. Which, admittedly, isn't very fast because even though I'm kicking up sand and feel like I'm flying, I get three feet from the shoreline when Carter scoops me up into his arms, and I scream as if I'm being murdered.

As his feet splash in the water and he gets waist deep, enough for my butt to get soaked when a wave comes in, he says, "Looks like it was a tie," then leans down and his lips touch mine.

My hand finds the back of his head and I bring him closer to me, deepening our kiss. Every important part of me breaks out in goosebumps, and I pull back, our foreheads touching, both of us breathing quickly.

Even though the water is cold and I'm pretty sure my butt is numb, the rest of me feels like it's on fire. He sets me down in the water in front of him and kisses my forehead.

I shiver. "I don't think I need to freeze my eggs anymore. This water definitely froze them for me."

He shakes his head and slaps the water, splashing me right across my chest.

My forearms go up instinctively to cover my boobs. "Oh, alright, dude. Are you trying to make me freeze?"

"Yeah." He dodges my splash by moving to the right. "Then I get to warm you up."

I saunter toward him as if I'm going to do something sexy. He looks at my body as I close the gap between us. Then I jump up and push on his head until he slips in the wet sand and goes underwater. When he comes up, wiping his face free from water, he says, "You're naughty. You better run."

"Oh yeah?" I hop back and forth on my feet and wiggle my brows. "I dare you to get me."

I run toward the shore, dodging him beside me and sprint as quickly as I can in water. If you just picture the slow motion *Baywatch* scene, that's what I look like, but I'm not in slow motion, just a turtle runner.

He shouts, "Better run faster than that, *chica!* There's sharks in these waters."

I get just out of the water when he grabs my waist from behind and spins me around, lifting my feet off the ground. I'm giggling like a kid, and I don't even care that there's another family that just arrived a few minutes ago giving us strange looks because this is the most fun I've had since—Well, since before my dad died.

"Are there really sharks in there?"

His eyes light up in amusement. "Haven't you ever heard of the Red Triangle? Bodega Bay is full of sharks."

My eyes widen, and I mentally commit to punish him for this dangerous escapade later.

Carter sets me down, and I rub my hands across his warm pecs and look up at him.

He kisses my hair. "Happy birthday. For real, Les. You deserve the happiest of birthdays."

I bite the side of my cheek. "Thanks. And thanks for bringing me here. I like it, even if it is full of sharks."

He laughs against my lips and gives me a quick peck. I'll be damned if it doesn't make me curl my toes in the sand wanting more. "Well, I like you a lot."

My heart feels strange, as if there's a thousand pound weight on it but it's light as air. I stand on my tiptoes until our noses touch before I whisper, "I like you a lot, too."

He grips my hips and pulls me closer until our lips touch again. There's a mixture of sighing with a taste of ocean water, happiness entwined with giddiness. I push against him, and his abs are hard and warm, though the air is cold around us. When we break, my chest heaves against him, and I catch him sneaking a peek downward.

Carter winks—which is inappropriate because I already told him he shouldn't be allowed to wink—and I sit down on the towel before our make out sesh turns into a something-more-right-on-the-beach-in-front-of-an-innocent-family sesh.

Settling in next to me, he bumps my shoulder with his. I smile and wiggle my toes in the sand, just excited to be here, doing nothing with a fun hot dude. "You know, I was a bit worried about how I'd spend my birthday this year."

He glances at me with squinted eyes as the sun shines in front of us. "How come?"

I shrug. A few seagulls caw loudly, but Carter waits until I break the silence. "I always spent my birthdays with my dad. And since he's, you know, gone...I, uh, I just didn't know what I'd do this year. Figured I would've spent it at home eating a pint of ice cream."

He leans forward and bends his knee, wrapping an arm around it. "That's still not off the table. I'm really good at pity parties. We can head out, grab some ice cream, get in our grungiest sweats, and watch some lame-ass movie with an 'I finally realized I love you' airport scene that every rom-com seems to have."

"Hey, those airport scenes all deserve Oscars. They are the best of the best."

He chuckles.

"You'd really have a pity party with me? That seems so... depressing."

His brow furrows and he rakes a hand through his wet hair. "I don't think you missing your dad is depressing, Les. So, yeah. You wanna have a pity party? *Estoy listo.*"

I bite my cheek to keep from grinning. "I don't think I want to have a pity party right now. You're doin' a pretty good of cheering me up."

The sun is near the water, and soon, the sky will light up in pinks and oranges. It'll be the perfect spot for a rom-com scene where the two characters start falling in love.

If only I were a character in a rom-com, right?

Carter puts his arm around me, and I lay my head on his shoulder. "My dad would've liked you."

"I am pretty great, huh?"

I flick his chest. "No. You're, like, barely a five on the scale of greatness."

He gasps. "At least a six."

"Four?"

"Eight!"

I laugh. "Seven."

"*Bien.* But hey, that'd be nice to have a parent actually like me. You know, unlike your mom."

Burying my face against him, I groan. "I'm so sorry."

His abs flex as he laughs, and I'm not leering. I'm just making sure that my studio audience gets a glimpse of this perfection too.

"I swear, my dad was a much better person than her."

"Ah, come on. Your mom isn't that bad of a person."

"Ehhh, don't tiptoe around me, babe. What happened was *bad.* With a capital B." I pull back from him and cup his cheek with my hand. "But I appreciate you not automatically hating her, even if you should."

I kiss him quickly and then go back to burying my face because these are not the kind of kisses you give someone you wanna hook up with. They're too...intimate. In a weird way. I don't know how to describe it. All I know is I want to keep kissing him, but I need to pull back before I get in too deep.

He puts his finger under my chin and lifts me up out of hiding. "Well, let's forget about her. Tell me about your dad."

"Okay," I whisper. And I'm not sure why, but for once, I actually *do* want to talk about him.

Chapter Ten

I'm still buzzing from my birthday high. Carter and I have been texting non-stop since he dropped me off. I almost invited him up, but...I chickened out. Instead, I just stayed up until 3 AM texting him about random stuff that shouldn't be exciting or fun to talk about. Except it was. Because it was with Carter.

Now, walking into calculus, I'm pretty sure nothing can ruin my day.

But cue the *womp-womp-womp* soundtrack because the whiteboard has *Quiz Day* written on it. I forgot, I'm sleep deprived, and also didn't study. Crap, I cannot fail this. Attendance is only 10% of our grade, and I'm pretty sure a 10% isn't going to get me into med school.

Tucking my hair behind my ear, I try to swallow the beach that has appeared in my throat. My hands are literally shaking as I sit down.

Candy says hi, but I can't even focus on her because Professor Butler hands out the scantrons and quizzes. The only good thing about this is that after the quiz, we're free to go to have a "personal study" day.

I rummage through my backpack, but my addiction to pens is catching up to me. "Gah."

"What's up?" Candy whispers.

"I don't have a pencil. The stupid scantron won't work with a pen." I place my hands on my thighs and breathe. "Do you have one I can borrow?"

She grimaces. "No, I don't." Turning around she whisper-shouts, "You got a pencil?" to Carter.

He doesn't even look up from the papers he's grading as he

throws one like a spear (which is incredibly dangerous), and Candy catches it. "Here ya go."

She smiles and puts it on my desk in front of me, then pats my leg.

I start filling out my name and student ID number on the scantron.

"Okay, class. Remember, you're allowed to go once you turn in your quiz. This is one of four that will account for eighty percent of your grade with your attendance and final rounding out the other twenty percent. Are there any questions before you get started?"

I want to throw up my arm and ask what calculus is, but I stay quiet.

"You're free to begin."

I turn over the quiz and my heart sinks.

s(t)=(8−t)(t+6)3/2

Compute (accurate to at least eight decimal places) the average velocity of the object between t=10 and the following values of t...

And that's the first question? I don't know it. Oh, no. I do not know it. What am I going to do? I'm going to fail the course, and I won't get into medical school. My mom will disown me, I won't get my trust fund, and I may be living on the streets or working as a stripper, throwing my dress at random people just like Carter said I was doing to him.

I skip to the next question, and the next, and the next, scrambling to remember what it was I studied the past few days and why I don't know any of it. Maybe because I've been shirking my school responsibilities like a freaking idiot.

It seems like everyone turns their quiz in before me, and I don't even have actual answers to turn in. It's just a giant joke. At this rate, I might as well just make a zig-zag pattern on my scantron and hope for the best. Actually, can you all come to life like the demons behind Ouija boards and guide my hand to the right answer?

No? Crickets? Cool.

So against all my better judgement and my mom's chastising, I make a one-sided Christmas tree with my bubbled in answers. And yes, I know you're disappointed. I'm disappointed in myself too.

"Results will be posted this afternoon online."

"Thanks," I mumble, slipping the scantron face down on Professor Butler's desk. I just need to make it out of this room before the tears fall. It's a ten-minute walk to my internship. That's five minutes to cry, two minutes to talk myself out of misery, and three minutes to fix my makeup. I've got this.

Three more steps. One...two...thr—

Footsteps echo behind me. I shouldn't already know the pattern of his walk, but I do. "Hey, wait up."

My dignity falls from my unsteady hold and shatters on the floor. I shake my head and keep walking into the hallway, tears streaming down my cheeks. Then my nose starts running, and I do one of those super sexy sniffle-snorts. A hand touches my shoulder, but I shrug it off.

Carter shuffles in front of me, slinging his bag over one shoulder. He places both his hands on my shoulders. "Hey, what's goin' on? Why are you upset?"

The words of what's really going on bang on the roof of my mouth but I swallow them. "I gotta go." I gaze to the gray walls beside us, desperate to make it outside of the halls and into the fresh air.

"Did something happen?" He squats down as if I'm a child and gets level-headed with me, cocking his head to the side with adorably pouty lips.

I don't need this right now.

"Yeah, Carter, something did happen. I just freaking failed that test, and I need this class to get into medical school."

"Don't worry, it's just the first one. You'll pick it—"

"No! I won't." I swipe at my cheeks with the palm of my hand. Ben was right. I shouldn't have taken this class so soon. I should've done Math 1010, retaken precalc and trig and then tried calculus. Now I'm going to fail the course, which is a permanent grade on my record. I'll lose my internship, kissing my dreams goodbye. "Seriously, I've gotta go. I have my internship."

I refuse to look at him.

"Okay." He drops his hands, and I feel the loss of his weight like a piece of me. "Okay," he says again, quieter this time. Then he runs his hand through his dark brown hair. "You know I can tutor you, right?"

I walk backward toward the set of double doors that leads uphill to the hospital and laugh. But I bite on my lip to stop another set of tears from falling. Just like Ben, thinking he's smarter than me. "So you can prove you're better at math than me?"

He shakes his head slowly and furrows his brows. "No, Les, I'm just trying to help."

The door opens as my backpack hits it, and a wave of cool air blows my hair in front of my face. "I don't need anyone's help."

But it's not true, and I don't know why I say it.

Tears fall hot and angrily down my face, as if they can't wait to get away from my eyes. I swipe at them, not caring at all about the people who look at me as I walk past them. I'm not the first college freshman to have a breakdown, and I certainly won't be the last.

Look the freak away, kids.

This isn't one of those oh-no-I-failed-my-test-but-will-actually-pass-it situations. I legitimately failed, I know it. How could I have been so stupid? My whole career is riding on these four years in college, and the first few weeks, I just give it all up? Act like it's nothing?

I walk mindlessly, determined to forget any of it happened in the first place. There's nothing I can do right now that will fix anything that happened this morning. I'm fresh out of tears. Remind me to hydrate more later.

By the time I make it to Dr. Guilliod's office, I've become numb.

A slender, Black woman reaches out her hand. "You must be

Les."

I give her a flat smile and shake it. "That's me."

"Well, what can I say? I won't be expecting anything Les than greatness from you. I'm Dr. Guilliod." She winks and hands me an iPad.

Mark that as 389 times I've heard that joke. If I wasn't all emotioned out, I'd probably get annoyed.

"We're going to go over some lab samples today, so if you could write down the notes I tell you as we go, that'd be great. Here, follow me. We're going to head to the second-floor research wing."

"Okay." My feet pad behind her, following her through the lobby. Piano music plays in the background, and with a deep breath, I begin to remember my people skills. "Oh! Congratulations, by the way. I heard your wife had the baby. You must be so—"

"Sleep deprived? Absolutely."

I laugh. "Yeah, I bet. Boy or girl?"

She presses the button on the elevator and it lights up white. "Boy. Named him Atlas."

The metal doors open with a ping and a few men in white coats step out, talking about their fantasy football lineups and who won that week. Once we get into the elevator and it's quiet, I say, "Cute name. I like it."

Dr. Guilliod fiddles with the nametag attached to her scrub's chest pocket. "So, how's school going for you?"

I make a little squeak, then let out an, "Oh, great. Yeah, going really good so far." It's just us in the elevator. I clear my throat. "Um, did you, by chance, hit the button for the second-floor?"

She startles and mumbles something, leaning forward to press the button, but the elevator doors whoosh open, and a screaming couple come in. Well, the guy is screaming. The girl, she's just super pregnant and cradling her vagina while waddling, which does not seem like a good sign.

I scramble back as Dr. Guilliod presses the number three for labor and delivery while saying, "We'll catch another elevator."

But as Dr. Guilliod gets out, the pregnant lady's butt blocks me in, and the elevator doors close. I'm stuck with a guy screaming, "It's fine! We're almost there. Squeeze your Kegels, the baby can't come out yet!" and a girl shrieking, "Just shut up already, Daniel! You don't know a damn thing about Kegels!"

I try to slide past her, but she's got me cornered here. The elevator bumps as it begins moving upward, the guy goes flying into the wall with the elevator buttons, and the whole elevator comes to a screeching halt.

"Oh, you've got to be kidding me. I have the worst luck ever," I whisper, balling my fists until my nails press against my skin.

"Well, thanks, lady, for getting into the elevator with us then!" The woman groans, then she drops her sweatpants to the floor, granny panties the only thing keeping *a freaking human inside of her body.*

"Wait, no, you heard the guy." I point at Daniel where's he's frantically pressing the help button to try and talk to the fire department. "He said hold it in."

She grips my wrist, and I cower. Without a word, she squeezes it harder. I'd start to think this is all a bad dream, but I don't need anyone to pinch me. This chick's about to break my wrist and I definitely feel it.

"There is no holding it in," she stutters out between shallow breaths.

I'm about to explain that she has to because I have no idea what I'm doing, I'm not a doctor, and she's going to have this baby in a dirty hospital elevator, which is probably very unsanitary, but thank the freaking Lord the elevator starts moving again.

A few seconds later, the doors open and the woman waddles out, me behind her, and she shouts at the top of her lungs, "My baby's coming out!"

I whip my head back to find Daniel, but he's on his knees

with his head down as if he's about to throw up. Crap, that cannot be a good sign. "It can't be happening. Don't all those labor books say it takes, like, days with your contractions and stuff?"

She glares at me with the force of Lucifer himself. "Apparently not."

The woman's still murdering my wrist, so I squeak out a, "Sorry!" and watch in horror beside her as she squats.

I crouch down to make sure everything's good, but a baby's head is visible and I'm staring at a stranger's vagina. So, no, everything is *not* good.

Now would be a really great time for a commercial break.

Two nurses rush in, slapping towels on top of my iPad and falling to the ground as the woman literally gives birth to a child in front of me in under a minute. She finally unhands my now-swollen wrist, and they place this squirming, tiny, alien-looking newborn into the towels that *I'm* holding (I mean, shouldn't I have a license for this or something?). Then the nurses lay the woman down on another set of towels all while ushering me next to her because this slightly-purple *live baby* is in my freaking arms and still attached to this woman's body via umbilical cord.

What (and I cannot stress this enough) *the hell* did I get myself into?

The nurse in hot pink scrubs rubs my back while the other nurse props a pillow under the mom's head. "Congratulations, you two. You've given birth to a beautiful baby girl."

A record scratches.

Say what now?

And then it all clicks. The woman careens her head toward me.

I whip my head toward her. "No, no, no. Oh, no. I'm way too young for this!"

"Give me my baby!" the woman shouts. "Daniel!"

The nurses gasp and wrestle the now-crying baby out of my arms, but they could've just asked because I would've gladly handed her over. "Um, congratulations." I wave and run in the other direction, this time taking the stairs to the second floor. The whole way down, I hear the woman cursing out Daniel.

For real, though. Do I just have *'include me in crazy situations'* tattooed on my forehead? I mean, the baby was weird. The whole process was yuck. My hands need to be scrubbed for an entire hour. It was all wiggly and slimy and strange, and kind of...interesting. It all happened so fast. Doctors and nurses literally bring life into the world multiple times a day. That's... okay, that's pretty cool.

And I could *never*.

But, still, being in that moment, sorta, in a way, makes me look forward to everything medical school will offer me.

I find Dr. Guilliod waiting by the second floor elevators. I quickly recount the story while we walk to the lab.

"I wish my wife's labor was that fast."

"Yeah, I think the woman almost broke my wrist, and I nearly dropped the iPad when they gave me the baby, but I guess it was kind of cool."

She unlocks a door with her badge and we enter into a room filled with microscopes, fridges, and test tubes. "If only research were that exciting on a daily basis. Let's have you scrub up over there." She points to a sink.

I spend five minutes in near-scalding hot water, scrubbing my hands up to my elbows.

Once I'm finished, we go through the three data sets of a clinical trial that's currently being tested on lupus patients. For the next two hours, she talks casually, but I hang on her every word, writing down the notes in the database and looking through the microscopes to see the different blood samples.

It's fascinating.

Still, a part of me goes back to the craziness of the baby. Not the actual child, but just how fast-paced and exciting it was. One thing is for sure: I'm going to be a doctor.

By the time my watch dings with an alert that my shift is

over, I feel good. I can do this. I *will* do this. I just have to buckle down and study. Calc won't bring me down.

I say goodbye to Dr. Guilliod and make the trek back toward where my car is parked on the opposite end of campus.

My phone buzzes with a new email, so I open it and click the link, not really thinking much of it. Putting in my student ID and password, it's not until I see the course name pop up that I realize what it all means.

I got a 46% on my calculus quiz, and Professor Butler wrote a comment on the grade saying, "We need to talk."

Chapter Eleven

Professor Butler's words echo in my ears. *May be best to with-draw from the course...statistically speaking, most people don't get much better...this was testing your knowledge from past courses... midterm grades...academic probation...loss of school-funded in-ternship.*

Maybe, just maybe, she should've held the quiz *before* the deadline to drop the course passed. Professors, am I right?

Candy waves in front of my face. "So? What are you going to do?"

I put the TV remote on my coffee table. "Huh?"

She throws a piece of popcorn at me. "Are you going to drop the course?"

"I can't. The deadline to drop courses was last week. Now, I'd have to withdraw. My mom would kill me. I can't have a 'W' on my transcript. And if I drop below fifteen credits, I'm no longer eligible for my internship. I just need to focus. Study more. Get a tutor." But it's all I've thought about for the past few days. Dropping the course means losing the internship I spent a year applying and interviewing for. But failing the course means being put on academic probation and also los-ing my internship.

The only option is to pass.

Chris Harrison comes onto the TV and announces, "Ladies, it's the final rose of the night."

Even quivering men and women on *Bachelor in Paradise* can't help me feel better. Especially when I look down to my vibrating phone and see *Mom* at the top of the screen.

"I gotta take this," I sigh. "Hey, Mom. What's up?" I don't have the energy to fake being happy that she's calling. She's probably returning the voicemail I frantically left her a few days ago. I purposefully left it then because she had a 30-hour surgery and wouldn't be checking her phone for at least two days.

"You need to get in contact with the TA, have them tutor you. It's best to get on their good side since they'll be grading many of the tests." She rambles for once in her life.

I snort. "I'm going to need another tutor. The TA won't help me."

"Unacceptable. I'll call the university."

"No." I rub at my eye as Candy mouths 'what's going on?' Her pink hair blurs in my vision as I shake my head. "I just—I can't ask the TA to tutor me."

"*Hola, chica loca.* What're you talking about?" Candy asks. "Carter will totally tutor you."

Why is her voice so loud? I jump on top of her and cover her mouth with my hand. She swats at it but I hold my grip as she rolls her eyes and stops fighting.

Mom clears her throat. "Hm, yes, that won't work. Les, it's time for you to reconsider your friends. You're a smart girl."

Which is honestly the first compliment she's ever given me.

She continues, "You don't need to be around people like them. I'll find a tutor and send him or her your way tomorrow. Have you given more thought to St. Maarten with—"

"Gotta go. Bye, Mom." I press end and climb off Candy.

"*¡Ya!*" Candy sits up, digging her claw nails into my couch. "You could've killed me. What is wrong with you? Stop being so *fresa.*"

"I'm not being...whatever you just said I'm being like." I slump back into the couch and turn the TV up higher. "Forget you heard that conversation."

"No, *muchacha.* I ain't forgetting it. Why are you so weirded out with Carter tutoring you?"

I've successfully avoided talking, thinking, or interacting with him for the past few days. So, it's not really something I want to get into with his twin. "I'm not. I just think I need more tutoring than he can provide, so…"

She stares into me with burning eyes and I worry she may have superpowers because my cheek is hot as I watch a new couple make out in the Paradise jacuzzi. "*No me gusta todo esto.* Girl, you lyin'."

"Well, has Carter said something to you or something?"

"Duh. We're twins. Can we pause this already? Let's go out and get some food or something."

"Fine." I aim the remote and pause Hulu. "Let's go."

"Cool. I'm driving." She bounces up from the couch and snatches her keys.

"Okay, let me just grab my helmet."

"Oh shut up." She groans, slipping on her Jesus sandals. "Are you going to change?"

I look down at my joggers and tank. "Um, no? I look like freaking Kim K in Kanye's line right now."

Candy draws up her mouth and looks like a blobfish. You know, if a blobfish could be hot and had pink hair…and an impressively intimidating stare. "I'll say this much—your butt definitely doesn't look like Kim K's."

Ouch, I can hear the, "Ooh, roasted!" from my studio audience loud and clear. I slip on my Birkenstocks. "Whatever. Less is best."

She squeals, "*Ay!* Just like your na—"

"Ah!" I scream and cover my ears. "Stop! That's why I refrain from using the word *less* at all costs."

We walk outside and she won't quit. "Seriously, that's so cute. That could be your tagline. Oh-em-gee, give me your phone. Is that your Insta handle? Make it your Insta handle. Or at least put it in your bio."

She unlocks her crappy Kia and I get in. Unlike Carter's car, it doesn't smell like cinnamon. It smells like flowers and… something else I'd rather not say.

I lean on the center console. "Knock it off, already. But yes, it *is* my Insta handle. Okay, where are we going to eat?"

Cranking the car, she stomps on the brakes and throws it

into drive before I even hear the engine turn over. Then, she peels out of the parking lot. Thank all things holy that there aren't children around.

She pulls up to a stoplight, nudges my elbow off the center console and opens it, digging around until she pulls out Hubba Bubba which is, and I'm not exaggerating, the exact color of her hair. "I know a great little place. You'll love it."

Her driving makes me nauseous, so I pull out my phone and stare at the ominous twenty-seven unread text messages. Granted, like fifteen of those are from a group text between old high school friends, but the others are from Ben and Carter. Might as well open them. Ben's have been sitting unread for over a week, since my birthday, 'cause I ditched him to go to the beach with Carter. Carter's texts I've been opening, but he sent one about an hour ago.

Carter: *Hey señorita, can we talk?*

I want to talk to him, I really do. But there's so much going on, and I don't know how to say it all.

Ben: *We still good for tonight?*

Ben: *Soo should I just come to your place?*

Ben: *Wtf, Les. Where are you?*

Ben: *Guess I can't get mad at you since it's your birthday. Just thought you'd want to spend it with me…*

Ben: *Hey, what happened last night?*

Ben: *So you're just going to ignore me in class too? Tf did I do?*

Ben: *Did you block my number again?*

Ben: *?*

Ben: *Hey, what's up?*

Ben: *I'm so confused.*

Ben: *We need to talk.*

Candy slams on the brakes, and I go flying forward, hitting my fist on her dash and my forehead on my fist, leaving a blossoming pain right above my nose. "That is definitely going to leave a mark."

She lets out a 'hee-hee' awkward laugh and turns off the car. "*Lo siento. Pero*, we're here," she sings.

Whatever she meant by "here" can't really be *here*. "Why are we at the baseball stadium? It's fall, there's not going to be anyone here."

"Look around you." She points to the dozens of cars. "It's an exhibition game."

I clutch my phone like a 1920's stars clutches her pearls. "Then, my question still stands. Why are we here?"

"*¡Ay Dios mío!* Get your white ass out of this car and let's go. The stadium has great snacks."

"What is up with you and your brother commenting on my white butt? And don't you know baseball games are notorious for peanuts? Are you trying to kill me?"

She bangs her head against her headrest. "Do you think I'm stupid? I put in a favor with the snack bar dude. They're not selling peanuts today."

Blowing my hair off of my forehead, I ask, "How do you even know the snack bar guy?"

"Do you really want to know?" She wiggles her eyebrows.

"No." I yank on the car door's handle, but it pulls free, and I turn around in horror to Candy.

She death stares me. I slowly start shrinking into my shoulders. She stares harder and her left eye squints. I hold up the handle so it covers my eyes.

"*¡Hijo de puta!* Do you have the strength of Thor?"

"I'm sorry! I barely touched it."

She rips the handle from my fingers. "Said every guilty person ever."

Which is true, but how was I supposed to know it'd break free? "Stop being so dramatic, I will pay for it."

"That's so offensive that you would even offer to pay for it. You don't think I can afford it? Am I just a charity case to you?"

And this is my worst nightmare (or, you know, at least top fifty). "No, that isn't what I meant."

She cackles. "I'm just kidding! You didn't even break it. I broke it sophomore year of high school while *bom-chica-wow-wow* with Tom."

I laugh and bury my face in my hands. "You're literally the worst. Do you know that?"

"Worst, best, *mas o menos*, it depends on your perspective. Just press your finger into the little hole part on the door and it'll pop open."

Sticking my finger in holes is not really something I like to do, but alas, here I am. I do as she says. The hole is sticky, but it does open the door. The whole ordeal distracts me enough that once I close the door and realize I'm standing at the baseball stadium entrance, I try to get back into the car. But Candy has a smug grin on her face and locks it.

"Candy," I whine. "I really don't want to be here. I shouldn't have even left the house. I need to study."

"Says the girl who was watching *Bachelor in Paradise.* You're avoiding both guys, and you know it. Time to figure your *ish* out, girlfriend." She pulls out two tickets and hands them to the man at the front. Which means she came prepared. Which means she was planning this all along.

"How far in advance did you plan this?"

She stands on her tiptoes and throws her arm around my shoulders. "I'm taking you to the game. Enjoy a girl date. Get out of your head, and let's have fun. Plus, what's better than staring at men's butts in baseball pants?"

"True. You got me there." Plus, I never do get to go to many baseball games 'cause of all the peanuts there. Thanks to Candy, it won't be a problem.

We find our seats, and since the stadium's fairly empty, we have the perfect view of West's team. It's easy for me to pick out Carter's lean frame. Of course, he's a pitcher. A super-sexy-watch-how-good-of-an-arm-I-have pitcher. After one inning, I'm ready to call my lawyers because I'm all hot and bothered.

The teams switch, and Tom's up to bat first. Candy tenses beside me, but when I cock a brow and elbow her, she mumbles something in Spanish and sticks her tongue out at me.

His first swing is a strike, but he hits the second pitch solidly, and Candy's demeanor eases. A few others I'm not familiar with bat before Rykard, who I haven't interacted with since the hot springs, goes to bat. Unfortunately, he sucks and strikes out. And yes, I know that doesn't mean he sucks-sucks, but still.

But now it's my turn to tense because Ben's up next. We're sitting close enough that I can make out his heart-shaped birthmark on his hand. He hits the first ball deep down the left field line and makes it to third base, bringing in two runners. The score goes to 4-0.

The game continues on, Candy and I share Skittles, and it's the bottom of the fifth inning when something happens. Problem is, I don't know what that something is. West and the opposing team start shouting at each other. They break off into little groups of testosterone and the umpires head toward them, breaking up the ones they can.

"That's not good." Candy stands and climbs onto her seat. "Ooh, yeah, that's really not good."

"What?"

She points toward the field where a white uniform with the number one on it shoves a guy in green. "What is his problem? Does he want to get kicked off the team?" she mumbles.

It's Carter.

The guy in green shoves Carter harder, but Carter pushes forward and raises his fist. And of all people to try and stop it, it has to be Ben.

Ben gets between the two and is tossed around, but he pushes Carter toward the rest of the team and shouts something. Carter's back is to us, but whatever Ben said didn't help because Carter's fist collides with Ben's eye.

Ben's hand shoots up to cover where he was hit, and he shakes his head and walks past Carter, past the rest of the players, and disappears in the dugout.

What. Is. Going. On?

"Come on, they're both going to be kicked out of the game," Candy says, pulling my hand. I follow because I have no idea what else to do.

She leads me around a few corners and into a cement hallway where two coaches shout while gesturing wildly with their hands. Carter is surrounded by a few other guys and Ben is on the opposite side with one other dude I don't recognize. When one coach shouts, "Go home. Now!" the players all flinch.

The coaches walk past us and Candy goes straight to Carter. But he isn't looking at her. He's looking at me with wide green eyes and crossed arms. I glance to the side and there's Ben, a bruise already forming under his right eye, staring at me as well.

I feel stuck. If I had my own car, I'd walk right out and leave without talking to either of them because choosing to talk to one and not the other feels like a decision I'm not ready to make. I go back and forth a few times, but neither of them break eye contact with me.

I walk to Ben, glancing one more time at Carter, but he's talking to Candy.

Ben slides his arm around my back and pulls me in for a side hug. "Hey."

I shake him off. "Are you okay? What happened out there?"

He shrugs. "I'm fine. You need a ride home? As it turns out, I'm banned from the game."

I pull away from him. "Uh, yeah. Yeah, sure. That'd be great." Turning toward where Candy and Carter stand, I yell out, "Hey, I'll catch you later, Candy. 'Kay?"

She cocks her head and raises a brow, then mouths *text me later.*

Nodding, I wave goodbye, not daring to catch Carter's gaze.

Ben puts his arm back around me as we walk toward the dugout. Grabbing his bag amongst the five others thrown out by the coaches, he says, "So, how've you been? You've been avoiding me." He touches his eye and winces.

Which isn't wrong, but also not entirely right. "I've just been busy. Classes are really hard and—"

"Right," he says, clenching his jaw. He leads me to the back

121

parking lot and unlocks his white, Mercedes G-class.

The smell of new car and leather seats hits me the second I open the door. Something I used to revel in now just makes me feel the weight of Ben's privilege attached to it. I get in, put on my seatbelt, and pretend to look at something on my phone. He opens the trunk and shoves his bag in the back. When he gets in the front seat, he looks exhausted. There's dirt on his pants, he's wearing his cap on backwards, and his lips look dry as he licks them.

"Why'd you blow me off on your birthday?"

"I think we should talk about your eye instead." But he doesn't budge. The temperature just climbed ten degrees, and I think a calculus problem might actually be easier for me to solve than it is for me to say, "I was out with Carter."

He presses the start button and the car purrs to life. "Okay, but why? I literally asked you to hang out and you said yes. Then you ditched me without any warning."

"It wasn't intentional. It just...happened. I'm sorry, okay? I didn't mean to blow you off."

"Alright." He backs out and we're silent as he drives. His parking pass swings on his mirror as we make our way over the speed bumps in the road.

Half-bare trees pass outside the window with piles of red and brown leaves. A couple of people are on the sidewalks, smiling and laughing. One throws a frisbee and another catches it then flips him off.

And yes, I'm noticing these things because this car ride is awkward AF. Don't judge me.

"You gonna tell me what that fight was about?" I turn toward him, and he opens his mouth slightly with a smile.

He has a spattering of freckles on his nose. He also has another birthmark on his right shoulder, but it's not heart-shaped like the one on his hand. He has a scar on his knee from when he fell at a soccer game when he was eight. And if you look closely, there's a small scar on his elbow from the time he got cut open by my snowboard after I promised him I could jump a rail.

I couldn't jump the rail.

Ben's not a mystery to me, nor is he someone to get to know. I already know it all. If only I knew how that makes me feel. There's a sense of calm with knowing someone. It's a lack of excitement that's replaced with a sense of ease.

"I'm really not sure what the fight was about." He leans back into the seat, waiting for the light to change. "Carter said some dude on the other team said something to him, but who knows."

"Then why'd he punch you?"

"Cause I was in the way?" Ben puts his elbow on the center console and holds up his hand like he wants a high five.

I place my hand against his and he intertwines our fingers then lays them down on the console. "B, I highly doubt Carter hit you for being 'in the way.'"

He's silent for the next five minutes until he pulls into my apartment complex and sighs. "Why? 'Cause he's so perfect?" He snorts. "Carter isn't as great as you think he is. You don't even know him."

Maybe he's right. I don't know him—not like I know B. But I feel like I know Carter, and I don't understand why he would punch Ben. As he parks, I pull out my phone and open up Carter's messages.

Les: *Are you okay?*

"Les, did you hear me?"

I flinch. "Sorry, what?"

He massages his forehead with his thumb and forefinger. "Can I come inside?"

"Yeah, for sure. Why even ask?"

"Because you've been avoiding me for a week. Sorry I'm not going to assume that I can just come inside with you."

"Don't snap at me," I say, getting out of the car.

He locks it with a '*beep*' while we walk up the stairs to my apartment. I punch in my lock code and walk inside. Ben wanders ahead of me and into the kitchen to find a glass and get some water. He's still in his baseball pants, and as you can see, he still has a great butt. A little too good of a butt.

I glance away before he catches me.

The apartment is silent. There aren't even people yelling or laughing outside, and the sun filters through my shutters and lends a golden shine to Ben's hair. "So, whatcha wanna do?"

He finishes the glass of water and shrugs. "Hell if I know."

"This is...kinda awkward."

He lifts his hat, fluffs his hair, and then replaces it backwards again with a laugh. "Yeah, sort of. Listen, I just want to spend time with you. We don't have to put a label on it. But we've been best friends forever, Les. I miss you." He glances at me with a pained expression. "I miss everything about you."

My pulse echoes in my ears. I clear my throat. "Um...You want some ice for your eye?"

"Nah," he sets down his glass, "I hear all the chicks dig a good black eye."

My lips quirk. "Definitely." I look around the room and settle on the few boxes still fully packed. "Want to help me unpack the last of the boxes," I air quote, "best friend?"

As he walks toward me, the sun moves over his face, lighting his brown eyes, and his biceps flex when he places his hands on my waist. "Mmm, I don't like those words coming out of your mouth."

"What are you doing?" I whisper.

He leans down, and his chin trails from my collarbone to my ear. Though he looks clean shaven, there's a bit of scruff that tickles my neck on the way up, but like the good actress I am, I control my breathing so I don't sound like a starved dog.

"Helping you unpack," he whispers, then drops his hands and walks away from me, toward the boxes.

I squeak and while his back is toward me, grab at my tank's collar and fan myself. I can *feel* him smirking from across the room.

He places his hands down on one of the boxes and some muscle I don't know the name of tightens at the back of his arm and—Okay, you're right, I need to stop looking at his muscles.

But as soon as he opens the box, I forget about the muscles anyhow and remember why I haven't unpacked any of these belongings.

The boxes hold everything I can't handle. On the top is a photo of me and Ben from prom night—before he dumped me—and our crowns from being crowned king and queen. He pulls them out and places the crown on my head, putting his on top of his hat. "I can't believe you kept these."

"Why?" I take off my crown and his, placing them on the floor. "I can't erase you, Ben. You were my whole life the past two years. Even before we were together, all of my memories are with you. It doesn't change because we broke up."

He places the photo to the side and grabs a scrapbook. And yes, my mom has told me many times that I could've purchased a book that printed my photos for me, but I like crafting. Or, I used to.

Ben sits cross-legged on the floor and opens the scrapbook to the first page. It's me, him, my dad, and my mom in Hawaii. The sunset is cotton candy pink and waves crash in the background. My mom and dad look at each other, grinning, and Ben and I both smile innocently, but we were really grabbing each other's butts. He laughs. "That was a good trip."

"Yeah, it was. Remember when we were deep sea fishing and you were scared of the mahi mahi that the guides caught, so my dad threw you overboard? You came up gasping for air and all like, 'William, I'm going to sue you!'" I laugh so hard that my abs burn, and it's the first workout I've had in weeks.

"It was not funny." He gives me a chastising glare but chuckles. "Your dad was a riot."

I lean my head on his shoulder. "Yeah, he really was."

Ben flips the pages, and almost every photo has him in it. More pictures from Hawaii, pictures that he took of me and my dad when he was diagnosed, asleep on the hospital bed, photos of just him and my dad together.

How did things turn so crappy? The tears fall fast and silent, trailing down the side of my face and landing on Ben's uniform. "I miss the way things used to be."

He sets the book down and slides me up and over his thigh until I'm sitting between his legs. Hugging me from behind, he places his chin on my shoulder. "I know. I do, too."

"It really sucks. He's not going to be there for my graduation. Or my wedding if I ever convince someone to marry me. He's not going to be there for me when I have a kid. If I even w-want one." The words drop like the first hill of a rollercoaster, and I can't stop them. "I'm never going to take another trip with him. I literally have no family left. My grandparents are dead, my dad is dead, half the time I wish my mom was gone, and I have no siblings. I have *no one*."

"Les, come on." He touches my shoulder and turns me around to face him, brushing my hair to the side. I probably look like a bloated blueberry, but it doesn't matter because he's seen me cry so many times. "You have me."

But, do I?

Without thinking, I kiss him. Our lips clash together, and it's a desperate plea for him to take everything away. Remove the pain and the memories of how perfect turned to disaster, and to feel something other than sadness and confusion when I'm around him.

I throw off his baseball cap and thread my fingers through his hair, pulling him closer. He smells of the ballfield and his sweat, a scent I didn't know I recognized until now. Ben stands and places me in front of him, never breaking our kiss. My arms tingle, and I press my hips against his. He grips my waist and then moves his hands up to the curve of my spine.

Breaking the kiss, I look up to his wild eyes searching my face.

"Les, I don't think we—"

I yank him down to my lips again and swallow whatever it was he was about to say. And my pain is replaced with the quickening of my heart. "Come on," I say against his mouth and walk backward down the hall and toward my room. I don't want to feel anything, but I need to feel *something*.

The second I step through my door's threshold, my phone chimes with a new text. But I'm too deep to care.

Ben steps in behind me, wetting his lips as his gaze travels from my head to my toe. Then, I close my bedroom door.

I can't show you *everything*.

Chapter Twelve

Ben's napping beside me in my bed, his soft breaths humming against the pillow. His eye is swollen and seems to be getting darker by the second. His golden skin is peppered with the occasional freckle or mole, and I think back to all the days that I had dreamed of being his.

He's handsome, and he was right—he has always been there for me. So why do I feel like crap?

And why do I want to text a different man than the one I'm lying beside?

Nothing happened, I assure myself. But that's not true. Ben may have stopped us, but letting him hold me while I cry seems a lot more intimate anyway. I bite my lip hard to try and ground myself.

This isn't me.

I turn over slowly, change into some shorts and a tee, and get out of the bedroom, heading to the kitchen. My phone has a message from over two hours ago, before my epic meltdown.

Carter: *I'm fine. How are you?*

He's just responding to my earlier question of how he's feeling after punching Ben in the face. If only I knew why he did it.

Les: *Can we talk?*

Immediately, he calls me.

"Hey," I whisper, checking the time. It's just about five. This may go on record as the longest day of my life.

"Hey, so, funny thing happened." Carter's voice is smooth and warm. "I was taking a drive, and my passenger seat was empty."

Despite my sour mood, I smile. "Is that so?"

"Yeah. And, it just felt wrong. I kept thinking that there

should be a hot girl sitting there, chastising me for getting kicked out of my game for punching her ex. So I did something crazy."

"What's that?"

He awkwardly laughs into the phone. "Let's just say, I'm in the neighborhood. Care to go for a drive with me?"

"Yes." The word flies out before I think of the repercussions. "I'll be right there."

I sneak into my room to grab my sandals and double-check that B is still out. This is stupid, right? I have one guy literally in my bed and I'm going to see another one.

But apparently, stupid is my middle name. It's like I'm sneaking out of my parents' house, but it's my own apartment. Any time my feet make a noise, I cringe and hold my breath just in case I hear him waking up.

By the time I open the door, Carter is standing against the railing, and I can finally breathe again. The breath I held whooshes out of me.

"Hi." Carter's in navy UA basketball shorts and a plain, white tee. He runs his fingers through his hair. Peeking out from his sleeve, I can see his insulin pump. His dark brown hair is mussed, and his left hand is taped up.

I close the door behind me and point at his hand. "Are you hurt?"

He waves me off. "Nah, Coach made me tape it. Sorry, I didn't mean to show up unannounced. I was driving around, and..."

Though he doesn't finish it, I can hear the unspoken words. The lighthearted tone from the phone call is gone, and the real us is here. He's confused, maybe hurt.

I nod. "No, I'm sorry. I shouldn't have yelled at you when you were trying to help me last week. And, I'm sorry about whatever happened at the game today."

He leans against the railing and grips it. "*Está bien*. Honestly, I get that you're overwhelmed and stressed out with every-thing. It's a hard class. I'd freak out too if I failed a test. But, I guess I just don't understand why you've been ghosting me."

Ugh. His voice is so sweet, and his lips are barely pouting, but not even on purpose. And gah, I can't handle it. "I'm not ghosting you. I promise. I don't want to ghost you. I really, really like you, Carter."

And now there's a million pound weight on my chest because I don't know. I literally don't know what to do. I shouldn't have left with Ben. I shouldn't have kissed him or cried with him or let him in at all.

"But Ben." He hooks his thumb over his shoulder. "His car is sorta hard to miss."

"I don't know what I'm doing," I whisper and gaze to the floor. I pick at a string on my cutoff shorts because I don't want to see the disappointment in his eyes. "But I know I don't want you getting caught in the crossfire."

He clears his throat and reaches his hand out to me. I grab it and he pulls me close. And because I clearly can't control myself, I take a big whiff of his shirt, and he laughs.

"Remind me to thank your ex-girlfriend for your cinnamon scent."

He doesn't laugh at that joke, though. Instead, he brushes his fingers through my hair, but it's pretty much impossible to brush through, so he just sort of limply plays with it. My ear is pressed against his chest, and his heartbeat is sure and solid. It's comforting, and I can't help but wish it was him in my bed instead.

"Do you love him?"

His heartbeat is drowned out by the thrum of blood pounding in my ears. "No."

"No?" Carter lifts my chin until I'm gazing into warm, brown eyes rimmed with dark eyelashes that any girl would kill for.

I shake my head. "No, I don't."

"*Gracias a Dios.*"

I hate to say it to him, but, "It's more complicated than that, though."

He tucks my hair behind my ear and leans down until our noses touch. "No, Les, it's really not. Tell him to leave and come with me."

"I can't."

"Why?" he groans.

"Because he's literally in my bed right now." And I don't know how that makes him think of me, but maybe that's the point.

You could hear a pin drop, and our lips aren't even an inch apart. My confession doesn't faze him. "I just want a chance. Don't count me out of the game before it's even started. Come on. Text him, tell him you'll be right back, and let's go for a drive."

I want to. So, so, bad I want to go with him. Reason tells me not to. Reason tells me that I have another guy in my bed, a good guy who knows me and everything about me. But maybe love's not reasonable because I find myself saying, "Okay."

Carter grabs my hand and leads me down the steps, jogging, which means I'm practically sprinting, as if he thinks that I'm going to change my mind before we get to his truck. He opens my door, lifts me up into the seat, then races over to the driver's side.

"Slow down, Usain." A laugh bubbles up out of me.

He flashes me a grin and winks, backing out of the parking spot. When his phone hooks up to Bluetooth, NF blares through the speakers, and he turns it down. "Sorry. Thanks for coming." He squeezes my thigh and then goes back to the wheel.

"Don't thank me. Thank your parents for making you sickeningly attractive." The car hits a bump, and as we lose the last bit of daylight, he turns on his lights. "So, what happened today? I don't really want to talk about *him,* but why'd you punch him? Please tell me it wasn't because of me."

"Definitely not you." He glances toward me and then covers with, "Not that you wouldn't be worth fighting for. But, no, you weren't the reason."

"Okay, then what gives?"

He taps his fingers on the steering wheel. "He's a racist coward, that's what."

I flinch. My watch dings with a notification, but it's a text from my mom with a tutor's number, so I quickly dismiss it. Ben's not a racist. At least not from any encounter I've had with him. "How is he racist?"

He scratches his chin and yawns. "I don't want to get into it. The kid's just pissed me off from the second he started training with us. He's entitled and thinks he owns the team. And when that douche from Davis told me to go back to where I came from, I..." He shakes his head and tries to suppress a smile, but it doesn't work, and he ends up sucking his lips into his mouth. His shoulders shake.

"Oh gosh, what?" I'm guessing he didn't say something too nice back.

"Well, I told him that the only time he's been successful was when his mom's birth control failed."

I bury my head into my hands and groan while giggling. "Boys are so weird."

"And for some reason," he starts, "apparently, that was offensive. So he came at me with his fists raised, and Mr. I'm-Perfect steps in between us and tells *me* to calm down. When I told him I got it, he said, 'Stop with your feisty Mexican heritage.' So, I punched him."

And rightfully so. I get it now. I would've knocked Ben out too. Except, you know, I probably couldn't unless I had a beer bottle or something other than my fist.

I sit back up. "He actually said that?"

"Yeah. And he said it to the wrong twin. Like *I'm* feisty." He purses his lips and shakes his head.

I wiggle my shoulders. "You can get feisty with me."

Don't roll your eyes. It was a cop out, I know. In a perfect world, I would've known what to say to him. But, I'm human and still learning. I can't pretend like I know what it's like to be a minority or marginalized group. Heaven knows I didn't grow up around many. The worst part is I think he *knows* it was a cop out.

He half-heartedly replies, "Don't tempt me, *cariña.*" But it lacks its usual flirty tone.

A few moments pass. I grab his hand and squeeze. "I'm sorry he said that. There's no excuse for it."

Carter nods. "Yeah, it's messed up. But whatever."

We pull into a parking lot on a hill, overlooking the valley and all the lights below. The stars are coming out and there's still a purple haze in the sky as it fades to black. I direct the conversation back toward happier things. "You know, you're always saying 'don't tempt me' but maybe I want to tempt you. Ever think about that? Come on, Carter. Show me what you've got."

He turns the truck off and moves his seat back. Then, he reaches over and lifts me up over the center console and into his lap. Normally, I would've hit my head on the ceiling, but this Mexican love god has it all figured out. I straddle his waist and he places his hands on my thighs, gripping them just hard enough for his fingers to dig in.

His mouth finds mine in the shadows of the truck and he kisses me, parting my lips with his tongue and truly showing me what he's got. I'm almost regretting asking him because the second his hands move up the back of my shirt, I know I'm screwed.

Not literally, but because these touches are giving me twice the amount of feeling that I felt a few hours ago. My nerves are a livewire, and when he breaks our kiss, my heart feels like it's synced up to EDM. He trails down my neck then up to my ear, where he bites gently, fiddling with my hoop earring between his teeth.

He hugs my lower back, pushing our waists together, and crashes into another kiss, both of us stealing the air the other breathes. I wrap my arms around his neck and lean back, pulling him with me. He shifts his weight and cups my cheek, his tongue—

HONK!

"Oh, crap!" I scramble forward and Carter places a hand between my shoulder blades. Our foreheads touch. "Now anyone that's here knows what we were doing. Look, even the windows are fogged."

He pulls back and laughs. With his index finger he traces on the window, "DON'T WORRY. WE'RE NOT F**K!NG."

"I appreciate the censorship. Heaven forbid a kid reads this. Now with two letters missing, they'll never figure it out."

"Hey," he shrugs, "I do what I can. Plus, I did an exclamation point for the 'I.' So that's a whopping *uno, dos, tres* letters." Then he smiles, lips swollen from our kiss, and nods his head to the side. "Come on, I brought sustenance."

"Ooh, boy. I knew I could count on you. Whatcha got?"

He pulls the handle and pushes the door so it swings open. I get off of his lap, and then he follows. "You'll see."

In his truck bed is a cooler, and when he opens it, my body tingles all over. Because he brought cookies. Dang good cookies, too. He pulls out Goodie Girl Mint Slims, which are basically allergy-friendly thin mints. "I even brought you some hipster, VSCO-girl, whatever-you-call-this-crap sparkling water." He points his finger to the sky. "But wait, there's more."

Two chocolate milks sit on the bottom in ice, and it's so stupid, but it's like the sweetest thing anyone's ever done for me.

"How'd you know I was going to say yes to coming?"

I lean into him and he kisses my forehead. "Just had a feeling, *mi amada.* Come on, there's a spot up here where we can look at all the city lights."

A couple yards ahead, there's a large rock with enough space to lay on. A few other people are around, one group has a small fire, but it's not very loud, and the view shimmers in front of us like a living portrait of glitter. You know—if glitter wasn't the worst craft supply of all time.

The rock is cold against my thighs, but it almost feels good considering how worked up I was earlier. It's probably best for me to cool down—temperature-wise and sexy-Carter-wise.

"Look, I appreciate the cookies, but I hope you know that just because you brought cookies doesn't mean that you're going to get to eat any of them." I take a sip of my chocolate milk through the straw and feel like a kindergartner.

"Aw, come on, girl. I'd rather eat a different cookie anyway."

I snort and chocolate milk dribbles out of my nose, burning my nostrils. And, now I don't feel like a kindergartner at all.

He rolls his eyes. "Chocolate chip! Candy made chocolate chip cookies earlier. Gosh, get your mind out of the gutter, Les."

Giving him the hand, I say, "Cool it, dude."

He laughs, and the sound could easily get on the Billboard Top 100 because *whew*, it's all I want to listen to. Bumping his shoulder against mine, he says, "Hey, just showing you what I got."

I dig my finger under the cardboard of the cookie box and lift until the edges separate. "Yeah, well, it turns out you got a little too much."

His leg straightens as he digs into his pocket and pulls out his controller for his insulin pump. After pressing a few different buttons, he snatches the cookies away from me.

"Hey! I thought you brought those for *moi*." I pout. "Am I going to have to steal them from your mouth?" To hell with everyone watching. I straddle him and suck on his earlobe.

"Unless you want me to take you to the truck bed and show you what I'm really made of, I suggest you get your *nalgas* off of me and eat your *galletas*." He puts a cookie in my mouth.

"I like truck beds," I mumble with my mouth full.

"I'm sure you do, *señorita*."

The cookie is my one true love, but it's gone before I can really appreciate it. Thankfully, there are like thirty more. "I have a confession."

He puts his fist to his mouth and coughs as if he choked a bit on his cookie. "Alright, shoot."

"Every time you call me *señorita*, I feel like Camila Cabello."

"*Ay Dios mío.*" He folds in on himself and laughs. "Is that even a good thing? You're such a dork."

"I know, I know. Just let me feel like a hot Latina woman for a second." I throw half of a cookie up into the air and catch it in my mouth. 'Cause I'm a boss like that.

"Well, I hate to break it to you, *amor*, I think you're about as white as it gets. But, we could put a little Latino in you if you know what I'm sayin', okurr?" He mimics shooting a free throw.

I gasp. "Carter's got the dirty jokes, eh? Alright, alright. I can roll with it. But you didn't have to go full-on Cardi B on me. *Okurr?*" I mock and snap my fingers.

His nose crinkles as he smiles, and even though we're at a cool hill with lots of pretty lights, I think the real view is him, right in front of me.

And shut up, I know that was cheesy.

I intertwine our fingers, and my hands buzz with excitement. Everything with him is fun. It makes me forget about all the worries that I have, which is probably a bad thing. Because this is real life, not some fairytale.

"I worry about this," I blurt out, then cover my mouth with my hand.

He furrows his brow. "*Por qué?*"

I shrug, and a breeze blows through, giving my upper arms goosebumps. I rub them out, but it doesn't seem to help. "You're, like, way too good for me. I'm a mess, and my life is a mess. I don't want to hurt you, and I feel like you're the type of person I could easily just..."

"Just what?" He rubs his thumb over mine.

"Like, fall for. You're the type of person I could easily fall for. I mean, we barely know each other."

"Barely is a bit strong. I'd say we definitely know each other."

I roll my eyes. "You know what I mean. We haven't known each other that long, and I'm already dreading leaving you tonight."

I look over at him and legit, the only way I can describe his face is from that stupid SpongeBob meme where he has that smug look with his smile nearly underneath his nose. That's what Carter looks like. "Why is dreading leaving me a bad thing?"

The cookies don't sound that great anymore as a sense of wrong makes my heart beat faster. "Because someone else is waiting for me at my apartment."

Carter closes his eyes and lets out a breath. "Come on, I don't want to talk about him."

"I don't either, but we have to because it's the reality of the situation here. I texted him and told him I'd be back. He might be there when you drop me off. What am I supposed to do? What am I supposed to say?"

He runs a hand through his hair and shakes his head. "Tell him it's over."

"But it's not over, Carter." It's as if someone throws a bucket of water on top of my head. "At least not yet."

As he sets down his chocolate milk, he bends forward, and now that he isn't looking at me, I want to cry. But I've cried too much today, and I'm a self-proclaimed non-crier.

"Why isn't it over? I don't get what you see in him."

I want to answer *the past*, but it's not a good enough response. "I don't know what to say."

He lets go of my hand. "You said you didn't love him."

A new crowd of people walk past us to one of the fire pits, and we fall into an uncomfortable silence until they all are far enough away again. I sigh. "I don't."

"Then what's the deal?" His elbows are on his knees and he gazes at me sideways. "You've got so much more going for you than him."

For some reason, maybe because of earlier, I get defensive. And I regret it before it even leaves my mouth. "Like what? Maybe I want to be with him."

He looks out to the city and lets out a sarcastic laugh. "Yeah, no. Otherwise, you wouldn't be here." The silence grows between us, and it's enough that I can hear crickets amongst the other people. "Why does it have to be him? Of all people, why choose him?"

"So this would be different if it wasn't Ben?"

He turns back toward me and thrusts out his hand. "Of course it would be!"

Is he for real? I brush my hair away from my face. "So you're saying you'd be fine with me hanging out with anyone else as long as it wasn't Ben?"

"Sure." He crosses his arms.

"Wow. Okay. So what is this?" I motion between us. "Is this just some longform game to get back at Ben for whatever crap you have between the two of you?"

He loses his smug expression. "*Qué mierda*, no, that's not what I meant. It's because I think you can do better than him."

I stand up from the rock and snort. "On what grounds?"

Carter gets up too, towering nearly a foot over me. "On every ground, Les. On *my* ground. I can treat you so much better than that racist asshole. He's—"

"I don't want to hear it anymore!" I throw my arms up. "What he said wasn't okay, I get that. But whatever else is going on between you two is *your* thing. Leave me out of it."

He tries to hug me, but I shrug him off.

"How am I supposed to leave you out of it when it's *you* that's between us? Come on, Les, I don't want to see you with anyone else. *Especially* him. From the second we met, I told you I was interested. I had no idea you were his ex."

"And from the second you found out, you started to pursue me harder. So honestly Carter, is this just some game to you? Because I don't have time for games right now. I don't have time for *this*."

He shakes his head. "Fine. If that's how you feel, let's go. I'll take you right back home to your *ex*."

My eyes fill with tears. I don't want to fight with him. I don't want to even go home. But I'm the only one to blame here, so I follow him to the car.

He stomps around, muttering stuff in Spanish that I can't pick up on and puts away everything he brought before opening my door for me. I tell the guy I don't have time for him and he still opens my door.

"Carter—"

"Forget it, Les." His voice is full of dejection, and I feel so dumb.

I get into the car and swipe at my eye as the first tear falls. When he starts the truck, I look out the passenger window so he can't see the second and third.

The car ride to my apartment is silent. The whole day repeats in my head from Ben to Carter to this fight. And even though I made all of the decisions that led me here, I can't help but feel like it's out of my control.

There's a flighty feeling in my chest, and my ears ring. I'm overwhelmed. Too much is happening too fast, and I can't keep up.

When we pull into my apartment's lot, Ben's Mercedes is still parked in the guest parking, which means he definitely hasn't left. Carter must see it too because he white knuckles the steering wheel and clenches his jaw.

He turns the truck off and lays his forehead on the steering wheel. "I'm sorry. I didn't mean those things I said."

The fact that he's apologizing to me just shows that he deserves better. "You have nothing to be sorry for. I'm the one who should apologize."

He rolls his head to the side and looks at me. "I don't want whatever this is to be over."

I shrug. "No one says it is."

"Then why does it feel like it?" he whispers.

I shrug again.

"Come here." He holds out his arms and I lean over the center console into him. But when I smell his shirt, another tear falls. What is happening? Over or not, it shouldn't hurt like this. I haven't even known him that long.

He's everything good in the world, and I don't want to ruin that. Every time I'm with him, it's fun and carefree. And every time I'm with Ben, I end up yelling or crying. It's clear: I should choose Carter.

But with a guy like Carter, I shouldn't be conflicted at all. He doesn't deserve that. Plus, Ben has two people cheering for him—my mom and dad.

"I don't know what to do," I mumble against his shirt. "I feel like I'm in over my head with all of this, and I know that's a crappy excuse."

He rubs my back. "Look, I don't want to make you cry. It's not worth it." He guides me gently to the side of him as he looks at his watch and sighs. "Can you hand me something from the glovebox? Blood sugar's on its way down."

"It's 'cause I hogged all the cookies, huh?" I sniffle and rub my nose, open the glovebox, and hand him a juice box.

His hands shake slightly as he undoes the straw wrapper and pokes a hole in the juice box. A few gulps later, he discards the empty container in his cup holder. "No, I probably just dosed too much for the back end."

I don't know what he means by that, but I just nod.

"Come on, I'll walk you up," he says, pulling the key from the ignition and getting out.

"It's fine, really. I don't want…"

He clears his throat and absently gazes at Ben's SUV. "Right."

"I'll talk to you soon, though?" I know it sounds horrible, but I don't know what else to say.

He leans across the console and places a hand on my cheek. When our lips touch, I know. I'm falling hard for Carter, but I'm scared.

"Don't give up just yet." His voice breaks the silence.

I squeeze his hand, lean up and kiss his nose, then get out. "I'll call you."

Jogging up to my apartment, I mentally prepare myself for what I have to say to Ben. Carter or not, it's time to end this. I'm pretty sure my mom is going to kill me, but I'll deal with that later.

I punch in the code and the lock grinds open. This is it. Rip it off like a bandaid. Quick and easy. I push open the door and Ben's pacing the kitchen on the phone.

"Yeah, sure, Dad. Bye." He hangs up and grips the counter-top, staring between his hands. His muscles are taut and his black eye looks way worse than it did a few hours ago.

"Is everything okay?"

He glances up and some hair flops down across his forehead. "No, it's not. My mom's been having an affair with the freaking gardener. I think they're getting divorced."

Chapter Thirteen

I fully planned on coming into my apartment and breaking up with Ben. After just a few hours with Carter, even with our fight, I still want him. So, tell me why I'm currently making this fool (AKA, Ben) a cup of tea.

Because I have issues, obviously. I mean, we all do. But somewhere in my mediocre life, I was guilt-tripped one too many times and now I don't know how to deal with things. Like when your boyfriend—ex-boyfriend—tells you that his parents are knee-deep in counseling working through his mother's affair, it just doesn't seem right to say, "Ooh, rough. Well, I need you to get out 'cause I'm going to date your teammate that you hate. That's life, bruh. Sorry."

So instead, I made tea. And by "made," I mean I placed a glass of water in the microwave and stuck a teabag in there.

"Are you sure your mom is having an affair with your gardener? As in, like, Josh, your gardener? Don't get me wrong, your mom can get it, but Josh is next-level hot. Plus, I thought he just got married to that one girl down the street? What's her name...Penelope? You know, the blonde chick who was always super snooty at neighborhood parties? Why would Josh —"

"Les!"

I flinch. His jaw is agape, and he shakes his head like I'm an idiot. Not that I blame him. I mean, I was just rambling about how hot his gardener is.

Sighing, I say, "They're trying to work it out. That's good, right?" I dunk the teabag a little too aggressively and some of it spills onto my hand.

He glares at me as if I'm stupid, brows knitted so tightly

they look like one of those birds you draw in elementary school. "No, Les, that's not 'good.' Apparently, the trip to St. Maarten is now some last-ditch effort to save their marriage."

Is it bad that I'm thankful? 'Cause now that means now I don't need to—

"You have to come with me. I can't be with them alone. Do you know how awkward that would be?"

Not gonna lie, it'd be pretty awkward. Ben's parents are like Cinderella and Prince Charming—for real. They're perfect and so in love. They're the couple that you look at and wonder if anyone else is truly in love because they're so googly for each other that every other relationship looks sad. So truthfully, this information is pretty shocking to me. I never would've guessed in a million years that B's parents could possibly be getting a divorce.

I grimace. "Just focus on your TikTok account. You still into that? Think of the content you could get while in St. Maarten."

"Yes, I'm 'still into that.' I'm one of the largest TikTok influencers now. How do you not know that?" He scowls. "That's beside the point. I need you to come with me. Please, Les."

My right eye twitches, and I wobble my hand. "Uh, er, that's a few weeks away. Let's talk about it then."

"Babe, I need you. I'm going to be thrown around like a ragdoll between the two of them anytime they fight."

Don't think I didn't catch that 'babe,' 'cause I definitely did. "You said you didn't want to label things."

"It's St. Maarten. It's not wedding bells." He scoffs.

Yeah, maybe so, but it sure feels like a ball and chain to me. "I don't think you need me. You are a strong, confident man who doesn't need a woman."

"What the hell? Can you be serious for one moment here?"

I glance at the floor, wanting out of this conversation so I can just go to sleep. "I mean...I'm sure this whole news is surprising to you. Maybe going to talk to someone about it would help?

He holds out his hand. "Yeah, I'm talking to you."

"Ooh-kay." I give him the cup of tea. "Sure. Look, I have a ton of studying to do the next few days…"

"Yeah, ditto. I've got early morning weights, too." Glancing at his phone, he says, "It's late. You want me to stay here?"

"Nah, it's all good." I smile and pat his shoulder once, then pull my hand back. "Maybe another night," I add, trying not to sound rude.

"Sure. I better get going then. I need to wake up early. Thanks for being there for me." He throws back the tea like a shot (is that a sign of a future serial killer?), sets the glass on the counter and walks over to me, lifting me up underneath my butt and twirling me around before kissing me. I turn my face to the side, and it lands on the corner of my mouth.

When he sets me down, I stumble a bit from the spinning.

Slipping on his shoes and swinging his uniform top onto his shoulder, he heads to the door, abs flexing for all to see. "See ya later. Love you."

I gasp, but then try to play it off like it was a cough before grimacing, a half-smile filled with terror. He grabs the door handle. "Forget I said that. Habit. Bye," he says, rushing to close the door.

"Mhmm, yep. Sure. Anytime. Bye, B." I wave.

But before he turns, a dark red blush crawls up his neck and into his cheeks. Though I may not want to be with him, it's still pretty cute.

∞∞∞

Over the next few days, I'm nose deep in my calculus book. My mom's "approved tutor" is an old lady who used to teach the course, so she definitely knows what she's talking about. However, her voice is so monotonous that I find myself fighting to stay awake, and some drool pools on my granite countertops.

"What can you compute T to?" Hold up, I know what she sounds like. Her voice is basically that slug secretary thing in *Monsters, Inc.*

I pinch my arm to try and wake me up. "Umm…" I look over the problem and start working out the answer on my paper.

She points at two different numbers. "No, right there is where you got it wrong. You have to change this value."

I work at it again, and again, until I get it right. It's ridiculous that this one course takes up eighty percent of my time. I don't have problems with any of the other classes except this one.

Another hour later, my tutor leaves my apartment. On the dot, my mom's phone call comes through.

"Hi, Mom. How are you?"

She sighs. "Fine. Are you prepared for your next quiz?"

"Yeah, hopefully." I put my books in my bag and grab my laptop. "I was actually just about to head to the library and do some more studying."

"Great."

"Mhmm." I search the counter until I find my keys.

"There's a gala coming up the second week of October."

Oh, come on. "Is that so?"

The phone is silent for a few moments. "This year, it honors your father."

I drop my keys, so I have to swing my bag onto my back as I bend down to reach them. A book slides out and hits me at the nape of my neck, making me groan.

"An inappropriate response, like always," she huffs.

"N-No, I just…I hit my head. If it honors Dad, then of course I'll be there."

"Alright."

The call ends without either of us saying goodbye. Who *does* that?

Whenever she calls me, I feel like a failure. Nothing I do is right. She cuts me zero slack. It's not like we were best friends growing up, but I always studied hard, I was dating the boy next door, the son of her best friend, and she really had nothing to complain about. And fine, if I'd broken up with Ben, maybe she could be upset. But *he* broke up with *me.* He never once tried to get me back this summer.

I guess now, I'm not her perfect daughter. Or maybe I never was. Maybe Dad always stood up for me when he was alive. Who knows. At this point, I'd rather she just not call at all.

I head out the door and drive to the library. There's a group of reporters on the main road leading toward the school. Probably another stupid crash from people texting and driving. I swear, every week there's another minor fender bender thanks to some idiot sliding into DMs or tweeting while driving.

I park in the lot closest to the library and head that way. A girl with long legs that I'd kill for and seriously gorgeous kinky hair hands me a piece of paper. It reads:

PROTECT CALIFORNIA
FIGHT AGAINST ILLEGAL IMMIGRATION
FRIDAY, 4 PM
HEAR REP. JOANNA MARX SPEAK ON CAMPUS

Eek, Joanna Marx? No, thank you. She's the former governor, and she's running in the special election thanks to a senate vacancy that just opened. The previous representative was caught talking to an underage girl online. Super gross, but believe me, Joanna Marx is not anywhere near better.

I go to hand the girl back her flyer, but she's already gone. Since littering should be a crime (Hush, I know it is. But like, a legit crime.), I take the paper with me to the library and put it into the recycle bin.

Groups of people sit at booths studying, and when I see a bob of pink hair, I immediately gravitate towards it.

I slide in next to Candy and throw my arms around her. "I think you're super hot. Can I take you out sometime?"

She pulls out an AirPod, looks me up and down, and says, "Not while you're feelin' up my brother, you can't."

"Ouch." I swing my bag off my shoulder and set it on the black, round table. "And for the record, I was not feeling your brother up."

"Well, he reeked of your perfume when he came home the other night, so…" She nonchalantly flips a page of our Business 101 textbook.

"Yeah, well, let me tell you how you got me into major trouble, thank you very much." I recount what happened with Ben and Carter.

"*Mira*, I'm not judging. Two hot guys sounds enjoyable, honestly. But maybe if you dropped that annoying lil' Benji, you could live happily ever after and we wouldn't be having this convo," she rushes out.

"Candy," I warn.

She holds her hands up. "Hey, I spent my night listening to Tom and a giggling girl in the room next to mine, so I'm pissy."

I give her sad puppy eyes. "Aw, babe." I pull her into a hug.

She fights it like a fish fights leaving water. "It's fine. I'm fine. Everything is *fine.*"

I mock an explosion by opening my fists and giving spirit fingers. "But everything was not fine." I talk as if I'm the narrator. And I *am*, just not for her story, so I make my voice deep like that one buff dude in *Emperor's New Groove.*

She glares at me. "Whatever. I'm focusing my energy on something else now."

I bellow a laugh loud enough that the two people at the tables closest to us turn their heads. "Sorry," I whisper. "Okay, so what is this new thing you're focusing on?"

She pulls out a crumpled piece of paper and tries to iron it out with her palms. "There's some racist rally going on this Friday. So, I want to protest it."

I look at the same poster that woman handed me a little while ago. "Okay, I'm listening…"

Candy waves her hands as if she's Picasso of the air, explaining all of her plans. And I am *here* for it. "I'm in. I'm so in." Who cares if that means I have to cancel a tutoring session?

She does a little dance with her fists up high and laughs. "My Twitter followers are gonna eat this up. Now come on, let's round up the other gringos to come along."

∞∞∞

Over the next few days, Ben's on me like a koala on a tree, and it's taken everything to avoid him. Alright, actually, it just took me mentioning PMS and 'so much blood' and he's stayed at his own place. But still, he's sent one too many lovey-dovey texts.

Carter, on the other hand, is awkward. We both stumble over each other multiple times when hanging out with Candy. Last night, us and their game night crew got together and made posters for the protest, and though we hardly talked, I couldn't help but feel like his eyes were on me. Every time I turned around, we'd lock eyes for just a second before he'd go back to his poster.

But now I'm currently sitting next to him in Tom's Jeep, and our thighs are an inch apart from each other. I keep readjusting how I'm sitting because being near him is almost too much. Everything tingles and burns, and I want to touch him so bad that I bite my tongue to try and focus.

Being that Candy planned this all, she basically made it like Coachella. She tweeted to her hundred thousand followers about it, and people from surrounding cities are coming to participate. She's dressed in a crop top MEXICO tee with cutoff jean shorts and red, white, and green stripes painted on her upper arms.

Carter's in a plain white tee and olive green shorts but has two stripes under his eyes like a football player that are painted red, white, and green. The rest of us are practically carbon copies of them, and Candy was the one who chose it all.

My mom would probably kill me if she saw what I'm wearing.

When we pull up to campus, there are thousands of people

already here. Since all the parking spots are taken, we have to park in a lot half a mile away. Candy squeals with excitement, grabbing onto Tom's shoulder and squeezing. I don't miss the look he flashes her when she's gazing out the window—the man's got it bad. So why don't they just get together?

Yes, I realize the irony of *me* saying that.

Carter gets out of the car and holds the door open as I slide from the middle seat. The sky is overcast, and it's cool enough that I get a few goosebumps on my skin. Carter says his first few words to me all day. "I have a jacket in the car if you need it."

"Nah, I'll be fine. Thanks though."

He nods, but doesn't say anything else.

Candy skips toward campus (literally) and Tom chases behind her like a dog stuck on a leash. Rykard and the other guy that came in Tom's jeep exit the trunk and branch off, leaving me to walk beside Carter.

"So," he says, kicking a rock, "I'm sort of surprised that you came along."

I snort and the action makes me pull back my chin, so I sport a really sexy double—okay, triple—chin. "Why would me coming along surprise you?"

He shrugs. "Your mom, your money, the people you grew up around."

By *people*, I'm assuming he means Ben.

"You think they're all racist." It's not a question, but a statement. He's right. As much as I hate to admit it, my mom has always been like that. In fact, if she knew I were here right now —like I said, she'd kill me.

"You could say that." He smiles, but it doesn't reach his eyes.

"Well, I guess it's time for me to show everyone how I'm different." Our hands brush accidentally, and the zing that travels to my elbow gives me courage. Because I'm a glutton for punishment, I gently tap his hand with mine again.

He takes it and intertwines our fingers. "We should talk."

"Yeah, probably so."

He stops walking and picks a daisy from the landscaping near the library. Tucking my hair behind my ear, he places the daisy with it. "*Qué linda eres.*"

"I hope you didn't call me an ugly slut or something."

He laughs and pulls me along the sidewalk, toward the outdoor steps that go to the first floor of the library. "Never."

We climb the stairs, Carter two at a time and beating me by, like, a full minute. When I reach the top, he wraps an arm around my waist and pulls me close. All the awkwardness is gone, and it's like we've been a couple forever. It feels good—a little too good.

But an underlying sense of guilt gnaws at me. I'm going against my mom's wishes. I've been lying to Ben. What would my dad say?

Today is not the day for that.

I push those thoughts away and focus on the happy fluttering in my chest. I like Carter so, so much. He glances at me and smiles, and I notice a small freckle beneath his right eye. I could study him all day long.

"What'd you want to talk about?"

He shrugs. "Us."

I bite my lip to keep a smile from sneaking out prematurely. "Is there an us?"

He stops walking and pulls me toward him. "*Sí,* I'd like to think so."

"Okay," I say, knowing I can figure it all out later. My nose crinkles from my pinched smile, and it breaks out into a grin.

He cups my cheek. "Okay?"

I nod. "Yes."

With a kiss on my forehead, he says, "Aight, good."

We catch up to the others, and I can feel the blood flowing through me in anticipation. I'm excited to be here with *Carter.* And I'm mega excited that we're holding hands. Who knew there's like five million nerves in my hand and that Carter ignites every single one of them?

I'm excited to protest with all of them.

Until we actually *get* to the protests. Thousands of people stand around, but it appears as though the opposing sides are split pretty evenly. Posters and painted faces, people shouting, and people laughing exist on both sides. It's two polar opposites in a crowd, and it's clashing.

Candy made it clear on Twitter that she wanted everyone here to be calm, happy, and spread love rather than the hate the other side is spreading. But kill 'em with kindness doesn't seem to be working—it seems like it's a rallying cry to be bullied.

Someone on the loudspeaker announces that Joanna Marx will be arriving for photos in ten minutes, and some people enthusiastically cheer while others shout boo.

"I can't believe West even let her present here. She's the worst of them all." Carter squints as he looks out into the crowd and shakes his head.

I'm not an idiot, I've read the news about her. Buzzfeed practically crucifies her on a daily basis for the stuff she says. She's been filmed saying racist slurs, she constantly puts down other women, and her platform is built on keeping the children of America safe—the ones that are white, of course. Her battle cry is to weapon up, shoot down the haters, and make the rich richer.

As I see someone hold up a poster of her face, I can't help but think that she sort of looks like my mom. And now I wonder if my mom voted for her. Please say no.

Tom walks around the crowd, weaving in and out, signing up people to register to vote. Candy pulls out a megaphone (from who knows where) and shouts things like, "We're all immigrants." "Caucasia's not even a place." And, "America wasn't yours to begin with."

For every one thing she says, the other side says five very colorful, very racist slurs. There's so much going on that it's a bit of a sensory overload.

We follow Candy to the front of the crowd. The two sides of the protest are separated by a walkway and ropes, where Joanna Marx will walk down.

I'm in awe watching Candy, who wholeheartedly knows who she is, what she wants, and how she'll get it. It makes me want that assuredness, to know exactly what my life will become. Instead, it's like I'm wading through never-ending confusion.

I'm so distracted by her that I almost miss the man across from me say, "Hey, blondie. What're you doing muddying up your bloodline with people like them?"

Like I said, I *almost* missed it. But I didn't.

And neither did Carter. "*Chingate.*"

"What did you say?" I ask the burly, beer-gutted, way-too-old-to-call-me-anything man, who scratches his beard.

"He's an idiot. Just forget it," Carter says, squeezing my hand.

But it's not okay. I'm not going to stand by him and say nothing just like I did when my mom was racist. I'm sick of it.

I cock my head at the beer-gutted guy. "How's this for muddying up my bloodline?" I jump into Carter's arms, straddling him.

He groans in surprise but helps lift me, gripping my thighs. Wrapping my arms around his neck, I wink. Then, I pull him close and give the idiot something to *really* talk about. But just in case that wasn't enough—I flip the guy off while intertwining my tongue with Carter's.

There's a few whoops and hollers, and also one, "*Dios mío*, get a room." But it's from Candy, so...

His kiss makes me forget the haters or that we're even in public. I want to take him back to his bed and explore him from head to toe. His hair is sheared short in the back, and I run my hands through it.

We unlock our lips and he sets me down. I feel like I just chugged an energy drink after that kiss. When I look across the aisle, the guy is gone.

Right on time, Joanna Marx and her security team walk toward the library's auditorium, waving as if everyone should praise her.

Her smile is clown-like, she wears a navy dress with red heels, and her hair is pulled up into a gray chignon. On her way down, we catch eye contact, and it's almost familiar. Not in a I've-seen-you-on-TV way but in a have-we-met-before way? I think she feels it too because she cocks an eyebrow, looking me up and down, before plastering her smile back on and facing the other crowd.

As the doors to the library open and a blast of AC hits me, I shiver. Though I'm not so sure it's because of the air.

Once Joanna Marx is inside, the crowds die down—mostly because all of the ignorant people go inside to hear Joanna speak. A few against Joanna's policies also go in to ask questions, including Candy.

I think about going inside with her, but karma decides to rear her ugly head from lying to Ben about starting my period. When I feel that telltale gush, I decide it's time get the hell home.

"What's wrong?" Carter ruffles my hair and I glare at him.

"Pretty sure I just started my period."

Carter laughs and holds up a finger. Reaching into his pocket, he pulls out a small black makeup-sized bag. He unzips it and hands me a tampon.

You guys, I'm not even kidding. "Why the hell do you have a tampon and a makeup bag in your pocket?"

He holds my non-tampon-holding hand and pulls me away from the library where everyone else is and toward the nearest building. "First of all, equality. Men can have tampons too."

"Of course."

He winks. "Second of all, I have a demanding twin sister who makes me carry around a tampon for her just in case."

"And the makeup bag?"

"All of my diabetes stuff."

I feel like I'm looking at one of those memes that says, "The perfect man doesn't exist—" and then it shows a picture of Carter. He's becoming my favorite man on the planet. (Sorry,

Shawn Mendes.)

"Well, you are just somethin' else, aren't you?"

He shrugs. "I like to be prepared. You'll never guess what else I have in there."

I laugh. "Oh, I'm sure I can." At the entrance of the building, I drop his hand. "I think this is where our journey ends. I'm gonna catch an Uber home after this." I wiggle the tampon in front of his face.

"You sure you don't want me to wait?"

"Nah, I'm good." A quick glance down shows I definitely leaked through just a bit. "You go be a political mastermind and listen to the horrible Joanna."

"Fine." He hooks his fingers through the belt loops on my shorts and pulls me toward him. "Can I text you later?"

I get up on my tiptoes and kiss him. Then, I give him the millennial version of commitment. "Oh, baby, you can even call if you'd like."

"Deal." He steals one last kiss and walks away.

I take a quick moment to admire his butt before I rush into the bathroom to stop the red sea. After the situation's moderately handled, I call an Uber and walk to the nearest street to hop into the black Honda driven by Marshall.

"Hey, how are you?" I ask as I get into the car.

"Good." He's a nerdy guy wearing a *Legend of Zelda* tee.

The few minute drive is silent, but as he pulls into the parking lot, my phone buzzes multiple times.

"Bye, thank you," I say, exiting the car and gazing at my Apple Watch.

Ben: *WHAT THE HELL?*

Ben: *Image attachment.*

I sigh and pull out my phone, opening the messages to see the image.

It's a screenshot of Candy's Twitter profile. Her top tweet reads: MAKE LOVE, NOT WALLS.

Underneath that is a photo of me and Carter, lips locked, his hands on my thighs, my hands tangled in his hair. His brown skin mixed with my (embarrassingly) white skin, is the exact message she wanted to relay to her followers.

The tweet already has 25.3k likes, 1,000 retweets, and 97 comments. Ohh shut the front door, Carter and I went viral! I've never gone viral. This is *awesome.*

But...then I remember who sent it to me.

Oh *crap.* Carter and I went viral.

I really hope my mom isn't on Twitter.

Chapter Fourteen

If I didn't think the viral situation could get worse, I was an idiot. Because the next morning, Buzzfeed posts about the interracial couple that everyone wants to be. By lunchtime, local news posts about the protest against Joanna Marx. An hour later, the New York Times comes out with an article about West University's fight against the right. Guess what the cover of the story is?

Yep, mine and Carter's photo. Now usually, I'd be fine with this. I look good in the photo. Carter looks even better. The problem is that my mom's a racist and my ex-boyfriend thinks we're currently rekindling our relationship.

Hey, can you get my PR person on this?

Ben: *We need to talk.*

Carter: *I'm sorry, Candy asked if I was cool with her posting the photo, and I said it was fine. I should've checked with you. I had no idea it was gonna blow up like this.*

And my mother is calling right now.

Literally, right now.

I should ignore it.

But I can't. Because the last time I ignored her call, I missed my father's dying breath.

"Hi, Mom! How are you?" I rage-clean my countertops, scrubbing away at non-existent stains.

There's a pause. It's the calm before the storm. I can feel it building up in the expanse of nothingness, drowning me in fear. And then it explodes. "*That's* why you cancelled your tutoring session? After everything I've done for you, Les, how could you embarrass our family like that? You come from a good family. Associating with radicals like this is asinine.

Now this *photo?*" she spits. "Proof to the world of your failures? And protesting *against* Joanna Marx?"

"Mom, it's not—"

"You're uninvited to the gala."

I drop the rag and lean against the counter. "Hold up, what?"

"Joanna Marx is one of the top contributors of the gala. BC Warriors, the non-profit running the event, is ran by her son. You disgraced our family and our name."

You've gotta be kidding me. There's no way Dad would think like her. But it's not like I can ask him because he's not freaking here. My heart rate speeds up as if I'm running. "Mom, I didn't know. Please, you can't just kick me out of an event honoring Dad. This is ridiculous." I pace back and forth, twisting my hair.

"I have never been so disappointed in you," she hisses. "If you don't get your act together, Les, I swear, there will be consequences."

I can't take it anymore. Everything I do ends up getting me into more trouble, more chaos. I'm at college. I should be able to have fun and live my life. *Who does she think she is?* "Because I kissed Carter, who just happens to be Mexican, you're going to act like you're about to disown me?"

She tsks. "You know that is not the reason, and I don't appreciate you talking to me like that."

I throw my hand up even though she can't see me. "No, I don't know! You were rude to him when you met him, and ever since you've been making snide comments about who he is and what he's doing. He's a good guy, Mom. I don't get why where he comes from matters. I know Dad would love—"

"A good guy?" She laughs, which is a bit creepy in itself. "Les, you wouldn't know a good guy if he hit you in the face."

Okay, does she seriously not see what is wrong with that comparison? "So, what about Ben? What was he?"

"Ben is different. You two were raised together. He's family. But yes, you *should* be asking yourself about Ben. From what I hear, he has a horrific black eye because of this 'Carter' you've been gallivanting around with."

She has me so frustrated that my voice becomes thick. "Is that what this is about? It's because I'm not with Ben? Because I'm shirking a family friend, who dumped me if you forgot, and going after someone I truly like, and he's not rich, white, and an automatic millionaire. That's what this is about?"

"I am not going to feed into your manic, passive-aggressive behavior right now. This has gone on long enough. Do I need to book you a psych appointment? I have important things to get done."

This time, *I* laugh. "Do you even hear yourself right now? Ha, wow. This is so typical. You always have something that's more important than me, right?"

I'm being petty.

I probably shouldn't be so rude to her. But every word is a shot to the gut.

Finally, she says, "I'd be careful with your tone. Don't bite the hand that feeds you. Your apartment, your schooling, your special tutors. You think your free internship pays for these things? You need me, Les."

My ribs feel like they're pulling away from my sternum. "Yeah, Mom." A tear slides down my cheek. "I'm well aware. Thanks for reminding me of my stupid reality." I sniffle and wipe at my nose. She doesn't respond, but when I pull the phone away from my ear, the call is still connected. So like the good daughter I'm supposed to be, I do what I have to. "I'm sorry. I want to come to Dad's gala. Please, just tell me what I have to do to fix this," I say, like the marionette puppet that I am.

"End this, Les. Focus on your school, stop hanging around political radicals, make some actual *good* decisions in your life. I don't want to hear a whisper of anything else. If Joanna Marx finds out that photo circulating is you, she could cancel your father's gala. Are we clear?"

Her words are like a slap to the face. I hate disappointing her. Even though she wasn't the main person who raised me, it's as if my inner child can't say no to her. Maybe she's right. Maybe getting caught up in this whirlwind romance was a mistake. Really, who do I think *I* am? I've been parading myself around like a hot commodity, going back and forth between two guys, playing with their emotions.

I've never been that type of person. And my mom is right, I do need her.

"Yes," I say. "We're clear." I'm betraying myself, and I don't even have a good reason except that I can't have the last member of my family abandon me. I hang up the phone, slide down against the cabinets, and cry.

This should be a happy time in my life, but instead, it's overwhelming. Why do I feel like this is just a preview of what she's capable of? If I don't do what she says, I'm screwed. I wish I could be like one of those TV heroines who disobey their moms, get their happily ever after, and somehow have everything work out in their favor. But I'm not.

I'm a freaking failure.

As deep, wracking sobs overtake me, all I want to do is call my dad. I want him to tell me that Mom is having a hard time, that things are going to get better, that *I'm* going to get better. That it won't always feel like I'm walking around with a hole in my lungs, unable to breathe. That somehow I'll forget the pain and remember everything happy.

He's the only person I want to talk to, but he's never going to be here again. Why did I have to be born into a family where both of my parents were only children? I have no cousins, no aunts, no uncles, no grandparents. Do you understand what that's like to realize that the only person I can reminisce about my past with is the one person I've been pushing away?

My whole life has been written out for me. The plan was set from the time I said my first word. Everything I've ever done was to please everyone else. The only thing I've ever wanted for myself was to become a doctor. But, was that even my idea? Honestly, probably not.

I don't know who I am anymore. I hate disappointing

people, and right now, I think I hate myself. I can't do it. I can't have my mom mad at me, disappointed in who I am and what I've become.

What would Dad think right now? If he were somehow here, maybe he'd be disappointed in me too. All I want to do is make him proud. And according to my mom, I've failed.

It's only 8 AM, and already, this day sucks. To make matters worse, I have a calculus quiz in thirty minutes.

I push myself up from the floor and drag myself into the bathroom. I look how I feel—like crap. Swiping some concealer under my eyes, I rub it in and then put on a layer of mascara. Using a tinted lip gloss, I pass as somewhat okay. You know, if okay was a rabid dog.

Already dressed for the day, I grab a granola bar, my keys, and head out the door. Could this day get any worse? Cue the sad *aww* from my studio audience, please.

I place my forehead on the steering wheel and groan. Not looking at the ignition, I search for the button blindly until I find it, press it, and the car rumbles to life, blaring "Death Bed" by Powfu.

It gives me a new sense of direction.

Plot twist: Once I get to class, I'm going to murder Candy.

I mean, she's the real cause of this all. In fact, if she'd never had a twin, none of this would've happened. So really, she's extremely guilty. She should definitely have to pay. But then I'd miss her too much, so I guess it's not an option.

Fine, cancel the plot twist. I'm not really in the mood anyway.

I lift my head up and look into the rearview mirror. "Alright, everyone, I'm going to go to class, ace this calculus test, and then make my parents proud." I'm just manifesting what I want into the air. That's how it works, right?

A really sexy, red indent across my forehead mocks me. Maybe it will make Carter think I'm unattractive. Keeps me from having to break both of our hearts, right?

Backing out of my parking spot, I gaze behind me and see a

cute woman walking her tiny dog. Maybe that would solve all my problems. Instead of a cat lady, I can be a dog lady.

I drive mindlessly.

Yorkies are pretty cute. Maybe a Pomeranian. Really, huskies are my favorite, but I've never trained a dog, so that seems like a bad choice. Chihuahua? I could show Candy and Carter how cute my teeny tiny dog is.

But that would mean Carter would still be talking to me. Ugh, Carter holding a chihuahua. That thought should be illegal because it'd be so cute and sexy that I could probably die.

Horns honk, snapping me out of my internal monologue.

The telltale sound of grinding metal pierces my ears as two cars ahead of me slam into each other. I stomp on my brakes to avoid the wreck and hit my head on the steering wheel.

Ouch. Now I'm really going to have a permanent red mark on my forehead.

Rubbing at my brow, I look up. Right at the notorious texting and driving spot is another car crash. A silver Honda and red convertible are crushed like empty beer cans. I put my car in park, press my hazards button, and run toward the accident. A guy gets out of the convertible, holding his forehead, his other hand on his chest.

"Are you okay? I'm calling 911," I shout, signaling the SOS on my Apple Watch.

"I don't know, my airbag didn't deploy. I slammed into the steering wheel." He lifts his shirt and there's a dark red mark across his sternum. Underneath his bellybutton, a seatbelt burn bleeds.

I point at him. "Sit down!"

"911. What's your emergency?" the operator's voice comes through my watch.

I jog toward the silver Honda. I can't see the driver inside, but the airbags deployed.

"Uh, there's been a two car crash on the corner of Jacobson and Mulberry on West's campus."

"Were you one of the cars involved?"

"No. One person is out of his car, but he's got a bad seat-belt burn, bruising, and swelling across his chest. The other," I yank on the Honda's handle, but the driver's door is stuck, "is still stuck in their car. Airbags deployed, and the door won't open." I can hear my voice getting higher. I'm freaking out.

"Ma'am, try the other doors."

I pull on the passenger door, but it looks like the doors are locked. "I can't. The locks are on."

An elderly man, maybe a professor, jogs up to the other side of the car, trying those two doors. He shakes his head.

"None of the doors will open," I say.

"Paramedics are on their way."

"Okay." I brush my hands through my hair and take a deep breath. I choke on the smell of gasoline.

I look toward the gray-haired man. "Do you smell that?"

"Hold on, I have a tool to bust the window in my car." He runs, shouting, "You still good?" to the other car crash victim who nods.

"I think gas is leaking. The smell is really strong," I say.

"Okay," the operator responds. "You're sure there's a person in there?"

"Yes."

Within seconds, the Maybe-Professor is back with a hammer-looking tool with a pointed piece of metal on the end. "I'll break the window back here."

The glass shatters in sparkling pieces, falling to the ground like crystallized sugar. "Hello? Can you hear us? Are you able to move?" he shouts into the window.

No one responds.

"We need to unlock this door." I point to the driver's side. "Can you open your door and unlock the others?"

His shoes crunch on glass as he yanks on the backseat handle once, twice, flinging it open and stumbling back. Ducking his head, he wiggles his hands toward the passenger front seat and reaches toward the buttons.

When I hear the thunk of the unlock, I try the driver's side door again. It still won't budge. "I need some help over here. I still can't get it open."

Another passerby comes up, pulling at the handle. He looks like he does body building in his spare time, and after he grunts one too many times, the door unlatches, and he pushes it aside.

Bodybuilder groans as he leans against the airbag, revealing an unconscious woman in the front seat. Her scalp has blood dripping from the top of her head down to her neck. Her forearm is bent in half, and there's a sharp piece of yellow-ish white sticking out from the bloody wound.

That does *not* look good.

"We have an unconscious woman," I tell the operator

Without the airbag pressure, she falls to the side an inch before Bodybuilder catches her.

"Should we move her? It smells like gasoline!" I shout at my watch.

"If the car is at risk of catching on fire, yes. Try to keep her head still as you move her."

Maybe-Professor holds the woman's head and Bodybuilder lays her down on the street a few yards away. I hardly think that would've stabilized her neck, but we don't have another option.

"I'm going to check on the other victim," the maybe-professor says.

"There's a fracture on her left arm. It looks like the bone may be sticking out. Her head is also bleeding, like really bad." I hesitate to touch any part of her. She looks so delicate.

"Does she have a pulse?"

I lean down and touch her neck, feeling for the soft flutter against my fingers. "I-I'm not feelin' one." That's bad, right? Yeah, why am I even asking. That's bad.

"Start CPR. You'll need to do thirty compressions to two rescue breaths—"

"I'm CPR-certified. But what about her neck?" How do I know she doesn't have a cervical fracture?

"Focus on the compressions." The operator is so at ease.

Me, on the other hand, not so much. "Okay."

The paramedics better get here soon.

I position my hands over her sternum. As I push into her chest, I pray to God I'm not doing something wrong. The wound in her arm gushes blood, staining her shirt. But I focus on pressing down and up to the tune of *Staying Alive.* It's harder than I thought it'd be, and it takes more force and pressure than I'd imagined.

Leaning down to give her the rescue breaths, I cringe when I see her nose dripping blood. I swipe at it to clear the space to her lips and breathe into her once, coming up for another breath, and leaning down once more.

I start the compressions again, tasting metal in my mouth. Her arm is right against my thigh and I can feel the side of my pants get wet as I focus on not doing more damage to this poor girl. Gosh, she's gotta be my age. This could've been me. Had I left earlier...*this could've been me.*

Giving her two more rescue breaths, the telltale signs of sirens sound nearby.

The 911 operator says, "Keep going until the paramedics tell you to stop."

My mind quiets, going into a calm state in line with the rhythm of compressions. All the chaos and the noise settles, and I'm no longer nervous or even scared.

This woman needs me.

When an EMT touches my shoulder and says, "We'll take it from here," I stand up, step back, and watch the paramedics work. It happens in merely a few seconds as they stabilize her neck, get her onto the gurney, and transfer her into the back of the ambulance. The paramedics do the same to the man who was in the convertible, putting him into a different ambulance.

They speed off with their lights on, and the energy seeps out of me. If this were a show, I'd hop in the ambulance with them, somehow saving the woman's life even though I'm not medically trained.

But, it's not a show, so I watch as the flashing lights fade. My hands shake, and my legs feel weak. Bodybuilder walks right in front of me and squats down, hands to his knees. "Are you okay?"

I flinch and shake my head. "Yeah. Yeah, I'm fine."

"Okay. You're covered in blood."

I look down at my pants where a softball-sized stain of blood is on my jeans. My shirt has a few trails of blood as well, but it's hardly *covered in blood.*

The maybe-professor walks toward us. "You may need to be checked out. There's a risk of blood pathogens and infection because of what you did."

A woman cop waves, flagging us down as she moves toward us. "I'm Officer Peyton. I need to get a witness account from the three of you."

We recount what happened from start to finish, and she takes notes. She asks us for our phone numbers to follow up with us and dismisses the others. "The hospital will test the victim for any diseases right away, and I'll call to let you know whether you'll need bloodwork done. The risk is low, so you should be alright."

"Okay, thank you."

She smiles and nods—just another day at the job for her. "Go home, take a shower, and take it easy, okay? You did a good thing here, no matter the outcome."

I lick my lips and hold out my hand to shake hers. "Thank you. I'll wait for your call."

Walking back toward my car, a million feelings and thoughts run through my mind. What if I had left my house earlier? That could've been me. What if I hadn't known CPR? What if the woman dies? Who even caused the accident? *What* caused the accident? Was it another case of texting and driving?

I let out a shaky breath and hop into the driver's seat. When I place my hands on the tan steering wheel, they tremble, and I see just how caked in blood my fingers are. They're dry, but the spot on my jeans isn't. I think my jeans fall under: throw the whole thing away.

Imagine if Mom saw me now, covered in blood and dirty. She'd turn her nose up of course. Mom only works with the finest of medical problems. The brain is her one true love.

Even though I'm filthy, I don't know, it felt good—really good—to help. It was sort of exciting and riveting, and...I really hope that woman's going to be okay.

It makes my worries this morning seem like a joke. And really, they are. My mom's words grate on my mind, but she was right about one thing: I need to focus on myself.

The thrum of adrenaline is gone, and I'm left feeling loose and cold. But despite it all, I love it. Who cares if my mom and dad pushed me into wanting to become a doctor? I *do* want to become one—their opinions be damned.

Maybe I just found the field I want to pursue, too.

I pull into my parking spot and turn off the car. I'm going to be a doctor. An actual, saving lives, really cool, doctor. Yeah, research is cool. Studying with Dr. Guilliod is a dream come true. But that feeling that I experienced back there?

It can't be beat.

As I get out of the car, semi-laughing to myself over my epiphany, a man does a double-take. But instead of a checking-me-out-smirk, he gasps and speed walks away like he's going to the next Olympics.

What's his problem?

Oh, wait, okay. I get it. He probably thinks I'm a murderer.

I *am* "covered" in blood, after all.

"Hey! When you're about to die, you'll come see me! And I'm going to save you!" Snorting, I brush some hair from my forehead.

There's only one problem. I just missed my calculus test.

Chapter Fifteen

Carter: *Are you okay? Dónde estás?*

Carter: *You know there was another quiz, right?*

I stare at my phone, towel wrapped around me, fresh and clean from my shower. The blood from the accident is gone. It's time to clean up the other mess—my grade. Problem is, my syllabus is nowhere in sight. Probably threw it away by accident. I bite my nail, then type.

Les: *Yeah. Long story. Do you have Prof. Butler's number?*

After setting my phone down on the counter, I walk out of the bathroom to get dressed. I throw on some sweats and grab an old hoodie. It's not until I put it on that I realize it's one of my dad's old ones. I put the cuffs of the sleeves halfway down my hands and sniff.

It doesn't smell like anything. Not that I was expecting it to, but still. Even if it did smell like him, I'm not sure I would realize it. I don't think I remember what he smells like anymore.

A sharp pain hits me in the gut.

I grab my phone from the bathroom and sling myself onto the couch, pulling a furry blanket on top of me.

Carter: *Yeah, here it is.*

Carter: *Jane Butler*

Les: *Wow, first name basis huh?*

The dots appear on the screen.

Carter: *She is a student teacher after all. Feels weird calling her professor.*

Les: *Mhmm. I'm sure.*

I tap the contact attachment and press on her number. The line rings twice before she answers. "Hello, this is Jane."

I sit up. "Hi. Hi, Professor Butler, it's Les. I'm in your calculus class on Tuesdays and Thursdays."

"Right. Les. What can I do for you?"

"I missed class today. I was actually on my way there when I witnessed an accident on Jacobson and Mulberry." I pick at the blanket bundled at my lap. "I was hoping I could make up the quiz that I missed today. I know you have a strict policy, and normally, I wouldn't even ask. But I'm struggling in this class and really need to do well. I've been working hard, and I was prepared, but then that accident happened."

There's a pause on the other end before she responds with, "I heard about that crash from a coworker. I hope everyone is okay."

I sigh, and my hands finally stop shaking. "Yeah, me too."

"Could you meet me Friday? Maybe around eight? Just this once, I'll allow you to do a make-up quiz."

My internship Friday doesn't start until nine. "That'd be perfect. Thank you so much for understanding."

"You're welcome." She pauses, and I don't know if it's one of those awkward hang-up-without-saying-bye type of calls. But the line is still connected, so I wait. "Les, now that I have your record pulled up, I actually need to talk to you."

Oh, *great.* "Really? What about?"

"I need to submit midterm grades, and you have a D minus."

My breath comes out shaky, and I bite the inside of my cheek. "So, what does that mean? Just because I didn't take the second quiz, right?"

"Well, no, not exactly. I haven't put those grades in yet. Currently, it means you'd be put on academic probation."

Which, if I remember right, would be bad. Like, really bad. As in, meet with my counselor weekly and have to stop my school-approved internship bad. That *cannot* happen. I worked my butt off to get that internship. It's what I'm relying on for med school applications. "I'll pass the test."

"I'll do everything I can to help you should a different outcome occur. But, I know you've got this Les. You can do it."

I smile, but I don't feel it at all. "Thanks, Professor Butler. I'll see you on Friday. Bye."

My internship is the best one at the school. If I lose it, I wouldn't be accepted into the program again. Academic probation will set my goals back by too much.

Texting my tutor for a last minute study session, I will myself not to freak out. And we all know what happens when you tell yourself not to do something. So, instead of stress-crying, I grab the TV remote and turn on an episode of *Bachelor in Paradise* that I'm behind on. There's nothing that can't be fixed by the smooth voice of Chris Harrison.

Mind-numbing TV. This is what I need.

Jenna, the hot commodity of this season, is choosing between two guys: Chad and Mike.

"Don't choose Chad. It's always the Chads that suck," I say, throwing my hand in the air.

On screen, Jenna bites her lip, rose in hand. "I, um. I-I can't do this."

Chris Harrison comes from the side and places a hand on her shoulder. "Jenna, who would you like to continue exploring things with?"

I grab my half-empty water bottle off the table and take a swig.

"I choose...no one."

The water sprays from my mouth, all over myself and the couch. "How did I not see this on Reality Steve's website?"

I immediately dial Candy's number. When she answers, I squeal, "Did you see that Jenna chooses no one?"

"*¡No me digas!* Are you freaking serious? I haven't watched the episode. *Te voy a matar.*"

Another voice in the background says, "*Con quién hablas?*" Pretty sure it's Carter.

"Les. She just spoiled Jenna's ending."

Their voices go in and out as I wait. "Hello, I'm still here, ya know."

She mumbles something else in Spanish that I don't catch.

"Pause the show. We're on our way."

There's some sort of loud commotion on her end of the phone call, and it sounds like someone shattered something.

"*Dios mío, eres un idiota*," Candy groans. "Fine! You can come. Hey, Rykard's coming too."

"Oka—"

"Um no, you're not coming," she snaps.

"Who else?" I stand up from the couch and grab a few discarded granola bar wrappers.

She literally hisses into the phone. "I guess Tom and Jared are coming too."

I snort. "Alright. Wait, who's Jared?"

"You know Jared. He was at the hot springs. In our car."

I somewhat remember another person besides Rykard, but couldn't pick him out of a lineup. "Alright, see you soon."

"Bye, *amiga*."

Thankfully, there isn't much to clean. Still, I go around the house and grab a few random things. As I walk into my bathroom, I step on a pair of bright purple underwear, and since I don't need any more jokes from Carter about being a stripper, I pick them up.

Knocks that sound like they came from twelve different arms sound on my door, probably waking up everyone in the cemetery a mile away.

I throw open the door to five smirking faces.

I give them an Oscar-worthy Jim Halpert face. "Get in here, fools. Preferably before someone calls the cops for a noise complaint."

Candy snaps and dances her way through my doorway. "Never seen this many males so excited to be a part of Bachelor Nation."

"I'm here for the hot girls." Tom says, walking in behind Candy.

"I'm here for Chris Harrison." Jared waves (and yes, it turns out I *do* recognize him when he shows up. How could I forget that perfectly coiffed hair and way too many muscles?).

"I'm here for all the hotties." Rykard winks, high-fiving me on the way in. "Well, and the food. You're gettin' food, right?"

"Hey, why not?" I laugh.

Carter's last, standing there in joggers and a long basketball tee. He shrugs. "I'm here for you."

The four voices behind me go, "Aww." And I'm not going to lie, it scared me for a second. It was as if my studio audience came to life. Thankfully, the voices in my head are staying in my head.

Carter raises his brows and pulls me into a side hug as he comes in. It gives me *all* the tingles, but I (metaphorically) step on my vagina and tell it to hush. Repeat after me: I cannot get on academic probation. I am focusing on myself. I will not let rock hard abs get in the way of my dreams.

Candy and Tom sit on the loveseat bordering the wall, Rykard and Jared sit on the large couch in the middle, and Carter sits in the recliner, throwing his hands behind his head. I see a spot open next to Jared, so suddenly the guy I didn't know at all becomes my new BFF and I sit down next to him. "Should we get some food?"

"*Por supuesto.*" Candy grabs the remote and presses random buttons, but nothing happens.

"You have to"—I point to the bottom of the remote where it says Hulu—"push that."

"*Genial.*" She gives me duck lips. "I know how to work the remote, by the way."

Carter chuckles. "No, you don't."

"*Cállate,* or I'm finna kick you out," Tom says, pointing at Carter with a goofy grin.

Candy mock gasps. "Don't you dare think that using Spanish is going to make me like you right now."

Tom slings an arm around her. "*Pero cariña, te amo.*"

Apparently, that wasn't good. Because now they're shouting at each other in Spanish.

I crinkle my nose, and Jared looks toward me. "Don't worry," he says, "I'm as lost as you are."

I nod. "I'm picking up on some of it. *Cariña* is some form of endearment. I mean, unless Carter was calling me a whore all this time."

Rykard throws his arm over Jared's shoulders and taps my arm. "We all need to hold Spanish classes together or something."

"Just press play!" I shout over Candy and Tom's bickering.

Candy and Tom both shut their mouths and sit back. After saying something else I don't catch, she presses play on the same episode I was watching before they got here.

I rewatch everything, and the whole time, I can't help but look at the back of Carter's head. Every once in a while, he turns toward me, and I catch his eye. I gotta get out of here.

"I'm going to grab a drink and order food. What do you guys want? Is pizza good?"

They mumble various yesses, and I walk into the kitchen so that I can finally breathe again. Even though I was only a few feet away from Carter, I swear I can still smell the cinnamon.

"Hey."

Or, maybe it's because he's right next to me.

I start typing in Palio's Pizza on Grubhub, feigning nonchalance. "Oh, *hola*. What's up?"

He walks up behind me, lacing his arms around my waist.

My breath catches but I swallow it down.

"I'm sorry about the photo."

I turn toward him—big mistake—and set my phone down on the counter after placing an order for a few regular pizzas on the app. "You're sorry? There's nothing to apologize for. We look great in it."

He squeezes my hips. "Yeah, but I didn't realize it'd go so viral, and I was the one who gave Candy permission."

"It's fine." And then I hold my breath because he smells so good and looks so good, and I'm seriously falling for him really hard. Why couldn't we have met just like six months later? I'd happily fall in love with him then.

"Ah *mierda. Esto no me gusta.*"

"What?" I take a little breath and hold it again.

"You realize Candy and I are twins, right? I'm like a quarter woman. So 'it's fine' means it's not fine."

I glance toward the living room where Candy yells at the TV in Spanish. "Come here." I nod my head towards the hallway and my bedroom.

He puts his hands in his pockets and then walks beside me. Once we get to my room, I gently close the door.

"Les, *qué pasa?*"

I sigh. He's standing in the middle of the room, tall and muscular, but his shoulders are slumped ever so slightly. There's a crease on his forehead and his lips are drawn up in a pout. I don't want him to be mad at me.

"I just—I don't know." My voice breaks on the last word. "Today was bad," I whisper.

He takes his hands out of his pockets as he moves toward me and wraps me in a hug, placing his chin on the top of my head. I lean my forehead against his chest and feel his heart beating.

"What happened?"

"I was one of the first people on a scene of a bad car crash."

Carter rears back to look at me. "Are you alright?"

"Yeah. Yeah, I'm good. It's just, I don't know. I think in a way it really cemented things for me. I really want to be a doctor, and school isn't going great. I'm at risk of losing my internship if things don't change. Everything is really overwhelming and my mom is mad at me. I just feel really, really bad." I wipe at a tear that trickles out of my eye.

I sigh. "I really like you."

"But? I know there's a but." His voice rumbles against me.

My hands go cold, and my breaths come in shorter and quicker. Then it spills out of me. "I don't think I can do this anymore. If I fail this upcoming quiz, I get put on academic probation. I worked my butt off to get in with Dr. Guilliod in the first place, and," I rub at my eyes, "I'm rambling, I know. I just, I don't know, I think I need to focus on myself and maybe press pause with us. I don't know what I should do." I draw out the last word with a choked whine.

Carter doesn't move or say anything, but his chest rises and falls with a deep breath.

"I literally feel so bad," I whisper, biting my lip.

He drops his arms from around me and I shiver with the loss of his warmth. Running his hand through his wavy hair he says, "I mean, I get it. But…Okay. No, I understand." He drops his hand to the side. "But are you sure? I can help you with calculus."

I shrug. "My mom already got me a tutor. And no, I'm not really sure. Like, yeah, when you're not here, I am. But then you walk in, and you're perfect, and I'm an idiot, and then I'm like, why am I doing this?"

He groans something in Spanish. "I don't want to be pissed. I know you've got a ton going on, but Les, come on. It's been back and forth with you so many times already. If you want this to be over, okay. I know it's for a good reason. I'm not faulting you for that. But you have to see where I'm coming from too. It's confusing. So if it's over now, I'm really done. I can't keep doing this."

"I get it. I-I don't know what to say except I'm sorry, Carter. I really, really like you." My heart feels like someone is squeezing it in their bare fingers. "I'm so sorry."

I reach out to his arm but he shrugs it away and shakes his head. "I thought at the protest things became different between us. I thought you felt the same as I did."

Everything in me stills. "They did become different. How do you feel?"

He shrugs. "Doesn't matter now, does it? It's stupid, but I was gonna ask you to be my girlfriend. I fell for you."

My pulse thrums in my ears and my eyes start to water. He wanted to be in a relationship? "I'm not trying to hurt you. I feel the same."

"It's whatever, Les. Like I said, I get it. It's not like I want to get in the way of your dreams."

"Carter," I whine. "It's not like that."

He lets out a sarcastic laugh. "Yeah, it is. But by the way, I never asked you for more time than you could give me. I offered to help you with calc. I was all in, Les. But it's not a big deal. Let's just forget this"—he motions between me and him—"ever happened, and we'll go back to being friends."

Every kiss, every touch, every conversation and text flashes in my mind. I don't want to forget it. But what else was I expecting? I can't expect the guy to wait until I'm ready for him. He's not Tom, and I'm not Candy. There is no saving him for later. There's only a goodbye. So I say, "Okay."

"Cool." He raises his wrist and glances at his Apple Watch. "I'm gonna head out."

He pulls me into a side hug, but I'm limp against him. It lasts for a second too long, so I bite my lip as my chin starts to quiver. "Bye, Les," he says, opening the bedroom door.

He heads down the hallway and disappears from sight. I can't help but feel like he's taking a piece of me with him.

"Bye, Carter," I whisper, but it's too late for him to hear it anyway.

$$\infty\infty\infty$$

A few days pass, mostly with me holed up in my room, calculus book in hand. I fit in three sessions with my tutor. Candy comes over once to watch another episode of *Bachelor in Paradise* with Chinese takeout, Jared, and Rykard. I don't ask her why Tom is missing, and she doesn't ask me why Carter is missing. Granted, she probably knows the answer to both of those questions.

Ben keeps texting. I keep ignoring. He's dropped his crusade over the photo and is now back on his campaign to get me to go to St. Maarten. I ignore that too.

Now I'm getting ready to make up my calc test and go to my internship. My apartment is dreary and lonely. A cold front came through, and the weather outside is chilly and silent.

Everything is silent.

I lock up and go to my car, wrapping my sweater around me as I go. Once in, I drive the short distance to the parking lot nearest my calc class. I walk past the library, past the spot Carter and I kissed, and into the warm math building with its heat blowing.

But once I get into the classroom, my fingers go ice cold. Because it's not Professor Butler there, but Carter.

Does the director of my life hate me? They must.

I awkwardly smile and walk toward the front of the class. "Hey."

He stares at the stack of papers. "Sorry, she texted me last minute and asked me to administer the make-up exam. Since it's my job, I couldn't exactly say no."

"Right." I nod. The fact that he had to explain that sucks.

"Here." He hands me the test without looking at me. "You have forty-five minutes."

"Okay." I sit down at my regular seat and get to work on the questions. Thankfully, the first question is actually one I know. It's exactly what I studied at my tutoring session, and I regretfully thank my mom for getting me my tutor.

A few of the questions I don't know, but I work through the problems and finish the test fifteen minutes early, hoping that I somehow passed it with at least a B.

"Thanks." I hand it to Carter.

"Sure thing," he says, grabbing it and setting it on the desk where he's grading other papers.

I'm about to leave for my internship, but my heart betrays me and I say, "Carter."

He glances up and our eyes meet for the first time. "Mm?"

I wring my hands together, not entirely sure what to do with them. My cheeks heat from his stare, and I miss the nights we would text until two in the morning. It's been a few days, but I miss so much already. "I am sorry."

"*Yo sé.* Let's not do this today, Les."

My throat tightens and I clear it. "Okay. I'll see you around?"

He takes his finger and salutes me. "I'll be here."

Walking out of the classroom, the cold bites at the tip of my nose. I rub it to stop it from running. When I get to my car, I turn my seat warmer on and hold my fingers up to the vents so the hot air can heat them up.

Choosing myself is the right decision. I know it is. I just wish the emotion-side of me would agree with the rational-side of me. Maybe I just need to get laid so the emotion-side quiets.

I'm kidding, *relax*.

Definitely not doing that again for a while. Time for my internship. I'm gonna crush some research. Woohoo! So pumped.

Yeah, I'm overselling it, I know.

I drive up to the hospital and find Dr. Guilliod in the research wing, head down as she types away at her iPad.

"Hi, Dr. Guilliod."

Her head snaps up. "Les! Hello. How are you?"

I genuinely smile. For a researcher, she sure has an aura that makes me feel better. "I am…good. Or, I will be. I just took a hard test. How are you?" I place my bag on the counter and grab another iPad on the lab table next to her.

"Great. Still a little sleep-deprived, but good. I feel worse for my wife. Her boobs will probably fall off from how often she has to breastfeed."

I cringe. "Yikes."

"Indeed. So today, we'll be taking our first set of samples and comparing them to the baseline samples here." She points to two different sets of vials of blood. "The others are in the fridge." She explains the different tests she ran on each vial of blood.

A little while later, I ask, "So, why lupus?"

She holds up a vial that she mixed with lupus antigens. "Well, I've worked on a variety of autoimmune diseases throughout my career. My mom died when I was sixteen with complications from Guillain Barré. So, that's why I became a researcher."

I put my iPad down. "I'm sorry to hear that. My dad recently passed away. I'm not sure it's something I'll ever get over."

"You're correct." She puts down the vial and taps at her screen. "Losing someone we love is unbearable. But somehow, we bear it. Time does make the sad fade, though. I'm sorry about your father."

"Yeah," I tuck some hair behind my ear, "me too. I actually had an experience earlier this week that made me think I might know what I want to do as a doctor."

"Is that so?"

"Mhmm. There was this accident, and it was messy and sort of crazy. I don't know, I really liked it. I think I might want to be an ER doc."

Dr. Guilliod lets out a chuckle. "I could see that."

"Really?" Surprise stains my voice.

She shrugs. "Definitely. I saw the way your eyes lit up when talking about that unexpected birth in the hallway. People in the ER love the unexpected."

I laugh. She's right. "I do love the unexpected most of the time."

"So, how are your classes going? Freshman year is always a hard transitioning time."

If only she knew. "Most of them are good. I'm struggling a bit with calculus."

Walking to the sample fridge, she shudders. "Don't remind me. I hated calculus. It's useful, don't get me wrong, but I still hated it."

And somehow, that makes me feel just a little bit better. "It's the bane of my existence."

She reaches toward the back and grabs two more small vials of blood. Holding them up to the light and reading the tags, she brings them back over to the table. "You'll be fine. Just stay focused on your end goal. But, don't let it rule your life. You've got to live a little too."

"Yeah, I suppose so." I fiddle with the string bracelet that

Carter tied on my wrist all those weeks ago. And even though it sucks, I know it will all be worth it.

Actually, could you write that down somewhere? I think I'm going to need picture proof.

Chapter Sixteen

Next Tuesday, Professor Butler hands us back our tests. Nope, not gonna look.

"I'm gonna freak out. I can't," I tell Candy.

She rolls her eyes, snatches it out of my hands, and turns it over.

I squeal, and the rest of the class turns toward me. "Sorry." I wave.

But the squeal was well deserved because I got a 78% on my test. Which, in no world would that help me get into med school. But, it does help me get my grade above the C- threshold needed.

Professor Butler doesn't have to report me to academic probation. At least...not yet. It's probably the only good thing about today. I'm feeling out of sorts. Sad, frustrated at the world, and insert-other-teen-feelings-here. But joking aside, no one knows what this day means to me. It's just me, with my thoughts and emotions, missing my dad.

But I try to think of what my therapist, Judy, would say. Well, actually, she would tell me to give my emotions some attention. But, she also told me I didn't have to think about my triggers, so...

Maybe I can distract myself instead. Push the anxious feelings aside, and focus on other things. Yeah, that's what I'll do.

After class, I get together with Candy.

"Wanna go get waffles at Anna's?" She wiggles her brows.

I laugh and crinkle my nose. My other plans were to sit in the dark and cry, but waffles can have my focus instead. "Sure."

We walk down to the diner, shrugging our shoulders up high to keep our ears warm. The cold front never went away. It looks like Fall is finally upon us.

I blow on my fingers to warm them up. "So, how are you and everyone else over at Candyland?"

She waves at a passing girl who says hi. "It's, uh, it's good. But...confession time. I had a moment with Tom."

I grab her arm. "What do you mean 'a moment'?"

"Chill out, *chica loca*." She snorts. "We like, barely kissed."

"You kissed?" I shout, and my jaw literally drops. Then I playfully smack her arm. "What the hell? Why are you just telling me this now?"

"Because you've been holed up with your calc tutor and mourning the loss of *mi hermano*."

I roll my eyes. "Your *hermano* shouldn't blab so much."

"*Mi hermano* has been going through *chicas* like he's dying."

I trip on a crack in the sidewalk. "Are you serious?"

She winks and smacks her gum. "Kidding! Just gauging *tus sentimientos.* Anyway, yes, me and Tom kissed. But we've kissed like a thousand times before."

"Okay, I'm calling bull. When was the last time you kissed him?"

Two people head out of the diner, and I catch the door with my foot. Candy sidesteps me and walks inside, shivering. "Like, a month ago? I don't know. It's not like I keep track of these things."

"The man is in love with you. I don't get why you don't just get with him."

Candy slides into the worn, red leather booth with her back facing the door. Orange lights are strung up around the diner with jack-o-lanterns and candy corn signs posted on the walls.

I sit opposite of her and grab a menu, glancing over the different options. But we both know what we're getting. The chef back there knows me by name as the peanut allergy girl.

She snaps her fingers. "*Podría decir lo mismo de ti.* You're the same with you know who."

I set the menu on the table. "You know that's not the same. Tom is a sweetheart. Ben is Ben."

"Mr. I'm-so-famous-because-I-have-followers-on-Tik-Tok." She rolls her eyes. "On the outside, everyone's a sweetheart, aren't they?"

She has a point, I guess. My fingers twitch. "Fine. I actually wanted to talk to you about him for a minute."

"Tom?

"No, Ben." And even saying this feels stupid. "Uh, today's my Dad's birthday."

Candy reaches across the table and squeezes my hand. "Oh my gosh, Les, I'm so sorry. Are you okay?"

I shrug. My life might be a little crazy and unpredictable, but the last thing I want to do is cry in a diner. At that point, my mom would probably disown me. "Yeah. It's just..." I sigh. "I think Ben might be the only person who will understand me today. I haven't talked to him since before the rally, though."

"It doesn't make you weak to reach out to him, *amiga*."

"I don't feel 'weak.' But, I think I feel bad. Like, I broke things off with Carter, and things were never *on* with Ben, but I don't want Carter to think that I'm jumping back into his arms or something." I spin my phone on the table and watch it as it goes around and around.

Candy sputters. "Carter is the last person you should be worried about today. I know how much you loved your dad, Les. If you want to talk to someone who understands, and that person is...Ben," she grinds out, "then do it. I don't like him. But, I like you, and I don't want you suffering today. You can set boundaries with Ben, you know. He doesn't have to be cut out of your life completely."

I nod, but maybe I'm being crazy. It's possible that Ben doesn't even remember it's Dad's birthday today. Ugh, this brunch was supposed to help get my mind off of today, not make me feel like I'm going to cry. "Thanks, Can-Can. But let's talk about something else. Tell me about your crusade against Joanna Marx or whatever it is you do for a living."

"*Muahaha.*" She twiddles her fingers. "First of all, I'm a very underpaid, and by underpaid, I mean free, activist. But, *perra*'s going down. We got a bunch of news coverage thanks to our little protest."

"Yeah, I know." I circle my own face. "My make out session is now licensed by public domain."

She pulls out her phone, glances at it, then says, "First of all, you're welcome." She types out something and then slides it back into her bag. "Second of all, *gracias, mi amor*. I hope it stops people for voting for her. And third of all, *mi hermano es el mejor* dude in *Los Estados Unidos*. And you're my best friend. That picture is adorbs. But someone is going to snatch my bro up quickly if you don't go after him."

The waitress brings us some water and takes our order.

I purse my lips. "You just told me not to worry about Carter! Support me being a feminist, Candy. I'm choosing myself. I'm acing my class. I'm going to be awesome. You should be proud."

She points at me with a long, pink fingernail. "First of all, I am happy for you. Second of all, I freaking love you. Third of all, sorry for wanting my best friend and my annoying brother to be an item, okay? But fourth and final, you go girl, choose yo'self. Plus," she mumbles, "I'll forever hold out hope for you and Carter happening one day."

I roll my eyes, again, and my special peanut-free waffles that come with this cute little pink flag on them with an X over a drawing of a peanut save me. "You're really into lists today. Just continue on with your political talk, please." Anything to get the *yes, choose Carter!!!!* fans out of my mind.

(Kidding, you know I love you all.)

Candy takes a long, drawn out sip of her water as if it's the best margarita she's ever had. When the straw slurps and bubbles, I set my fork down and say, "Oh, come on, already."

She giggles. "So, news coverage was great. I got my face out there, and my Twitter following grew by a hundred thousand in this week alone. I'm so pumped. I even got an email from Vice. They want to interview me. I have a meeting with them tomorrow. *Me siento muy* excited. So that..." Her grin falls, an almost indecipherable drop of the corners of her mouth.

I cut off another bite of syrupy waffle. "That?"

"That's when the kiss happened. But it's not going to go any-where anyway, so…"

Not wanting to prod again about their relationship, I nod and stuff my face full of waffles. I get it, though. Because for the briefest moment this morning, I wanted to text Carter. I wanted to tell him about my Dad's birthday like I told him all those stories back on the beach. But, that's all they'll ever be. *Stories.* I got halfway through a text before I deleted it. If we *were* an item, I could have told him. That's all gone now. Like he said, it's really over this time. Still, I twiddle with the string bracelet he tied on my wrist.

My watch dings, so I glance at it.

Ben: How are you doing?

Not Carter. (Insert sad studio audience *aww* here, please.) Three dots flash on the screen.

Ben: I know today has to be hard.

I grab my phone. He *does* remember.

Les: Honestly, trying not to think about it much.

Putting my phone on the table, I push his texts out of my mind as much as humanly possible. Which is, you know, not possible at all.

Candy and I eat in near silence, which shows how much is wrong with today. I wish I knew what to say to her about Tom, but obviously, I don't.

"Need a ride home?" I ask, signing my name on the diner receipt.

"Actually, yeah. *Gracias.*"

I grab my bag and sling it around my shoulder. Following her out of the diner, I feel my phone buzz two more times.

When the cool air hits my face, I cower. Does it really have to be this cold out? I mean, sure, it's only like 50°F, but still, I'm in danger of boob-frostbite.

Candy sighs. And it's one of those sighs that means she wants me to ask what's wrong.

"What's wrong?"

"*Me siento estúpida.* I feel stupid." She rubs her hands together and blows on them. "I shouldn't even be talking about this to you with everything you're going through."

"No, believe me, it's fine. But, I don't get it. You're the one who wanted to 'save Tom for later.' If you've changed your mind, why don't you just tell him?"

Two guys shout at each other, laughing as they run down the sidewalk toward us. One of them accidentally bumps Candy, knocking her into me, which makes me drop my phone, which shatters my screen *again.* "You've got to be kidding me," I groan.

"*Vuelve aquí ahora mismo,* you idiots!" She tries to chase after them, getting about a foot away before I grab her backpack and pull her towards me.

"It's fine. Seriously." I brush aside some of her stray hair that is caught in her lip gloss.

"They just broke your phone screen!"

I laugh. "Yeah, and I'll get a new one. It's not a big deal."

"*Ricos estúpidos.* All I'm saying is I could've blasted them on Twitter and gotten you a phone screen." She shakes free from me and heads back the way we were going.

I shake my head and follow. "No, thank you. After you blasted me on Twitter last time, I almost got disowned by my mother, so..."

Candy snaps her head toward me. "I knew your mom was the reason you broke up with Carter!"

"First of all, we weren't together. I don't think we could even classify this as a break up." Even *if* I felt more in those few weeks with Carter than I ever did in two years with Ben.

"It was a situationship. I think it counts as a break up." She grabs some Hubba Bubba from her pocket, and it's so on-brand that I chuckle.

"What in the world is a situationship?"

She works her jaw around as she chews the bubblegum. "Well," she pushes the gum to the side of her mouth, and I know, because her cheek's bulging like a squirrel's with a nut in it, "Twitter calls it that. It's like when you're in a relationship with feelings but not an actual classified relationship."

Um...okay. I mean, it makes me feel a little bit better to say it was *some* sort of relationship with how much I've been mourning the loss of that sweet butt of his. "Alright, whatever. But anyway, my mom is not the reason. I'm nearly failing calculus, Candy. I barely escaped academic probation this time. I can't focus on someone new right now." My phone buzzes again, which reminds me of someone old.

As we step into the parking lot, I fish around in my backpack until I find my keys. I press unlock and zip my bag up again.

"I know, I'm just giving you crap. Now, don't get all emotional on me because I know I've never said this before..." She grips my shoulders and takes a deep breath then exhales forcefully. "*Pero, te amo.*"

My face breaks out into an actual grin. "Aw, I love you too, you cute little pixie chick." I pull her into a hug and squeal.

She groans, wrenches free, and goes to the passenger side. I get in as well, and start the car. One hand on the wheel, I sigh. "You know that you can talk to me about Tom anytime, right?"

"*Sí,*" she huffs, "I will. But not today." She looks out the window and doesn't say another word.

I drive the short distance to her house, pulling up to the entrance closest to her apartment. As she gets out, Carter walks in front of my car.

"Eff. My. Life," I groan. "Can this day get any worse?"

Our gazes meet, and then his gaze shifts over my face. When we catch eye contact again, he nods. I lift a hand from the steering wheel and wave, doing that straight, sorta grim smile that Americans seem to be known for.

He looks good, and his joggers hug his butt in a way that makes me totally want to check him out. When he turns, one backstrap strap hung on his shoulder, I see where he's looking back to. Or *who* he's looking back to.

A pretty girl with long black hair and a full-lipped smile throws her hands up and giggles. Her backpack is on the ground, pencils rolling across the parking lot. Carter laughs at it and walks back to help her. "Girl, you're clumsy."

The chick giggles. "You love it."

I lean over the center console to the open door. "Candy, who is that?"

Candy rolls her eyes. "Family friend. Kriti." Candy sticks out her bottom lip and pouts.

I put on a fake smile and wave her off. "I'll talk to you later, okay?"

She nods and closes the door.

Before I start feeling sorry for myself when I'm the one who put me in this situation, I drive away, not glancing back.

I get two streets away before my phone buzzes. Leaning over the center console at a stoplight, I dig inside of my backpack until I find my phone. The screen is shattered bad, and a small shard of glass pricks my finger.

"*Ugh.*" I slide across the screen. "Hello?"

"Hey," Ben says. "Let's go do something."

And I know he's trying to help, but I don't feel like it. "I don't think today's a good day."

He sighs. "I know it's not. That's why I'm calling you. Come on, Les. Let's go do something to celebrate. Your dad would want that."

The stoplight turns to green. "Where are you?"

"I'm at my place."

Which I've never even been to. Weird. "Okay. Send me your address."

"No, Les. I mean it. Let's go out and do something. Something that your dad would've wanted to do."

I chew on my lip as I pass West, and my eyes burn. This is why I haven't thought about it all day. I don't want to cry today. Dad wouldn't have wanted that. A tear drops, and I swipe at it. But it doesn't help because a few more fall. "I don't know what to do, B."

"I know. I don't either. Have you talked to your mom today?"

I think back to our last conversation over a week ago. "No. I don't even know what I'd say."

"How about we go and get some froyo? You never did take me up on that date. While we're there, we can brainstorm for ideas." His deep voice reverberates through the phone, and it's comforting.

"Okay. How about TCBY? I'm passing it right now."

"Cool. I'll be there in five."

He hangs up, and I park my car facing the street. As I watch the cars pass, I give myself just one moment. I go to my photos and find the last picture I took with my dad. He was hooked up to an IV at home in his hospital bed. My head is on his shoulder, and my brow is furrowed. You can't tell from the photo, but I was sobbing. I asked Ben to take one last photo of me with my dad because I wasn't sure how much longer he'd be alive. But I didn't have the energy to smile or be happy because Dad was a shell of the man that I used to know.

I wipe the tears from my eyes as I remember. Later that night, he died. I wasn't even there for it. But I don't want to think about that. Not now, not ever, and certainly not on his birthday.

A knock at my window startles me, and Ben places his forehead against the glass. I turn the car off and open the door. I barely get out of the seat before Ben wraps me in a hug, covering my face with his arms as I bawl. He squeezes tighter as my back shakes with each sob.

"I hate this. I'm so mad that he isn't here." I sniffle against Ben's shirt. "He should be here."

Ben runs his hand over the back of my head, smoothing out my hair. "I know. But for a second, just imagine if he saw us in the parking lot of TCBY crying. He'd be so disappointed."

Cue the laugh track. "He'd probably say something stupid like, 'I'm going to upload this to my Facebook so Harvard Medical School knows who not to accept.'" I pull back and wipe my nose with the palm of my hand.

Ben cups my face in his hands, wiping the tears from under my eyes with his thumbs. "He'd send it to Coach Wilkes and tell him to suspend me for five games."

I thought that joke would make me feel better. But, it really doesn't. Everyone says to not be upset, but how can I be okay? I don't even have a word for what I'm feeling. I'm devastated, and sad, and anxious, and so freaking mad. I smile, but it wavers, so I bite the inside of my cheek. "We are going to eat froyo, and we are going to get weird flavors like my dad always did, and we're gonna enjoy every bite." Even though I don't feel like enjoying anything.

He nods. "And then we're going to go skydiving."

I deadpan. "No, we're not."

"You know your dad would want to. But your mom would probably kill us."

I shake my head as I walk into TCBY. "We are not going sky diving."

"We'll see," he whispers in my ear.

Grabbing the biggest cup of froyo they have, I survey the flavors and let out one more shaky breath. I'm not going to cry anymore. "Okay, what are the two grossest flavors we could get?"

Ben grabs a cup of his own and squints as he reads over the flavors. "I dunno about you, but I'm definitely going New York cheesecake and avocado."

I cringe. "Avocado froyo? Who does that?"

He smiles and points at himself.

"Oh-*kay*. I'm gonna go with cotton candy and salted caramel."

"I feel like that's cheating," he says, raising his eyebrows and sucking in his lips.

"Me? Cheating?" I mock gasp. "On my father's birthday? Ben, how dare you accuse me of that." Before he can say anything else, I talk to the TCBY employee about my allergy. She goes in the back and gets me half cotton candy and half salted caramel. And sure, they're my favorite flavors, but that doesn't mean I'm cheating. Combined together, they're gross. So…

He tsks but minds his own business, going a bit heavy on cheesecake and a bit light on avocado. Not that I blame him.

We put every single topping on (well, every topping that I can safely have from the back) and pile our yogurts up as high as they can go. When we check out, the total comes to $29.84, which is a little ridiculous for frozen yogurt, but oh well.

I grab us two spoons and we find a booth in the corner of the store. There are a few other people sprinkled around, but with just B and me, it feels private. And if I'm being honest, it was nice of him to call. "Thanks for calling. And for the yogurt." I hold up my cup and wiggle it.

He takes a bite of yogurt, grimaces, and swallows loudly. "You're welcome."

"It's crazy, right? This is the first birthday without him. I don't even remember what we did for his birthday last year."

Ben points his spoon at me. "You forced me to scheme. How could you not remember that?"

I rear my chin back. "Scheme? What do you mean?"

"You wanted it to be the best birthday ever, and you had me decorate the pool house like a nightclub. I had to steal a bunch of top-shelf liquor from my parents. We threw your dad a rave." He's looking at me as if I've lost my mind.

But now that he mentions it, I do remember. "I think I've just like blocked some stuff out. Or maybe it's just the stress and how sad I've been about it. I don't know. But yes, I remember the rave. We wheeled my dad around in his wheelchair because he was too weak to dance."

Ben smiles. "Mhmm. And you sat on his lap as I twirled you guys around to old school hip hop." Digging in his pocket, he says, "I have a video from that night."

"No way?" My stomach drops, and I smile. "Gimme, gimme!"

He hands over his phone and I press play.

Blue, purple, and pink lights flash. In leather pants and a cropped tee, my hair is thrown up in a side ponytail. I run across the wooden floors of the pool room, pushing my dad in his wheelchair.

Dad holds two shots up high in the air. "Come and get some of this, Ben! No way am I missing your first shot."

"Uh, yep." The picture shakes as Ben props the phone up on something. "This is totally my first shot, George."

I widen my eyes, shushing and drawing a line across my throat. "Of course it is. Here, give me one of those."

Dad cackles, throwing his head back. "Alright. On three. One… two…three!"

Ben does his shot first, and I follow, swallowing it all in one gulp. "Um…" Ben starts.

"Dad…What was that?"

"Water from Roxy's bowl."

Ben retches, and I gasp. He runs back to his phone, saying, "Gross, man. After we throw this whole party for you?"

Dad laughs. "Sorry, B. Had to get you one last time before I kicked the—"

The video ends.

"Okay," I clear my throat, "that's probably why I forgot. I can't believe we drank dog water."

Ben chuckles. "Ah, I'd do it again."

"Me too," I whisper.

"You're a lot like him. You know that, right? Les, he'd be really proud of you. I mean it."

I push some boba to the side and find a strawberry to eat. "Thanks." I glance up at him with his big brown eyes and shaggy hair. His eye still has just a bit of yellow from that punch he got a while back. "I'm sorry, by the way."

He shrugs. "What for?"

I clear my throat. Saying sorry really isn't my specialty. "Uh, I don't know. For, um, I guess for leading you on."

He sucks in air through his teeth. "Ah, there it is." A blush blooms on his cheeks and he scratches at his nose, that heart birthmark near his thumb catching my attention. I used to stare at that all day long sophomore year. He was it for me. Ben was everything I wanted. But now I think he was just comfortable, and I don't think he'd be enough anymore. "Let's not do this just yet."

Ben still loves me. But I'm not in love with him. Whether I like it or not, Ben's life is entwined with mine. He lives next door, our parents are friends, and I don't want to hurt him.

I lick my lips. "I don't want you out of my life. We were friends for fifteen years, Ben. What is Christmas without the Maldon family party?"

He smiles.

"But, I can't do whatever you think this is right now. I'm not in a good spot with everything going on."

Pushing his yogurt away, he nods. "I'm not asking for a relationship. Look, I'm sorry for how things ended with us. I should've been better and handled things differently. I love you, Les. And I'm here for you with whatever you need. Especially for things like today. Anything with your dad, I'll always be here for. I loved him, too."

"I know you did." I mix my froyo into a puddle of mush. And though I may not want to admit it, Ben's being really nice today. He does get it. We both loved my dad, and we're both mourning him. And he hasn't mentioned Carter or St. Maarten at all. Which is why I say, "I don't know if you've heard or not from your parents, but BC Warriors is throwing a charity gala, and my dad is going to be the honoree. Would you—" I clear my throat. "Would you want to come with me?"

Ben leans back in his chair, throwing his hands behind his head. "A charity gala? That's basically our playground."

I groan. "Don't remind me."

He laughs. "The answer's yes. Yeah, absolutely. I'd love to go with you."

Chapter Seventeen

I do what I told Candy I was going to do—I focus on myself.

All I've done is study. Okay, that's not totally true. I did go Halloween costume shopping with Candy, Rykard, and Jared. I'm gonna be the hottest mouse you ever did see.

But besides that, I've studied. I've texted with my mom a few times, basically just trying to get on her good side, but I still haven't talked to her on the phone since before my dad's birthday.

Yet for the first time in forever, I'm actually wanting to talk to her. Maybe it's some weird childhood thing, who knows. But, I don't think twice as I pace in my kitchen and dial her number, waiting for her to answer.

"Hello?" Her voice sounds hesitant, with a small lilt at the end, as if she thinks I'm butt-dialing her.

"Hey, Mom. I'm about to go to class and take my next calculus quiz. I'm feeling really good about it."

There's some road-noise on the other end, and I hear a clicking sound, as if she's using her blinker. "That's great, Les. You're done with that little rebellion of yours?"

Is she...joking...right now? "Why do you have to say stuff like that to me? I'm not rebelling, Mom. I literally dated someone else besides—You know what? It doesn't matter. I wanted to call and have a nice conversation, but I guess that's not possible, is it?"

"Les, wait."

My finger hovers, readying to hand up. "What?"

"Please let me know how your calculus test goes."

I let out a defeated laugh. "Okay, Mom. Since you said please. As far as the gala goes, I'm bringing Ben. I'm still invited since I did what you said, right?" I know my voice is sarcastic, but she's pissing me off.

She lets out a breathy sigh, and I can almost taste her relief through the phone. "You're bringing Ben? Of course you're invited. I will send you an email with the info tonight. Have a nice day, Les."

"You too, Mom. Love you." I hang up and swipe my keys off the counter. "Have a nice day, Les," I mock in her uppity-rich-people-accent voice.

Am I looking forward to this quiz? No.

Do I have to take it? Yes.

Do I have to pass? Abso-freaking-lutely.

I lock up my apartment and head down the stairs to my car. On the windshield is a flyer for BOGO sushi, so I grab it and throw it in the center console. I'd be an idiot to complain about free sushi.

Throwing on some Marshmello to get me hyped (okay, and because it reminds me of Carter), I go into Candy mode. "Think like Candy, be like Candy, take over Candy's brain, and eat Candy's soul. Kidding, everyone! Totally kidding. Except...it would be nice to live in her brain for a day. She probably has a ton going on in there."

At the stoplight, I glance to the car idling next to me, and the girl is looking at me like I'm crazy. "It's fine." I wave her off. "Everyone talks to themselves!"

She quickly looks forward and her hands seem to tighten on the steering wheel. There's no way she could've heard what I said. For real, why is everyone in this world so against talking to themselves? It's a normal thing to do! At least, that's what my therapist used to say to me.

"Oh-em-gee. Did Judy lie to me all this time?" I think back to all our sessions. "Nah, Judy was cool AF." I turn into the parking lot closest to the math building and search for a spot. With so many cars here this early in the morning, it'll be a miracle if I find a spot at all. Why do I pay over four hundred dollars a year for parking? Seems excessive.

Well, except my mom pays for it. But still. I should probably start adding up all this stuff in case she "disapproves" of me once more. I'll be all like "Ta-ta, Ice Queen, I'm outta here!"

Ah, nothing like a Tuesday morning dream.

Finally, this snowball-looking girl in a white puffy coat zipped up to her nose waves a mitten at me and points to her car. See, this is the kind of women solidarity I need. I give her a big thumbs up and creep behind her feeling oddly like Joe from *You*. It's kinda awkward.

She gets in her car and backs out, and I pull in with five minutes to spare before class starts. So I grab my bag and get out of the car, realize I forgot to turn off said car, get back in and turn it off, then book it like my life depends on it.

By the time I make it to the classroom, I pause outside the door and try to catch my breath. Key word: Try. I could probably huff and puff and blow the three pigs' houses down from how hard I'm panting. But I'm three minutes late thanks to my far away parking spot. I can't go in there sounding like I'm two seconds away from an asthma attack.

"Doin' okay there, cute thang?" A tall, Black, and handsome guy with tattoos and a football jersey smiles as he walks backwards, checking me out in my near-death state.

And ohh, if I hadn't sworn off men to be totally alone, I'd climb that like a tree. "Yeah, hot stuff, I'm good. Now run along before I do something embarrassing."

He chuckles and turns around, so I take ten more seconds of false-privacy before I throw open the door to the classroom.

Professor Butler stops talking mid-sentence, and everyone whips their heads back to the door as if I'm the worst person in the world. I lean back and slowly, stealthily, slide my feet across the floor and ease into my seat without saying a word.

"Just pretend I'm not here," I say, and mouth *sorry*.

"Alright, as I was saying," she continues.

I unzip my backpack, and she goes quiet again. I look up. Everyone is staring at me. Candy has her fist over her mouth, and I can hear through her quiet snorts that she's trying to not laugh.

Professor Butler smiles, and it crinkles her normally large eyes into small slits. "We'll wait."

"Sorry, sorry," I sing, finding my pencil and placing my backpack on the ground. "I'm done. For real this time."

"Okay, then." Professor Butler tucks an errant curl behind her ear. The movement offsets her glasses and she readjusts them. "Mr. DeLeón is going to hand out the scantrons. Once you've finished the quiz, you're free to go. Test results should be posted tomorrow."

A guy throws up his hand and shifts in his seat. "What time tomorrow?"

Professor Butler rolls her eyes. "I don't know, Ethan. Whatever time I get to it."

Candy snickers, and Ethan sends her a glare, to which she winks, and a blush appears on his cheeks.

Can we just get the freaking test already?

Thankfully, it seems I also play director because as soon as I think that, Carter gets up from his seat with arms full of scantron sheets.

He passes out the tests to each row of students as Professor Butler hands out the printed quiz. It's only ten questions long, which is nice, but also sort of scary because if I get one wrong? Fine. Two wrong? Eh. Three wrong? I can hear the chastising from my mom already.

It's too bad I don't have the ability to "phone a friend" and ask my studio audience to google the answers. I'm kidding, I know y'all wouldn't know the answers either.

When I get to the first question, I'm a little relieved. The limits are easy to work out, and it's not even that hard. Every single question, I find the answer in the multiple choice answers. Which is good, because before my tutor, my answers were never one of the four choices. So I must be doing something right, *right?*

As I finish the last graphing question an hour later, Candy stands to turn her test in. I'm weirdly anxious about being accused of cheating, so I wait another minute or two before standing and turning in the quiz.

Determined not to make an exiting scene as well, I tip toe up the stairs. I glance at Carter, who's staring at me while biting on the cap of his pen, and he smiles. Lifting my fingers in a small wave, I grin back before heading out the door.

He's not mad anymore?

Maybe we can really be friends after all.

I quietly shut the room's door and turn around.

"Woo!" a voice whoops.

My feet slip on the worn down slick tile, but I catch myself. "Gosh, you scared the crap out of me, Candy."

She giggles. "*Lo siento.* I've been waiting out here for you."

"Need a ride?"

"No, I'm waiting on Carter. Twin bonding time, ya know?"

I purse my lips. "Um, no actually, I would not know. 'Cause I'm not a twin."

"Remember how you said I could talk to you about Tom at any time?" She grabs my arm and I pause, elbow deep in my backpack looking for my keys.

"Yes?"

She sighs. "I need you to come to my sister's sex reveal party."

I glower at her. "Like, baby sex reveal? What's that got to do with Tom?"

Throwing her arm over her eyes, she sighs again. "Carter is bringing Tom. I need you to be a buffer."

"It's a *baby party!* Nothing is going to happen at a freaking sex reveal." My phone buzzes, but it's just a text from Mom asking how the test went. I quickly reply *okay* and glance back to Candy where she's putting on an Oscar-worthy pouting performance. I roll my eyes. "Fine. I will come to the party with you. Surely, it won't be that big of a deal."

∞∞∞

Boy (or girl), was I wrong.

Carlotta, Candy's sister, is having a sex reveal party alright. It hasn't even started yet and chaos is all around me. Spanish is flying so quickly that the only words I'm picking up are *fiesta, asada, dulces,* and *piñata.* Small children run with arms full of steaming hot food, bowls of chips, and hundreds of decorations. And in the back, there's a very pregnant-looking woman fanning herself when it's not even hot inside the event center. Because it's not being held at the DeLeón's. No, it's being held at a legit, rented out, party space.

I thought these things were usually, like...small?

Candy waves at a tall, pale blonde woman holding the start of a balloon garland in her hands. "*Hola, Mami. Qué pasa? Necessities ayuda?*"

The woman puts down the bunch of balloons and her face breaks into a huge grin, showing off perfectly white teeth. She pulls Candy into a side hug, saying, "Hi, love. How are ya?" When she lets go and spots me, she gives me an open-mouthed smile. "Oh, you must be Les! I've heard so much about you from the twins."

"As in both of them?" I grimace. "Well, Mrs. DeLeón, hopefully all good things."

She waves me off and her flannel sleeve slips down from her elbow. "Of course. Please, call me Cassie."

Definitely will not be calling her Cassie to her face. Sure, she looks young enough to be one, but it feels weird calling older people by their first names. She's an adorable mom, though, and she has Carter's eyes.

"So, do you need help?" Candy asks, setting her bag on a table near the side of the large, rectangular room now filled with décor.

I follow suit, and now I don't have anywhere to put my hands, so I just awkwardly place them at my side.

Cassie shakes her head. "No, I don't believe so. Carlotta

might need help. You know how she gets. All the women in this family are so dramatic."

Candy snorts. "Like that should be a bad thing? Puh-lease, I'll build my career on drama."

Picking up the balloons, Cassie tapes two ends together until the garland is now twice its size. "Candy, go help your pregnant sister. Now, *por favor*." And I may not know a ton about Spanish, but that woman sounds just like Candy, so her accent must be impressive.

"*Sí, sí, Mami,* you don't have to use your stern voice on me." Candy grabs my hand and stomps off in the direction of the now beet-red and clearly overheated, Carlotta.

We get halfway across the room when two identical boys come running through shouting, one holding a bowl of chips, and the other holding a baseball bat. His curls are wild around his face, and they flounce with each step as he dangerously swings the bat.

The side door bangs open and Carter yells, "*¡Paralos!* Carlotta, do something!" He continues sprinting after them. "*Necesito una chancla.* Tell them to knock it off, they're giving me a heart attack!"

I can't help but smile. I knew the boys looked familiar. Those must be the nephews from Carter's phone screen. "Nephews?" I ask Candy.

"Mhmm, chip-boy is Mateo. Baseball-bat-boy is Adrian. They're identical, so good luck." She stalks toward the boys and snaps at them before pointing a long, red fingernail in their direction. "Knock it off, now."

"Sorry, *tía*." Adrian hangs his head low.

Carter protests. "No, no, no. Do not fall for that. They just apologized to me a minute ago and then started running again as if this is some freaking Kentucky Derby with preschoolers."

Carlotta walks over to her two boys and pouts. "*Tío* Carter is so mean. *Pobrecitos.* How could you say that about these sweet, sweet boys?"

He throws his hands up in the air. "I'm watching you two."

He motions to his eyes and points toward them.

They snicker and saunter off, everyone enamored with their cute little brown curls. "In their defense," I say, "they are pretty cute." I close the gap between us all and stand in between Candy and Carter.

Carlotta nods and pushes her dark, golden brown hair off of her shoulders. "Thank you," she says, putting on a duck face and staring at Carter. "I'm glad *someone* thinks so."

Carter scowls. "Those curls hide devil horns."

"*Necesitas ayuda?*" Candy stands on her tip-toes and slings an arm around her sister's shoulder.

"Actually, yes." She glances my way. "Les, right?"

"In the flesh." I circle my hand in a good-natured bow.

"Nice to meet you. Sorry it's under these circumstances." Carlotta points to her stomach and sticks out her tongue.

I laugh. "You kidding me? It's great. Seems like I've been around a lot of baby-related things recently."

"*Blech*. Must be something in the water." She winks (clearly a familial trait) and says, "Could you help Carter with the treat station? I need Candy to"—she whistles—"help me into a different dress. I underestimated the size of this stomach."

And under normal circumstances, I'd probably say no to me and Carter being alone, but to a pregnant lady? You have to agree. "Yeah, totally. I will see you in a bit." I wiggle my pointer-finger guns toward Candy. Which is awkward. Why am I being awkward?

"*¡Vámonos, chica!*" Carter turns toward the side door he came from and walks, albeit a bit too fast, so I have to hurry to catch up.

He leads me into the event center's kitchen, where a bunch of others hang out and talk. Tapping on an older man's shoulder about the same height as him, he says, "*Oye, papi, este es mi amiga,* Les."

A man, who I'm gonna assume is Carter's dad, turns around and stares. Doesn't frown, doesn't smile, just sort of…acknowledges. After setting down his drink, he sticks his hand out and I shake it. Judging by his build, he probably played sports growing up. If I had to guess, seeing Carter play college baseball at West is probably a big deal for him because he's wearing a West baseball shirt, so he's clearly a fan. He's handsome too, which, *obviously* 'cause Candy and Carter are hot as hell.

"Hi, nice to meet you. I'm Les."

He lets go of my hand. "Hello, Les. I'm Cisco."

Ah, so everyone in the family has 'c' names. Carter and Cisco talk back and forth in Spanish too quickly for me to even hear what they're saying, but Carter's cracking up laughing at the end of it, and Cisco raises his brows once with a grin and turns around to the others in the room.

I feel sort of out of place. If I had my phone on me, I'd probably be googling *Spanish classes near me* because I'm feeling like an idiot.

As if Carter senses that, he says, "My dad was just saying he was proud of me for securing someone 'out of my league.'" He chuckles. "I then informed him that I had actually failed to secure you."

"Oh, whatever." I laugh. "Don't be dumb."

We hold each other's gaze and it just so happens that my lips are dry and need to be licked, but I swear, it's not because I want to kiss him.

Don't roll your eyes at me.

"So," he runs his hand through his hair, "let's get this candy set up, shall we?"

I reach for the nearest glass vase that's filled with rainbow gumballs. "Hell yeah, we shall. So, what do you think your sis is having?"

He picks up a bowl stacked high with different Mexican candies and leads the way out of the room. "Plot twist: She's having another set of twins and it's one girl and one boy?"

"No way, for real?"

He turns his head until he catches my eye and clucks his tongue. "No. She'd lose her freaking mind."

"Yeah, I'll say. You almost made my balls drop." I hold up the vase and wiggle it.

Carter bursts out laughing, nearly breaking the bowl as he sets it on the table too hard. When he looks back at me, I wink and place the vase of gumballs next to his bowl. My arm brushes his, and it sends a zing from my elbow to my shoulder.

So I quickly step away. It's then that his Apple Watch sounds off an alarm and he sighs, grabbing out his little pouch of diabetic supplies. I can't imagine having to constantly track every bite of chocolate or every gumball I eat. It has to be exhausting. Then again, I guess having a peanut allergy is pretty exhausting too.

Like right now. I bite my lip. "So, awkward question, but… Will there be peanuts here tonight?"

He unwraps one of the caramels from the table and pops it into his mouth. With more force than is needed, he puts his stuff back in the pouch, zips it roughly, and shoves it into his pocket. "I don't think so. Candy told my parents beforehand. I'll double check with *mi papi* just to make sure."

He heads back to the kitchen, so I follow him and grab another bowl of candy. We continue back and forth, setting up the table until it looks like I copied and pasted it straight from Pinterest. I stand quietly as he pulls out his controller, retests his blood sugar, and clears his throat.

"We did a good job," I say, whistling as I step back from the table.

He put his hands on his hips and nods. "Yeah. We make a good team."

His cheeks have the slightest blush on his brown skin, and a speckling of freckles on his nose crinkle as he smiles. And part of me whispers that maybe I made a mistake. That being with him wouldn't be so hard. I'm already here. What would be the difference if I were here as Carter's girlfriend?

But whoa, okay, pretend I didn't just think that because, girlfriend? I'm getting ahead of myself. Like, way ahead. We weren't even in a relationship to begin with. Plus, he had that girl (Kristy? Karen? Okay, fine, I'm not fooling anyone. I went home and insta-stalked her. *Kriti.*) over at his house the other day.

Oh no, why does my face feel like it's on fire? And why is he looking at me like that? He's giving me eyes. Heavy-lidded, smokin' hot, let's-meet-up-in-my-back-seat eyes.

There's just one problem: I'm imagining it all.

Carter's not mine. He never was mine. And he's not going to be mine. So I brush my hands off on my jeans and say, "I better go find Candy."

And if it weren't for the smell of tacos and tamales bribing me to stay here, I'd just go home.

∞∞∞

Carlotta stands with her husband, Antonio, in front of a semi-creepy baby face piñata. It's easily five feet tall and swings from a tall ladder with a piece of plywood across the top of it. Both of them have a hand on the two strings, which when pulled will open up the baby's chin and spray pink or blue confetti.

"One..." everyone yells.

"Two..."

"Three!" we shout, and Carlotta and Antonio pull the strings.

Everyone is screaming and cooing, waiting to see what they're having, but instead of colored confetti and sprinkles, the two strings detach from the bottom of the piñata and nothing happens.

"Oh, come on!" Carlotta groans. She storms off to the side of the room where Mateo and Adrian stand. It isn't until I see the burning in her eyes that I realize what she's going for.

The baseball bat.

Pregnant woman that she is, she yanks the bat out of Adrian's hands and stomps over to the piñata. Antonio scurries to the side right as Carlotta holds the bat over her head and—

SMACK!

SMACK!

SMACK!

Yeah, the piñata definitely isn't breaking. At this point, I think we're all enthralled in what she's doing, and everyone is almost silent.

"*Dame ese escalera, Antonio,*" she says, pointing toward the ladder. "I need to get higher to really hit it."

"*¿De qué hablas?* Are you crazy? You're not getting on the ladder." Antonio tries to take the baseball bat from her but she, quite literally, growls.

Producer, zoom in on Carlotta's face and cue the laugh track.

The two bicker back and forth, so when a hand pushes me gently aside, I don't realize who it is until Carter is walking in front of me, toward the couple. Without a word, he takes the baseball bat from Carlotta.

Before anyone can protest, he swings the bat once.

The giant baby head bursts open and pink confetti flies everywhere.

Carlotta drops to the ground sobbing. "*¡Es una niña! Ay Dios mío,* it's a girl! I'm s-so happy," she cries, and Antonio wraps her up in his arms and laughs.

I turn toward Candy, who's wearing a shit-eating grin. "That little baby is gonna be spoiled rotten."

"Indeed. This was so—"

Music blares through the speakers set up in all four corners of the room. There's suddenly a DJ in the corner and he shouts into the microphone, "It's a girl! Congratulations. Let's get this *fiesta* started."

Everyone moves away from the broken piñata and toward the center of the room where people begin dancing. The song is in Spanish, but the energy is contagious. I feel like I could start singing even though I don't know any of the words.

I'm ready to party. Candy holds out her hand, palm up, so I take it and she leads me to the dance floor. She shimmies and twirls, and with every movement, she's pulling me closer and we get put into a line of ladies circling Carlotta and singing lyrics I can't comprehend.

My face hurts from smiling and my toes tingle with energy. It's not even possible to feel down or sad when you're surrounded by this much excitement and fun. I'm doing the cha-cha, grinding with Candy, eating tacos while dancing, and it's pretty much my dream.

I'm so into it all that I almost forget why I'm here in the first place. But then the record scratches in my mind and I'm like *wait, hold up.*

"Where is Tom?" I have to shout so that she can hear me.

Candy stops dancing, one foot off the ground and hands out to the side. Her smile turns upside down and her brows crash together. "Uh, *no hablo ingles.*"

"Candy!"

She backs away and resumes shimmying backwards. "*No sé.*"

"Candy, what the hell?"

Holding up a finger phone she says, "*¡No puedo oírte!*"

"Yeah, you better run!"

Someone grabs my hand from behind and spins me around. "Who?" Carter asks.

He rolls his shoulders and hips, moving to the beat of the mariachi song and alright, the boy's got moves.

Since Carter's in front of me, I might as well dance with him. "Candy. She told me Tom was going to be here and that's why I needed to come tonight."

His chin lifts toward the ceiling as he bellows out a laugh. "No way. Tom is banned from family parties for at least another year after what he did at the last one." Carter pulls me toward him, then spins me to the side.

"Uh-oh, what'd he do?"

He glances sideways as if remembering and goes from a smirk to a full grin. "Let's just say a Christmas tree ended up in flames."

"Oh gosh, do I even want to know?" We straighten our arms and then he pulls me toward him so we're chest to chest.

"Probably not, no." He cocks his head to the side as we sway back and forth. "Although, it was partly my fault too. I was the one who supplied the gasoline."

I ponder why the hell two guys would need a Christmas tree and gasoline, but at the same time, I don't even question it. Guys are weird. "Well, your fault or his, I don't know why Candy would claim he was here when he wasn't."

Carter stands back and claps as the song comes to an end. "Ah, she probably just wanted to hang out with you."

I gesture to my sides like a circus director. "Well she isn't here, is she?

Not that I really care because I have a feeling that no matter where she is, she's probably up to no good.

A slow song begins playing, and Carter arches a brow. I shake my head and waggle my finger. "Absolutely not. Friends don't slow dance."

He holds my hand and pulls me close to him. "Sure they do. And stop giving me those do-me eyes, that ship has sailed."

I can't help but shake with silent laughter. "That quick huh? A few weeks ago you'd pick me up for romantic nights out but now hooking up is off the table?" And because I have serious problems, I allow myself to sniff him.

"*Sí, mami.* I've moved on." He feigns nonchalance, shrugging his shoulder and raising his brows once as if to say you snooze you lose.

"You've moved on. I guess I'm becoming a nun. How did we get here, Carter?"

He chuckles, and I stumble on a step, pushing us closer than before. My chin is right below his shoulder, and I stare at all the other couples dancing.

Most of them are older, but I catch Carlotta and Antonio dancing, baby bump to crotch. Yeah, no thank you. But they look so happy. She has this cute grin on her face like everything is right in the world.

How crazy would it be to actually feel...okay with your life? To not be upset or down, missing people all the time, and to just be happy? And not just while you're surrounded by crazy fun people, but when you're by yourself, too.

Has Carter seriously moved on? Does he not miss me at all? Our late night texting sessions? The day at the beach? Whispered confessions on long car rides? None of it? All I smell is the cinnamon surrounding him, and it chokes me. I *haven't* moved on. I don't even *want* to move on. Being pressed against him right now isn't helping.

I can feel his heat through his thin shirt, feel the scruff on his jawline against my arm, so I wish I could plant my lips there, trailing from his mouth to his jaw to his abs.

My skin breaks out in goosebumps. He whispers in my ear, "Are you cold?"

I want to say *yes, I'm cold, warm me up.*

His heavy weight pushing me against the wall, a mattress, the back of a car, literally anywhere would be acceptable. Bodies touching, lips telling silent secrets, hands roaming. Forgetting why we ever stopped and agreeing to never press pause again.

"Can I cut in?" The woman's voice startles me.

I flinch away from Carter and glance toward my fantasy-crusher. And what do you know? It's the cute girl from the parking lot the other day.

"Um, sure." I take another look at Carter, whose beaming face tells me everything I need to know.

He wasn't lying. He *has* moved on. I'm just the weird friend who talks to herself and ruined her chances.

"Absolutely. Yes. Here." Stepping away from him, I let go of my hold and plaster on a fake, probably crazy-looking, grin.

"Les, this is Kriti. Kriti, Les," Carter introduces us.

"Nice to meet you, Kriti. You guys have fun."

It's as if his body relaxes the second she touches him. He seems to go from taut to loose when one of her slim, brown arms swings around his neck.

She's hot. With a butt that I thought was only trademarked by the Kardashians and long, black hair that nearly reaches her waist, I'll admit it, I'm jealous. But it goes beyond her hotness. Her eyes crinkle with joy, and she has no problem diving right into a conversation with him that makes him gaze at her with adoration.

Plus, Carter invited her. He didn't invite me because I'm the idiot that let him get away. He deserves to move on. He *deserves* to be happy.

So...why does it feel so bad?

After breaking things off with him, I shouldn't be allowed to feel this way. I wish I didn't, but I guess you can add that to the long list of my flaws.

Looking away before they catch me leering at them like a grade A creep, I search for Candy in the crowd. Weaving my way through couple after couple, I find her dancing with her two nephews.

I can't be mad Carter has moved on.

I can't be mad that the girl who he moved on with is a sexy goddess.

I am not going to let a guy ruin my evening.

"Hey! Can I get in on this action?" I ask.

Candy lets go of Adrian (I think) and pushes him toward me. "Come on, Les. Prove to him that white girls really can't dance."

I roll my eyes, but her comment elicits a snort. "Get over here soon-to-be big bro. You ever seen the Sprinkler? It's gonna rock your world!" I dance like no one's watching, white girl be damned. I'm sure you think I look ridiculous, and I probably do, but hey, you can't feel sad while dancing, right?

Chapter Eighteen

Today is my father's gala, and I'm brushing through my tangled hair, listening to Olivia O'Brien's "Trust Issues," when I get a text from Ben asking when he should pick me up. We have a three hour drive, so really, he should've picked me up like twenty minutes ago.

I grab my makeup bag and some snacks for the road, and fifteen minutes later, I'm getting into Ben's G-wagon and turning on the seat heater. "Hey."

"You could sound a little more depressed to see me, Les." He puts his hand on top of mine.

What does he think he's doing? I pull it back and give him a, "Hardy har-har. Very funny."

Frankly, I'm not in the mood for his antics.

We drive toward home, weaving into some snow-dotted canyons along the way. We stop at Starbucks, get gas, argue about the choice of music, and relax. I have my feet up on the dash, and the windows fog slightly as I gaze out of them. It reminds me of that night with Carter when he wrote on his car window.

Granted, they were fogged for a much different reason. Is this how it's gonna be? He's now forever branded as the one who got away? Blech. I need a reshoot of this episode of my life. I'm being drama over a guy I dated for a few weeks.

Eager to change the topic of my own internal monologue, I turn toward B. "How are your parents doing?"

He shrugs. "My parents? What do you mean?"

Is he for real? "Um...with the affair?" I wish I had telepathy to see what was going on inside that mind of his 'cause right now, I'm thinking it would just be crickets.

"Oh, yeah. They're, I don't know. They're my parents. I don't really want to think about my mom spreading her legs for some other guy's—"

"Okay, for real? You don't have to be so crass." I huff while gazing out the window, and it leaves behind a circle of fog. Then I feel bad because I know it's just a defense mechanism of his. "How are you doing, though?"

He runs his hand through his hair and glances at the rear-view mirror. "I'm fine."

"B, come on."

"I don't know. It's weird. What do you want me to say?" He pauses. "You're still coming on the trip, right?"

I take a sip of the herbal tea we picked up from Starbucks an hour ago. It's lukewarm. "Um, I never agreed to that."

A few snowflakes fall on the windshield, so he turns on his wipers and they clear. "Yeah, but my mom already bought the tickets last Christmas. We've been planning it for forever."

"Yeah, when we were together." I set the tea back into the cupholder. "Come on, man, don't make this awkward. Don't make me have to remind you that we broke up."

He chuckles and elbows me good-naturedly. "Whatever, weirdo. You can still come with me as a friend."

His grin makes me blush. "I don't believe that."

"You don't believe what?"

"That we'd go as friends."

He snaps his fingers and dances like he has some weird white boy swagger. He *doesn't*.

"Put your hands back on the steering wheel, you're going to kill us!" I whine.

"Look, baby girl—"

"Yuck."

"—you still got the hots for me."

I laugh incredulously. "I mean, I'm not gonna lie and say you aren't attractive. You could probably convince the Queen of England herself into bed."

"Hey, that old hag? She can still get it."

"Who are you?" I faceplant into my palms. "You're insufferable. I can't believe *I'm* saying this, but Ben, this is not some sitcom. The camera isn't going to cut from us arguing to us in bed naked with pre-recorded *oohs* and *ahs*."

He twirls his finger at my forehead. "I'm not ruling anything out. I know you've got your studio audience up in there commenting on all of this. Some of them are probably chanting my name. Hashtag Team Ben."

Can someone else tell this kid to knock it off? *Producer, producer! Kick him off of set, please!*

"You're driving me nuts."

"You like it," he challenges.

I humph and cross my arms, conceding in this one thing. But the rest of the drive is mostly silent with Ben's weird music in the background. Thirty minutes later, he punches in the gate code for our neighborhood. As the wrought-iron fence opens without a creak or rumble, he drives with his window still down, letting in freezing air that smells like the literal personification of *winter is coming.*

Another mile later, Ben turns right into the driveway that leads to the large, modern home with more glass than walls. "Home, sweet home," he says, parking the car in front of the garage.

"My home, you mean."

He shrugs. "Practically mine, too." Which, if I'm being honest, I guess isn't too far off. But really, his home is next door—literally.

"Are you running home to change?" I ask, pushing the garage code in.

"Nah, I've got it all here. Plus. The 'rents are gone. Dad's on a business trip and Mom's visiting Lizbeth." Ben's sister is ten years older than us, so I sometimes forget that she's even there.

"Yeah, my mom told me. She was 'oh, so disappointed' that they wouldn't make it to the gala." I pass by the sports cars that belonged to my dad. I'm actually a bit surprised to see them here in the garage. Mom was supposed to sell them last I heard.

Ben whistles. "I'd love to get my hands on that Porsche."

I snort. "Pretty sure my mom would give any of them to you if you asked. You're her favorite child."

He comes up behind me and playfully pinches my arm. "And don't you forget it."

Thankfully, he ditches me for the big screen TV while I head upstairs to my room where my mom said she laid out my dress. I glance out my bedroom window, relishing in the view of Lake Tahoe. The blue water, the dusting of snow that leads to its banks, and the mountains all around. It truly is beautiful.

For the next hour, I curl my hair, do my makeup, and put on the sparkly gold dress that hugs my hips and dips low in the front. Paired with the white fur jacket, I look good enough to seduce myself.

As I come downstairs, Ben's in his tux with his hair gelled to the side, standing and watching the last of a football game. Because proper rich kids know not to sit down in their tuxes.

He glances my way, back to the TV, then back to me again. "Damn, girl, you lookin' fine as hell."

I roll my eyes and laugh. "Let's go."

We head toward the garage, but I take a detour into my dad's office. It's stale, and there's hardly anything in it since he hadn't worked for so long. Déjà vu hits me. The last time I was in here, it was a few days before my dad died. He wanted one more drive through the canyon, so when my mom was in surgery, I snuck him out. It seems like so long ago now. But I can't have another breakdown tonight. The wall of keys is still there, so I swipe the Tesla ones and walk out.

Ben's jaw drops. "You're gonna let me drive the freaking Tesla?"

"In your dreams, lover boy. I'm driving."

∞∞∞

Ben and I step up the marble staircase that leads to the second-story ballroom. The building smells like nothing. No faint scent of cleaner and no smells of food (that I'm sure is being served in the ballroom) exists here. It's sparkling clean and sterile, like a hospital.

My heels clack against the hard floor, and Ben places a hand on my lower back as we cross the hallway. It opens up into a grandiose room with ceilings five stories high that end in a dome. Old artwork hangs on the walls, and probably a billion dollars' worth of clothes drape across rich people, smiling without wrinkles. But it looks so natural you'd never know they pay for that Botox every twelve weeks.

A black curtain and photographer greet you the moment you step in, taking posed photos of you. Not to mention the dozen photographers snapping candids after that. The flashes blind me with every step, and I stumble into Ben's side, turning my face away from the nearest camera.

I glance toward the front where a slideshow of photos of my father, as well as photos of other brain cancer survivors, fade in and out. It seems as if every time I blink his face is up there again.

What am I doing? A caterer bumps into me, and a bit of champagne spills on my dress.

"I'm so, so sorry, miss. Are you okay? Here, let me get that." He hands me a napkin, and I blot at the spot.

"It's fine. No biggie." But when I glance up to him, it's clear that it *is* a biggie—at least to him. I smile. "Seriously, you're okay."

The guy nods stiffly and hurries off. Not that I blame him— no doubt 90% of the people here are like my mom and would freak out if champagne spilled on them. Which is ridiculous, because 100% of these people can afford the dry cleaning to clean said spill.

Ben chuckles. "Man about crapped his pants."

"Indeed." Not that I really feel like laughing right now. Actually, all I really want to do is leave. I turn toward the entrance, but Ben grips my arm—a little too harshly, if I'm being honest.

"Don't do it. You'll regret not being here," he whispers in my ear, and my skin burns as I flush.

"Why would I regret it? My dad would hate being here right now."

Ben's grip loosens and he moves down to intertwine our fingers. "Would he though? The man loved attention. He'd probably enjoy this."

No, I don't think he would. Yes, he liked attention (don't we secretly all?), but not this kind of attention.

"We're already here," Ben laments. "We drove all this way, so the least you can do is wait it out until your mom speaks."

My studio audience must be conflicted 'cause one side of me says *get the hell* out and the other part whispers *stay*. Ugh, I guess Ben's right.

A caterer walks by, and I grab one of the fruit kabobs covered in chocolate that she's parading around. "Fine. I might as well enjoy this fruit. Probably costs a hundred dollars a bite."

Ben grabs a drink with a melon ball sticking out of it. We all know they're not carding at a high-dollar event like this. He could get away with anything. "You're gonna love driving the G-wagon home."

So...I guess I'm the designated driver. "How nice of you."

He shakes his head. "Relax. I'm kidding. It's for her," he mumbles, gesturing behind me.

"Ben. Les." My mom's voice laces up my spine.

I turn toward it and find her dressed in a black, short sleeve dress that cascades to the floor in a layer of lace. And she's my mom, so of course she looks good. "Hey, Mom. Everything looks great."

She dips her chin. "Of course. I'm glad you made it."

Ben gives her the drink and a hug. "Glad I was invited. You ready for your speech?"

"I am." She glances to her side then holds up a finger at us. "If you'll excuse me."

As she disappears, I take my first breath. Then I take another look around the room. Something is bothering me, and I don't even know what it is. But it's that itch you can't scratch, the thought on the tip of your tongue, and it has me once again wishing I could phone-a-friend for the answer.

Violins play softly in the background, but no one dances. "It's weird, right?"

Ben brushes at his gelled hair. "What's weird?"

"That this isn't the first gala we've been to. That it won't be the last. That we literally grew up in this." I gesture to the obscene flower arrangements and tables dressed in linens.

He shrugs. "I guess? I mean, we don't know any different. Just seems natural. Why are you freaking out?"

I roll my eyes. "I'm not 'freaking out.' I guess it just seems weird. Maybe it's just me."

Ben puts his arm around me and seems to ponder for a second. "I think you're overly stressed because it's honoring your dad."

The air feels like it's being sucked from my lungs, and another photo of my dad smiling right after his first brain surgery flashes on the screen. He has two thumbs up and half of his head is shaved. "Yeah, I suppose that could be it."

We sit down at our assigned table, and the nametag next to me is my mom's. After what seems like an hour, people start sitting down as well, filtering into their seats as the music comes to an end and dinner glasses are set on the table.

Waiters place plates of appetizers on the center of the table: A line of spoons each with sautéed greens and a lone scallop on top, charcuterie boards, oysters, and sourdough slices. I avoid the oysters (definitely don't need those tonight while sitting next to Ben) and go for a scallop. It's all so pretentious with the small servings and individually plated items that I have to contain an eyeroll.

Mom sits down, and a handsome, young man sits next to

her. They chat about the gala, and I eavesdrop, putting two and two together. He's the CEO of the nonprofit BC Warriors. Which means...he's one of Joanna Marx's sons. And he looks awfully young for being *any* CEO.

Now I get why people say screw rich people.

We're waiting on the first course when Joanna Marx herself sits down, and my fingers go cold. She glances my way as she scans the room, then her eyes zero in on me. "Have we met before?"

Thankfully, Mom pipes up for me. "Governor Marx, this is my daughter, Les."

"She's not governor anymore," I mumble and flatten my lips in an attempt at a smile, but the way Joanna's eyes flash with amusement, it's clear I'm not succeeding. Ben puts his knee against mine and pushes, which is his signal to say *stop it.*

It's vain, but all I can think is how bad this will look if pictures of me and Joanna Marx get out after I was branded as the face of Candy's protest against her. Not to mention, what would Candy think? Carter? Literally *all of my friends* who were at the rally?

A photographer comes creeping around the table and snaps a photo as I turn toward Ben to try and hide. Once they're gone, I lift the napkin from my lap and dab my lips. "If you'll excuse me."

I grab my wristlet and head to the bathroom. Once I confirm no one else is in here, I let out a breath I didn't know I held, whip out my phone, and text Candy.

Les: *Full disclosure, I'm at a gala, and Joanna Marx is here. They're taking pictures, and I don't want you to have to do damage control if they get out.*

Three dots immediately appear on the screen.

Candy: *Blech. I'm sure it will be fine. Why are you there?*

Les: *My dad is the honoree.*

Candy: *Lo siento, bb. That's gotta be tough. Don't worry about the pics. Text me after?*

She sends a kissy face emoji, and I send two hearts back before exiting the stall. When I get back to the table, I distract myself through four courses by letting Ben talk about the latest baseball stats. He rambles on about players I don't know a thing about, but I find comfort in the rhythm of his voice as the backdrop to my own thoughts.

After dinner, Ben and I dance to a few songs played by the string quartet. When it's just me and him, I loosen up a bit. I couldn't count on two hands the number of galas we've been at with each other, so it feels natural. For the briefest of moments, I look into his brown eyes and think *would a future with him really be that bad?*

I wouldn't have to dedicate much time and energy, I'd have someone to hang out with, someone to cry with about my dad, and someone to complain to about my mom.

I want that. I want to have a person to do all of that with.

But the person I want to do it with isn't here.

Ben must mistake my feelings for Carter as desire for him, and he leans in for a quick peck on my lips. Yeah, it's not giving me a lady boner by any means, but is it bad? No. Being kissed by someone like Ben can't be *bad*. He's a great kisser.

Could I fake it till I make it? Could I be with him, make my mom happy, and be the perfect little rich girl with the perfect little rich boy?

For once in my life, my mom saves me. She gets on stage, and the music stops. Ben and I make our way back to our seats as she waits for everyone to sit down.

Mom smiles without it reaching her eyes. Or, maybe it does, but the Botox she has is preventing any emotion from showing.

"Thank you all for coming tonight to BC Warriors. Tonight's gala honors all those who have had brain cancer, both treatable or not. The specific honoree tonight is my husband, George Watkins." She stops speaking, and if I didn't know her, I'd almost think it's because she's choking up. "He was a wonderful father, friend, and doctor."

With a composing breath, she delivers the punchline to

every gala. "Please, tonight we ask you to open your hearts and your wallets for donating to BC Warriors and funding brain cancer research to prevent devastating deaths like the one that's hit our family."

Aaand, there it is. Ben squeezes my hand as if the mere mention of my dad will make me fall apart. But it's not the mention of him that has tears stinging in my eyes, it's the fact that he would hate this, and my mother is using him as a charity case. I thought that this would make it all better. That seeing his name and photo and all of these people honoring him would feel good. It's why I fought so hard to come here.

But now? *Why?*

I never should have come to begin with. The only thing anchoring me to my seat is the fact that I don't want to be labeled as a "spoiled rich girl" having a "sad breakdown" over her "dear father's" death. I don't need them talking about me at the Christmas party, or brunch, or whatever stupid events they're putting on.

So I bury it.

While Mom drones on, I stare at the back of Joanna Marx's perfect head. Her hair secures at her neck in a chignon, delicate diamonds framing it. I don't look away as my mom concludes her speech. I don't look away as Mom sits down next to me. I don't look away even though I feel Mom's eyes boring into the side of my head.

As soon as the slideshow and auction are over, I stand. My chair squeals and Joanna turns, our eyes meeting. But I don't care to fake it anymore, so I fight back the urge to politely smile.

Ben stands, pulling at my hand. "Beautiful gala. But I can't help myself. I need a minute alone with this gorgeous girl." He smiles with every shiny, rich-boy white tooth, and speed walks down the hall, nearly dragging me.

It doesn't matter because I'm thankful. And as misguided as he usually is, even a broken clock is right twice a day.

"I'm gonna lose it."

He whistles. "Yep. Saw that coming from a mile away. Let's get out of here."

"This was horrible. Why did I want to come?"

Stopping at the top of the marble steps, he cups my cheek. "Because it's your dad, Les. You wouldn't miss it."

I shrug and glance away to see if anyone is coming. Then I whisper, "I hated it. *He* would've hated it. I think I might hate my mom. B, am I bad person?" I bite my tongue so hard, I'm surprised I don't taste metal.

He sputters and laughs. "Shut up. You are not a bad person because you hated a pretentious gala."

Wiping at my eyes, I say, "Don't tell me to shut up. You shut up."

He rolls his eyes, but a grin creeps up on his lips. He nods to the staircase, and I hold his hand as we make our way down the steps, perfectly in my heels. Because what Ben said was true—I've basically been groomed for this my whole life.

I'm numb the whole way out, and it's not because it's chilly outside. As we wait at the valet for the Tesla, I'm just...out of sorts. I'm sad and frustrated. I wish my dad was here. And at the same time, I feel stupid for not being "over it." It's been months. Shouldn't the pain be leaving instead of getting worse?

One more tear slips out, and I'm sure you're all feeling pity for me. Maybe that makes things worse.

"You wanna drive? I'm good if you want me to do it," Ben asks.

I shake my head and sink into the passenger side. He practically salivates at the car, so it seems fitting to let him drive. Silence blankets the car as we get away from the gala. Ben keeps glancing at me, but I bite at my nailbeds. My nail tech would be so disappointed in me. Just add her to the long list of people who are.

Ben clears his throat, and it's so loud in the quiet that I flinch. "Hey," he starts, "I don't know if it will help or not, but I have more videos of your dad on my phone. There's a bunch of old TikToks that we recorded when I insisted on going viral."

Oh man, do I remember that. I snort. "You never did go viral, did you?"

He licks his lips then smiles. "Actually, we did. I think it was our...fifth water chugging video that did it. Your dad choked so badly on the water that it came out his nose."

I sigh. "Hand me the phone, please. I don't want you texting and driving."

"It'd be TikTok and driving, thank you very much." Before he hands it over, he taps on the screen a few times and puts it on do not disturb. Finally, he hands it over with his account pulled up.

"You upload on here a lot, huh?" The latest video on his account is me climbing the steps at the museum, my dress draping behind me. "Thanks for asking for my consent."

He squeezes my thigh. "Your face is never shown."

I'm not really sure why that matters, but I was joking anyway, so...

I scroll down through his videos, seeing thumbnails of his face and baseball, some guys on the team, a huge group of dudes with a pretty redheaded girl in the middle, and random things, like ice cream. But way, way, way down are his first videos on his Tik Tok, and all of them include my dad.

I click on the first one.

"We're chugging water until we're viral, right?" Ben says.

"Hell yeah, Ben. Three...two...one!"

They both place the water bottles to their lips and chug. Ben wins by a mere half second.

"Tune in tomorrow, and we'll chug more water."

The video replays its 15 seconds two more times until I go to the next one.

"Les, baby girl, whatcha gotta say to my followers?" Ben says.

The camera turns toward me, dressed in a tight bodycon dress and a high ponytail that reaches midway down my back. I waggle my head back and forth, snorting. "You'd need to have followers for me to say anything to them."

The camera pans to Ben's pouty face, bottom lip drawn up to his nose. "She's so rude to me, guys."

Dad grabs the camera. "She's the best thing that ever happened to you, idiot." He bops Ben's head.

I go to the next video.

Whitney Houston blares in the background. Ben and Dad are dressed in white tuxes and black Ray Bans. Two mics stand in front of them.

Ben yanks his toward him. "And I will always love you!"

Dad snaps along to Ben's singing before taking his own mic. "I will always love you!"

I giggle. "Why on earth were you two singing Whitney Houston, and where the hell was I?"

Ben shakes his head and grins. "Honestly, I have no idea." Punching in the gate code to our neighborhood, he says, "If I had to guess, probably studying or interviewing for that internship of yours."

I suppose I did do those things a lot. "Yeah, probably so." I hand him back his phone. "Don't ever delete those. I need you to send them to me."

He nods. "You got it."

We pull into the driveway, and he parks the Tesla in the garage, behind the BMW i8 and next to the DB11. Though it's nearly ten, I'm ready to go back to my own apartment. As we make our way into my house, Ben pushes me through the door. When I turn around to scold him, he plants his lips on mine.

I sense a slight buzz, not strong enough to be a tingle, but a reminder of the past. And I don't know whether it's the surprise of the kiss or the fondness of the memories, but I kiss him back.

Chapter Nineteen

It's Halloween. I'm supposed to be at Candy's house getting ready for a party. But am I? Nope. I'm right on my bed. After two weeks of parties with the sex reveal and the gala, I'm emotionally drained. A heavy weight pulls at my chest.

Last Halloween, my mom, dad, and I went to the hospital and passed out candy to the children's cancer wing. This year, I'm supposed to go out and celebrate as if nothing is wrong. Something *is* wrong. A constant worry boils beneath the surface of my skin.

The problem is I don't know how to fix it. I haven't been crying. But, the laugh track hasn't been playing either. I've just... existed, pushing away the worry as best I can. Forgetting that it exists when possible. Doing everything I can to avoid it.

Sorry, I guess this is one of the crappy episodes of my life. Every show has them.

My phone buzzes, and Candy's name appears on the screen.

"Hey," I answer.

"*Hola, muchacha.* You comin'?" Candy asks.

I pick at a throw pillow on my lap. "I'm not feeling too well. I think I may have to miss out on the party tonight. I'm sorry."

"Oh no, are you okay? Is it your knee again?"

Stop looking at me like that, okay?

I cringe at the myriad of excuses I've given everyone the past week. "Yep. Yeah, it's my knee. That workout really did a number on me." And by workout, I mean sitting in my pajamas, binge-watching *The Bachelor*. Not even the current *Bachelor in Paradise*. Nope, I went straight back to an oldie but goodie: Jason Mesnick. Anyway... "But you go and have fun! Call me after? We can have a sleepover."

A clatter sounds on the other end, and Candy curses. "Okay. You should ice it or something. Happy Halloween, Les!"

"Happy Halloween to you, too. Bye, Can-Can." I hang up, curling in on myself.

The child in me wants to call my mom since she's all that I have left. But if I do, she'll just ask if I'm experiencing one of my "moods."

For someone operating on the brain, she sure is clueless.

Ben hasn't sent me the videos of my dad, and pictures won't do on a day like this. It's a grief so strong you have to live in it, feel it, and bear it.

So instead of having fun, instead of being a regular college girl, I pull out my calculus book under the guise of studying. And for one moment, I let myself feel the weight of the world as my tears soak the pages.

But I have to push it away, so after draining my eyes of all moisture, I *do* study. My last quiz before the test is coming up. I can't fail it. If so, my internship really is gone. I'll have nothing.

I'll end up sacrificing love for zilch.

Even the thought of how my mother would respond to me failing my test is enough to make a sharp pain pass through my head. Yeah, I don't need that on top of everything else.

I pour myself into the equations, writing them out and working through them from every angle. It challenges me, pulls at my mind and makes my brain hurt, but it's a welcome pain. The equations require my full focus, dissolving the memories of my past.

Sadness becomes confusion, which becomes understanding. Seconds become minutes and minutes become hours. When I blink, I see derivatives. When I breathe, I mutter functions. My eyes strain from staring at small numbers and letters all night long.

I yawn and check the time. It's nearly midnight. My stomach growls, but a part of me thinks I should just fall asleep hungry. I'm exhausted, and my brain is mush.

At least I'm remembering some of what I learned. Maybe,

just maybe, I'll actually pass this last quiz, pushing me up over a C before the final. A girl can dream, right?

My phone vibrates, and I flinch. Candy's calling.

I clear my throat. "Hey!" I cringe at the sound of my raspy voice. "How's the party?"

Candy makes a strangled sob sound, but that can't be right because she doesn't *cry*...unless something happened to Carter.

Flashes of him passed out and unconscious fly across my mind. Did he have a severe low? Was Candy too distracted to see what was happening to him? I should've been at the party. No, no, no. This can't be happening. Not him. Certainly not when I'm away, unable to help. I know he's moved on. But *I* haven't. He's still on the forefront of my mind, and if he's out there, hurt, I'll break. "What happened? Is Carter okay?"

I hold my breath, biting on my lip until I'm sure it might bleed. My hands shake.

Candy sniffs. "C-Carter?"

My heart races as I throw off my notebook and bed covers, scrambling to put on pants for the first time today. "Where are you guys? I'm coming."

Candy shouts, "Screw Carter!"

I pause, leg halfway in and halfway out of my leggings. "What is going on?"

"Carter is gallivanting around with a bunch of women, so screw him!"

Welp, that's a shot to the heart. I sigh. "What's going on then? I thought you only cried over Carter."

"The problem is Tom! *Lo odio!*"

I let out a shaky exhale. "Okay, I don't know what that means."

"I hate him!" she screams. Then, she begins sobbing again. "I hate him. We were playing beer pong and he won. Some chick jumped onto Tom and began making out with him right in front of me. I'm so mad. So, so mad. I know I shouldn't be mad. But I am. And it's surge pricing for Uber," she cries.

"Babe, I'm sorry." I finish putting on my leggings and head out of my room into the kitchen. "Can I come pick you up? We'll forget this stupid holiday exists and drown ourselves in ice cream."

"Okay," she concedes. "I'll send you a pin."

My heart still pounds, hands still a bit wobbly. But this isn't a death or something bad. This doesn't involve my unrequited feelings for my best friend's brother. It's typical college drama. I can handle this. "See you soon."

∞∞∞

A pint of Ben & Jerry's Half Baked and my allergy-friendly Wink Cinnamon Bun later, we're lying on Candy's bed, watching a late night rerun of *The Nightmare Before Christmas.*

It isn't until the creepy green, candy-filled character comes on the screen singing his song that we hear Candy's apartment door open, footsteps shuffle, and close. She stiffens beside me, but there's no way for us to tell which guy, or guys, just came through the door.

Voices mumble down the hall, and I think I make out Carter and Jared, but the third is too hard for me to tell whether it's Tom or Rykard. But no matter who it is, I brush through her hair. "You know you're gonna have to face Tom at some point. You guys live together, Can-Can."

She waves me off, eyes not leaving the TV. "It's whatever. He can be with whoever he wants. We're not together."

I grab the empty ice cream container from her and set it on her nightstand, sitting up as I do so. "But even if you're not together, it can still hurt seeing him with someone else. Especially since you just kissed him not that long ago."

"It's not my place to be angry with him."

"Candy, this is not normal. You can't just 'save someone for later.' It's going to destroy you."

Rolling her eyes, she turns off the TV, then turns away from me. "*Y tú*? You say you're choosing yourself, that you ended things with both Ben and Carter because you wanted to succeed in your class. But that's a lie because you just kissed Ben, and your little freak out about Carter on the phone just proves you're not over him. You're the last person I should take advice from. Don't pity me, Les. I made my bed, I'll lie in it."

I have no idea how much she drank tonight, but even with that, where is this coming from?

"What the hell does that have to do with anything? I'm trying to help you. You get all bent out of shape whenever Tom does anything with another girl, but you won't lay claim to him yourself either. You're just as much of a hypocrite as I am. Don't call me out when you won't look at yourself. You have no idea what's going on behind the scenes with Ben." I get that she's hurt, but did she really have to say all that crap? Ben is Ben. I don't want to be with him. But most of the time, he's just…there. And he's so interwoven in my past that I can't unwind us. This is freaking dumb. I *know* I shouldn't have kissed him the other night. It was a mistake, but that was all it was.

She rolls over and glares at me, unshed tears shining against the nightstand light. "You want to talk about behind the scenes? I heard that Ben is seeing someone."

I laugh. "He's probably telling people I'm his girlfriend now. Ignore it!"

She shakes her head. "Not you. Someone else."

"Okay, well, that's a dumb rumor. He just proclaimed his love to me a few weeks ago. At the gala, he kissed me and said he'd wait until I was ready to start a relationship with him again. Trust me, he's not seeing anyone else. Not that it even matters. Believe me, I realized that mistake the second I kissed him. Not happening again. But we're not talking about me. We're talking about you!" She's beginning to piss me off.

Candy twists her hair and puts it on the top of her head in a bun. "Tom cheated on me. That's why we broke up. So stop pushing with all the Tom crap!"

My anger bleeds out and is replaced with shock and confusion. Why would Tom cheat on...You know what? That's her story, not mine. "I'm sorry. I didn't know."

"Yeah, well, now you do. I'd like to think that one day, after we've both run around enough and gotten everything out of our systems, that we can be together. That he'll have experienced enough that he won't cheat on me again."

I don't think that's how relationships work. And I've never seen Candy insecure like this. Tom hurt her...*bad.* "Have you even been with anyone else since him?"

She gives me a dead stare and points at herself. "*¡Claro!* I'm basically a Victoria's Secret model."

I shake my hand. "I mean, like, maybe? If you cut a model in half?"

It's enough that she lets out a small snort. "*Cállate.* I'm not that short." She shuts off the nightstand lamp, and I lay down.

Now that it's dark, she whispers, "For the record, I'm sorry. I know it's hard with Bruce because of your dad. I shouldn't have blurted out all of that. You're right. It probably is just some dumb rumor someone started."

"Ah, and I thought you finally gave up on not calling him odd names."

She reaches her hand out to me and slaps me until she finds my hand and squeezes. "And I know despite everything, you really are *trying* to choose yourself. You're pulling a Jenna, and I admire you for it. Girl power and all."

I fluff the pillow and settle in. She's starting to sound *really* drunk. Like, I probably shouldn't have trusted anything she said tonight drunk. "Jenna?"

"Yeah." She yawns loudly. "From *Bachelor in Paradise.* You know, how she had the two guys and she chose no one?"

Right...how did that episode even end? "Huh. You think she still has dirty thoughts about the guys though?"

Candy punches my arm. "*Dios mío,* gross. If you have dirty thoughts about my brother, keep them to yourself."

I laugh.

JESS CARPENTER

The conversation ends there, as it always seems to end on a random note when you're all partied out and tired. What seems like seconds later, Candy's soft snores fill the room. Nothing sounds beyond the door, so it looks like everyone else has finally gone to sleep for the night. I know I should sleep too, but I think my ice cream gave me a sugar rush.

All these thoughts are flowing through my mind with no rhyme or reason to them. When I close my eyes, it's as if I can see the cluttered landscape of my brain. I wasn't totally honest earlier. Last year, we did hand out candy in the cancer wing, but after that, I went to a party with Ben.

We fought halfway through because I wanted to go home, and he then called me out saying that I was never *any fun anymore*. Like, for real? Obviously, I wasn't fun. My dad was freaking dying.

This Halloween I haven't even heard from Ben. Besides seeing him in class, I've hardly talked to him at all. The last text I got from him was yesterday with a picture of St. Maarten asking me to shine up my bikinis and get ready.

Honestly, I don't want to go. But if I don't go, Ben's parents will probably throw a fit to my mom, who will then write me out of the will for disrupting the peace of the neighborhood and ruining her life by consorting with brown-skinned individuals.

Ugh, people are the worst. My *mom* is the worst.

I grab my phone and put on my sleep playlist—AKA Netflix's new murder documentary. It's about some dude who would skin his victims. The crazy part is that all his victims were his roommates. Hoping the murderer story will put me to sleep, I watch it for the next thirty minutes. But it backfires, because it's actually really interesting. Now, I'm wide awake.

I'm also kinda hungry. I didn't eat anything for dinner. Knowing that sleep isn't coming, I grab the empty ice cream pints and spoons then silently tiptoe down the hallway. All the doors are closed, and it's dark, silent, and slightly eerie. It's weird knowing other people are sleeping in this household.

Maybe I kinda like living alone.

I don't want to turn on the kitchen light and wake anyone, so I pull out my phone to use as a flashlight. I shine it toward the living room and pan across to the trash can.

Eyes glare at me from the corner of the kitchen.

I drop my phone and let out a garbled, "Gah!" It lands flashlight down, so I'm covered in darkness again. My socks slip on the tile as I careen to the door, ready to leave Candy and all the other hooligans without saying goodbye. I never should've agreed to sleep in apartment 13666. I knew it. This place is full of creepy ghost devils who probably think I'm a delicious sacrifice to Lucifer himself.

My knee bangs against the tile, which is why you should never wear socks to bed in case an emergency like this arises, so I army crawl my way to the door, knowing any second I'll probably be murdered. This is what I get for watching a murderer show on Halloween, the night that most murders occur.

Okay, fine, I made that statistic up.

Will anyone even miss me? My mom's crappy, Ben just wants me for my butt, and I'm sure Candy will be the next person murdered after me.

The kitchen light turns on.

"What. The hell. Are you doing?"

Nike socks are all I see as someone stands in front of me. I will myself to glance up, up, over the gaping boxers, and into the face of a very confused, very handsome, very non-murderous man.

I clear my throat. "Carter. Nice to see you at this hour."

"Is there a reason you're army crawling across the floor?"

Getting up on my hands and knees, I shake my head. "No, not particularly, no. Just, uh, wanted to make sure you all are vacuuming enough." I swipe my finger across the floor. "And it looks great. Nice job, really."

He crosses his arms. "*Qué chingados*. White people, I swear," he mumbles.

Should probably get up, so...I stand and cross my own arms,

realizing I'm definitely in sleep clothes and definitely not wearing a bra. "Fine. You scared me. I saw you lurking in that corner." I point. "So naturally, I thought I was about to be murdered."

"Oh yeah, that's a completely normal reaction." He deadpans. "I wasn't lurking. I was having a snack."

I sputter. "Who has a snack at," I glance at the microwave clock, "three in the morning?"

Carter scoffs. "Apparently, you!"

"Well, we just established I'm weird!" I lean against the kitchen island.

"You are." He chuckles.

"So are you."

He points at his Apple Watch. "I have an excuse. Just hit a low, needed something to bring it up so diabetes doesn't, you know, *actually* kill me. Unlike your fake murderer."

"Well, you might as well share your snack since I'm already here."

Opening his mouth and closing it like a fish, he then shakes his head and laughs. "On tonight's menu of Carter's Three AM Diabetes Scare, we have," he pretends to do a drumroll, "Halloween candy, a chocolate protein shake, and, you're in luck, peanut-free granola bars!"

"Wow, what an assortment."

He turns on his phone flashlight before shutting off the bright kitchen lights. I turn mine back on as well, and we put them face down on the counter, basking us in an unhealthy-looking blue glow.

Handing me a granola bar, he asks, "So, how was your Halloween?"

I tear it open. "Uh, well, I think I did enough studying for the whole calculus class. Definitely different than last year's Halloween, that's for sure. My dad was pretty sick then."

He pops an M&M into his mouth. "I'm sorry."

"Yeah."

"Are you doing okay?"

I don't know, am I? The granola bar feels sandy in my mouth. "I'd like to think it's getting easier. Not really sure that's true though." I rub at my eye. "Some days, it feels like I've accepted it. That he's not coming back. Other days, it's…hard. Lately, I've sort of hit a block it seems. Can probably chalk that up to major anxiety or something. Who knows." I awkwardly laugh.

Carter doesn't bristle when I say that. Instead, he just nods. "I'm sorry."

Clearing my throat doesn't help the mound that seems to be stuck in it. Even though it's easy to talk to Carter about this, it feels weird. Like I'm telling a secret that I shouldn't. He wasn't part of my little life-circle. Carter doesn't know all the pain that surrounded my dad's death. When we were together, I was happy to share. But now?

He doesn't need to know that I feel like a basket case most of the time because my mom acts like I have all of these issues. So, I change the subject. "Anyway, how about your Halloween? Spend it with that girlfriend? Heard you had a few ladies on your arms."

He cocks an eyebrow and takes a sip of his protein shake. "Girlfriend? Definitely not."

My little Grinch heart beats with excitement. "No girl-friend? How's Kriti?"

"She's still around. Just, not my girlfriend."

Grinch heart shrinks once more. "Oh, cool cool."

"So, you studied tonight? You ready for the next quiz?"

Blech, way to suck all the fake sexual tension I was picking up on out of the room. "Eh, I wouldn't go that far."

He shrugs. "You'll get the hang of it. My offer still stands if you want me to help tutor you."

I reach around him for another piece of candy. "*Gracias*, but no thanks. I don't think I could focus on the calc problems while around you." The words slip out effortlessly, which, duh, I'm an idiot. I should not be talking to him right now. I feel all bubbly and good and energetic, and I'm beginning to think something was in my ice cream.

Maybe I'm just a little relieved from seeing him. When Candy called, I was for real concerned. My feelings for Carter are definitely not going away. Not in the slightest. In fact, they've only grown.

He gulps the rest of his protein shake and tosses it into the trash next to the kitchen island. And because he's a college baseball pitcher, it easily goes in despite the room being dark. "Couldn't focus around me? *¿Por qué?*"

I glance away from his cutesy-boy smile because now I'm embarrassed. "Just...couldn't."

"Why?"

I can feel his stare on me, which isn't good, 'cause y'all, I'm getting those tingles. You know the ones. The really good, really strong tingles all over my freaking body. So, I do something stupid. I turn toward him and look into his eyes. "You know why."

He leans forward, barely a movement, but it puts us less than a foot apart. "I don't think I do."

"I still think about you." I shuffle my feet and move a few inches closer, nearly closing the gap between us. This is a bad idea. A voice in my head (and yes, it sounds like my mother) is telling me that I'm a bad person for wanting him. Because I can't want him and be successful in calc. Those two things don't coexist. It's me, or it's Carter.

But I've tried so hard to push him out of my head and out of my thoughts. It's not working. He's still there, like a favorite memory pulsing against my conscience.

"What kind of thoughts?" His head dips down, so he's talking right into my ear.

A shiver courses through me. "I don't know."

He doesn't move, and something tells me, deep down, that he's not going to. He's not going to be the one to close the final gap. To make that choice. It has to be me. I tentatively reach out my finger toward the palm of his hand. When I touch it, it's like a living energy. I feel it from the tip of my finger, up my arm, right into my stomach. I swallow to try and wet my dry throat.

"Carter, I think I made a mistake. I underestimated my feelings for you." By the time I get the words out, I'm breathless. I need him.

His finger intertwines around mine, and it makes me crave him more. I close the gap between us and our foreheads and noses touch, lips barely an inch apart. The air between us is warm and hot, and I want to take the breath from his mouth.

So, I do.

I reach my hands up to his cheeks and pull him into me. The kiss is heavy and frantic, as if we're making up for lost time. He tastes of unlimited possibilities and hope, wrapping me in a cocoon of warmth and the feeling of rightness.

I forget the worries and hardships and am filled with effervescent desire when his tongue meets mine. The kisses slow to become languid and peaceful, exploring. His hand travels from my hip up my back, pushing me closer into him. Our bodies fit together in a way that feels as if we were made for this exact moment.

Wrapping my arms around his neck, I part his lips with my tongue. He moans, pushing me up and onto the kitchen counter. My legs spread, and I push his hips into mine when I bind my ankles behind him.

I crave more, and I moan his name, breaking our kiss.

He pulls back slightly. With his lips still brushing against mine, he whispers, "You didn't make a mistake."

Everything stops as our chests push and pull against each other with our breaths.

"Wait...what?"

He exhales shakily and places me back on the floor. "It wasn't a mistake to press pause on things."

"What do you mean?" I'm too close to him to see the expression on his face.

"You deserve to get your dream, Les. I meant what I said that night. I don't want to get in the way."

My fingers go cold, and I wrestle out of his grip. "What? Why did you just kiss me then?"

He runs a hand through his hair, and I see a scrape on his elbow. "I don't know. Because you're you and because my blood sugar made me feel all…"

I glance toward the floor. Or, I mean to, but I get stuck on Carter's boxers. "What does that even mean?"

"I still like you. That doesn't disappear in *uno o dos días.*"

My heart is beating erratically, and I'm so confused I have no idea what anyone is thinking at this point. Commercial break? Scene reshoot? Literally anything to get me out of this?

"I still like you too!" I whisper-shout. "I'm sorry, what was your endgame here?"

He releases a breath that ruffles his hair. "My endgame was to get my blood sugar stabilized. I didn't plan for you to come out here, dressed in one of my old shirts, and make out with me. You're going to wake up in the morning and realize you've made a mistake."

No, I won't. 'Cause choosing Carter could never be a mistake. "And if I don't?"

With a groan, he says, "Five weeks, Les. That's all you have left of the semester. Don't ruin it."

"So, you're just gonna act like the kiss didn't happen? Go back to Kriti and all your other 'not girlfriend' girls?"

He leans against the counter. "You can't be mad that I'm moving on. What do you want me to say? Do you want me to claim that every time I'm with another girl I'm wishing it were you?"

Yes. But that's not fair to him.

"No. I don't know. I-I just…I don't know, okay? I miss you." I want to be *his.* I want him to be *mine.*

Gesturing to the side, he shakes his head. "I've been here. I've been your friend. I've stayed away. I've done everything you said you wanted."

"I don't want that anymore." This is getting uncomfortably vulnerable, but I don't even care. I want the best of both worlds. I want to pass calculus, make my parents proud, and be with Carter. I want it all. I want him. My throat clogs with emotion. "I want you," I whisper, my voice breaking.

He picks up his phone and shoves it into his pocket. "You know what *I* want? I want to stop playing tug-o-war with your mind, Les. Ugh. I deserve better than this."

He's right. I don't have anything to say to that. He does deserve better. And I made a mistake. I can't just want him back because he has someone new. It's not fair. All I've done is hurt him or get in the way of him moving on. It's not right.

Candy's words from earlier ring in my ears too. I said I was choosing myself, but I've still been playing with fire, keeping Ben and Carter on short enough leashes in case I change my mind.

I'm the problem here, not them.

Carter sighs. "You've got five weeks, Les. Finish it out and pass the course. I know how much it means to you and your family."

He begins to walk away, then runs his hands through his hair and turns around. "I'm sorry I kissed you. Are we cool?"

"Yeah." I bite on my lip. "Yeah, it's no biggie. We're cool."

Carter doesn't want me.

Totally cool.

I only have myself to blame.

Even cooler.

I repeat these like mantras in my brain.

From now on, I'm focusing on myself for real. He rejected me. It's over.

I don't need Carter.

As I watch him walk down the hallway and into his room, my heart still tries to reach for him. It's fine though, 'cause my brain shuts it down. Who needs a heart anyhow?

Chapter Twenty

I dunk the tea bag into my water and lean against my kitchen island. It's dreary today. Though all the curtains are open, gray still blankets the apartment from an overcast sky. November came with a vengeance, and the outside air is icy. It makes me even more tired.

It's been nearly a week. I feel fine. Hollow, but fine. Mostly, I focus on school. Nothing else holds my attention. I don't think too long or hard about anything. I guess that's what happens when you shut your heart off.

Call me the Tin Man. Or, wait, no. The Lion? I don't even know.

But today, something important has to be done.

I stayed up until three in the morning reading all about the different politicians and opinions because for the first time, I get to vote. Before this year, I never even gave it any thought. I blindly followed whatever my parents chose. Now? I know what I want to do. Candy and I are planning on going together today.

My phone vibrates like a jackhammer against the granite, jolting me out of my thoughts. Mom's name lights up the screen. I take a deep breath, trying to gather enough energy from around me to get through this phone call. "Hey, Mom. How are you?"

"Fine, Les."

A pause follows, and I'm not sure how to fill it. "So...what's up?"

Mom clears her throat. "Right. I just got off the phone with the head of the Marx campaign. They've invited us to their campaign celebration."

Come *on.* I'm so sick of hearing her name. "What is she celebrating? Voting hasn't closed yet."

"It's the close of the election. To celebrate her win, supposedly."

I don't want to fight with her, but I'm also not going to sit here and take it. "Yeah, don't think I'll make it with my last calculus quiz, unfortunately. You know how seriously I'm taking this class." Get her off topic, get her off topic.

"Of course. I will pass it along. And you believe you'll pass the course?"

"That's the plan, Mom." This time, I do smile. If I don't, she'll *hear it* and say something about me being disrespectful or something.

"Good. I don't need to remind you how important..."

A knock on my door muffles what she says.

"Hey, Mom? Someone's here. I gotta go. Love you." I hang up the phone before she can say anything else, which means that she's probably going to send me a passive aggressive text about it later.

I set my phone down and walk toward the door. Checking the peephole, I breathe a sigh of relief. Not really for him, but for the fact it's not an axe murderer or something. Don't roll your eyes at me. Everyone knows overcast days are perfect for crime.

I swing the door open, and Ben barges into my apartment. "Hey, I was in the neighborhood."

I cross my arms. "Sure, come right on in, why don't ya?"

He glances at his phone as I shut the door. "You been getting my texts?"

When he looks up, I smile sweetly. "Sure have. Guilt tripping me into going to St. Maarten. Is there anything better?" I bat my eyelashes.

Tossing me a smolder, he says, "Come on, babe—"

"Not your babe."

"—you know you want to come. Think of how much fun we'd have. Remember the last time we were there?"

I throw my hands up, make my way over to the couch, and sit down. He's got five minutes before I toss his butt out of here. "Of course, I remember. I love St. Maarten."

He nods and sits down next to me, folding one leg on the cushion so his knee butts into my thigh. "Remember the yacht?"

What normally would be a pull in my belly is now a roiling sickness. Yeah, I don't want a repeat of the yacht because I don't want to be with Ben. I never should've let it get this far. Now my mom is going to be pissed that I'm not jumping back into his arms. "Look, I don't think I can go on the trip with you. It'd send the wrong message. And that would leave my mom home alone on Thanksgiving."

He waves me off and shakes his head, which doesn't move a single coiffed hair. "Don't worry about that. She gave her blessing."

Of course, she did. "Yeah, but she'd never say no to you and your family. You know that. I think that deep down, she'd want to spend Thanksgiving with me."

His voice goes high-pitched. "Do you? 'Cause it's not like she's been that happy with you lately."

Um, yeah, cue the *is he kidding?* from the crowd because for real? This is so not his place. I can feel my face pinching, and a brief flash of *something* crosses his eyes as if he actually knows he made a mistake for once.

He places his hand on mine, and it feels clammy. "I didn't mean it like that. I really want you to come. I *need* you to come. How am I supposed to be there with my parents alone? Les, come on, you know I can't do this without you."

Now his face is pretty genuine. His lips purse as his brown eyes swirl with pleading. But this is a classic case of if you give a rich kid a dollar, he's gonna bankrupt you a million.

I do empathize with him. Being there with his parents is going to suck. So...why would he want me to have to endure that too?

Squeezing my hand, he says, "With you, we can do our own

thing. If I'm alone, I'm going to be stuck in the middle. Please, Les. We've always been there for each other."

We've always been there for each other. Have we? He wasn't there after we broke up. He didn't show up to my dad's funeral. But now he wants *me* to be there for him? Every time I broke down about my dad this semester, Ben *has* been there. But he just insulted me earlier too. So, do I really owe him this?

No.

I give him just enough so he'll get off my back. "I'll think about it."

His face splits into a smile. He's handsome and charming, but he's also easy. That's literally all I can think about. Life with him is no challenge. Our families love each other, we know everything about each other, we'd have no highs. We'd have no lows. It would just be mediocre.

I don't want mediocre.

My mom's voice in my brain says *yes! This is the best thing for you!* But my brain's a liar because we broke up for a reason.

I'm inching my hand away slowly from his, and when he leans in to kiss me, I turn my head to the side and cough. "Sorry, I don't feel that great."

He flinches away from me like I just said I had leprosy. "Oh. Why didn't you say something before letting me in?"

"I didn't let you in," I mumble.

Ben continues as if he didn't hear a word I said. "I better head out. You need anything?" He's already up from the couch and walking toward the door. "I don't want you to spread it to me. No point in us both being sick. Happy to get something delivered here for you, though."

And the sight of him recoiling after one cough is enough to almost make me laugh, but I stomp it down and put on a sober face. "No, hopefully it's just allergies or something. Thanks though."

"For sure." He points at me. "Remember what I said about the trip, 'kay? What better way to rekindle this blossoming romance than a hot yacht?"

"It's not a blossoming romance!"

With a smile, he says, "You know we still love each other."

"That's not—"

He's out the door before I can finish saying, "Yo, Ben. Actually, no I'm not going on the trip, and I'm breaking up with you even though we're not really together-together."

Obviously, only the studio audience hears me, and Ben is long gone, but at least I said it. Blowing out through my mouth to make my lips vibrate, I realize how dumb all of this is. I feel like the Grinch where he screams, *I'm an idiot!* But instead of a yodeler yelling back *you're an idiot!* it's my studio audience saying it.

It's okay, I forgive you. I'm calling myself stupid too.

I get up, grab my phone, and press Candy's contact.

It rings twice and then, "*Qué tal*, boo?"

"That's exactly how I wanted to start the phone call."

She laughs. "You ready to go vote?"

A warmth spreads across my chest because this is the one thing I feel sure about. I've picked all of my choices, I put the time in, and I get to vote for the people I think are best. Not who my mom thinks is best, and not who anyone else does. It's like it's the one thing in my life that I can control. And truthfully, had you asked me six months ago, I probably would've had a different answer to who I'm voting for today.

"I'm ready." I smile. "You want to drive or should I?"

"I'll come to you. Today's been weird over at Candyland."

I thought she'd given up on calling the apartment that. And what does she mean by weird? "Alright. Text me when you're here."

∞∞∞

I put the "I voted" sticker on my thumb and thrust my thumb out with a kissy face for the photo.

Candy snaps it. "Ew, no. *Uno más.*"

After *three* more, she posts it to her Twitter and Instagram. She's up to like half a million followers, which is insane, but I don't blame any of those people because she's pretty cool.

She turns toward me and places a hand on my shoulder as if she's going to tell me some lifechanging thing. "We're having a game night at our house. If it's too much for you, you don't have to come. But if you want to, *está bien*. It's just gonna be the roomies. Plus you, if you want."

It's getting dark, which should be a sin because it still feels like it's early. Stupid daylight savings. But, as much fun as a game night sounds, it sounds more fun to not be publicly hanged, and that's probably what my mom will do if I don't pass my test. So... "I would. But we have that calc quiz coming up. Last one before the final, and I'd really rather not fail. Think I'm going to call in a last-minute tutoring session for the weekend."

"No, come on!" Dropping her hand, she cocks her head and gives me a small smile. "What if we make game night a study session?"

I look away, feeling the blush crawling up my neck. "I'm not sure I want to be around Carter right now."

She sighs. "Come on! Hoes before bros!"

"That is definitely not how that saying goes." I laugh. "Candy, believe me, we did not end things on good terms the other night."

Waving me off, she says, "I know. He told me all about it. *Mira*, wouldn't it be more beneficial to work with others on calc problems? You can only learn so much by yourself."

She's making me give up. Surely, I can avoid Carter. Old lady tutor or hot guys teaching me calc? I might regret this, but the choice is clear. "Fine."

She squeals, her pink hair floating up and crashing back on her shoulders as she jumps. "*Vámonos!*"

It's as if she's filled with some kind of voter-high, and I guess for an activist like her, she probably really is. It's contagious, and we half-run, half-walk toward the car. We get in, and she blasts the music the whole way to her apartment. It reminds me a bit of the day we met.

"Do you still carry mace in your bag?"

She cackles. "Duh. And if you don't, you should. People are creeps."

Her car backfires as we pull into the parking lot, but I'm so used to it now that I hardly react. I mean, I react a little bit, but not shove my head down to my knees sort of react. The moment we open the door to the apartment complex, muffled shouting comes from the end of the hallway.

"Uh, what's going on?" I ask, following her now-brisk pace down the hallway.

She rolls her eyes and sighs. "Today's been weird all day long. It's like the guys are working out some strange bro-hierarchy or something. I think Jared and Rykard are fighting, and they never fight."

"What's up with those two? I always pick up on some tension between them, but then Rykard hooks up with someone else."

Shrugging, she says, "*No sé.* Those two are either gonna be endgame or burn this apartment to the ground."

With each step, the shouts get louder. Candy pushes open the door to Rykard pointing at Carter, shouting, "I know he's mafia, and he's a liar!"

Carter hangs his head then turns his attention toward Rykard. "I told you, man, I'm a civilian."

Okay, so, this looks like a normal night. Just a couple of guys shouting at each other, playing Mafia.

"*Hola,* party people. I brought our favorite girl." Candy squeezes me.

Jared smiles and waves, Rykard lifts a hand, and Tom raises his brows.

"'Sup, Les?" Carter nods, and it takes me a little by surprise 'cause we haven't talked in the past week. Our gazes lock for a second too long, but that's all I get, and he's back into the game. Butterflies tickle my stomach, but I push them down because I'm not a masochist.

Tom rubs at his temples. "Time's almost up. I'm calling it. Carter's the liar. We all know he's mafia."

But Jared is sitting on the couch, super quiet, which is *super* suspicious.

The phone in the center of the coffee table says, "It's time to make your guesses."

Everyone turns on Carter, and he just shakes his head lowly. "You're all *idiotas.* I'm not freaking mafia."

I shut the door behind me and watch as the rest of the game plays out. They flip over their cards. Jared laughs like he's Maleficent, and Rykard gasps in horror. Carter groans, and Tom slams his hand on the table.

"Why are you surprised?" Candy asks, sitting down next to Carter. "It's always Jared."

I sit down next to the mafia man. "But Jared looks so innocent. Just look at this little face." I squeeze his cheeks together, and he plants a kiss on my forehead.

"The man is six-three. He's not little," Carter points out with a lopsided grin.

Candy rubs her palms together and juts out her chin, smiling an evil smile. "I have a request for game night."

All the guys groan in-sync with various forms of, "What do you want?"

"Our *chica,* Les, here, needs some of our help. You see"—she stands up grandly to her full height—"she is struggling with an evil nemesis of us all. *La clase de* calculus."

Carter rubs at his eyes. "*Dios mío.* Is this gonna be a whole 'thing?' If so, I need a snack break."

She spins gracefully and turns her nose up as if she's some 1920s detective. "You may gather your snacks, but if, and only if, you agree to help create calculus games to help our girl study for the upcoming quiz."

He glances at me (and I think my bones melt) then he glances back at Candy (and my bones work again) and then back at me (bones are now jello). "Fine. Only because I feel like it's my duty as the class TA. Come up with the plan. Les, help me grab snacks?"

And because I'm a glutton for punishment, I forget to say no. "Um, sure."

"*¡Perfecto!*" Candy turns toward the other guys and starts planning a game.

I follow Carter into the kitchen, knees shaking because why does he want to talk to me? This is A-W-K awkward.

He tosses and glance at me, his gaze roving from my head to my toes, but he's not checking me out, he's obviously questioning why the hell I'm here. And that smolder in his eyes is not a smolder but rather an annoyed glare. Then his ogling catches on my wrist, where the bracelet he gave me for my birthday is. Something passes across his face, but I don't know what it means. It almost looks like he's mad that I still have it on. It's gone in a second, and his face is back to neutral. "So, about the other night."

My gaze shutters. "Can we not relive my most mortifying moment, please?"

When I open my eyes, he just stares at me, and that same expression is on his face. Mad? Annoyed? I don't know. But finally, after our impromptu stare off, he nods once and clears his throat. "So, snacks. Whatcha in the mood for, *señorita*?"

Cool, so now my knees aren't working. Apparently I'm a cliché, because he calls me *señorita*, and I'm all goo-goo-gah-gah for him. Being here is dangerous. He just rejected me. And here I am all up in my feels. "Uh, um, you know, whatever."

He sidesteps around me to the fridge and reaches above to the cabinet. A little piece of skin shows right above where his pants sit and oh, Les, focus. Say it with me: *FOCUS!*

We will not be swayed by hot abs, brown skin, and a delicious smelling body. No, no, we will not. Especially when we made a fool of ourselves in front of him by begging for him back.

Grabbing some popcorn, he asks, "You have Thanksgiving

plans?"

He hands me two packs, and I check the label to make sure it doesn't contain peanuts as he opens the bags. "Um, yeah, I guess. I'm gonna hang out with my mom. Not really sure what we'll do though with it being our first Thanksgiving since my dad died." I internally shrink away from the "d" word. It's so harsh and final.

"Aw, *lo siento.*" Here comes the pity. It's written right in his eyes.

I wave him off.

We stare at each other, and once again, I have no freaking idea what he's thinking. "If you change your mind about going home for Thanksgiving, I know Candy would be down to have you at our house. We make *tamales, pozole, menudo,* and a few different American dishes too. Otherwise. my mom would flip." He rolls his eyes, but he does it with a grin because his mom is awesome—unlike mine.

It's funny how easy it is for me to *want* to go with Carter and Candy to their house. Except, he didn't invite me. He said *Candy* would be down to have me. I smile, knowing that I won't make it. "So, we've got popcorn. What else?"

"After the day we had here today, I'm inclined to say we juice up their food with laxatives. You know, to get the bull-shit out of them."

I snort. "Oh my gosh, did you just make a joke?"

He flips non-existent hair, and I immediately know what's coming. "Um, duh, I'm like, so funny," he says with his best valley girl accent.

I playfully slap him with the bag of unpopped popcorn. "I do not sound like that!"

With his hands up in surrender, he raises his brows twice. "Never said you did." Then he goes to the microwave and puts three bags of popcorn in at once.

"Gah! Take those out! You can only do one at a time."

His face pinches up. "No, that can't be right."

I growl and take the extra popcorn out myself, shutting the

microwave door before pressing the popcorn button with *one* bag in the microwave. "Candy would've been pissed had you blown up Candyland."

"But, I probably could've pushed the calc quiz off for a few days while we recovered in the hospital."

I make a grab for the bags. "Give me the popcorn back!"

He laughs and holds it way higher than I'll ever be able to reach. "Are you for real worried about the quiz?"

My shoulders slump with the mention of the stupid test. "How about we change the subject. What happened here at Candyland today?"

"Eh, something happened between Jared and Rykard. It'll blow over in a few days like always." He points at me. "Your turn. Last I heard, you'd been studying pretty hard. You're still worried?"

I ignore the fact that he might be keeping tabs on me. In reality, it's probably just Candy's loud mouth spilling too much. "Yes. It's the last one before the final, and you've seen my grade."

"Believe it or not, Les, I don't actually memorize everyone's grades. *Pero,* that's what I'm here for as the TA. You know I'm down to help you." He ruffles my hair, and I just sarcastically laugh while I die inside 'cause, *hey y'all,* I'm back in the friend zone.

He grabs a bowl from one of the cabinets and sets it down on the counter. But...the bowl is covered in like a thousand Nicolas Cage faces. This apartment is so random.

I point at the million Nicolas Cage faces. "Let me guess. You and Tom?"

Pouring the popcorn into the bowl, his lips quirk up. "We do a big white elephant gift exchange every year. I don't know why, but Nicolas Cage seriously creeps me out. So naturally, Tom decided to give me this bowl."

I tsk. "Girlfriends assaulting you with cinnamon, roommates giving you bowls of fear. Carter DeLeón, I think you need better friends."

"Hey," he throws a piece of popcorn at me, "ex-girlfriends. Now, what's an inflection point in a function, and how would you find it?"

Funny that he assumes I know that off the top of my head. Who stores random calculus information in their brains? I scrunch up my nose and yank the popcorn bowl from him. "Oh boy, you have your work cut out for you."

Chapter Twenty-One

As I sit down to take the last calculus quiz before my final, flashes of calculus game night go through my head.

We played Go Fish with calculus problems, and I think it actually kinda worked. We had to solve the equations and ask everyone else for the answers to make a pair. It took forever. Like, way longer than playing Monopoly.

I've had four more tutoring sessions with my mom's tutor this week. I'm feeling good.

Good enough that I also decide today is the day—I'm officially going to end things with Ben. He's been hounding me like crazy over the stupid Thanksgiving trip, and I'm not going. First of all, I don't want to be with him. Ben's charming and cute, so spending a week together sharing a yacht room while I'm mourning the loss of Carter? Ha, yeah, no thank you. Second of all, I don't want to be in the middle of his parents' affair and working their crap out. Can you say awkward?

We need a clean break. No being friends. *Nothing.*

Maybe for once in my life, I'm prepared for the day. I'm gonna crush it so hard.

Candy groans and lifts her head from the desk. "You're gonna crush what so hard?"

Hold up, is Candy my studio audience? Can she read my mind?

Her voice sounds full of sleep when she says, "Les, you just mumbled that you're gonna crush it so hard. What the hell are you talking about, and why are you crushing anything so hard this early in the morning?"

Note to self: Stop mumbling thoughts aloud. "The test." I look around the room and everyone is focused on their own stuff, so I add in a whisper, "And I'm gonna kick Ben to the curb today."

She gasps so strongly that her hair gets caught in her mouth and she sputters. "My prayers have been working. *Gracias Madre María.*"

I laugh. "Thank you for keeping me in your prayers, Father Candy."

Professor Butler sets down a stack of papers and the class snaps to attention like a rubber band. "Before we start, I want to remind you all that next week's classes will be study sessions for the final. With Thanksgiving being so late this year, the study sessions will be your second to last opportunity to study. After the break, we'll have one more study session before you take the final." She grabs a whiteboard marker and writes. "Your final's been scheduled for Friday, December 5th at 10 AM."

A shiver laces down my spine. No, I'll be ready for the test. All I have to do is pass calculus. It's not like I need an A. Not even a B. I just need to pass so I don't get put on academic probation. With all my other classes being As, my GPA won't suffer *that* much.

Carter heads to the front of the class and grabs the scantrons from Professor Butler (who cheeses like a little girl when he smiles at her) and begins handing them out. When he gets to us, he tosses a scantron to Candy, and she scrambles to stop it from sliding off the table. "*Idiota,*" she mumbles, but Carter just chuckles.

He hands one to me, and his hand accidentally brushes against mine. I quickly pull back. At the last tutoring session, he had mentioned he was going out with Kriti afterward, so I guess things are back on with them. Or maybe they were never off. Our late-night kiss on Halloween doesn't count. Please, I can't even remember half of it.

(Stop looking at me like that, okay? I can remember it, I lied.)

Professor Butler passes out the actual tests, and when I turn mine over, the heavens part. Or my studio audience really knows how to hit a note because there's a choir singing *Hallelujah!* in my ear.

I KNOW THE ANSWER TO THE FIRST QUESTION!

And the second...not the third...but the fourth, yes. And it goes on like that for the rest of the test. I'll spare you all the calculus details, but like I said earlier, I'm freaking crushing it.

I even turn my test in before Candy. Texting her that I'll meet up with her later, I head out toward the library, filled with renewed purpose. I don't know what I was so worried about. I've never failed before. Why would I suddenly start failing classes now?

Okay, I'm giving myself too much credit. Step aside arrogance. Buckling down and not getting (too) distracted by hot men is probably the reason for my most recent success.

I'm so entrapped in my personal monologue that I tune everyone else out.

Until I slam into an old man holding a cup of iced coffee. It spills in an explosion of ice and mocha, drenching my long sleeve white shirt in cold brown liquid as I fall to my butt on the ground.

"Oh. My. Gosh." It's already cold outside. Now? I brush off ice and shiver. "I am so sorr..." The words die in my throat as I glance up.

Graying brown hair. Light blue eyes with wrinkles. Slight bump in the bridge of his nose. A polo tucked beneath a cashmere sweater. Tailored jeans with brown leather dress shoes. He looks...who is this guy?

"Are you okay, miss?" He holds out a hand to help me up, a kind smile on his face.

I slowly shake my head. "I, uh. I'm sorry. I shouldn't have been...been uh, walking, so...so fast. And I, um, yeah..."

A lump in my throat won't go away. I can't swallow it, and it almost feels as if my airways are closing. But I haven't had any peanuts. Okay seriously, I can't breathe. My breaths are whistling, and each inhale is shaky. "Were there peanuts in that?"

He shakes his head. "No, it's keto iced coffee. Are you okay?"

It feels as if a hundred pounds is crushing my chest, and the man keeps asking me if I'm alright. Why does everyone ask if I'm alright?

I'm not alright. *I can't freaking breathe.*

I stand up without touching his hand, picking my bag up off of the concrete. I have to get out of here. I need to get away from him. He looks like the past, like all of my memories.

He looks like my dad.

A whimper escapes my mouth as I push on my chest and speed walk away, not daring to look back. I hear him call out "Miss!" a few different times.

To my car. I just need to make it to my car.

Am I dying? My head spins, and each breath is like breathing through a straw. As I stumble down the library steps and into the parking lot, my vision blurs. My eyes close, and I put out a steadying hand to balance myself.

Breathe.

In.

Out.

Breathe.

But it's not helping. I rip my keys from my bag, pressing the unlock button, and shuffle to my car. I yank on the handle and get in the driver's seat. My hands begin to shake.

My dad. How did he look so much like my dad? I bring my trembling hands in front of my face. Each breath takes three inhales. I put my forehead on the steering wheel and squeeze my eyes shut.

I feel the two tears fall down each side of my face. I focus on the feeling, of the now, and try to breathe without my heart failing. It stutters in my chest, like it can't catch up with my brain. My whole body is on fire and freezing at the same time.

This isn't an allergic reaction. It's something else.

Panic.

I should've seen it coming. Seen the signs. Anxiety's been creeping up on me the past few months, and each time, I've shut it down.

A horn honks, jolting me. I look over my shoulder and there's a guy in a red truck waiting for me to back out of my spot. One more deep breath and then I back out of the spot, still shaking and shivering as I drive.

And I drive.

I drive through the shaking breaths and the painful heart palpitations. I drive through the shivering and the nausea. I drive, and I drive, and I drive. Because focusing on the road helps me forget what's causing this panic in the first place.

Hours. I think I'm gone hours by the time I pull into the gravel parking lot of the cliff that overlooks the city. The one I came to with Carter months ago. The sun is setting, shimmering warm oranges and pinks against the clouds, and I stare at it until my eyes burn. Until tears form and stream down my face again. They mix with the tears of sadness and hurt and frustration and anxiety until my cheeks are wet and sticky with salt.

I'm not sure I blink until the sun disappears and the sky is bathed in gray. And it's then that I can breathe. When the sun has gone and left behind nothing but shades of black and white, colors devoid of emotion. When the sky matches the empty shell of me, my breath returns.

I don't understand. How do you go from doing so well to so terrible in seconds?

I sniffle and wipe my nose with my sleeve. I inhale and smell the coffee, remembering. My lips quiver, but the tears are gone. There's not enough water in my body to produce them at this point.

These past few months, I've been prancing around, trying to be happy.

Was it all an act? 'Cause I can't even get through a run-in with a middle-aged man, so something must be wrong with me. It's been months since I last went to therapy. Maybe Judy helped more than I thought.

Is this what grief is? Is it mountains and valleys and insurmountable hope for a better future that never comes?

Will I always struggle like this? Will I be anxious, worry all the time, and forever be branded as the "anxiety-ridden girl?"

I'm in the trenches of it right now. It's usually easy to get out of them, but the doppelgänger was like an electric shock to my triggers. The second his voice reached my ears, I recoiled. Because it wasn't my dad's voice. But the real reason is I don't even think I remember what Dad's voice sounds like anymore.

When two cars pull up beside me, filled with teens ready to have actual fun–bonfires and laughing and everything normal college students do–I leave.

The last thing I want to do is taint someone else's fun with my anguish.

A week goes by. The box of my dad's things lies in the corner of my living room. They're the last things I have from him. Some photos of my father and me in their frames, a few pieces of his clothing, and his coat. It all mocks me. They'll never be enough. None of it matters. None of it is him.

I want him here. I need him to give me advice, to laugh when stupid stuff happens to me, and to joke when I don't feel like laughing.

I want to erase the last few months, forget all of the stupid decisions I've made, and just, I don't know. Just redo it all.

Do you have one of those movie-clapping-things? Where I can yell, *cut!* and we can reshoot the past few months? Look at me, still talking to you all as my studio audience. Maybe I really am crazy.

I take a shaky inhale.

Will I ever get better? This whole semester showed I can't be trusted with making decisions. Back, forth, back, forth. If my mom isn't whispering in my ear, who even am I?

A fool.

"you were good to me" by Jeremy Zucker and Chelsea Cutler plays for the tenth time. Pretty sure my Alexa is getting sick of me asking her to replay the song.

I collapse onto the couch and pull out my phone, mindlessly scrolling through Instagram. Anything to get my mind off of the itchy feeling inside of me.

A throwback photo with me and Candy at the hot springs back in September is the first thing on my feed. I forgot how demanding she was that night, but I guess it worked because Rykard took a good picture. Maybe I'll have her send me the others.

I come across a photo of Sheila from high school. She had her baby and is apparently "so happy" and "so in love" with her new husband. Awesome.

Then there's a photo of Kriti and Carter, smiling—wait, what? I scroll back up. Kriti uploaded a photo of her and Carter yesterday, smiling at a basketball game. Cool. Literally, so cool. I dumped an awesome guy, then he rejected me, and now he's with an awesome girl. And if she's uploading a photo to Insta, that pretty much means they're official.

An awesome, *freaking* couple.

So glad that everyone is so happy! And yes, I'm obviously being sarcastic. Can't you tell?

I groan because all of this is my fault. Karma is back to bite me in the butt, apparently.

My phone dings with a text from Ben telling me he called my mom. *Freaking kiss ass.* So I missed a few classes...and didn't respond to any of his messages. But who cares? He's not my boyfriend. So why the hell is he meddling?

And what's my mom going to do anyway? The only thing she did back in March was push me into Judy. Not once did she talk to me about Dad's death. She compartmentalized and forced me to deal with it on my own.

If she found me crying, I was "weak." If she saw me staring off into nothing, I was "depressed." If for whatever reason I actually tried to talk to her, I was dealing with a "manic episode."

Mother of the year, everyone.

But now she's calling me, and like Pavlov's dogs, I answer. "What?"

I can feel her bristle through the phone because I'm the most disrespectful person in the world. "Ben called and said you were upset again. What is it about this time, Les?"

"I'm fine, Mom."

"So you'll be going to St. Maarten with the Maldons?"

I snort, but it sounds like a cry. "No. I don't want to leave you on Thanksgiving."

"Don't worry about me."

I'm gonna lose it. I want to say something stupid like *okay, boomer,* but obviously I can't do that. "Look, Mom, I'm sad because I miss Dad. It's our first Thanksgiving without him, and I don't want to spend it with my ex-boyfriend and his family. I want to spend it with *my* family. What don't you get about that?" The second the words leave my mouth, I flinch. "I'm sorry. I'm sorry, I didn't mean that. I-I just, I don't know. I'm having a hard time. Ever since I ran into Ben this semester, it's like things somehow came back."

Tears stream down my face. I need her to be there for *me.* Not for Ben. Not for the stupid rich people in our neighborhood or dumb political parties.

She sighs. "It's childish to try and blame your state of mind on another person. If you're struggling, then maybe you need to see Judy again. Or maybe you need something stronger. Is that what you want?"

I guess she's right. I shouldn't be blaming things on Ben. He's been here every time I broke down about my dad. "Okay, just forget it. I'm fine," is all I have to say.

A knock sounds on my door, once again saving me from her. "Mom, I have to go. Someone's here. And knowing how you two work in sync, it's probably Ben." I wipe at the tears on my face. "I'll see you soon."

I end the call and walk to answer Ben, my sweatpants dragging on the floor. But when I swing open the door, it's definitely not Ben.

It's a short, redhead chick with pinched lips and fidgeting hands.

"Uhh, hi?" I cross my arms over my shirt because I'm definitely not wearing a bra.

She looks to her side and then back at me. "Are you Les?"

"That's me."

"Can I come in?" she asks.

I should say no. I don't even know her name, but it's freezing outside, and I'm pretty sure my nipples could cut glass, so I sidestep and let her walk past me like the doormat I've reverted to.

"So, not that I mind girls dropping by my apartment, but like, who are you?" I stay near to the closed door just in case I need to make a run for my life. She's like three inches shorter than me, so I'm pretty sure I could take her.

"Right. I'm Alice." She fidgets her hands once more.

If she thought I'm supposed to know who she is then she's smoking something. "Ookay, Alice, nice to meet you."

She nods, and it bounces her auburn curls. She tucks a few strands behind her ear where multiple earrings line the cartilage. "This is so awkward." She then proceeds to laugh, *awkwardly*. "Um, so I was told that you're Ben's ex."

I frown and straighten my shirt out. "Sorry, but where are you going with this?"

"Right." She pulls her phone from the back pocket of her jeans and presses the side button so the lock screen shows. It's a photo of her and Ben, her hand over his heart, him with a backwards baseball cap, standing close together. Like, really close.

I rear back a bit, but then I scoot forward because what the hell? Is this legit? "I'm sorry, who are you?"

"Alice," she says slowly, like I'm a child. Normally, I'd give her side eye, but I'm dressed one step above homeless and keep asking her weird questions. "Ben's girlfriend."

Chapter Twenty-Two

Ben...has a girlfriend?

"Ha, no way." I laugh, but then remember that Alice can hear me laughing and zip my lips. "Didn't mean it like that. But, um, I really hope you're not Ben's girlfriend?"

She swipes up and taps on the screen. Facing it forward, she goes through photos of them at a football game, golfing, dressed up for Halloween, *kissing in a bedroom,* and a thousand other things.

But there's no way. I mean, he uploaded videos of me to his TikTok! Is this woman an idiot? How did she not know about me?

And then everything else dies in my mind because *hello,* how did I not know about her? This is...not something I was prepared for. Like, what do I even say to her?

I take a step back because now I'm suddenly scared this girl came to cat-scratch me. "Who did you think I was?"

She shrugs. "Friends. I know you two are still in contact. But...then he told me that you're going on a family trip with him and his parents, and it seemed weird. So while he was in the shower this morning, I looked at some of his texts between the two of you, and he called you 'babe.'"

Oh honey, he did a lot more than call me babe. "Oh. Um, okay. Uh..." I'm having a hard time putting all of this together. He's been over here so much. He's been everywhere. How could he have a girlfriend?

I put the heels of my hands into my eyes and press *hard.* Ugh. This is not happening. "Why aren't there photos of you on his Instagram at all?"

She furrows her brow. "There are." She goes to his account

and shows me the photo of her lying down, him taking a body shot off of her.

Oh, so she's the girl I cried over this past summer. Super *kewl.* "But, that was like, months ago."

"Yeah...well, he's a TikTok-er, so, there's more of me on there. We started dating when he was out here for spring training."

Hold up, what? "Like, back in freaking March?" While my dad was *still alive?* How did no one mention this to me? He cheated on me.

Alice puts her phone away. "Yes, back in March."

It echoes in my head like a chant. *He cheated on me. He cheated on me. He cheated on me.* And here I was, feeling bad that I didn't want to get back together when he seriously cheated on me while we were still together in high school. "But no one knows about you!" I shout.

Apparently that was not the right thing to say because she scowls. "Who is 'no one'?"

Um, all of my friends who are on the baseball team with him? I'm not handling this well, I know, but *what the hell is going on?* I catch myself playing with my bracelet and drop my arms to my side. My head spins as I try to think back to those weeks after spring training. The last days I spent with my dad were always spent with Ben too. Ben, the same guy who came over the night Dad died and held me for six hours straight as I sobbed, cheated on me two weeks before. And I never had any clue. I glance back at Alice, who casually twirls her hair, like she doesn't know she just gutted me.

I clear my throat. "The baseball team. None of them have mentioned an Alice at all."

She gives me a wry smile. "Yeah, I'm more of a football and basketball girl. I don't think I've met any of them."

My brow furrows. "What about his roommates?"

"He's in the athletic dorms. Rooming with Jay and Alex. Basketball team."

I lick my lips, but my tongue is dry. "You should break up

with him."

She flinches. "Um, who the hell do you think you are? I'm not breaking up with him."

I run my hand through my hair. "He told me he loved me."

Now she's looking at me as if she's concerned for *me*. Like she pities *me*. "He would never."

Well so much for women solidarity. "Sis, you're the one who came to me. Why would I lie?" Especially when my whole world is dropping out from underneath me. Ben's scum. But how did I not see this? Am I really that stupid? "Look Alice, I don't know why you came here if you think you know everything."

"To make sure you weren't a threat." She looks me up and down. "And once I saw you, I realized you weren't."

"Um, ouch. First of all, if you're together with Ben, you should be having this conversation with *him*. Not me. This is his fault, not ours. And by the way, I've been mourning my dad's death, okay? Sorry that I'm in sweatpants."

Alice smiles as if it pains her to do so and shakes her head. "Honey, it's not the sweatpants."

My jaw literally drops. Did she just call me...ugly? Don't get too excited. I'm not going to fight with the girl. Apparently, her and Ben both suck.

I take a deep breath and try to exhale her negativity. I'll deal with the ugly comment later. "Well, I appreciate you coming here even though your intentions were backwards AF and also sort of creepy."

She opens her mouth to speak, but I hold a finger up. "And you can rest assured I will not be going to St. Maarten with Ben and his family."

"Thank you." She smiles. "I appreciate you keeping your distance."

I grin back, but I know I'm overselling it. Don't lie, *you* love this drama. "Sure. Now, please, for the love of all that's holy, get the hell out of here and forget my address. 'Kay thanks."

Her gaze is screaming *you're crazy*. And maybe I am a little crazy, but I'm pretty sure *she's* the weird one. Alice stomps away, out of my house, making sure to slam the door loud enough to rattle the picture frames behind me.

I run back to the couch and pick up my phone, pressing Candy's contact in my Favorites. It rings twice and, "*¿Qué pasa, cabrona?*"

"I've ruined my life," I whine. Had I known Ben cheated on me in March, I never would've been in half the positions I've been in this semester.

She tsks. "Well, we're awfully dramatic today, *eh?*"

"Ben cheated on me."

"I mean," Candy's voice gets high pitched, "did he? I thought you didn't like him."

"No! Back when we were still together. Before my dad died, he came out here for spring training, and he cheated on me."

She whistles. "*¿Qué mierda?* You're for real?"

"Apparently." I throw my hands in the air, but forget that I was holding the phone and it clatters into my lap. I scramble to pick it back up. "His *girlfriend* of *several months* just showed up at my place."

"His *novia? ¿Tiene una novia?* What the hell!"

"You were right. He is seeing someone. But it isn't new. It's been going on since March."

"*Dios mío.* I wouldn't have thought that *pinche* boy had it in him."

"It's not a freaking badge of honor, Candy!" I groan.

She laughs sarcastically. "Yeah, yeah, I know. What're you gonna do?"

I lie down on the couch. "Forget the coward ever existed? Throw a pity party to end all pity parties?"

"No." A noise like metal hitting metal comes through the line.

"No, what?" I pout, even though I know no one can see me.

"*Ay, pobrecita.* You are not throwing a pity party for Ben. You're going to get out of this funk, sit your white ass up, and wait for me to pick you up so that you can go tell this *pinche pendejo* off!"

Her anger makes me smile the slightest bit. "I can't. I don't even know where he lives. Plus, I don't want to tell him off. I want to cry about how I'm an idiot and my life is forever ruined because I'm probably going to fail calculus, my mother is a horrible person, I broke up with Carter because of my own insecurities, and—"

"*¡Cállate, carajo!* I can't fix your mom, but I'm your best friend. I'm your *familia* too and you're going to shut up and tell Ben off. You are not going to fail calculus, I promise you, we will work on that next. The Carter thing? Agreed. You were stupid on that, but nothing else. Now, get dressed in something hot. I'm coming to get you."

"Okay, bye." Oddly, I do feel a little bit better. Candy basically commanded me, and I must follow. Maybe I'm an inner mushy person because her calling me family has me all teary-eyed. But I don't have time to cry because Alice called me ugly, so I'm about to slather on some makeup to show everyone that I *am* a threat.

Well, not to Alice, apparently.

But I'm going to get dressed in some sexy, reasonably-warm-because-I'm-not-an-idiot, clothing and rip Ben a new one.

I put on some leggings and a tunic, but they're tight and show off my "non-threatening" body. After three swipes of mascara to make my lashes reach my brows, I put on some lip gloss. The telltale three honks outside are obviously from Candy, so I grab my thigh-high boots and head out the door. Her old Kia rumbles in the parking lot, and her game face is on.

"How will I tell him off if I don't know where he lives?"

She glances at me as I buckle my seatbelt. "They're at practice, *muchacha.* They're playing a pickup game today at the stadium."

As she drives, she puts her hand on my own and squeezes. "You're going to go in there and tear Brody a new one. It's going to be bad, it's going to bad*ass*, and it's going to be lit."

"Please, do not ever become a motivational speaker."

She laughs. "*Basta,* I'm obviously going to be a social media influencer."

I roll my eyes. "Whatever. Call me when you get invited to the White House, Ms. Political Activist."

The car ride doesn't last long enough before she parks at the near-empty stadium and nods. "Go get him."

Nerves claw at my stomach and flutter to my throat. "You're not coming with me?"

She pulls out her phone. "*Lo siento.* Did you want another Buzzfeed article about you? 'Cause if I come, I'm gonna have to film that disaster. *Amiga,* you've got this."

"No. You're right. I can do this. Thanks, Candy." I wipe my clammy hands on my pants. I can't pretend anymore. It's time for Ben to be cut off completely.

"Nothing to thank me for."

I reach for her over the center console and give her a hug. "Actually, yes, there is. You've totally changed this year around for me. If I hadn't met you, I don't know what I'd be doing right now. I love you."

She squeezes me tighter, pulls back and puts her hands on my cheeks. "*Te amo,* Les. Now, go on. Get out of here. I'll leave the car running."

I hop out of the seat and shut the door quietly behind me. Checking my watch, I find it's only been a half hour since everything changed. What if Alice hadn't stopped by? Would I have been guilt-tripped by my mom, Ben, to going to St. Maarten? And then what?

That bastard cheated on me. He cheated on me while my dad was about to die. While I was home, crying about my life forever changing, he was scoping out his newest conquest. And then we broke up one week later, the night *after* my dad died. But, we didn't break up because of Alice.

I make it to the bottom of the stadium where the guys are playing. As they break to switch teams, I hop over the stadium's railing and walk right toward third base where Ben is talking to a guy I don't recognize.

Rykard stands in the outfield and nods toward me. "Hey, Les, what's up?"

Jared is beside him, and he cocks an eyebrow. "Les...what are you doing here?"

I wave but don't answer. Just keep walking. Ben looks up and spots me, breaking into a large grin. But when I don't smile back, he looks around as if he might need reinforcements before his smile shakes and falls.

"Les, are you okay?" Ben asks.

And the way he lifts his arm as if I might need to be steadied pisses me off. Everything with him is a perfectly constructed lie. "Oh, don't even start with that crap. You don't care whether or not I'm okay."

He takes a step toward me. "I don't know what you're talking about."

I scoff. "The *audacity*. Saying 'we've always been there for each other.' Saying you need me to come with you to St. Maarten. Always calling my mom like some toddler tattleteller. Telling me you love me and that you'll wait until I'm ready for a relationship. You made me think you were a good guy. But it's all a lie. You haven't been there for me since day one!"

"Calm down, Les. What're you talking about? I meant what I said." He steps closer and his voice gets low. "Is this some medication side effect or something?"

I laugh, and the wind blows some of my hair into my face. "Screw you, dude. You're a liar, an asshole, and a garbage human being!" My shouts carry through the open stadium, and the rest of the team realizes that something is going on, so like cockroaches, they come closer. "Do you even remember why we broke up, Ben?"

"Are we really going to do this, babe? It doesn't matter why we broke up. Okay? I said I'd be the bad person if you want me to be. That's in the past."

"No, it's not in the past! We broke up *because* you are a bad person! You got mad that I didn't give a speech after getting the stupid homecoming crown. You were mad that I wasn't happier on prom night. You were mad that I wasn't the perfect little girlfriend you always had draped across your arm."

He sighs. "That's not how it went down at all. You're not remembering right. It was an emotional time for you."

"Excuse me? Of course it was an emotional time for me. But don't gaslight me into thinking differently! That's exactly what happened. I told you I wanted to go home instead of going to the after party. Ring a bell?"

Ben glances at his teammates. "Why don't we go somewhere more private?"

I don't even deign that with a response. "Do you remember what *you* said? You told me that my dad wouldn't want me to be sad. Then you freaking tried to reach up my dress and start something! While. We. Were. Dancing. Who *does* that? I told you to stop. You said, 'Well, maybe we should see other people.'" My cheeks burn from the cold, and I smile against the numbness. "And I said you're right, we should. Because I was done, Ben. I was so done with your whiny butt. And at the time, I didn't even know about Alice."

He freezes. For half a second, his face is the epitome of surprise. His lips part, his eyes widen, and his brows raise. Then he blinks and it's gone. "I don't know what you're talking about."

"So you didn't cheat on me when you came out here for spring training?" I circle my hand toward the field. "Your girlfriend—thanks for giving her my address by the way—would say otherwise. And really, you deserve each other."

"Les, wait, you're getting this all wrong."

I glance around the field, at the twenty or so other guys standing there snickering, talking, or agape, and I shake my head. "No, actually, I'm not. You're getting it all wrong, Ben. I needed you. My dad had just died, and my mom forced me to go to prom. I needed you. I needed to know that you were there for me, even if I was deep in the depths of grief." My voice cracks, and I shake my head. "But you weren't. Because while I was sobbing, literally thinking I was breaking apart from grief, you were here, sleeping with someone else."

My eyes well up with tears, but I shove them back down. "I thought that it meant I really was a failure. That you were right. I *was* stupid. Or dumb enough that I couldn't even see you had someone on the side this whole semester. And ya know? Maybe I am a little bit of an idiot. I never should've let my mom or you guilt me into trying us again. But it says a lot more about you than it does about me. And the fact you thought that you wouldn't get caught? That shows you're the real idiot here."

He holds out his hands. "But we weren't together. We'd broken up. And you were hooking up with Carter, too!"

Rykard smiles and steps up to Ben, slapping him good-naturedly on the shoulder super passive-aggressively. "I'm tellin' you, bro. You don't wanna go there."

I literally guffaw. "Well, if this conversation's told me anything, it's that I should've kept hooking up with Carter and gotten rid of you! You told me you loved me while you were in an actual relationship with Alice. So, no, not the same. Nice try, though." I roll my eyes. "I'm done, Ben. Give me your phone."

He rears back. "What the hell? No. I'm not giving you my phone."

I step up to him and push his chest with my pointer finger. "Give. Me. Your. Phone."

"I don't have it." He swats at my hand. "Stop."

"Where is it? If you don't give me your phone, I swear Ben, I will metaphorically tear your ass up right here, right now." And with how frustrated I am, I really will. "Remember 7th grade? Ooh, how about senior year? Aw, remember how you cried after we had—"

"Just stop." The words sound pained, as if they were torn from his soul. But he'd have to have a soul for that to happen. "It's in my practice bag. Which I do not have." He holds his arms, showcasing the field.

"Then go and get it."

He shakes his head. "No."

I glare at him. "I know nearly everything about you. I could make your life a living hell. You're going to give me your phone, right now. After that, we're done. And if you even try to contact me, I will file for a restraining order. We wouldn't want your parents to have to deal with an affair and all of that, would we?" My hands shake, but I drop my gaze to that birthmark of his that I used to love so much. Now it just looks like a speck of crap from him not washing his hands well enough.

Someone holds out Ben's phone. I look up his arm to my sidekick, and Carter smirks. I smile and take the phone.

Ben groans. "You're a simp, DeLeón."

Carter chuckles. "Hey man, I'd be a simp for Les any day."

I turn to look at him, brows drawn together. Carter nods, whispers, "I see you, señorita," and walks away.

Yeah, we're gonna unpack that later.

I focus back on Ben. "What's your password?"

Ben crosses his arms like the petulant, spoiled rich kid that he is. "I'm not giving it to you."

I exhale loudly. "I want my dad's videos, Ben. Believe me, I couldn't care less about whatever stupid conversations you're having with your side chick."

I try 1-2-3-4, but it doesn't work. This idiot had to choose something easy.

0-0-0-0. The phone unlocks. Stupid.

I go to his videos and scroll through them until I find the ones from the past few years of us and my dad. Sucks Ben is in all of them, but as much as I'd like to, I can't erase him. I send them to my email before deleting all of them. I erase them from his email outbox, his phone back up, and his TikTok. He doesn't deserve to have a piece of the best man who ever lived.

He's mumbling crap that I'm not listening to, but some of the other players are saying things like, "You messed up, dude." And, "You should be groveling, man. You're an idiot."

With a final burst of sass, I go to his contacts and delete my number, our text messages, and clear his phone calls so he can't ring me. Throwing the phone on the field in front of him, I say, "And if you even *think* about calling my mom, or anyone for that matter, before I get the chance to talk to them, I will sign up for Tiktok and expose you in a tell-all for what you did junior year. I even have video from that night."

He blanches and nods, his Adam's apple bobbing as he gulps.

"Take this as my no-way-in-hell am I going to St. Maarten."

As he leans down to pick up his phone, I mutter, "Bye, Ben," and walk away from him, forever ending that episode of my life.

I need to work on the new, and better, version of me. It's time to call my therapist.

Chapter Twenty-Three

I pack up my things and head to my car. It's going to be nice to have the long drive to think while I head to my mom's house.

A new resolve is burning in me. I still haven't told my mom about what went down with Ben. I think that's a conversation best had in person. Driving toward the mountains, I turn on my Dean Lewis Pandora station and let the soft music trail over me. I wonder what my show's soundtrack would be. Ben was always so critical of me, saying I was wrong for talking to myself.

I guess I should thank him for you, my studio audience. You're the real MVPs.

Even though my dad liked Ben, I think he'd be proud of me for ending things. I deserve better than someone who cheats on me and wants me to "get over" my grief before the funeral even begins.

A lot of anxiety is still swirling in my gut. I called Judy to talk about it all, and I'm not really sure why I ever stopped going to therapy.

Everything that happened with Ben brought up everything that happened with Carter. I still feel like I made a huge mistake. What if I never find someone to love again?

What if I end up just like my mom—alone and bitter?

Judy's been talking to me a lot about making choices for myself. With such a "strong-willed" mother, I've basically been bullied into everything I've ever done. This semester was a prime example of that. It's going to take a little while to grasp that control over my life.

I wish I could go to my mom and tell her, "Hey, I broke up with Ben. And I'm dating Carter. He's awesome and exactly who I want to be with. Oh, and I passed calculus, so suck on that."

But life doesn't always turn out how you want it to. I got the break up with Ben, and it looks like I'll probably pass calculus too after all my study sessions. As far as I know, Carter is still with Kriti. Not gonna lie, it hurts. I should've been more direct with what I wanted from the beginning. Shouldn't have let my mom and Ben win.

Judy's words come to me: *Focus on the here and now.*

So, I do. I try my hardest to calm my constant monologue of thoughts, focusing on being mindful and *alive.* I see the trees, the mountains, and the snow. I glance at other cars, appreciating the other people. I zone in on the road and out of my thoughts.

The drive goes by in a whir, and I punch the neighborhood gate code in with shaking hands. My mom is going to be mad. I can feel it like a kick to the shin.

It's freezing here, and fresh snow is starting to fall. I'm just glad the roads were all plowed. I pass Ben's house and cringe. He's probably coming home tomorrow so they can leave for St. Maarten.

I park my car in our driveway and head around to my trunk to get out my overnight bag.

"Les, honey, hi."

I flinch as I turn, slinging my bag on my shoulder. Ben's mom stands there in a pink dress, hair perfectly coiffed, a large briefcase slung on her arm. It looks like she just got back from work, but geez, I didn't even hear her come up to me. She's almost as sneaky as her son is.

"Hey, Mrs. Maldon, I was actually hoping I'd see you." I mean, not really, but it has to be done. "I'm so sorry, I can't come to St. Maarten."

She hugs me and pulls away with a small frown. "I'm sorry to hear that. We'll really miss you. How are you doing with everything? How's your mom?"

How's my mom? Oh, you know, acting like nothing happened and she's been a single parent her whole life and is my momager. "Uh, we're getting there. Yeah, it's been a tough year, but I think we're on the up now." I smile. I really do feel like it's gotten better. Maybe that panic attack was what I needed to accept everything. My heart hurts and still feels broken, but I can do this.

I can get better.

Alright, let's be honest, it's gonna take a lot of therapy.

She squeezes my shoulders. "If you ever need anything, you let me know. Okay?"

I nod. "I-I, um." I clear my throat. "I don't actually think I'll be around much anymore. Ben and I have broken up. For good now."

Her lips purse. "Is that so? He was just telling me how much he cares for you, honey. You know we love you like a daughter."

I swear these rich parents all have doctorates in guilt-tripping. "Honestly, it's for the best. He's even dating someone new. You should ask him about her." I'm respectful, but hey, I can still stir up a *little* trouble.

She raises her brows, but of course, no wrinkles show on her forehead. "Interesting."

I shiver against the cold. This conversation needs to end. I nod. "And I'm sorry to hear about you and Mr. Maldon. You two were always the couple that I looked up to." Which is true. They were always so in love that I can't imagine them getting a divorce. But I guess I would've said the same about Ben cheating on me.

Releasing my upper arms, she cocks her head. "How do you mean, darling?"

Give me an A! Give me a W! And a K-W-A-R-D! What does that spell? Awkward! (Sorry, I wasn't a cheerleader.) But, is she really going to make me say it? "Uh, the whole, you know"—I lower my voice to a whisper even though I can't see anyone else around (rich people also have dog-level hearing)—"the affair."

She puts her hand to her heart and gasps. I swear, she'd be clutching her pearls if she wore them. "Who's been having an affair?"

I'm basically that monkey meme with the side eye. "Um... Ben told me that you were having marital problems due to your affair with the gardener."

Mrs. Maldon, quite literally, chokes on her spit. "He *what?* Honey, there's no affair."

I grimace. "Um, okay." She probably just doesn't want to admit it, and I'm fine with that.

Her cheeks redden and I see a blush crawl up her neck as well. "That *boy*," she spits. "He is going to be in so much trouble."

She brushes hair off of her shoulder and exhales forcefully, probably to regain her perfect composure. "That is completely false, dear. I don't know what would make him say that."

Truthfully, she does seem *pretty* shocked. Huh, figures he'd lie about that too. I shrug. "Hmm, well, make sure you add another dose of punishment on top for him cheating on me."

Her botoxed bottom lip pushes out as she shakes her head. "It pains me to hear that. That is not the boy that we raised. I promise you, he will be in trouble. Take care of yourself, Les. I better go, I need to speak with my husband before Ben gets back."

With a sigh that transforms into a mini-cloud thanks to the cold, I head on inside. Fool me once, shame on you. Fool me twice, shame on me. Fool me five hundred times? I guess we'll just call me the world's biggest fool at this point. I'm glad to be getting away from the Maldon drama, honestly.

I open the front door, and the smell of Christmas hits me. The tree is set up in the living room, adorned with beautiful ornaments. It's a late Thanksgiving, but Mom never allowed Dad to decorate for Christmas until December first. I drop my bag and look at the shining globes. The tree is all done up in gold this year, with cascading glittering ribbons and a crystal star on top that sparkles as the sun filters in through the window.

"Do you like it?" My mom's hesitant voice comes from behind me.

I turn around. "Yeah, it's beautiful, Mom. Dad would've loved it." Christmas was his favorite. He would always try to decorate right after Halloween, but Mom's rules won. I guess this year she made an exception.

She nods with a flat expression on her face.

I clear my throat. "Um, we should talk."

Without a word, she walks toward the kitchen and I follow like the evil witch's tiny monkeys. She puts a kettle on the stove and gets two mugs out. The kettle is kind of a "thing" with her. It's much easier to just stick your mug of water in the microwave, but she'd probably throw up if I suggested that.

"So," I start. "Ben and I are done. For good this time." Might as well rip it off like a band aid.

She sets the mugs on the counter and the sound has me cowering. With a look in her eyes that conveys complete and total disdain, she hisses, "Why?"

I snort. "Not that I need to give you a reason, but for starters, he cheated on me."

"And you didn't? With that other boy?" She glances at me and then back toward the mugs.

"Um, no. I mean he cheated on me when we were together in high school. Like two weeks before dad died. And he's been with that girl since."

"That's absurd." She sighs.

"I know, right?" We're just gonna pretend she's actually believing me here.

"There's no way he's been with someone else."

Aaand, there it is. I'm sure there's a bulging vein on my forehead from the amount of self-restraint it's taking to not yell at her. "I'm telling you that's what happened. If I'm saying it happened like that, it happened."

"Don't raise your voice at me. It's disrespectful."

"I didn't—" I laugh once. "You know what? Okay."

The kettle whistles, and she turns to pour the water in the mugs. She places loose leaf tea in the infusers and dunks them into the water. "Okay, what?"

"As in okay, Mom, I'm not going to. But I just think it's funny how you're so critical of me and not of Ben when he was the one in the wrong. He has a girlfriend. I kissed Carter when Ben and I were broken up. And that's all that happened." I don't know why I'm defending myself, but she makes me feel like I do everything wrong.

She fixes her pearl earring before handing me my tea mug. I'm gonna let it continue to steep because I don't have the appetite for it.

"You know I only want the best for you, Les."

Y'all, she is out of her freaking mind. I close my eyes for a second because at this rate, I'm about to fire out angry heat lasers. "No, I really don't. You want what you think is the best for me."

Taking a sip of tea, she rolls her eyes. "Please, explain the difference."

I place my mug on the counter. "You're not always right. This is my life. I want to build it how I want it. If that means I don't think the same politically as you, or I don't want to be the type of doctor that you are, or I want to date someone with skin that's a few shades darker than mine, then who cares! I don't need you breathing down my neck."

She raises one perfectly shaped brow. "So, that is why you really ended things with Ben? You're gallivanting around with the other man?"

Raking my hand through my hair, I say, "No, Carter has a girlfriend too. I am completely and totally alone. Just like you." I pick up the tea mug and lift it. "Cheers."

"I don't like how you're acting."

I look to my side but there's no one to back me up except the audience in my mind. It helps me anyway. "Well, I don't like *you*! I try so hard to make you happy and do what you want me to do, but it's tiring, Mom. I want to be my own person, and you're constantly shoving yourself onto me. I don't want to be a rich, racist, ruined human!"

It's silent. She stares at me without any expression, and internally, I shrink into my turtle shell. What I said was harsh, I get it. I should've handled it better. But she makes me so mad.

Mom looks at the clock on the wall, gently setting her tea down on a coaster. "Are you finished?"

"To be honest, probably not."

One corner of her lips quirk up. "You're just like your father, you know that?" She looks back at me.

"How nice of you to mention him outside of a charity gala." I roll my eyes.

She sighs. "I miss him, Les. You were always his girl. I don't know what to say to you. He wasn't the surgeon. He didn't have the responsibilities I had. He spent more time with you. And every time I look at you, all I see is him." She clears her throat.

"Mom, I miss Dad, too. But that doesn't make it okay to say the things you do to me. Or to my friends." My throat feels dry, so I swallow, but it doesn't seem to help. "I really liked Carter. Maybe even more than liked. And it felt different. It felt real."

My eyes start to burn, and I blink to clear it. "Deep down, I ended things with him because I knew you didn't approve. I tried to make things work with Ben. I kept him in my life because you liked him, but I wasn't happy. You have no right to treat me the way you're treating me. You've been so judgmental and always assume the worst of me. It sucks. And it hurts."

With a deep breath, she nods once. "When I see you making wrong life choices—"

I hold up my hand. "But I didn't choose anything wrong. That's the point. You seriously made my friends feel like they were wrong for being Mexican. And please, you have to see what's wrong with that. Their culture is amazing." I smile thinking of Carlotta's baby shower. I wish I could be there for their Thanksgiving. "I get that we think differently about some things. And for the record, I hate Joanna Marx. But, we're each other's last family. I don't want to constantly fight or feel like I'm disappointing you."

"You're not disappointing me." She puts her hand on my shoulder. "I am your mother and truly want what's best for you. Me and your father both do." Her face falls, and she bites her lip. For once, she's not composed. "I have something for you."

She exits the kitchen and walks down the hallway that leads to her room. What could she possibly have for me? It's just, I don't know. This all seems weird. But she's right, I spent all of my time with my dad. Maybe all of this is because we haven't spent much time together.

When she comes back, she holds a flash drive. "Your father, um, he left this for you."

I take it. "Wow, a dollar flash drive. Thanks, big guy."

She shakes her head because apparently, my humor still falls flat with her. "They're recordings. He spent every night recording videos for you." She purses her lips, but not before I see them quiver. "He loved you so much."

I take the flash drive, flipping it over in my hand. My vision swims. "Why didn't you give this to me earlier?"

She shrugs. "I don't know. There's a lot of things that you don't know about me. I cried too, when your father died. I didn't want you to see me like that. Why do you think I forced you to go to prom with Ben? I wanted to be strong. I needed to know that we'd be okay. I needed time to mourn him and miss him. I had a whole life with him, and then you came along."

She's sounding weirdly...jealous? What kind of mom keeps something like this from her daughter?

"So, you kept the videos he made? Because you had a life with him before I came along, and you got mad he did this for me? Do you not see what's wrong with that? Your husband's *dying wish* was for you to give these to me, and you failed. I-I just, I can't do this with you right now. That's seriously so messed up." I can feel the anger building up inside of me, so I run back to the living room, grab my bag, and head upstairs to my room.

"I'm sorry, Les," Mom says from the bottom of the stairs. But at this point, I don't even know what mistake she's apologizing for. She's made too many of them.

I sit on my bed and plug the flash drive into my laptop.

It appears on the side of the screen, so I click it and pull up the files.

Watch This First
For When You Graduate Highschool
For When You Go Off To College
For Your First Birthday Alone
For Your First Failed Test
For When You and Ben Break Up (Don't open if you stay together)
For When You Have a Hard Day
For When You Get Married
For Your Future Spouse (Don't watch this one!)
For When You Have Your First Kid
For When You Face a Big Decision
For When You Miss Me
For When You're Sick of These Videos and Want Me to Go Away

I roll my eyes at the last one. How did he know that I would need him so much? It's so unfair. He should be here. I want to watch all of them, but I know that would be cheating. So I click on *Watch This First*.

His face appears on the screen, smiling. Eyes crinkle at the corners and he wears a red polo sweater. "Hey, Les. It's me. If you're watching this, I guess that means I'm dead." He chuckles awkwardly. "Wow, didn't realize how weird it would be to make this. Alrighty, then.

"I'm making you a series of videos. Ones that you can watch when you have big life events or hard days. I wish I could be there for you, kiddo. Wish I could be there when you graduate." His voice gets thick, and he clears his throat.

He points at the camera. "No crying. That's more for myself than for you." He sighs. "Anyway, I love you, Les. And just because you have half a name doesn't mean I love you half Les. Get it?"

I laugh, but my eyes fill with tears.

"Just know, kid, my life was fulfilled. You made living life every day worth it. You're my baby girl, and I can't imagine what you'll go through without me. Or maybe you won't care 'cause I'm just your annoying dad."

I wipe at the tears falling.

"I had a whole script of what I was going to say. Of course, as soon as I pressed play on this camera, that all went out. Just know I am so proud of you, no matter where your life takes you, and I want you to have a fulfilling and happy life. And please, for the love of everything, keep laughing and making jokes. My bad sense of humor has to live on somehow." He swipes at his eye. "I said I wouldn't cry. I'll do better on the next one. I'd tell you to be good, but I gave up on that a long time ago. Be bad, Les. I love you."

I can barely see the screen through my tears, but I click on the next one: *For When You Graduate High School.*

"You did it!" He appears on the screen with a party hat and streamers. Blowing into a horn, he dances horribly. "High school is through! Oh man, I wish I could tell you it gets easier, but you're about to step into a world of pain. Just kidding. College is great. Your mom would kill me if I said anything otherwise. Although, I guess she can't kill me since I'm already dead...Bad joke, okay. First of all," he holds out his hands and then clasps them, "so proud. I am so, so proud. If I were there, I'd be giving you the biggest hug."

"And I would've embarrassed you while you walked across the stage. Shouted something like, 'You can do it honey, don't let the diarrhea you had this morning bog you down!' Ah, that would've been good." He wipes at his eyes, this time from laughing too hard at his own joke.

Wasn't even that funny, Dad, come on.

"I want you to go out tonight and have the time of your life. Go party at the richer neighbor's house next door—not Ben's house, we all know we're richer."

Weird flex, but okay.

"Just don't get arrested for trespassing or breaking and entering or anything like that. And no, I definitely did not get arrested the night of my high school graduation." He winks. "You did it, kid. Not gonna lie, right around third grade I thought, 'if this kid graduates high school, it'll be a miracle.' But look at ya. You stopped eating your boogers and turned it around. Go make your mark on the world, Les. You're pretty special."

The video ends and the tears are back. I think this is just gonna be my face now—waterlogged and swollen. I skip a few and click on: *For When You and Ben Break Up.*

He sits in all black, his head hung low. "This is your last warning. If you and Ben are still together, do not watch this video. I repeat, do not watch this video."

He lifts his head and smiles. Then he holds up a sign that says, "Congratulations, your real life starts now."

"I never liked the guy." He chuckles. "That's a lie. I loved the little devil, but I never liked him for you. I saw the way you acted with him, a little sad, a little repressed, like he stole a part of your light and wouldn't give it back." Shaking his head, he says, "Ben's a good guy. He's great for where we live and for getting you through high school, but I always knew you were meant for more. Life with Ben wouldn't have let you reach your full potential."

"Do I know what your full potential is?" He grimaces. "Definitely not, and I'm a little scared to find out. But I know that it's going to be amazing, whatever it is that you do. It's going to hurt for a bit. I know you liked him. But when he comes back and realizes the mistake he made letting you go, don't give in."

He takes a deep breath and sighs, pulling at his turtleneck. "Sorry, this is the only black thing I had and I wanted this video to look like I was mourning your breakup. Anyway, you always tiptoed around Ben. When he got mad, *you* always cheered him up. I mean, really, the man couldn't even lose a game without a full pouting session. I loved the kid, but man, Les, I want more for you."

"I want you to find someone who you can laugh with over stupid stuff and cry with when things get hard. Someone who isn't going to judge you or ridicule you. Someone who supports you, even when you stop supporting yourself. You need a confidant, a friend, and someone who makes you want to be a better person. Did Ben make you want to be a better person?"

No. My dad knew the answer is no.

"The person you fall in love with may challenge you. They will fiercely love you and want the best for you, even if they think it's not them. It may not be who you pictured, and it may not be the easiest route to get there, but I know that the person you fall in love with will be one of the good ones. With the person you love, you won't have to choose between loving them and being yourself. Those things can coexist, and a true love won't ask for anything more than you can give. Remember that, kiddo. And then tell the person that if they don't treat you right, I'll come back from the dead and haunt them. Okay? Love you, honey."

My heart beats rapidly, and I want to close the computer but also keep watching the videos all at the same time. It's so good to hear his voice, to see him and his mannerisms. How he sniffles whenever his nose itches, how when he laughs, he throws his head up as if the joy is escaping him.

I miss him so much. And I'll spend the rest of my life missing him. I think I'm going to save the rest of these videos for when I really need them, but there's one last one I want to watch: *For When You Fail Your First Test*

The video opens up with him sitting in his office chair, feet up on the desk, with a book titled: *How To Raise Your Daughter For Dummies.* He scrambles to drop the book, then puts his face in front of the camera, "So, you failed a test. Now what?"

This video must've been made later than the rest of them because his hair is shaved on the side, probably from when they tried to operate on the tumor.

"Now...nothing." He smiles so big his eyes nearly shut. "So, you failed a test. *So what?* It's not a big deal. But, I bet your mom is gonna make it one. Your mother probably hasn't failed one test in her life. Me, on the other hand, I've failed a lot. As in, I pretty much had to retake every class from my freshman year in college because I partied too hard and didn't study enough."

He points at me. "But you, kiddo, you study too much. You psych yourself out and then take a test, and you're so overwhelmed that of course you're going to fail." Gazing up at the ceiling, he chuckles and throws his hands behind his head. "I used to say I'd give anything to live in your mind. I bet you have a whole world up there."

He grins, and it's a sight that I want to pause. "Please, when you fail your first test, don't do something drastic. Relax, calm down, and take a breath. Failing is not the worst thing in the world. In fact, failing can teach us lessons that we never knew we needed. So cheer up, kiddo. Celebrate failing a test with a party or something. You're a college kid after all. And know that even if you get a big, fat F in a class, you're in good company."

He stands to shut off the camera. "Me. I'm that good company. Figured I better explain my jokes since I won't be around for you to ask about them. I love you, Les."

I close the computer and sob, but it's a mixture of happy and sad tears.

My mom should've handed me these earlier. They would've saved me heartache and hurt, but I'm not sure I have the energy to be mad right now. My dad was a great, incredible person, and she lost a husband. Does it excuse things? No. But maybe we can work on trying to mend our broken relationship.

Though if I'm being honest, that's not the relationship currently taking up most of my headspace. I did the opposite of my dad's advice. I failed a test and did something dras-tic. I thought I had to "choose" myself, but a real relation-ship wouldn't have needed me to choose anything. And Carter never asked me to choose. He offered to help, he respected my wishes, and he did what I asked him to do. He was supportive, even when I asked him to stay away so I could pass a class. He was a friend. He was someone I could talk to when sad. He was someone I could laugh with over dumb things.

But maybe most importantly, he made me want to be bet-ter for myself and my future. He challenged my views on the world (with Candy's help, of course), and he never once judged me or who I am as a person.

I did something drastic, and now I have to live with the re-gret of letting someone I love slip away.

A knock sounds on my door, and I turn over on my bed to call, "You can come in."

My mom opens the door and sits down on the edge of my bed, fidgeting with her hands. "I am sorry, Les. I made a mis-take not giving you the videos, I know that. And I would like to apologize."

I nod. "Yeah, Mom, you did. But, I got the videos, so..." Not to mention, there's about a thousand other things she should be apologizing for.

"You know, when I met your father, your grandparents weren't too keen on him."

I snort half-heartily. How could anyone not like my dad?

"They called him a dreamer. Flippant. Whimsical. Thought he was going to tear down all my dreams and destroy my life plan." She sucks in her lips. "But he did the opposite. He was the only person that could make me...feel like me. And losing him did ruin me. You were right."

I pick at my comforter. "I know."

She places a hand on mine, and I bite down the urge to flinch away. "I'm sorry about Carter," she says, and it comes out fairly sincere.

I feel a wave of emotion come over me at the mention of

him, though, and it turns out I have a few more tears left to cry. I bury my face into my pillow and choke out, "I think I loved him, Mom."

She rubs my back, but doesn't say anything else. I let myself feel the emotions of everything—Ben cheating on me months ago, my dad not being here, the fact that I let Carter go and lost my chance with him. I don't know how long I cry, but for once, she stays with me. When the sobs cascade down into sniffles and shaky breaths, I sit up, wiping at my swollen eyes.

We sit in silence for a few moments. I'm tired.

In her own way, maybe my mom mentioning Carter was her way of surrendering just a little bit of control over my life. She's the only family I have left. I'd like to think we can somehow figure out how to be around each other, but I'm not stupid enough to believe that it will be easy.

I clear my throat. "Would you be willing to go to therapy with me? I know that's a dirty word for you boomers."

She rolls her eyes but smiles in the slightest.

"But I think it could help us a lot. And...it'd be a way to see each other every week?" My mom may never change, but isn't it worth it to try? (In a non-biased environment, of course.)

Her fine-boned shoulders shrug. "I'll think about it."

Chapter Twenty-Four

"Good morning, everyone." Professor Butler claps her hands. "Thank you for being with me this semester and putting your best foot forward. Today is our final!"

People hoot and holler, and even Candy gives a little cheer. But I stay quiet. I don't want to ruin the calm and focus that's within me. I studied, went to my internship, had tutor sessions, and even stayed after with Professor Butler one day to go over my past quizzes and work through what I did wrong.

I'm ready.

"Good luck, everyone." She gestures toward the back where Carter sits. "Oh, and before I forget, the university has gotten a new standardized computer system. Mr. DeLeón will be taking the tests over once everyone finishes, so you can expect your test scores by two this afternoon."

Oh, great. No, I'm fine. Everything's fine. At least I'll know quickly whether I passed or failed. Right now, my grade sits at a healthy 73%, so this test pretty much makes or breaks me.

But I take a deep breath and calm down, remembering what my dad said. *Don't overthink it.*

Carter passes out the scantron sheets, and when he gets to me, he mouths *you've got this.*

I crinkle my nose and nod, adding in a wink for good measure. He clutches at his heart with a silent chuckle before moving on.

Ah, if only.

I start the test, glancing over the problems. And they all look…familiar. In fact, it's the same set of questions from each quiz, compiled together to become our final. The only reason I know is because I just went over all of these questions with

Professor Butler. Which means...I can totally do this.

I work through each equation, double checking my answers and work before choosing a multiple choice answer. An hour and a half and forty questions later, I walk toward the front of the class and turn it into the bin next to Professor Butler.

"It's been a pleasure, Les. Good luck," she whispers, nodding her head.

A smile escapes me. "Thank you. You too."

Candy turns in her test after I do, and I wait for her outside the classroom. When she rears her pink-haired head, I give a little, "Woohoo! We did it!"

She grins. "Freshmen."

"Aw, you love me."

"That, I do. That, I do. Anna's for waffles?"

I sling my bag on my shoulder. "Absolutely."

We get outside, and the cold December air bites at my cheeks and nose. Even my eyelashes feel like they're sticking just a bit, but we shuffle quickly toward the diner.

I blow warm air onto my hands. "So, what're your plans for classes next semester?"

Candy taps on her phone. "*No sé.* I've signed up for a few poly-sci classes, but I may rearrange my schedule during Christmas break. See what people drop or what classes open up. *¿Y tú?*"

"Well, it depends on whether or not I passed calculus I guess. I still have my internship with Dr. Guilliod next semester, but she decided to take that parental leave after all. She'll be out another six weeks. Other than that, I'm not too sure. But I was thinking...maybe I should take a Spanish class."

She stops, shakes my shoulders, and smiles. Some pink strands of hair get stuck on her lip gloss, and she sputters to get them out. "Uh, *sí*! Do it!"

I laugh and nod.

We turn the corner, and I see a flash of someone familiar.

It's Alice, she's walking alone, huddled in a large West hoodie, and our eyes catch.

I smile flatly and wave, but she stops to stare at Candy and me.

Candy elbows me. "Who is that?"

"Uh, that would be Ben's girlfriend, Alice."

Alice doesn't budge, but her lips pinch as if she can't decide what to do. She brushes back her hair and stomps over to us.

I nudge Candy. "Do. Not. Say. A. Word."

She huffs. "Fine."

Alice fidgets with her hands, which are covered with blue and purple striped gloves. She glances at me and her shoulders drop. "Ben and I broke up. It was all over TikTok. Not sure if you saw it."

Ah, influencers. I really hope it's not because of me. "I'm... sorry to hear that, Alice."

She smiles, and this time, it actually reaches her eyes. "Yeah, I'm not. I think we're both better off without him."

Truer words have never been spoken. "Definitely."

Alice rubs her palms together then holds out a gloved hand. "I should've believed you when I came to your house. And... I'm sorry for the whole stalker-getting-your-address-from-Ben thing. We cool?"

I shake her hand. "Yeah, no biggie. We're cool." Even though you called me ugly, I add in my mind. I link my arm in Candy's. "Well, we better get going. It's freezing out here."

"Same. Merry Christmas, Les. "Alice waves.

"You too!" I call out after her.

Candy squeals as we walk away. "Good thing, right? It's a happy ending. Ben is all alone."

I think of the *real* happy ending I'd like, and it doesn't end with karma kicking Ben's balls. I mean, it does, but it goes beyond that. Beyond Ben. But finals are over, it's almost Christmas, and I'm with my best friend about to eat waffles. So, I nod. "Yes. A happy ending, most definitely."

We stroll toward where Anna's shines amongst the gray, dreary weather. Lights outside twinkle red and green, sparkling against the metal exterior. And inside, right in the center, is a large Christmas tree with clunky handmade ornaments.

Once we step foot in the heated diner, I nearly curl my toes. I mean I would, but they're frozen. We take a seat at our usual booth, and when the waitress comes to us, she already knows what we're ordering. She even paraphrases my five-minute soliloquy of *please do not kill me, keep everything separated and use your peanut-allergy-friendly waffler*. I'm gonna take that as a sign I should probably change my diet next year. Maybe a New Year's resolution? Less waffles, more vegetables.

"What're you doing for Christmas, Can-Can?"

She groans. "Don't call me that. And we'll be making *tamales* and having a big family party like always. You wanna come?"

I shrug. "Yeah, maybe. My mom and I are trying to work on our relationship, so I'll probably spend a day with her. We have our first therapy session. But both Christmas and Christmas Eve may be asking for a bit much. Plus, I know my mom's going to the Maldon's Christmas party, and I'm definitely skipping that this year."

"*Bien.* Well, *mi familia* and I would love to have you. My mom can't stop talking about the 'cute blonde girl' I brought around." She rolls her eyes. "She sees one white person, and I swear..."

Laughing, I grab my plate from the waitress balancing our waffles and French toast. "So, who else will be at your Christmas party? Is there a certain man with a name starting with the letter 'T' who may be in attendance?"

She shakes her head. "No, he's banned."

"Ah, right. I forgot. Carter told me about that actually. Though, Carter said he was partly responsible. I feel like he should be banned from your Christmas parties too."

With a bite of french toast in her mouth she says, "I know, that's what I said! My mom lifted the ban, but *mi abuela?* That woman brings the grrr to grudge. Especially because the Christmas tree lit up her porcelain doll collection. I won't ever admit it to her, but I was glad to see those things go. They were creepy."

I giggle into my drink. Setting the glass down, I pick at my waffles. I'm a little nervous about my test results from calc.

We eat and people-watch, looking at the different students sitting near us. There are a few couples, a group of guys who are definitely hungover, and even a crying girl whose friends are trying to comfort her.

Been there, done that.

Candy and I catch up on everything from Thanksgiving, like how her nephews managed to "accidentally" throw the turkey on the trampoline. It's a welcome distraction, and though it's been a crazy few months, if her friendship is all I got out of it, it was worth it.

Candy's phone vibrates on the table, and she slides open the text. "*Dios mío.* Carter texted me. He just got back from running our test results. Do you want to know yours?"

I hesitate. Do I? Not really. But, at the same time, I can't hide. No more hiding, no more burying feelings. I'm working with Judy on all of that. So I squeal, "Um, okay, yes! Tell him to send it over."

She taps on the screen. "He's responding." A few seconds later, "Okay, thank you *Madre Maria.* I got an eighty-five. One sec, he's typing."

She glances at me and then her phone vibrates again, so she looks back down. "Hold on, he didn't know you were with me."

The seconds stretch, and anxiety churns in my gut. Ugh, please don't let it be a failing grade. I knew all the answers. And yet...

Candy covers her mouth. "Shut up."

"Oh gosh, what? Did I fail? I failed, didn't I? Crap!" I put my head down on the table, but then quickly get back up because the table is probably pretty dirty, let's be honest.

"Um, no actually." She shoves the phone in my face. "You got a freaking ninety-six. You must've missed like one question!"

My whole body is alight with fire as I do a little dance,

throwing my arms in the air. "I passed! I passed. I seriously passed. OMG." I feel like I could cry and throw up at the same time. That grade should bring up my final score to somewhere in the B- range, I think. Maybe a C+. But that's good enough.

I did it.

I didn't fail.

"Congrats, *amiga!* We need to have a little party to cele-brate."

I nod. "Yes, yes, we do." My heart wants to celebrate with a special someone, but a party will do too. "Ah, tell Carter thanks for sending that over."

She puts the phone back down on the table and locks it, cas-ually moving her food around with her fork. "Or...you could tell him yourself."

Right. She's not my messenger. "Yeah, I'll text him."

"No, I meant, like, in person," she grumbles.

I glance up from my waffles, and she shrugs.

"Don't be starting trouble, Candy. Carter's happy. I'm not gonna mess with that." My stomach vehemently wants to barf on that answer, but I swallow it down.

"*Bien.*" She moves her hair off of her shoulder and to her back. "But, you still have feelings for him, don't you?"

A blush creeps up my face. "Me? I mean, yeah, I guess. He's a great guy. But I think I'll take a page out of your playbook and save him for later."

She bites her lip and smiles. "Whatever. You *lerv* my brother. Are you actually gonna see other people?"

I point my fork at her and laugh. "You know I won't. My heart lies with your annoying twin. Let's just pray to the uni-verse he doesn't like Kriti that much and it fizzles out before they get married and have adorable Indian-Mexican-Ameri-can babies."

The waitress comes to refill our drinks, and we fall into that awkward silence while we wait for her to leave. Once she does, Candy says, "You know, it's kinda weird. I heard this rumor."

I internally groan. "Candy! You and your rumors. What

now?" I set my fork down.

She takes the longest gulp of water known to man before saying, "Ah, that is some good *agua*."

"What's the rumor?" I snap.

"Remember Jenna from *Bachelor in Paradise*? You never did finish that episode." Her face is the epitome of coy.

Right now. She chooses *this exact moment* to bring up *Bachelor in Paradise*? Good gosh. "Okay? And your point?"

She licks her lips. "Jenna said she chose no one. That neither of the two guys were who she would end up with. But Chris Harrison did an update two weeks later. Jenna chased after Mike. It was sort of a 'thing.'" She air quotes. "Mike forgave her. Basically the cutest *Bachelor* couple ever."

Weird. But we all knew Chad and Jenna wouldn't have made it. He slept with like a dozen people at a music festival. "I don't see where you're going with this."

"Well, her and Mike got back together. You know, she'd spent time with the Chad guy before the show, but in the end, it just didn't work out. Her and Mike have been together since she chased after him." Candy places her hands under her chin and smiles.

I stab a piece of waffle with my fork and get ready to shove it in my mouth. "Good for her. Mike was a cutie."

Candy sighs. Probably because I don't understand her dramatic rumor that is not a rumor. She finished *BIP*, so did half of America.

"Carter and Kriti broke up."

My fork clatters to my plate. "Wait, what? Are you serious?"

I can literally feel my heart beating quicker. Because that would mean maybe it's not too late. That maybe things could work out. But I don't want to get my hopes up. "Don't mess with me, that's rude."

Throwing her hands into the air, she raises her brows at the same time. "I'm serious. To be honest, I'm not sure they were ever even *on*. She's been a family friend for ages and they never had any chemistry. But if you want to know a secret," she cups her hand over the side of her mouth, "they broke up after your showdown at the stadium. I guess you lighting into Ben's ass got Carter's heart rate up."

My fingers go cold, but my stomach burns with excitement. He's single.

This isn't a joke. Carter is totally, completely single.

Unattached.

I could go see him. No, I *will* go see him. "I-I have to go."

She grins widely enough that a dimple appears on her cheek. "Yeah, Les, go chase after your man."

I stand up, trip over my feet, and scramble for my bag. "Gah!"

Candy laughs. "Just get out of here! I've got the bill."

I grip her shoulders. "Are you sure?"

She grips my shoulders too. "Yes, I'm sure. Get the hell out of here and over to *mi casa*. Go get your *hombre*."

"*Te amo*, Candy!"

As I leave, she calls out, "I love you, too! We're gonna work on that accent of yours!"

I chuckle and run back toward campus to the parking lot. But my car is nowhere to be found. And I can't remember where I parked. So freaking typical.

I sprint up and down the aisles pressing the lock button and silently praying to the car gods until I finally hear a *beep, beep* a few minutes later.

Once I get in the car, I brush the hair from my face and grab the lip gloss from my bag. I look in the rearview mirror and slather some on before starting the engine. Then, I do what I should've been doing all along—I drive to Carter.

My nerves are at an all-time high.

This is the point in every rom-com where I should be running through the airport, trying to catch Carter before his flight leaves. But we're in college, so instead, I'm driving to his apartment to try and convince him to love me.

Ah, sweet, sweet romance.

With every red light, my studio audience bites their nails.

With every green light, *you* cheer. I know you're on the edge of your seat, waiting for me to reunite with the best guy we know. And trust me, I know you never liked Ben. You were always Team Carter. Thanks for that. I've finally seen the light.

I pull into his apartment complex, parking my car in the nearest guest spot. I can see Carter's truck, so I know he's here. I have no idea what I'll say or do or if it even matters. Does he even like me?

No! I am not going to overthink this. I get out of the car and jog to the apartment complex door. It's gonna be so romantic. I'll knock on his door, he'll open it with a smile.

I yank on the complex entrance.

It's locked.

Crap! I forgot I need someone to let me in. You've gotta be kidding me. I don't want to call Carter. That will ruin the surprise. I grab my phone and tap Candy's contact. But before it even begins ringing, I hear, "Yo, what's up?"

I turn, and Tom is walking toward me, gym bag slung on his shoulder. I could basically pee my pants I'm so relieved…and nervous, and okay, I'm just gonna stop here.

Sweat gleans on his face, but I give him a hug anyway. "You just saved my day. I'm about to go profess my undying love for your future brother-in-law. And, I'm going to ask him to be my boyfriend." I cover my face but peek through my fingers.

He breaks out into a smile and high fives me. "Hell yeah, girl."

I put my hands down and laugh. "It's not too forward?"

Tom readjusts his gym bag and grins. "Nah, go get him."

Whew, okay, good. I nod. "I'm trying. I need your key fob to get in."

"Oh, you right. Here." He holds it to the door and it unlocks. "You know what? I'll catch up with you two later. Let you have the apartment alone."

I point toward him. "You're a lifesaver."

"No prob," he says, walking back to his car.

I open the door, and the hallway stretches before me. My

feet stumble as I rush inside from the cold and lean against the wall. I take a deep breath before forcing myself to walk.

With every step, the tingles go from my center to my fingers and toes. My body is numb with desire and excitement.

The red door of the devilish apartment 13666 stands before me. I lift my fist, and drop it.

I'm scared.

What if he says no? What if he doesn't feel the same?

But as if someone pushes me from behind, I fall into the door and knock with my fist. Dang, did my studio audience just go all ghost on me?

The door flies open, and it's like our first meeting once again. His green eyes shimmer against the fluorescent hallway lights, and for a moment, I forget what I'm doing here. The words die in my throat as his gaze travels from my head to my boots and back again.

Carter cocks a brow but smiles. "Congrats on passing your test."

I finally remember to breathe, and the cinnamon scent of him wraps around me. Energy rises into my face, and I'm probably beet red. I've got to say it all before I chicken out or get nervous gas or something. We're here to make a good impression, not scare the man away *again.*

"Thanks." I wipe my palms on my pants and bite my lip. "But I didn't come here for that. I'm here to talk to you."

He leans against the doorframe. "Hmm?"

I take a deep breath. "Um, I-I'm sorry. I'm, like, really sorry. You're the best man currently alive, and I should've never let you go. I made a huge mistake. Candy told me you're single, and I couldn't help but come see you. I know you're looking at me like I'm crazy, and maybe I am, but I think I love you, Carter. And—"

He holds up his hand. "Slow down, Les."

Everything in me stills, and a blush crawls up my neck. My ears are basically on fire from the awkwardness. "You're right. Love? What? Ah, weird." I cough. "Anyway...um, you smell nice, and I like you."

He doesn't say anything, just angles his head to the side. A few seconds pass with him staring at me, and then he quirks his lips. His full, rosy, really delicious-looking lips. "I like you too. You also smell nice. But I meant slow down as in slow your words down. I wanted to savor your apology."

I deadpan and swat at his chest. "Whatever!"

Carter grabs my hand and pulls me closer. I look up into his eyes, and they twinkle with mischief. "Say that other thing again."

"You smell good?"

He shakes his head. "Before that."

I inhale. "You're right?"

He chuckles, and his chest rumbles against my hand. "Even before that."

My breath comes out shaky. "I...love you?"

"There it is." He drops my hand and puts his arms around my waist, pressing our foreheads together. "*Te amo* too, Les."

I let out a half-laugh, half-whimper. "Do you want to go out with me?"

He cups my cheek and nods. "*Sí*. But first, I'd really like to stay in with you."

His lips brush mine, and I stand on my tiptoes to deepen the kiss. It's everything I've wanted and feels so good, so right, so *earned*. This whole time, he was there when I needed him, as a friend or more.

He's my person, the one I want to spend my time with.

As his hands graze my back, I realize I need to get out of everyone's sight.

So, this is where my story ends. Hopefully in some other crazy world, my experience has made you laugh, cry, and learn a thing or two (*cough cough* don't be an idiot like me). But if not, if you're all in my mind, that's okay too. I'll just make sure not to tell anyone about it.

I break our kiss, pushing Carter through the door's threshold and into his apartment. With one last glance toward the

hallway and invisible cameras, I wink and close the door.
You know what they say...Les is more.

The End.

Epilogue – Carter

Les is passed out on my bed, wearing one of my practice jerseys. Her hair splays over the pillow, and she looks like a princess—if princesses snored as loud as bears.

She's everything.

I never thought it'd be like this. I just want to stare at her all day long. I'm scared that if I look away, she'll disappear.

Les has stolen my heart from me, but I don't ever want it back.

It took us a while to get here, but I couldn't be happier. Screw the last few months. They don't matter when the future holds us together.

I lay beside her, pulling her into me. Kissing her forehead, I inhale the scent of her shampoo and perfume. She smells like vanilla or something. Whatever it is, I want it all over my pillow, and sheets, and me.

The movement wakes her up, and she mumbles, "Are you okay? What time is it?"

I check my watch. "Just past two. Sorry, my Dexcom woke me up. Had to get a snack."

She sighs. "Did you bring me any?"

Chuckling, I put the fruit snacks in her hand. She doesn't even open her eyes, just shoves them in her mouth and snuggles into my side again. "I love you so much, Carter," she says, but it comes out more like *I ruff ew so muff* because she refuses to not stuff her face.

"You're gonna get cavities like that." I brush through her hair and kiss her forehead. "I love you too, Les."

She pulls back. "Say it in Spanish so I know it's real."

"So demanding when you're tired. *Te amo,* Les." I tilt up her chin.

Our lips meet in reverence, soft and still as the night. But she pulls me on top of her, deepening the kiss. She licks my bottom lip, and I'm lost in sweet seduction. In this moment, everything is perfect. Nothing could change the way I feel about her, and when she moans my name, I know it deep in my soul.

She's it for me.

I'm always gonna be hers.

Want more of Les and Carter? Keep reading for a bonus epilogue, *Christmas with Les!*

Read Candy's Book, *Sweet as Candy,* **now.**

Christmas With Les

Christmas Year One

The snow's coming down (okay, not really), I'm watching it fall (on the TV). Just my boyfriend around, baby please come home! It's you. You're "baby." And yes, I hope you're singing with me.

Call this my Christmas special. Christmas with Les. Ooh, yes, that's cute. Let's go with that.

Welcome back, studio audience.

I'm lying with Carter in his bed, one day before Christmas Eve, watching a cheesy movie on the big screen TV. It's only ten in the morning, but I've been making us watch holiday movies for a week straight. My eyeballs might have Santa and Christmas trees permanently burned into the irises, but it's fine.

The two characters in the movie just found out that they're made for each other. Sound familiar? I may cry. They're just so cute.

Carter groans. "You are not getting emotional over this Netflix movie, are you?"

I sniffle. "Of course not. I just, like, have something in my eye."

He chuckles and moves his body on top of mine, blocking my

view of the screen. "Okay, mi amor. You're lyin'." He kisses me on my nose. "You need a tissue for those tears?"

Slapping his chest, I say, "Oh, stop. Now move so I don't miss the airport scene."

"So demanding, ay, ay, ay." He rolls off of me and plays with my hair. "You still going shopping with Candy today?"

"Yep," I pop the 'p' and avert my gaze. If he looks me in the eyes, he'll know.

I have no idea what to get him for Christmas. I mean, what do you get a guy that you love but really you've only dated officially for like two weeks? Oh my gosh, this is why people hate insta-love, isn't it?

A thousand gift ideas have gone through my mind, but they all get branded the same: weird, too extra, or not extra enough.

He turns me on my side and becomes the big spoon, whispering in my ear, "Ooh, what're you gonna get me for Christmas?"

I sputter. "Um, what're you going to get me?"

"Already have it."

Of course he does. Because he's the perfect boyfriend. Shoot. A puppy is too extra, right? I don't even have to ask. Of course it's too extra. I play along. "Oh, well aren't you special."

"Sí, very, very special if we're going off of your—"

The door slams open and Candy appears in the doorway. "¿Qué pasa? Oof, blech, you're still in bed?" She glances up and down our bodies, and puts her hand over her mouth. "OMG, please tell me you're both clothed. I'll barf."

I throw off the covers as Candy shrieks and covers her eyes. "I'm scared to look."

"We're clothed, Can-Can." I sit up from the bed, and Carter pauses the movie. I point to the screen. "We're finishing that tonight."

He shrugs. "Amongst other things, sure."

My cheeks are not blushing, stop saying ooh. The heater just turned on or something, that's all. I give Carter a quick kiss and follow Candy out of the apartment.

She pops her gum and taps at her phone as she holds the door open for me with her butt. "So, amiga, where we shopping?"

I swing my purse onto my shoulder and sigh. "I have no clue. I don't have any ideas of what to get Carter."

She glances up from her phone and laughs. "You're seriously stressing over what to get him for Christmas? He's a guy. Get him socks or something, who cares. Everyone knows it's the guy who stresses over the girl for holidays. Not the other way around."

I pull at my hair as we get into her Kia. "Well, as your brother would say...equality. Women can worry too. And I am. I'm stressing hardcore."

Candy groans in tune with her ignition as she starts the car. "White people problems. I swear, you're like one of those Hallmark movies. Carter really won't care, believe me."

"Well, I care. My dad was a huge gift giver, and I got it from him. Carter needs the absolute perfect gift." I think back to my last Christmas with Dad, and it hurts that he won't be here this year. I'm going to my mom's house after Carter's Christmas Eve party tomorrow. She's going to the Maldon's party (shocker), but she didn't ask me to go with her. In fact, she hasn't mentioned Ben once since that day a few weeks ago.

Therapy with her has been good. We've only had two sessions, but I do feel like it might be helping. Only time will tell, I guess.

But I'm excited for the party tomorrow with Carter. His family is so fun, and I even picked out little gifts for his nephews, Adrian and Mateo.

Candy's gift was easy too. I got her this purse I kept seeing her gush about on Instagram and Twitter. If anything, that girl knows how to drop a hint.

Carter, on the other hand, is much more subtle. Tried seducing a gift idea out of him, and you know what he said?

The man said, "Tie a bow around your waist and I'll have you for Christmas."

I legit choked on a Rudolph sugar cookie.

Sighing, I buckle my seatbelt and begin googling Christmas gifts for boyfriends that you really love but, like, haven't spent that much time with but want to still impress without saying I'm a stage five clinger.

Shockingly, nothing comes up. Perfect.

Candy starts singing to a Spanish song that comes on her Spotify playlist, and the only word I catch is yo. It's a good thing

I'm taking a Spanish class next semester. I grab some chapstick from my bag and put it on. "Where are we going?"

She waves me off, and I check out her Christmas mani. It's got red, green, and gold sparkles on each coffin-shaped nail. Looks expensive. "The mall. Figured we better start there. With your indecisiveness, we'll be there all day. At least there's a hundred stores to choose from. You'll find something."

~~~

Well, Candy was right. I did find something. But that something was not worth the five hours it took to commit to it. And I'm pretty sure Candy was disappointed in my choice, but she was so tired of shopping with me that she just said, "Perfecto! Now let's go get some cheesecake."

Now I'm in Carter's room, wrapping the sad, sad gift.

I finish tying a gold bow, and dread sets in. Yeah, no, this gift definitely sucks. I toss back some Sour Patch Kids and grab my phone. I'll just order a little something extra, just in case.

But right as I press checkout, Carter comes through the door, gym bag slung on his arm, cheeks slightly blushed and sweaty, with a huge grin on his face. "Hola, cariña. What are you doing?" He points to the box. "Is that for me?"

And call him Rudolph because his face lights up as if Santa just said he's gonna be the leader of the pack tomorrow night.

I snatch the box and hide it behind my back. "Yes, yes it is."

He throws his bag and barrels into me, and I shriek and fall to the floor, laughing.

Brushing back my hair, he says, "What'd you get me?"

I roll my eyes. "You are one loco hombre."

Kissing my lips, he mumbles against them, "Hombre loco. Come on, girl, we've already discussed this."

But now I'm lost in his kiss. I grip fistfuls of his shirt and pull him fully on top of me, relishing in his body weight against me. He grabs the back of his shirt and yanks it up and over his head. I run my hands down his chest and abs. "Thank every deity in the world for your abs," I say as he kisses down my neck.

He pulls back and winks before rubbing his scruff against the sensitive spot between my shoulder and neck. "It's just your world and my abs are living in it, huh?"

I writhe underneath him as his breath tickles my skin. "Yes. And your lips, and your eyes, and those eyelashes I'd kill for, and your bi—"

He presses his lips against mine and puts his hands underneath me, rolling over so I land on top of him, straddling his waist. "Now what was that you were gonna say?"

"I was going to say your back." I suck on my teeth as he gives me a chastising stare.

"That is not what you were going to say," he mumbles.

"Fine." I hold up my hands. "I was going to say your big mouth that you're always running, okay? And then I was going to say that you need to take a shower because you're sweaty."

Not that I mind, but he needs to hurry up. We've got at least three more Christmas movies to conquer tonight, and we're doing a Christmas-themed game night with everyone.

"Está bien, I know you like it." He lifts me up off of him. "But, fine, I will shower. I got some asses to wax in Cards Against Humanity anyway."

I breathe a sigh as relief as he exits the room to shower. Hurrying over to my phone, I finish checking out with my gift. Please tell me my extra-but-hopefully-not-too-extra gift idea isn't going to end with my boyfriend dumping his lame white girlfriend.

~~~

An airhorn sounds, and I startle awake. "Merry Christmas Eve, amigos!" comes from beyond the bedroom door.

I rub at my eyes. "Why is your sister and my best friend waking up the whole apartment with an airhorn on Christmas Eve?"

Carter pulls the covers over our heads, encasing us in a little cocoon of warmth and his cinnamon scent. Who needs Christmas-scented candles when your boyfriend smells like this? He kisses me quickly on the lips. "No sé, and I plan to kill her for it later."

One of his arms disappears as he reaches out of the comforter. When it comes back, he holds his phone in his hand. Unlocking it, he yawns. Then he opens it to his Dexcom app. "Why'd we stay up so late last night?" he groans.

"Is that a rhetorical question or..."

The door slams open, banging into what I think is the wall, but I can't see anything except Carter's lit up face from his phone. He pulls the covers down. "Candy, cierra la puerta, now, por favor."

Candy looks like she just stepped off the runway, no joke. She has on a short gold bodycon dress, which makes her hair look even more perfectly pink, and has white pom-pom earrings on with over-the-knee white boots. Smiling, she says, "Merry Christmas Eve, Les! As much as your relationship with mi hermano warms my heart, so do our Christmas Eve traditions. So, Carter, apúrate." She folds her arms. "Mom will kill us if we are not there to start making tamales. The last thing she wants to do is be stuck with Abuela all alone."

"Bien." He covers his eyes with his forearm. "Can I just have one second with my girlfriend?"

"Aw, did I like interrupt something?" she says in a valley-girl accent.

I sit up in bed and shake my head. "I do not sound like that!"

Carter chuckles, and I playfully slap his chest. But seriously, I don't sound like that, do I?

She blows a kiss and closes the door behind her.

I brush back Carter's hair from his forehead, and his green-eyed stare shutters. "I hope you're ready for a crazy celebration."

"I am." Anything to save me from having to go to the Maldon party is fine by me. It could be the worst Christmas Eve in history, and I'd still be fine with it. "But just in case your nephews pull me away to dance with them, we better get a good make out sesh in right now."

He sits up and I climb onto his lap, wrapping my arms around his neck. "Merry Christmas Eve, Carter."

"Merry Christmas Eve, Les," he whispers, capturing my mouth with his. When he pulls back, his eyes search mine. "Come to Mexico with me."

Uh...what? "Like...permanently? Or..." I grimace.

He chuckles. "No. For New Year's Eve. I don't want to be alone when the clock strikes midnight."

A panicky feeling flies into my chest. "Um, a family vacation is probably a little too soon, yeah?"

"Nah. Parents already cleared it. Or, sorta. Candy and I each get to bring someone this year. I talked to her about it, she agreed, and we want you to come. So..." He kisses my cheek, and I capture a bit of a blush crawling up his neck. Aww, he's nervous! "Come with me?"

I bite my lip. "Okay."

"Yeah?"

I nod. "Yeah."

Candy's voice comes squealing from beyond the door. "Cancún better watch out! Oh, and can you finally just agree to move in with me? I know you hate that uppity apartment of yours."

I chuckle and yell, "Deal! Only because Christmas is a day of miracles!"

She whoops and kicks the door once. "Alright, I'm heading out. I'll see you in a few."

My breath comes whooshing out of me as I glance into Carter's sparkling green eyes. He's the best. "I can't believe that's my Christmas gift. It's way too much. I got you socks. Socks, Carter! I'm so lame."

His brow pinches, and he cocks his head to the side. "Socks?"

"Yes." I bury my face into my hands. "And then I panicked and got us tickets to Disneyland for Valentine's Day."

He bursts into a fit of laughter. I glance through my fingers, and he's holding his stomach as he continues to laugh. "Ay Dios mío. I love it. It's very you."

I deadpan.

"Hey," he pulls at my hands until I'm sitting in his lap, "I love you, señorita."

I succumb and shake my head, laughing too. "I love you, Carter."

"You know who else is coming to Cancún?" He bites his bottom lip as a laugh slips out of him.

Pretty sure I can guess where this is going. "Who?"

"Tom." His face is once again the SpongeBob meme smile.

I groan. "Candy's gonna kill you."

Christmas Year Two

I rush through the hospital after shadowing Dr. Guilliod. Crap, I'm going to be late. I already know what she'll say. "I thought we talked about your tardiness."

Pulling out my phone, I hop over a discarded teddy bear in the hospital lobby and nearly trip in my heels as I dial Carter's number.

He answers after one ring. "Hey, where are you?"

Oh no. That is not good. Is there a way to like transfer my studio audience to him? 'Cause he's gonna need you. "You're already at Anna's? OMG is she there? I lost track of time and... Ahh, I'm so sorry."

"It's all good," he says casually, but his voice is slightly more high-pitched than normal, so I know my mom is sitting across from him.

"I'm rushing, I promise. I'll see you soon. Love you." I hang up and pull up Uber. All the cars are at least ten minutes out. It's only on the opposite side of campus. What if...

So, yeah, with my heels in my hand, I run the half mile in a dress to Anna's Diner, where my mom is meeting Carter and I for Christmas Eve Eve's dinner. Don't laugh at me. Tomorrow we'll go to Carter's family's like always, and for Christmas Day, we're going skiing with some friends.

I rush through the door, sweating even though it's cold outside. My bare feet slap against the tile, and I slide into the booth gasping for air.

My mom furrows her brow. "Really, Les? You're going to get MRSA."

My hand waves, but I'm barely aware of it because I can't breathe. I need to work out more. New Year's resolution? Let's be honest, probably not. "I'm here. Merry Christmas, Mom."

Carter grabs my thigh under the table and squeezes it, and I lean over to give him a quick kiss.

He gestures to my mom. "So, your mom was just telling me about how you're planning to take the MCAT soon."

My chin disappears into my neck as I shrink away. I've been doubling up on classes and taking courses during the summer, so I'm technically a junior, along with Carter. And it's a topic we haven't talked about because hello, I don't know what his life plans are. "Um, yeah, probably. I might have to take the entrance exam multiple times, so just want to get a head start on it..."

Thankfully, the waitress comes up at that moment, saving me from the rest of the convo. We order waffles for me, french toast for Carter, and a chicken salad for my mom (typical). The dinner goes by with barely a bump. Most of the time, I don't know what my mom is thinking. But, things have been a lot better the past year thanks to our therapy together.

Mom invites us to spend spring break with her in Hawaii, and though I have no idea if we'll go or not, the fact she even wants to go on a vacation with Carter and me says something. And it makes me feel all warm and fuzzy.

I hug my mom goodbye before sitting across from Carter in the booth of Anna's like we've done so many times over the years, eating a special Christmas cheesecake the cook made for his favorite peanut-free girl (his words, not mine).

"So..." Carter smiles. "Were you gonna tell me about the MCAT?"

My sigh could blow out a small village. "I just didn't want to overwhelm you. I know you're graduating in finance, but I didn't know what your post-grad plans are. Obviously, I sorta have to go wherever I get accepted into medical school. Lo siento, I should've told you." Hopefully if I use the Spanish I've been learning, he'll go easy on me.

He licks his lips and nods. "You know I've been keeping my plans pretty laidback for a reason, right?"

What does that even mean? "Um, no?"

Our waitress refills our glasses of water and Carter leans forward on the table to get closer to me. When she leaves, he says, "I'm in this, Les. Always. Once we're graduated, I'm coming with you. Wherever that is."

I swallow through the rocks that are somehow now in my throat. "You...you're...wait, this has always been your plan?"

He shrugs. "If you'll have me, yes."

A squeal comes out of my mouth. "I love you. You know that, right?"

He chuckles. "I love you, too."

Christmas Year Three

"I'm scared," I whisper, holding the Stanford Medical School envelope in my hand.

Carter sits next to me on our bed, playing with my hair. It's been a year, alright. Carter tore his rotator cuff, and he hopes to recover for his senior year baseball season, but whether he will or not is a different story.

And I failed a course, so even though I have good MCAT scores and a relatively okay GPA, I've gotten a lot of rejections from medical schools the last few months. It's been rough.

I gulp.

He kisses my cheek. "Whatever is in that envelope won't change anything, Les. There are still a lot of schools you haven't heard from. Whatever happens, respira. Estarás bien," Carter reassures. "And if it's a rejection, I know some Mexicans who are always down to get drunk on Christmas Eve with you."

He's right. It's going to be okay. I think. Hope. I hope. Gah. Maybe waiting till Christmas Eve to open this was a bad idea. Who wants to ruin their favorite holiday? Unless...can I call upon my old studio audience to use X-ray vision and see what it says in the envelope? Save me from the dread? I'm hearing crickets to that question. Ugh.

"Okay. I'm gonna do it. Just rip it off. Like a bandaid." With a deep breath, I slip my finger under the envelope and tear. I peep at the paper.

Dear Ms. Watkins,

...pleased to announce you have been accepted...

"Ahh!" I scream, barreling into Carter.

He falls back into the bed, and I scramble on top of him, kissing all over his face. "I got in. I got in. I got in! Your boo is gonna be a doctor!" I squeal.

Our bedroom door slams open, and Candy comes rushing in, throwing her bag down. "Did you make it? These are happy tears?" she asks, pointing at my face.

I nod, and she jumps onto the bed and hugs me. "¡Felicidades! I'm so excited for you guys!"

Carter chuckles. "How'd you even get in here, Candy?"

She waves him off. "Les gave me a key to your apartment months ago."

Candy lets go of my arms and squeals. "I know you want to be an ER doc, but if you change your mind, might I suggest plastic surgery? I want discounted Botox."

I laugh. "I'm just glad we're gonna still be close by each other."

Carter slides off the bed. "Guess I should start looking at jobs in San Francisco, eh?"

I bite my lip and smile. "I guess so."

Candy pushes me away from her. "Your heart eyes toward each other are still sickening after all these years. Let's go people. Abuela is waiting."

I roll my eyes and follow behind her. Carter slings his arm around me. Te amo, he mouths.

Love you, too, I mouth back.

Christmas Year Four

Carter pops into our bedroom where I'm nose-deep in an anatomy book. "Estás bien?"

I nod. "Yeah, sorry, just studying a bit more before we go."

I glance up at him. He's wearing a tailored red sweater and black pants, and his hair has grown out a bit in the last year, making it really tempting to pull him onto our bed so I can run my hands through it.

My dress is hanging against the door, so I grab it down. Carter watches as I change into it, biting his lip. I laugh, knowing that I still have an effect on him with such a simple move.

"We're gonna be late if you pull that, cariña." His heated gaze says he's not lying.

Honestly, I'd take being late for that. Things have been a little weird with us the past few weeks. I've been slammed with school, and he's been slammed with work in downtown San Francisco. The company he works for is a startup, and it's an app for college athletes, so Carter really enjoys it.

We've grown up a lot in the last few years. But here's hoping we grow together rather than apart.

Maybe Christmas will give us the time we need to reconnect since he's been gone so much. I smile. "Let's go, shall we?"

The drive back home to Carter's family's house is nearly silent. We put on Christmas music, and it's raining outside, getting darker by the minute as the day stretches on.

Carter keeps wiping his palms off on his pants and clearing his throat as if this is awkward, but I don't know why a simple car ride with your girlfriend would be awkward.

Finally, I can't take the tension. As we pull off the freeway to his hometown, I ask, "Are we okay? Things have been kind of weird between us lately."

He puts on his blinker and slows down at an upcoming stoplight. "Sí, we're fine."

"Okay," I whisper. That's a vague answer. Everyone knows fine is not fine.

I don't say anything else until he passes by the turn off for his parents' house. "You missed your turn."

He smiles. "Humor me for a minute, okay?"

Is he trying to annoy me? I think he is. "Your parents are not going to be happy if we're late."

"We're not gonna be late, Les. Chill."

I gasp. Did he just tell me to chill? "You want me to chill? I just asked you if we're okay and you said we're fine. Everyone knows fine doesn't mean fine, Carter!"

He rolls his eyes, but doesn't respond.

We're traveling up a hill, and as the rain continues to fall, I can hardly see where we're going. It's worse than I thought. Our favorite holiday, and we're fighting.

But when he stops the car and reaches for my hand, I sigh and give it to him.

He gives me do-me eyes. "Let's get out of the car for a minute."

I give him my best side-eye. "You want to get out of the car. In the rain. After we got all dressed up for Christmas Eve. So that we can...what? Show up to your parents' soaking wet?"

His full lips tip up into a grin, and he begins laughing. "Just, come on. I promise, it'll be fine."

"Men!" I gripe as I get out of the car and into the rain.

In front of me are the sparkling lights of the city, and I shield my face from the rain with my hand. "Hey, this is where we came my freshman year, huh?"

He opens an umbrella for us and pulls out a cooler from the trunk of our car. Sitting in it are my favorite cookies and two chocolate milks. "I couldn't take you to the beach with it being winter and all without you raising a protest. But, I figured why not recreate one of our dates for Christmas this year?"

Most of my concerns bleed out (not all of them because... #anxiety). He's still my Carter, busy or not. Recreating one of our first sorta-dates is really sweet. Really, really sweet and my heart might actually melt.

"I love it," I say, smiling so big my nose crinkles.

"Vamos. There's a place over there where we can sit with the umbrella." He nods his head.

I follow behind him, watching my steps so I don't trip on the gravel in my heels. "How much farther..." I glance up, and my words trail off.

Lights sparkle on a hillside pine tree, glowing against the dreary rain. Red and green ornaments decorate the tree, adorned with photos of Carter and me. One from the time we went to Disneyland with Candy and Tom. A selfie from our first vacation together in Mexico. Pictures from football games, college game night, our first apartment together, and countless other memories. I step closer to look at them as Carter stays behind me.

These pictures tell a story. One that I'm so in love with. "Oh my gosh, Carter, when did you find time to do this? This is amazing."

I glance back toward him, but he's down in the gravel. On. One. Knee.

My hand covers my mouth as I gasp. "What're you doing? OMG, don't tell me. Wait, what? Shut up." I look to the tree, to him, to the tree, and to him. "Is this for real?"

He hands me the umbrella and reaches into his pocket. "You're the one who asked me to be your boyfriend. I felt that it's only fair that I get to be the one to ask you to be my wife. ¿Te casarías conmigo?"

It's a good thing I've learned Spanish the last three years because this man right here, the man of my freaking dreams, is asking me to marry him. "Yes. Yes, of course, I'll marry you!"

I toss the umbrella, get down to my knees, and throw my arms around him.

He puts a hand back in the gravel to steady us. "You haven't even seen the ring yet."

Kissing every part of him I can get my lips on, I mumble, "I don't care about the ring."

He stands, lifting me up into the air and spinning with pure ecstasy. "Dang, wish I knew that before spending a fortune on the thing."

I laugh, wiping at the tears that have escaped my eyes. "Show me the ring."

Setting me down, Carter opens the small box in his hand. On a delicate gold band sits a teardrop diamond surrounded by a halo of small pink jewels. I hold out my hand as he slips it on my finger. I wiggle it under the light of the Christmas lights, and it sparkles and shines. It's the prettiest thing I've ever seen. "I'm obsessed."

Carter kisses me, lacing our fingers together. "Good. I'm glad. Candy helped pick it out. I love you, Les. So much."

"I love you, too," I get out through stupid blubbering tears. I can't help it, I'm just so happy. "Is this why you've been weird the past few weeks?"

He laughs and picks up the umbrella I tossed. "You have no idea how hard this was to pull off with your nosy ass."

I grin. "How'd you even come up with this idea for the proposal? Those ornaments are like my favorite part. Now we have something to decorate our Christmas tree with each year."

As he sits down on a large rock next to the tree, he shields us from the rain with the umbrella. "Your dad, actually."

I lay my head on his shoulder. "What do you mean?"

"One of those videos he left to you was addressed to me, as your future spouse." He pulls back and winks. "When I watched it, he talked about all of these things, including asking you to marry me around Christmas, your favorite holiday. He also threatened to kill me if I hurt you, but ya know, let's focus on the good."

My eyes well up with fresh tears. I've watched almost all of my dad's videos now. But even from beyond, he's still here with me every step of the way. Carter swipes at the trail of water making its way down my face.

His phone vibrates, making a loud buzzing noise against the concrete. He pulls it out. "Sorry, everyone's asking me if I've done it yet. Hold up your hand."

I show off my ring and smile with Carter in our first engaged selfie. He sends it to the family group text. "I'll have to make an ornament of that, too."

"Best. Christmas. Ever," I whisper.

He leans in to kiss me, whispering against my lips, "Just wait and see what I have planned for next year."

The End.

Note from Jess

Hey, readers! Thanks so much for making it through to the end of my book. If you liked the book...me, my characters, and future books will love you forever if you write a review. This helps spread the word! And, I always love to hear from readers, so check out my Instagram, Twitter, Facebook, and website to talk more.

Peanut Allergy Note: Les has anaphylaxis to any form of peanuts. Even being in the room with someone who opens a bag of peanuts could kill her. At times, this has been used in novels in an unflattering light. I wanted to show that food allergies are a *normal* part of life. It doesn't make these people different—and no one should ever be fearful of dating someone with an allergy. That's ridiculous and discriminatory.

Les also talks about Spokin, which is a food allergy app, that helps her find safe restaurants and brands to use.

Type 1 Diabetes note: Not everyone's experience is like Carter's, nor does everyone get diagnosed late in life. However, there are so many people who have died or become very ill because the signs weren't recognized in the beginning by health professionals, especially in minority populations. Carter's diagnosis was inspired by my sister's late-onset diagnosis of type 1 diabetes. If you, or someone you know, have any of the signs below, please go see your doctor.

Signs of Type I Diabetes:

-Increased thirst.
-Frequent urination.

-Bed-wetting in children who previously didn't wet the bed during the night.
-Extreme hunger.
-Unintended weight loss.
-Irritability and other mood changes.
-Fatigue and weakness.
-Blurred vision.

Big fat thank you to:

So many people made this book what it is today. First and foremost, Mom, for always thinking I'd write a great book. I'm still not sure this counts, but you're my number one fan. You're the best.

Danielle, who I borrowed so many different things from to make both Carter and Les. You're my best friend ever. Kate & Anna, who I also borrowed way too many characteristics from to make Les. Love you!

Ryan, who would rather die than read a fiction novel, but who is just as much of a *Bachelor* fan as I am, I stared at your baseball jersey in our office for too long. ;)

Lisa, for helping me translate and fix everything. You jumped in at the last moment, and I'm so thankful!

Sarah, for the beautiful cover and bringing Les to life!

My writing group. Dave, for your dramatic commentary and loving my characters like they're your own. Jim, for being the king of proofing all of my grammar. Vale, for tearing this book apart, HAHA. Pat, for forcing me to add more plot development and reading it all without complaining. April, for knowing this book better than I did. Your insights, input, and questions legit changed this book and made it what it was. Best beta readers ever, and I could have never written this book without all of you.

And to all the future readers that love this book, I wrote it for you! Thank you so very much for reading. It's only going to get better from here on out.

Les is More Playlist

Songs Mentioned:
Trust Issues - Olivia O'Brien
One Thing Right - Kane Brown & Marshmello
Neon Circus - Amber Run
5 AM - Amber Run
Waves - Dean Lewis
DNA - BTS
Señorita - Shawn Mendes & Camila Cabello
death bed (coffee for your head) - Powfu
you were good to me - Jeremy Zucker & Chelsea Cutler

Songs That Inspired The Story:
Happier - Marshmello
Yo x Ti, Tu x Mi - Rosalía & Ozuna
i can't breathe - Bea Miller
Leaving My Love Behind - Lewis Capaldi
Back to You - Selena Gomez
I Want More - Kaleo
Yo Perreo Sola - Bad Bunny
All I Want (For Christmas) - Liam Payne

www.ingramcontent.com/pod-product-compliance
Lightning Source LLC
Chambersburg PA
CBHW021534250626
47154CB00006BA/2119